Sarah's
ORPHANS

Books by Vannetta Chapman

Sarah's ORPHANS

VANNETTA CHAPMAN

HARVEST HOUSE PUBLISHERS
EUGENE, OREGON

SARAH'S ORPHANS

Copyright © 2016 by Vannetta Chapman
Published by Harvest House Publishers
Eugene, Oregon 97402
www.harvesthousepublishers.com

ISBN 978-0-7369-5607-9 (pbk.)
ISBN 978-0-7369-5608-6 (eBook)

Library of Congress Cataloging-in-Publication Data
Names: Chapman, Vannetta, author.
Title: Sarah's orphans / Vannetta Chapman.
Description: Eugene Oregon : Harvest House Publishers, [2016] | Series: Plain and simple miracles ; book 3 | Description based on print version record and CIP data provided by publisher; resource not viewed.
Identifiers: LCCN 2016009186 (print) | LCCN 2016006006 (ebook) | ISBN 9780736956086 () | ISBN 9780736956079 (softcover)
Subjects: LCSH: Amish—Fiction. | GSAFD: Christian fiction.
Classification: LCC PS3603.H3744 (print) | LCC PS3603.H3744 S27 2016 (ebook) | DDC 813/.6—dc23
LC record available at http://lccn.loc.gov/2016009186

Printed in the United States of America

16 17 18 19 20 21 22 23 24 / LB-CD / 10 9 8 7 6 5 4 3 2 1

For my friends,
Bill and Connie Voigt

Acknowledgments

This book is dedicated to Bill and Connie Voigt. Both Bill and Connie have participated in mission work for many years. They have ministered to families in Honduras on six different occasions, Nicaragua on half a dozen trips, and an additional three trips to Mexico. They have also ministered to those here in our hometown. They are an inspiration and have helped me to understand what it means to be "the hands and feet of Christ" to others.

Thanks to my prereaders: Kristy and Janet. You both help me to write quality fiction, and you are such good friends. God blessed me richly with you two! I appreciate my family and friends who support me in this journey of sharing God's grace through fiction. I'm grateful for the help of my agent, Steve Laube, as well as the wonderful staff at Harvest House for publishing this story. I'd also like to thank Nelson Bynum for the use of his name. I think you'd make a great sheriff.

Lastly, I would like to express my gratitude to the Amish communities in Oklahoma. This is the third and last novel in my Plain and Simple Miracles series, and I have enjoyed the time I spent with you—both in person and on the written page.

If you find yourself near Tulsa, drive east on US-412 for forty minutes until you reach the town of Chouteau. There you will find the Plain and quiet community I refer to as Cody's Creek. You'll be blessed by your journey.

And finally…always giving thanks to God the Father for everything, in the name of our Lord Jesus Christ (Ephesians 5:20).

*We think sometimes that poverty is only being hungry,
naked, and homeless. The poverty of being unwanted,
unloved, and uncared for is the greatest poverty.*

MOTHER TERESA

Love your neighbor as yourself.

MATTHEW 22:39

PROLOGUE

Cody's Creek, Oklahoma
October

on't worry. I'll find him." Andy paused long enough to touch her shoulder, and then he too was swallowed up by the stormy night.

Sarah Yoder watched her brother disappear as the wind tore through the stand of elm trees to the south of the house. Lightning streaked across the sky, revealing a deluge of water.

"Is he going to be all right?"

She hadn't heard her youngest brother step out onto the porch. Was he asking about Andy or their father? She supposed it didn't matter, as she didn't know the answer to either. Instead of waiting for her response, Isaac sat on the floor, scooting until his back pressed against the house. Sarah remained where she was, staring into the blackness and wondering how her life had come to this.

She heard her brother sniffle, a small, broken sound, so she stepped back under the roof hang, shook the water from her dress, and sat beside him.

"*Ya*, of course he will."

"But it's so co-co-cold." Isaac swiped at his nose with the back of his hand.

The child was shivering. She should insist that he go inside, but inside was worse than the storm. Instead, she put her arm around him.

"Looks like we'll be having an early winter. You'll be able to sled down the hill before Thanksgiving."

Isaac shrugged, as if that wasn't his favorite thing to do from first snow until spring. The child could turn anything into a sled—a trash can lid, a discarded box, even feed sacks. There was no distracting him tonight, though. Not after what had occurred at the dinner table.

"What's *Mamm* doing?" she asked.

"Still crying."

"Henry and Luke?"

"Gone to the barn."

Her brothers often fled to the safety and peace of the hayloft during one of their father's episodes. Not Isaac. He was one to stay near Sarah and share her burden of worry. Perhaps that was a blessing.

What had the bishop said on Sunday? *Very few burdens are heavy if everyone lifts.*

In his own way, little Isaac was helping her lift the burden of their father—an impossible weight for either of them to carry.

Lightning once again split the sky, followed immediately by a deep, continuous rumbling that seemed to rattle the very boards of the porch. The storm was upon them. The temperature had dropped more than twenty degrees in the last two hours. Sarah wouldn't be surprised if frost covered the fields in the morning.

As the thunder faded, a crash came from inside the house. A dish thrown against a cabinet, if she were to guess.

Isaac tucked in closer to her side.

Sarah stared out into the night.

Together they waited for the return of their father.

CHAPTER 1

Tuesday morning, three months later

Sarah glanced out the kitchen window. Snow covered the yard, the clothesline, even the trampoline under the red oak tree. January's accumulation had broken the single month snowfall record in Cody's Creek. It was quite a sight, but it wasn't enough to close school.

"Are you sure, Sarah? Maybe you just haven't heard that the school is closed." Isaac had come downstairs in his oldest pants, which were a good inch too short, and three layers of his brothers' outgrown shirts—his version of sledding clothes.

"I'm sure. Now hurry upstairs and change before your *bruders* are back."

Her mother sat clutching a mug of coffee, neither participating in the conversation nor taking note of it. Deborah Yoder was forty-two years old with dull brown hair pulled haphazardly into her *kapp*. Her face was gaunt, and dark circles rimmed her blue eyes, but then her mother had always seemed unhealthy in some way. She'd changed considerably in the three months since her husband died, but it wasn't that she looked older or younger. No, the difference between now and before was that she gave the impression of being barely present. To Sarah it seemed that she drifted a little further from them each day.

Isaac began pleading his case for a snow day. Sarah marched him upstairs and returned to find Luke sitting at the kitchen table, sopping wet, a trail of water stretching from the back door to his chair.

11

"What happened to you?"

"Snowball fight."

"You're kidding me."

"*Nein*. While Andy and Henry were feeding the horses, I snuck around the back and worked on my snowball arsenal."

"Arsenal? Where did you learn that word?"

"You should have seen it, Sarah. I ambushed them."

"Ambushed?"

Sarah knew where the language was coming from. Luke had been at the neighbor's again the previous afternoon. No doubt young Ethan and Luke had spent an hour or so playing video games. It was a situation she needed to address soon, but it wasn't her most pressing problem.

"Upstairs. Change into dry clothes."

"Why?" Luke shrugged. "I'll just get wet again on the way to school."

"Not if you stay out of the snow."

"But, Sarah…it's everywhere." His arm came out to encompass the entire world, and he nearly knocked over the pitcher of milk.

She caught it just in time, and then she glanced down to see that a large puddle had begun to spread near his chair.

"Apparently it is everywhere, including in your pocket. Now upstairs and hurry, or you'll have no time to eat."

Her oldest brother appeared at the back door next. Andy nodded once and made a beeline for the coffee. Henry banged through the door the moment she set the large pot of oatmeal on the table. Henry had a sixth sense for when food was being served.

"Again?" Luke stood and ladled a giant helping into his bowl. "Fourth time this week we've had oatmeal for breakfast."

"You'll thank your *schweschder* for making your meal and be grateful for it." Andy's voice was stern, though the expression on his face was kind. He was a *gut* big brother and had stepped into the head of the house role without a single complaint.

Luke murmured, "I'm sorry," and they all bowed their heads for a moment of silent prayer.

Did her mother pray? Or did she continue staring into her cup of coffee. Sarah couldn't say. She uttered her own petition for strength and wisdom—two things that she needed an abundant supply of— and then she proceeded to pass around raisins, brown sugar, and thick slices of bread.

The two younger boys spoke of school and hopes for an early dismissal if more snow arrived as forecasted.

The two older boys spoke of their old horse, the tractor, and what work they planned to accomplish in the barn that day. Instead of eating, Sarah made sure lunches were ready for Luke and Isaac.

"You should have some breakfast, Sarah." Andy filled his bowl with a second helping.

"*Ya*, I will. Later, maybe." Sarah continued to struggle with the eating disorder she'd had for nearly ten years. She'd recently turned twenty-three years old. How the years had flown. And yet some things, like her difficulty eating and her family's challenging situation, remained the same.

She intended to go into town to speak with the banker once the boys had left for school. Just the thought of their financial troubles and sharing them with the world made her insides quiver. Their situation wasn't exactly a secret. Their father had apparently gambled away what little savings they had before he died. He was a troubled man, but as the bishop had reminded her just last week, it wasn't their place to judge.

A few moments passed in peace. Breakfast was one of Sarah's favorite times of the day. It seemed there were less problems early in the morning. By the evening she was often weighed down with them.

Andy and Henry donned their jackets and headed for the barn.

Isaac and Luke left for school, tossing snow at one another as they walked down the lane. The sight caused the band around Sarah's heart to loosen. Perhaps they would not be scarred by the sins of their father. Maybe they would grow up to be well-balanced adults.

Her mother joined her at the window. Any hope that she was enjoying the sight of her two youngest children quickly evaporated when she spoke.

"You'll remember to check the mail…when you come back?"

"*Ya*, of course." The box was at the end of their lane, a quick ten-minute walk that would have done her mother good. But she had no intention of stepping outside the house. Instead, she walked to the living room and stood at the large glass windows, staring out across the fields.

Sarah couldn't imagine what her mother might be expecting in the mail. Whatever it was, she hoped it would bring her mother back to them. It was hard enough losing one parent. She didn't know if she could survive losing another.

CHAPTER 2

Sarah sat across from Mr. Charles Dackery. The man had a large belly, causing him to sit slightly back from his desk. A bald head and wire rim glasses caused Sarah to think of an illustrated character she had seen in one of Isaac's library books.

"The money for your escrow account was due in October. It pays your insurance and your taxes. We've already given you two extensions." Mr. Dackery folded his plump hands on top of the loan papers and waited.

"*Ya*, and we appreciate that. The thing is, the first extension was before my father died."

"Such a tragedy—"

"I didn't even know about the extension."

"And yet it's still tied to your land."

"Of course." Sarah had known this conversation would be difficult. She'd had her argument plainly laid out in her mind, but the minute she'd stepped into the banker's office, all of those thoughts had fled. "I know we owe the bank, but we won't be earning any money until the spring when the winter wheat is sold."

"You and I both know that with the winter we're having there will be no winter wheat." He glanced out the window, where snow had once again begun to fall. "I'm sorry, Ms. Yoder. I feel for your situation, but there's simply nothing I can do. You're past due on both your taxes and your insurance. The insurance must be paid because your father

15

took a loan out against the new barn he built. Then he took another loan out several years after the first, against the equity. I wasn't keen on approving that loan, but there's a committee, and they have their way of doing things."

Sarah didn't know what to say to any of that, so she remained silent.

"The insurance is past due. We cannot, per banking regulations, hold a loan against a building that isn't properly insured. If you put off paying the taxes, the county will file a lien against your property. In addition, the next payment on the barn is due February 10. That gives you less than two weeks to come up with the money. If you're unable to do so, we'll have to put the property up for sale, and you will have to vacate the premises."

"But—"

"Ms. Yoder." Dackery removed his glasses, folded them carefully, and placed them on his desk. He leaned forward as if he needed to impress on her the importance of what he was saying. "Your oldest brother could get a job in the factory. It pays well. I'm sure there's a small home here in town you could rent. It's not the most terrible thing that could happen to you, to lose your land. A farm can be a burden, and it seems to me you've had more than your fair share of those." He cleared his throat and replaced his glasses. "Your mother should be the one here speaking to us. Her name is on the title now."

"She's not...she's not well."

He folded some papers into an envelope and pushed them across the desk to her. "Take those home. Show them to your mother. They explain the foreclosure process. It's something you should discuss as a family, and then you can come back and tell me how you wish to proceed."

Those words echoed through her mind as she stuffed the papers into her purse, cinched her coat, and made her way out into the cold morning. Instead of climbing into her buggy, she stepped in front of Dusty, their twelve-year-old gelding. Most of the other Amish in Cody's Creek drove their tractor to town, often with the beds of old pickup trucks attached to provide room for groceries, animals, or family members. Buggies were reserved for church, weddings, and funerals.

But the Yoder tractor had broken long ago. Andy said it was easier to keep a horse going than to fix an ancient tractor, but Henry was convinced he could repair the 1962 Ford. Someone would have to fix it if they had any hopes of planting a spring crop. The Oklahoma dirt held a good amount of clay, and tractors were necessary to farm it. Their community had made that decision more than a hundred years ago.

The horse stared at her with trusting eyes as she rubbed his neck, ignored the tears trailing down her cheeks, and whispered, "I'll think of something."

Ten minutes later, she'd regained her composure and was standing in the grocery aisle of Byler's Dry Goods. Rebecca had been helping an *Englisch* customer when she'd walked in, but now the dear woman made her way back toward her. When Rebecca enfolded her in a hug, Sarah did her best to hold a tight rein on her emotions. She smiled brightly—at least she hoped it was a smile—and said, "How are you? How is Joseph feeling?"

"He's *gut*. It's all I can do to keep him upstairs on the couch where he belongs. The heart doctors say another week and then he can return to work, but no heavy lifting. It's a real blessing that we have Paul, or I don't know what we'd do. The boys are all busy on their own farms dealing with all this snow and caring for their livestock."

Paul walked by at that moment, carrying a crate of flour and sugar. He was a large man by Amish standards—probably close to six feet tall—and he looked like an *Englisch* football player. Sarah guessed he was in his thirties, with curly black hair and no beard. It was no wonder he hadn't found a wife. The man never smiled. He passed them without a word and began to restock the shelves.

Sarah didn't know how good of a thing it was for Rebecca to have her brother-in-law helping. Though he was a good twenty years younger than Joseph, it seemed to Sarah that he had a sour disposition. Rebecca and Joseph Byler had always been a bright spot in their Amish community, their shop teeming with grandchildren and a brisk business.

Perhaps it was the day's gloomy weather, but the dry goods store seemed deserted.

"Do you have a list I can help you with?" Rebecca asked.

"*Nein*. Only…" Sarah studied the prices on the shelves, which hadn't changed since the last time she'd been in the store. She'd counted her money before coming in and knew she had enough for flour or sugar, but not both. "I'll take a large bag of the flour and a big tin of oats."

"That's all?" Rebecca asked as she motioned for Paul to pick up what Sarah needed.

"*Ya*." She forced another smile, followed Rebecca to the register, and counted out the total, closing her billfold quickly so that Rebecca wouldn't see it was now empty.

"You know our community is eager to help in any way—"

"*Nein*. We're fine."

Rebecca didn't argue, but neither did she nod in agreement. "How's Deborah?"

"*Mamm* is…okay, I guess. She seems to still be recovering from the shock of it all."

"A man should not grieve overmuch, for that is a complaint against God." Rebecca shook her head as she placed Sarah's money in the register and closed the drawer. "I heard that proverb all my life growing up."

"*Ya*. I've heard that one too."

"Not all proverbs are created equal, though." Rebecca pulled a stack of cookbooks toward her and began stamping them with price stickers. "Personally, I think grieving takes a different amount of time for different people. Your *mamm* has had a difficult life. It could be that she'll need longer to recover from the shock of losing your *dat*."

Sarah thought of that as she juggled her purse, the twenty-five-pound sack of flour, and the canister of oats.

"Paul could carry those—"

"I've got it," she murmured. She stumbled toward the door.

Paul was there in an instant, opening the door and frowning down at her. "Let me help—"

"No need. *Danki*." And with those words, she fled across the snowy parking lot.

CHAPTER 3

*P*aul stood at the door of his brother's shop, watching tiny Sarah Yoder stagger across the parking area to an old buggy and tired-looking horse. He'd had to pull his mouth down into a frown to keep from laughing out loud at her. She looked like a cartoon figure under a giant bag of flour.

However, the reality of it wasn't funny. She was pitifully thin. Did the family need money? Her Plain dress was clean and pressed, and she wore a coat that was perhaps sufficient against the cold, though it had no doubt seen better days. Her blond hair, precisely braided, indicated she was careful about her appearance regardless of her poverty. Sarah was a pretty young woman, and Paul had to wonder why she wasn't yet married. Not that he was in a hurry, and he had to be a good ten years older than her.

"She's a stubborn one," he muttered.

Rebecca had joined him, ostensibly to put the cookbooks in a turning rack by the door, but she was also watching Sarah.

"Terrible thing that happened to that family. Her father, Melvin Yoder, struggled all his life."

"From what?"

"Bipolar disorder, they say. In the old days we would have said melancholy."

"The first speaks of highs as well as lows."

"I suppose, but Melvin spent his highs in the casinos in Tulsa, which only resulted in more lows."

"He passed recently?"

"He did." Rebecca pressed her lips together, and Paul knew that meant she would speak no more on the subject of Mr. Yoder's death.

"Younger siblings?"

"Four."

"But she still has her *mamm*."

Rebecca nodded once, curtly, which said more than any words could have.

"Paul, would you mind watching the store while I go on an errand?"

"In this weather?"

"The roads are clear already."

"More snow is coming."

"I'll be back within the hour." She patted his arm, fetched her purse from behind the counter, and hurried out to their tractor.

Paul shook his head. Back in Indiana, all Plain folks traveled in buggies, most of which had heaters and all of which had doors that closed. Traveling in an open tractor through the snow? That made no sense. There was much in Oklahoma that puzzled him, but he was glad he'd come to help his brother.

One of seven boys, he wasn't sure there was anything for him back in Indiana. And land? Well, he couldn't afford that even after ten years of working in an RV factory building cabinets.

The community in Oklahoma might have unusual ways, but the land here was productive and inexpensive. Which were two reasons that Paul thought he just might be staying.

He spent the next hour stocking shelves, checking out the two customers who came in, and sweeping the floor. Rebecca returned, her cheeks flushed, in a cheerier mood. Whatever her errand had involved, it eased the worried look from her eyes.

He took his lunch upstairs with his brother. Paul was the youngest in their family, having just turned thirty. Joseph was the oldest. He'd celebrated his fiftieth birthday the week before.

When Paul had first arrived two months earlier, Joseph had looked pale, frail, and as old as their *dat*. The heart attack he'd suffered had been relatively minor, or so the doctors said. The open-heart surgery had left a scar the length of Joseph's chest where the surgeon had cut through his breastbone. Paul had seen it and blanched at the sight.

Five hours in surgery, eight days in the hospital, and then limited activity for four to six weeks, which had been extended to eight weeks when he'd contracted the flu as well. Things had turned around in the last few days. Joseph was quickly regaining his health and along with it, his stubborn streak.

"Couldn't you find any work to bring me?" he asked.

"I brought you the accounting books."

"Finished those by ten this morning."

"Perhaps you should have worked slower."

Joseph harrumphed at that, and they both shared a smile. It was the exact sound their mother made when frustrated.

"If you could help me down the stairs—"

"And risk Rebecca's wrath? Not likely." Paul had been putting together a sandwich—bologna, cheese, lettuce, tomato, and pickle, followed with more bologna and cheese. Now he realized he'd probably built it too tall.

"Sure you don't want one?"

"Already ate."

Paul carried the plate and a tall glass of milk over to the table.

"I could maybe sneak into the storeroom and do some reorganizing. If she doesn't see me—"

"Rebecca knows you're restless, Joseph, and she has her eye on you. Just do what the doctor said and rest. It's only another week."

"An entire week." He tapped his fingers against the table. "It's unnatural for a man to be idle this long."

The conversation died a natural death, and Paul enjoyed his sandwich. Giving it time to settle before making a decision on fresh oatmeal cookies, he eyed his brother and finally plunged in.

"Sarah Yoder was in the store today."

"*Ya?*"

"Small thing. She didn't buy much."

"Maybe she didn't need much."

"Could be." Paul crossed his arms on the table and leaned toward his brother. "Right after she left, your *fraa* went on a mystery mission. I'm thinking it had something to do with the family."

"Rebecca worries."

"Understandable." When Joseph didn't offer any details, Paul asked, "What happened to her father?"

"I suppose it was before you got here."

Paul nodded.

"Melvin had these episodes. He'd be right as rain one minute— well, maybe not exactly right." Joseph ran his fingers through his beard. "Everyone was aware that even his *right* was a bit odd. He'd be too happy, too full of energy, as if he had jumping beans inside of him. You knew when that happened a crash wasn't far off."

"What kind of crash?"

"Hard to say, as his wife, Deborah, never let on, but a few times the bishop had to intervene. He would take the children to stay somewhere else a few days. That sort of thing."

"Yoder was abusive?" Something in Paul's heart hardened toward the man, someone he had never known and now never would.

"I suspect the family took the brunt of his anger if that's what you're asking. Was he violent?" Joseph shook his head, but then he admitted, "Maybe once or twice. Mostly it was the way he treated his family— not with respect or even love. All of his anger would rush out toward them, exploding, and then disappear as quickly as it arrived. Like a storm passing through."

"But the damage would be done."

"Yes. He'd try to make up for his episodes. It all created a very unpredictable home for those children. I think Sarah—being the oldest— took the worst of it."

"How did he die?"

"Rushed out into a terrible storm. He was carrying on about how they all were trying to kill him. See, when Melvin took his medication, he was better, though it made his thoughts a bit cloudy. When he didn't take the medication, his thoughts would become crazy. He could be quite paranoid."

"And he ran out into a storm?"

"*Ya.* Andy, the oldest boy, hurried after him and tried to find him, but by the time he did, Melvin had already been hit by a passing truck. Died at the scene."

Paul nodded as if everything Joseph had shared made sense, but it didn't. A father claiming that his family was trying to kill him, running out into a storm, and being struck and killed by a truck? That was hard to imagine, let alone understand.

Paul made his way back into the store and busied himself with the afternoon tasks, allowing his mind to wander where it would. But it wasn't Melvin Yoder he thought of. Instead, he was seeing a whisper of a girl, bearing the weight of flour and oats, stepping out into a cold January snow.

CHAPTER 4

*M*ateo Lopez watched the dry goods store from the confines of the abandoned barn across the street.

"Mateo." Mia tugged on his shirt until he finally turned his attention to her.

He sank onto the floor of the barn and allowed his little sister to crawl into his lap. She was only three, and she had taken to fretting if he stepped out of her sight for even a second. Clingy. That was the word he had learned in school back in Texas, when they had lived behind the diner where his *mamá* worked.

She'd lost that job when she got sick, and now she was looking for another—or that was what she'd said when she left two days ago.

Mia coughed twice before sticking her thumb into her mouth and closing her eyes.

He would wait until she was asleep, until he had tucked her back into the old leaky trailer, and then he would sneak over to the dry goods store. He'd seen what the tall man had thrown in the Dumpster, and he had every intention of going to get it.

CHAPTER 5

Sarah, Andy, and their mother sat across from Bishop Levi. They had been finishing up dinner when Sarah heard the clatter of the bishop's buggy in the drive. He rarely drove a tractor, perhaps thinking that as the leader of their community it was up to him to maintain the old ways. Levi was probably in his fifties—white hair mixing with the gray and brown in his beard. He had a limp and always walked with a cane, and Sarah knew him to be a kind and fair man. When he said he needed to speak with them, she'd sent Henry upstairs with the two younger boys.

"Some in the community are concerned that you're struggling here."

"We're doing fine," Andy insisted.

Sarah was thinking that the bishop had seen the leftovers on the table—potato soup without cheese, crusts of bread, and milk. They would never starve living on a farm, but the children weren't exactly eating well, either.

"I know that you are working hard, Andy. I commend you for taking on the role of provider in this family. And Sarah..." The bishop turned toward her, and a wide range of images flashed through Sarah's mind simultaneously.

Bishop Levi, taking her to the hospital in Tulsa.

Bishop Levi, insisting they stay in a neighboring district when her father was having one of his episodes.

Bishop Levi, informing them that their father was dead.

"You're doing a *gut* job, Sarah. It's plain that the children are being taken care of, and Brian Walker told me just the other day that both Luke and Isaac are doing well in school."

Sarah only nodded, but she appreciated his kind words. She had no idea how to raise a houseful of boys, though some days it seemed as if she'd been doing it since she was a child herself.

The bishop blew a bubble, pulled the gum from his mouth, and wrapped it in a scrap of paper before tucking it into his pocket. They were to the serious portion of the conversation, the real reason for his visit.

"Deborah, my worries are that financially, you don't have the resources to meet your obligations."

Sarah's mother didn't answer, but she managed a shrug, which was more than she did when Sarah asked her a question.

"Now, I'm aware that Melvin took a loan out on your barn. Has the payment been made?"

"*Nein*, but we mean to. That is to say, we will." Sarah jumped in with the answer. She'd tried to talk to her mother about the meeting at the bank, but with no luck. Deborah had claimed a headache and retreated to her darkened room.

"I'm sure you will, given time. However, banks rarely have any extra of that to give." He smiled to show he was attempting to make a joke, and then he again turned serious.

"The insurance?"

Sarah and Andy both shook their heads.

"Taxes?"

Again, no.

"And how much money do you have for food, clothing, and such?"

Andy looked to Sarah. When their father had died, he'd told her that he would happily take care of the farm, the crops, the horse, and the barn if she would handle financial matters. They'd also agreed that Andy would look after Henry, who was closest to him in age. Sarah would look after Isaac, who was youngest. Luke was in the middle, which seemed to mean that he was Sarah's responsibility until he'd finished the school year, at which point he would probably be working on the farm with Andy.

Neither had even pretended that their mother would be of any use, though an unspoken hope had passed between them that someday she might be.

Sarah cleared her throat. "The neighbors are kind enough to provide us with some milk, and we have some things canned, of course—"

"So you have no money."

"No, but I have been able to mend some of Andy's old clothes for Luke and Henry and Isaac." She didn't add that she was worried about shoes. She'd noticed holes in the bottom of Isaac's the day before, and Andy's pants had been mended so many times they looked like something one might put on a scarecrow.

Bishop Levi nodded, allowing her words to fade from the room, and then he tapped his cane against the floor. "People want to help. They care about you, and we are a community. We lean on one another when there is a need, as there is here."

Andy looked as if he were about to argue, but Levi stopped him with an upheld hand. "Humility is an important thing to learn for each of us. There is no shame in accepting the help of others."

He stared out the window at the darkness. After a moment had passed, he returned his gaze to Sarah's mother. "We cannot help if we do not know. This is your responsibility, Deborah. To come to me, to come to your brothers and sisters in Christ, when you have a need."

Deborah nodded as if she understood and agreed, but she still didn't speak.

"I'd like to hear you say you understand." Levi's voice was soft and gentle.

"I do," she said softly.

"*Gut!*" He pulled a fresh stick of gum out of his pocket and popped it in his mouth, offering each of them a piece, but they all declined. "I will go by the bank tomorrow and take care of those obligations."

"We'll pay it back," Andy said.

"You already have. Your tithe has gone to help others all these years, and now it is their turn to help you. It's a simple thing when you think about it." He pulled an envelope out of the pocket of his jacket and handed it to Deborah. She practically threw it into Sarah's hands.

If Levi thought that odd, he didn't comment on it.

"There's enough there to see you through until spring. And if there is anything else you need, please do not hesitate to speak to me."

Once Levi's horse was again clip-clopping down the lane, Andy declared that work remained to be done in the barn. Henry and Luke and Isaac tumbled down the stairs and dashed out after their brother. Sarah thought her mother would mention the bishop's visit, or the unpaid bills, or the money in the envelope. Instead, she pulled a piece of folded paper from her pocket, the letter that Sarah had brought in from the mailbox. She stood there for a moment, staring at it, and then she turned, walked to her room, and quietly and gently shut the door.

CHAPTER 6

*S*arah was quite busy the next two days, perhaps too busy to notice what her mother was preoccupied with.

The morning after the bishop's visit, Sarah went back to the dry goods store. This time she bought more than flour and oats. Paul insisted on helping her load her purchases into the buggy, and he seemed worried that she wouldn't be able to unload all of the items once she got home. Sarah assured him that Andy and Henry were there to help her. The man appeared a smidgen less sour than he had when she'd seen him on Monday, but still he frowned and remained unusually quiet—even for an Amish man.

She decided not to let it bother her.

Had Rebecca told the bishop about their situation? Sarah didn't know and decided she didn't care. The important thing was that she now had food to put in the kitchen cabinets, and more than oatmeal and potato soup to feed the boys. She'd also purchased new fabric for clothes, although she was careful to buy only what was on the sale bolts.

Her happy feelings fled when Luke came home with a note from the teacher. "Could you stop by for a meeting?" was all it said. She assumed the note was for her, though it could have been for her mother. When she attempted to speak to her mother about it, Deborah had said, "I can't deal with that right now" and hurried toward her bedroom.

"What's up with her?" Andy had asked.

"I don't know. She barely speaks."

"And she spends an inordinate amount of time alone in that room."

Their mother had never been a typical Amish woman. Perhaps all the years enduring their father's spells had worn her down. Though Melvin's death was tragic, everyone had hoped Deborah would pop back now that she had the chance to live a normal life. But something deep within her mother was broken, and Sarah didn't know how to fix it. So she prayed for patience and wisdom, and she focused on stepping into the gap left by her parents.

Both she and Andy asked their brother what the note from his teacher was about, but Luke claimed he had no idea.

"I'll drive them in tomorrow and speak with Brian." Andy pulled out a copy of *Successful Farming* magazine and settled into the recliner.

The librarian in town had explained that she recycled any issues over a year old. Andy had told her that farming didn't change much over the course of a year, and he would be happy to take the old copies off her hands. Sarah had seen the way the librarian had looked at her brother, and she'd wondered if there might be some romantic interest between the two. So far nothing had come of that, which was probably a good thing as the woman was *Englisch*.

"Can you spare the time?" Sarah asked.

"More snow is forecast, and I'm nearly out of projects in the barn."

"The tractor's fixed?"

"Still waiting on a part."

It was settled. Andy would go into town for the teacher meeting, and Sarah could focus on her sewing. She was nearly finished with a pair of pants for Isaac and would like to complete a pair for Andy before Sunday. She'd also splurged on fabric for a new dress for her and her mother—more salvage fabric, but it would sew up nicely. She hoped she would be able to get to those the following week.

They settled into a quiet evening, but it wasn't destined to last. Twenty minutes later, Luke came tumbling down the stairs.

"He's brought a snake into our bedroom."

"It won't hurt you!" Isaac shouted from upstairs.

"I'm trying to sleep here!" yelled Henry, who shared a room with Andy and often went to bed as soon as it was dark.

The thought had crossed Sarah's mind that Henry was having another growth spurt, or perhaps he was upset about something. Surely he was only tired. He'd been hired on at the Dutch Pantry in town two days a week. No doubt he was resting up for that.

Andy sent Sarah a desperate look, but she shook her head. "Snakes fall squarely under your responsibility, not mine."

"But I'm more tired than you are."

"That's doubtful."

"No doubt it's a grass snake."

"Didn't look like a grass snake," Luke said. "Looked like a rat snake to me, and a large one at that."

"Why would he bring it into the house?" Andy muttered.

"Because he has no common sense." Luke was sitting on the couch, bouncing the heel of his foot against the floor.

Was that why he was in trouble at school? Because he never seemed to sit still? Andy put aside his magazine and headed upstairs to deal with the wildlife situation. Sarah couldn't imagine where her little brother would have found a snake in the middle of winter. No matter. Andy would deal with it. She decided to take the opportunity of their being alone to speak privately with Luke.

"So you really have no idea why Brian would want to speak with us?"

Luke shrugged his shoulders.

"You remind me of *Mamm* when you do that." She'd meant it as a tease, but somehow those nine words ignited a bitter fuse Luke had been harboring.

"I'm nothing like her at all! She's barely even here."

"Lower your voice."

"Why? You think she'll hear? You think she even cares?"

"I think you need to watch your words, Luke. What's said cannot be unsaid."

"What difference does it make, Sarah? You're always making excuses for her. She doesn't even care about us." He scrubbed a hand across his face, as if to remove tears before they even fell, and then he hurried out of the room, claiming he'd forgotten something in the barn.

Sarah's heart ached for her brother. Was this the trouble at school?

Luke's bitterness? They had been through so much, enduring their father's spells and then his death. Now their mother seemed unable or unwilling to care for them.

Isaac seemed barely to notice. If she were honest, she'd admit that he treated her as his mother, and he always had. She'd been fourteen when he was born, old enough to provide for most of his care. But she'd been only nine when Luke had been born. Her mother must have been more involved during those years, and perhaps that was why he suffered from her absence more.

Did she make excuses for her mother?

Maybe.

The year before, Sarah had spent three weeks working at the Texas coast on a mission trip after a catastrophic hurricane. That experience had given her a bit of perspective. She understood their situation was challenging, but they still had a home, still had each other, still had an intact community around them. She'd also had the benefit of *Englisch* counseling to help her deal with her mother and father. Perhaps she needed to seek the same for Luke. Although he didn't show any symptoms of an eating disorder like she had, obviously he was struggling with their situation.

Instead of running out after her brother, she remained where she was, sewing by the light of a gas lantern and praying for the restoration of her family.

CHAPTER 7

The next morning things went more smoothly. Henry ate early and then hurried off to work. Several of the Amish youth who worked at the restaurant in their small downtown area shared a ride. He had to be at the end of their lane by seven a.m.

Sarah thought that Luke seemed better this morning. Though he didn't apologize for his outburst the night before, he did thank her for his lunch, and he teased Isaac that at least he had managed to get them a ride to school in the buggy.

"I'd rather walk and not be in trouble." After he grabbed his lunch box, Isaac threw his arms around Sarah's waist, giving her a tight hug goodbye.

"Tell *Mamm* goodbye," she reminded him.

He'd waved awkwardly at Deborah, who was busy staring at a sheet of paper. Andy was already walking through the snow to the buggy. Although they'd had no new accumulation, the temperature hadn't risen above freezing for days. But this morning Sarah could see the snow in the road melting as the sun finally broke through the clouds. She was glad that Andy's forecast had been wrong. She'd had quite enough snow to last her for a few weeks.

Sarah cleaned up the breakfast dishes. She spent the next twenty minutes cutting up vegetables for a soup, grateful that she had ham to add to it and that they could have cornbread and fresh butter with the meal. Next, she fetched her sewing and spread it out on the kitchen table. Glancing up, she noticed that her mother had gone back into her bedroom and changed clothes. She was now wearing her Sunday dress. As Sarah watched in amazement, she carried the single suitcase they owned out of her bedroom and set it next to the front door.

"*Mamm*, what's going on?"

But instead of answering, Deborah continued to stare out the front window.

Sarah's stomach began to quiver, and she thought she might not be able to keep down the little she had eaten. She closed her eyes and focused on breathing deeply and calming her digestive system. Some days it worked. Other days she lost that fight, but she was determined to try. She would not be ruled by her illness as her father had been by his.

Opening her eyes, she saw that her mother had donned her coat.

"Where are you going?"

Deborah turned to look at her then, actually look at her for the first time in what seemed like months. Glancing back at the road, as if she was afraid she might miss something important, she walked quickly across the room and sat down next to Sarah.

"I'm leaving."

"What?"

"The letter—it was from my cousin."

"Your cousin?"

"Yes, and she's offered to let me come and stay awhile."

"What cousin?"

Her mother waved away the question. "I only took enough money to pay for the bus fare."

"You're taking the bus?" Sarah's mind was swirling. In fact, it felt as if the very room were tilting. She shook her head, aware that the situation was quickly spiraling out of control. "*Mamm*, where are you going?"

"To my cousin's, in Florida."

"But what about us?"

"You don't need me."

A shadow crossed Deborah's face, and Sarah was certain that she was about to shut down again. She'd uttered more words in the last five minutes than she had in the previous month.

"We do need you. How can you say that? You're our mother. You're—"

"Stop! Just...stop."

Sarah's heart skittered into a triple beat as a car vehicle pulled up in their driveway. She recognized Amelia Stark's van. The woman often gave rides to the Amish in their community for a minimal fee. She'd even driven to Tulsa to fetch Sarah the time she'd been in the hospital there.

"*Mamm*—"

Deborah turned on Sarah with the ferocity of an Oklahoma twister, and Sarah realized in that moment of complete honesty that her mother had been wearing a mask since her father's death. Perhaps since long before that. Gone was the blank stare. Instead, what she saw now was confusion and anger and, under that, determination.

"You are going to have to handle this. I cannot be here...cannot be here one more minute. Do you understand?"

Her eyes searched Sarah's. There was no tenderness in her expression—only desperation.

Before Sarah could respond, before she could even process what had just happened, her mother was out the door, down the steps, and climbing into the waiting van. Sarah ran outside, but Amelia was already driving away, and she was taking Sarah's mother with her.

She had to do something. She had to stop her. She had to at least try.

Sarah went back inside to grab her coat and purse. She ran back out the front door but then stopped when she remembered the pot of soup she'd left on the stove. She went back into the house and turned off the burner. Hurrying across the yard, she prayed that the tractor would start. She skidded to a stop when she entered the barn.

Andy had been working on the tractor because it kept stalling. What had he said last night?

Still waiting on a part.

Apparently he'd taken the engine apart to find out what was wrong, or Henry had—he was the mechanic of the family. The pieces were placed carefully across his workbench, and the tractor...well, the tractor wasn't going anywhere.

She'd walk.

Maybe someone would pick her up and offer her a ride to town.

She hurried down the lane, not even bothering to skirt the puddles of melting snow. The water splashed up and stained the hem of her dress, and her toes began to grow cold. Still she hurried on, her mother's words churning round and round in her mind.

To my cousin's, in Florida.

You don't need me.

You are going to have to handle this.

Was that what she'd been doing all these months? Planning her escape? What kind of mother left her fatherless children? What kind of person could do that?

She didn't realize she was crying until Andy stopped the buggy, jumped out, and ran up to her. He shook her by the shoulders, asked her something, and took off his coat to drape over her own thin one.

Slowly her presence of mind returned.

When it did, she looked up at her brother, wondering how she could cushion this latest turn of events. Finally, she settled for the truth and simply said, "She's gone."

CHAPTER 8

*P*aul had stopped by the feed store, which was located next to the bus pick-up and drop-off point. He glanced up to see Deborah Yoder stepping out of an *Englisch* van. There was no question that she was Sarah's mother—she was an older, more tired version of her daughter, but otherwise they looked alike.

Both had blond hair. Though Sarah's looked quite pretty peeking out of her *kapp*, Deborah's looked as if she'd barely had time to braid it with tendrils escaping from every corner.

Both were rather short. Paul had insisted on helping Sarah carry her goods to her buggy when she'd returned to buy more. He guessed she was no more than five feet two.

Both were slight. In Paul's family, the women were rather rounded—Plain food and a contented life could do that to a person. But Deborah and Sarah had a gaunt look to them.

Mother and daughter had a small, perky nose. Sarah had a sprinkling of freckles across hers.

Deborah hurried past him without a word, stepped up to the ticket window that fronted the street, and purchased a ticket for Florida. He wasn't eavesdropping, but he heard the ticket seller loudly say, "The bus for Sarasota leaves in ten minutes. You can wait inside if you like, or you can wait on the bus that just parked at the curb."

She must have said she'd wait on the bus. Without looking around, she accepted her ticket and change, picked up her suitcase, and practically ran to the vehicle.

Where was she going? Why the hurry? And why was she going alone?

None of those questions were his business, although the situation seemed mighty odd. He turned into the feed store and walked to the back, where the bulletin board was located. He found the notice he'd seen the week before, but he'd forgotten to bring anything to write on. So he went to the counter, asked for a pen and slip of paper, and returned to the board.

Still 87 acres.

Still a price he could afford.

Still for sale.

He jotted down the information, including the seller's contact information. The question was, what sort of shape was the place in? He was a fair carpenter, but he'd be putting down nearly all of his money to purchase the farm. He wouldn't have the resources or time for major repairs. Not the first year, and maybe not the second.

Returning the pen, he thanked the shop clerk and walked back out into the brisk February morning. The bus destined for Sarasota was just pulling out. As it passed him, Deborah Yoder glanced out the window, and for a fraction of a second, her gaze met his. Before he could think whether he should wave or not, she abruptly turned away.

That evening, as he was finishing dinner with his brother and sister-in-law, he pulled out the scrap of paper and handed it to Joseph.

He studied it a moment before passing the scrap to Rebecca, and then he reached for his pipe. For as long as Paul could remember, his brother had enjoyed a pipe after dinner—never during the day, never more than one bowl full—and yet he seemed to take great pleasure from such a small thing. Since the surgery he no longer smoked the pipe, but he still carried it in his pocket and took it out occasionally to study it.

It occurred to Paul that his brother was completely satisfied with his life, in spite of the fact that he'd nearly lost it during the heart attack. Or maybe because of that fact. Who could say?

"This is a *gut* price." Rebecca tapped the scrap of paper. "And eighty-seven acres, it's big enough but not too large."

"That's what I was thinking, and it's nearly half the price the same amount of land would be back home."

"*Ya*, La Grange County is a tourist mecca now." Joseph grunted and smiled around the pipe. "Our *bruders* seem to enjoy that."

"Sure. It's nice to have the restaurants."

"Pie from the Blue Gate tastes even better than mine," Rebecca admitted.

"But for a farmer, it's not so *gut*. I suppose since I'm the youngest, I felt the weight of that more than our *bruders*."

No one spoke for a few moments. Joseph studied his pipe. Rebecca stood and cleared off the dishes. She washed, Paul dried, and they both insisted that Joseph remain in his chair.

"You're spoiling me and treating me like an old man," he grumbled. He walked over to a small desk, pulled out a sheet of paper, sat at the table, and began to make some notes.

When Paul and Rebecca had finished the dishes and returned to the table, he rotated the sheet toward them.

"You told me that you had saved this amount." He pointed at the top number.

"*Ya*. That's right."

"And we owe you this much at least for your help since I've been sick—"

"You owe me nothing."

Joseph tapped the second number. "I would have paid anyone this amount, and we've made enough with the Christmas rush to cover it."

Paul nodded, though he wasn't sure he wanted to accept money from his brother. The doctor bills had been exorbitant. The community had held several auctions to help pay off the debt. He wondered if the money Joseph planned to give him would be better spent returned to the benevolence fund. Instead of arguing, he waited for his brother to continue.

"As far as I remember, the place has been empty for at least a year." Joseph glanced at his wife for confirmation.

"*Ya*. It has, and I don't remember the home being in such good shape even before Leon Fisher passed. Actually, we never saw much of the inside of the house. When it was Leon's turn to host church service, we always had it in the barn."

"So the barn was in *gut* shape?" Paul asked.

Rebecca and Joseph shared a look, which told Paul all he needed to know. Instead of depressing him, it made his palms itch. He hadn't realized how restless he felt until that moment. Definitely time to get to work, and not inside his brother's dry goods store. He'd enjoyed his time staying with them, but he longed for his own land, for the feel of dirt sifting through his fingers, even for the ache of sore muscles from a long day in the fields.

Joseph returned his pipe to his pocket. "Call this number tomorrow. Let's set up a time to go and take a look. You won't know what you should offer until you see the place."

Paul felt good about the plan. As he prepared for bed, he tried to tamp down his enthusiasm. There was no use getting excited about a place that might turn out to be a dump. On the other hand, Joseph would soon be well enough to return to the store, and Paul was more than ready to own a place of his own.

CHAPTER 9

*M*ateo sat watching the lights in the building across the street. He'd been able to figure out that the tall man and the woman lived upstairs in an apartment over the store. He'd also seen another man up there, sitting by the window during the day. As he watched, one by one the lights went out.

He felt more alone then.

His mind wanted to tussle with the questions he'd been trying to ignore. Questions like where was his mom? What if something had happened to her? And what was he going to do about Mia? His sister couldn't grow up in an abandoned barn or a dilapidated trailer.

The night before, he'd pulled out some of the boxes from the trash dispenser behind the store. The old trailer they were hiding in provided some shelter, even if there were holes in the roof and the glass in the windows had cracked and spidered. With the empty boxes, he'd created a sort of fort that he hoped would keep them a little warmer. That's where Mia was sleeping.

At least she wasn't hungry. He'd found cans of beans and loaves of bread in the Dumpster as well. Why would anyone throw out good food? He couldn't imagine. He'd stuffed as much as he could into the pockets of his ragged coat and hurried back across the road.

No, he wasn't worried about Mia being hungry.

But he *was* worried about the persistent cough that had begun earlier that morning. Touching her forehead, he thought maybe she had a fever. Wasn't it enough that they were homeless and alone? Did she also have to be sick?

It wasn't fair.

Mateo brushed away his tears, angry at himself for being weak.

Girls cried. Women cried.

He was supposed to be the man of the family. It was his responsibility to watch over his little sister.

The last thing his mother had said was, "*Cuidado con tu hermana,*" and taking care of his sister was exactly what he planned to do.

CHAPTER 10

*O*nce Sarah was sure that Isaac and Luke were in bed and asleep, she put on her coat and made her way out to the barn. Andy had been there since dinner. Henry had joined him soon after. Basically, they'd been hiding out.

During the meal, the younger boys had asked after their mother. When Sarah said, "She's gone away for a few days," no one questioned her. The subject was dropped, and everyone returned their attention to their food.

When she walked into the barn, she found Andy and Henry staring under the hood of the tractor.

"Shouldn't you be in bed?" She reached up and tousled Henry's hair. He looked the most like their father. He was also the most even tempered among them. Henry had that rare trait of being able to accept and roll with whatever came their way. He reminded Sarah of a kite in the wind, refusing to be overcome by its force.

"*Nein*. Tomorrow I am only a farmer, not a Dutch Pantry employee." He straightened up, combed back his hair with his fingers, and said, "Would you be sure you wouldn't like to try some of our fresh cheese with that?"

"Putting on the accent kind of thick." Andy didn't look up. Instead, he continued to hover over the tractor's engine.

Sarah smiled. "And you sound more Irish than Amish."

They all laughed, and then she marveled that they could. Perhaps they were past the point of grieving. Perhaps this latest blow was the one that would tip them over into some dark abyss. Or maybe they were simply enjoying a lighter moment, something they'd had far too little of in their life.

"I'd like to talk to you both about *Mamm*." Sarah upended a feed bucket and sat on it.

"That means she's staying, *bruder*," Henry said to Andy as he winked at her. "You may as well get your head out of that tractor."

But once they were all seated in a circle, the light from Andy's lantern slanting across the floor, Sarah couldn't think of how to start.

Fortunately, Andy saved her. "I told Henry what you told me—all of it."

"And I can't say I'm surprised. *Mamm*…well, she hasn't been quite right for a few years now." When no one responded to that, Henry pushed forward. "What I mean to say is, it seems to me that she emotionally distanced herself from *Dat* and at the same time from us. She's like a house with the shutters closed tight against a storm."

"But shutters also keep out the light," Sarah murmured.

"Indeed. But tell someone inside that—someone who is terrified and quivering." Henry shrugged his shoulders when they both stared at him.

"Our *bruder* may be only sixteen, but he has the makings of a bishop," Andy said.

"Or at least a preacher."

Henry was sitting on a bale of hay. He smiled and then reached down, plucked out a single straw, and stuck it in his mouth.

"Do you think she'll come back?" Sarah asked.

"Can't know for sure." Andy looked at Henry, who shook his head.

"But she has to come back eventually."

"Women have left the faith before, Sarah. Surely you know that." Andy held up a hand as she started to protest. "I know *Mamm* said that she left to see her cousin, but she wouldn't give you a name—that's suspicious. The only Florida community I know of is Sarasota, and it's like Amish Disneyland."

"Some share your opinion," Henry agreed. "Others say that even the Amish need a week's relaxation from rules and such."

Andy ran a hand across the back of his neck, spreading grease there that he obviously didn't realize had stained his fingers. "We could write some letters to family. See what they know."

"Not sure what good they can do. Most of them live in Ohio."

"And they might descend on us in droves." Sarah wrapped her arms around her middle. "I feel better taking care of things ourselves."

"I agree," Henry said. "Remember *Onkel* Herbert? Do we want him showing up on the doorstep offering to live here?"

Onkel Herbert had visited for their father's funeral. He'd brought his pet goat on the bus, though Sarah couldn't fathom how he'd managed that. He'd even insisted on bringing the animal in the house to sleep on a straw bed in his room. No, it didn't bear thinking about Uncle Herbert descending on them.

Mammi had attended the funeral as well, but she'd left somewhat abruptly. Sarah rather thought she could get along well with her father's mother. Still, it was a chancy thing, calling on family. There was no telling who would insist on helping them.

"Perhaps we should wait on any letter writing," Sarah said.

"Tell the bishop?" Now Andy leaned forward, his elbows braced on his knees.

"But she could come back! She could change her mind, and then…" Her brothers were staring at her as if she were hiding Herbert's goat behind her back. "And then we would have worried him for nothing."

Andy stood and picked up a grease rag off the workbench. "It's Friday. I think this is not an emergency, and it can at least wait until Sunday morning. If we haven't heard from her by the time the service is over, I'll speak with Bishop Levi."

Sarah returned the feed bucket to where she'd found it and dusted off the back of her dress. At least they had a plan, and they were all sticking together.

"You done here?" Henry asked Andy.

"Almost. Go on without me. I'll be in soon."

As they walked back toward the house, Henry shoulder to shoulder with Sarah, she asked, "Do you think we'll be okay?"

"Honestly?" He opened the back door for her, stomped his boots on the mat to knock off the mud, and headed straight for the plate of fresh baked peanut butter cookies. "I think we'll do better than when she was here." He stuffed an entire cookie in his mouth.

"How can you say that?" It felt like a betrayal to Sarah, though she'd had the same thought herself.

"Because it's true. Look, I know you love her. We all love her." Henry opened the fridge, pulled out the milk, and raised his eyebrows.

"No thanks."

He poured a glass full, returned the milk, and promptly drank half of it. Reaching for another cookie, he rested his back against the kitchen cabinet. "We all love her, Sarah. It's not as if I'm being disloyal by saying what we know is true."

When she still didn't respond, he glanced slowly around the room. "No broken dishes. No yelling or crying. No awkward silences where we wonder what she's going to do next. Maybe she wasn't as bad as *Dat*, not as violent, but she was as unpredictable."

"And now?"

"Now we have a chance to make the kind of home we've never had. I'm not saying it will be easy, but it will be better than what it was before."

"Are you sure you're only sixteen?"

"I'm wise for my age. Didn't you hear Andy? I might even be bishop material." Laughing, he rinsed out his glass, removed his shoes, and bounded up the stairs.

Leaving Sarah in the kitchen, studying a plate of cookies and envisioning a peaceful family life.

CHAPTER 11

The next day didn't start peacefully.

A coyote had found its way into the chicken coop. Several of the hens were killed, and the rest were scattered. Isaac was more than happy to look for them, but in the process he brought a lizard, a snake, and a rabbit into the kitchen. Each time Sarah shooed him out. Each time he stuck the critter in his pocket with a smile as he walked away.

Luke, on the other hand, was determined to sulk all day.

"It's not my fault you got into an argument at school," Sarah reminded him.

"It was about sports. *Sports*, Sarah. You're supposed to argue about sports. I was only saying that if Oklahoma had its own NFL team, we would have to endure less news about the Cowboys and the Saints."

"How would you even know that?"

"Guys talk."

"But we don't subscribe to a newspaper, and we certainly don't own a television."

"Tell me. The only way to see a ball game around here is to go to Ethan's."

"Do you think that Ethan could be part of the problem?"

"I thought you liked him." Luke finished wiping off a pair of boots and set them well away from the bucket of water.

"*Ya*, for sure he seems like a nice kid. But he's not Plain, Luke. We're

47

different, and I wonder if your spending so much time with him is a *gut* thing."

Instead of being angry with her, he offered his slow, charming smile. "Are you worried about me, Sarah?"

"Of course I am. You're my little *bruder*."

"Not so little now. Only four more months of school, and then I'll be free."

"Free to do what?" She handed him another pair of boots to clean.

Instead of answering, he changed the subject. "There are only five people left in our family. This is my sixth pair of muddy boots to clean."

"Andy has a couple pairs. Just, you know, in case he needs them."

Luke groaned as if he had a terrible stomachache, but he dipped his brush into the pail of soapy water and began to scrub. The sun was again shining on their snow-covered fields, and mud was everywhere. Though it was only ten in the morning, the temperature had risen to the midforties. With no wind at all, it was a beautiful day to be outside.

Luke's task was somewhat futile. They both knew the shoes would be muddied again as soon as someone slipped them on.

That was Andy's logic. To teach Luke the futility of arguing and also for using inappropriate language in school. Apparently, he'd had quite a row with one of the other boys. Had it all been over football, or was there more to the story? Isaac was still looking for hens. Andy was mending the wire around the coop, trying to make it coyote-proof. Sarah looked up to see Henry walking back across the pasture. He'd let Dusty out for some time in the field and had walked the perimeter to check the fencing.

"Problem with the fence?" Andy asked as he hammered more goat fence to the south side of the pen. They couldn't afford a new chicken coop. He was doing his best to mend the breaks in the board with old materials he'd found in the barn.

"No problem. It looks *gut*."

"Did you forget that you're supposed to be cleaning out Dusty's stall?"

"I didn't forget, *bruder*. But I thought you'd like to know someone is looking at old Leon Fisher's place."

Sarah had been attempting to coax one of the hens out of a tree. Andy was hammering the fencing. Isaac was adding a spider to the collection in his pocket, and Luke was scrubbing the last muddy boot. Everyone stopped and turned to stare at Henry.

"Fisher's place?" Andy readjusted his grip on the hammer. "It's been for sale a long time."

"*Ya.* I know."

Henry leaned against the chicken coop, and Sarah had the absurd notion the entire thing might fall over under his weight. But it didn't. It was sturdier than it looked, sort of like her family.

"Amish or *Englisch*?" Andy asked.

"They're in a buggy."

"Could you tell who it was?" Sarah asked.

"*Nein.* Too far away."

"Fisher's place is a mess." Sarah stood up on the tip of her toes, as if she would be able to see the old, dilapidated house, but it was on the opposite side of the adjacent farm. She couldn't see a thing except for fields. "I remember going with *Mamm* once to take Leon some fresh bread when he was ill."

"*Mamm* made bread for neighbors?" Isaac squatted down to study something under a rock.

"Actually, I made the bread, but it was her idea I take it over there. Then she didn't want me going alone and all you boys were helping *Dat* in the field, so we went together."

"What was the house like?" Henry asked.

"Falling in, practically."

"If it's that bad, whoever is looking won't be buying." Andy returned to mending the coop. "There are plenty of other places that wouldn't require repairing the house."

Sarah finally succeeded in coaxing the hen out of the tree. She gently set it down in the coop, warned Isaac to leave his critters outside, and hurried into the house to work on their Sunday clothes. Andy was probably right. It was unlikely anyone would want the Fisher place with its rickety house and rock-strewn fields.

But she rather liked the idea of having a new neighbor. Maybe it would be a young family, including a woman her age she could be friends with. Not that she didn't love her brothers, but sometimes she could use a little female companionship.

Her mind slipped back to her mission trip, sharing a room with Becca Troyer, now Becca Kline since she'd married Joshua. Sarah still visited with her after Sunday services, but their place was on the opposite end of the district. She couldn't run next door and borrow a cup of sugar.

As she sewed, she hummed, and she prayed for whoever their new neighbor might be, that they could be a blessing to each other.

CHAPTER 12

*P*aul put out a hand to stop Rebecca. "Don't step there. Wood looks rotted. Best to walk around."

She skirted the sagging portion of the porch, which was no easy feat because the entire thing looked about to collapse.

"The real estate agent said the place was unlocked," Joseph offered.

"No need to lock it. There's nothing here for anyone to steal." Rebecca followed Paul through the front door.

Paul noted the small size of the rooms, the major repairs that would have to be done if he bought the place, and understood that he would be living in the barn for the first few months.

Water pooled on the floor where snow had drifted through the roof and landed in piles. The cabinetry work looked good, but apparently mice had the run of the place. The windows were intact—that was a plus. At least he wouldn't need to put out money for new glass.

"I thought it might be bad, but I had no idea..." Rebecca turned in a circle. She reached out and touched her brother-in-law's shoulder. "I'm sorry, Paul. It wasn't well maintained when Leon lived here, but it's in much worse condition than I imagined. I guess a year with no one living here didn't help."

Paul walked to the back door, which had slipped off one hinge and was hanging at an angle. He stared out at the fields. They were nearly as decrepit as the house. The snow had melted, revealing rocks

51

throughout the field. The fences would need mending too. He saw all those things with his eyes, but his heart was seeing something else entirely.

He smiled at Joseph and Rebecca. "Let's go check out the barn."

The walk across the yard showed that the parking area would have to be graded. There were holes in some areas, made by burrowing animals, and piles of dirt in others.

But the building in front of them was in surprisingly good shape. They stepped out of the sunlight and into the barn.

"This is where we always had church service," Rebecca said.

"Looks like he lived in here." Joseph was standing in the doorway of an office. Most farmers had a room in the barn where they could take care of paperwork, make out their supply orders, and catalog the crops and the seed—what was planted versus what the land was able to yield.

Paul moved past him into the room. It was larger than he expected. More importantly, there was a potbellied stove, a cot, and a bathroom.

"I could live in here."

"But, Paul…" Rebecca allowed her hand to trail along the windowsill, thick with dust. "Where would you bathe? Where would you cook your food? I couldn't bear the thought of you living here in this little room."

Paul grinned.

Joseph grunted.

And Rebecca stared at them in amazement. "Tell me what I'm missing here."

"It's like a man cave, dear. You've heard of those?"

"I've seen them on the covers of magazines. A foolish way to spend money if you ask me."

"*Ya*, I agree, except it might make sense in Paul's case. This could be his Amish man cave."

"It wouldn't be forever," Paul rushed to assure her. "Just until I have time to care for the fields, bring in what animals I need, mend the fences, and get this place up and running again. Hopefully within six months—"

"More like a year," Joseph murmured.

"Within a year I could begin remodeling the house."

"You might want to just start over." Rebecca stood there with her hands on her hips, a frown creasing lines across her forehead.

Paul loved her for that look. He'd been a young lad when his oldest brother married and moved to Oklahoma. Because there was a good twenty years between them, he didn't know Joseph very well, and Rebecca had been a distant memory. But the woman in front of him was kind and hardworking, and she was plainly concerned about his welfare.

"We have a few things in our storage area," she admitted. "An old couch—"

"And that small icebox we used when we first moved into the apartment."

"Twenty years ago."

"Still works if you put ice in it." Joseph pulled out the sheet of paper he'd been figuring on the night before.

"This number?" He pointed to the asking price. "We all know it's too high. With what you save, you could hire someone to help you with the house."

"If I offer him twenty percent less, I wouldn't need the money you were going to pay me." He held up his hand to ward off their arguments. "You've provided me a place to stay and fed me for the last few months. I appreciate that."

"But you worked for us."

"Maybe you could give me some of that stored furniture for free. As far as the money, I'd rather you…" he crossed the room and pointed at another line on the sheet of paper. "Give that amount back to the benevolence fund. Someone may need it."

He left them then to wander the length and width of the barn. It was a good, solid structure, and it would serve him and any animals he would get well.

They were walking back to Joseph's buggy when he saw the horse in the adjacent property. Something about the tired gelding looked familiar.

"Who's the neighbor?"

"Yoder family."

"Yoder?" There were several Yoder families in their church district. He was trying to place the horse. He'd seen it recently.

"I believe you've met Andy Yoder. He's running the place since his *dat* died." Joseph climbed up into the buggy, a grin on his face. Plainly the day spent away from the store had raised his spirits.

Rebecca held up the hem of her dress to avoid the mud as Paul helped her into the buggy. She patted his hand, fighting a smile. And now he was convinced there was a joke he wasn't getting. But his attention was split between the house that might fall down, the barn that held his future, and the fields shining in the February sun.

Old gelding.

Andy.

Father died.

Rebecca laughed when understanding dawned on his face. "Yes, that Yoder family. You helped young Sarah just last week when she came in and restocked her pantry."

It would seem as if he was about to buy a piece of property next door to a farm full of orphans.

CHAPTER 13

Mateo had no choice but to break into the dry goods store. He'd watched the two men and woman leave earlier that morning. A teenager was minding the store. Mateo spent the rest of the day planning how he would do it. That evening, he bundled Mia in her ragged pink coat and carried her over to the barn. From there he had a better view of the dry goods store. He waited until all of the lights went out, though this seemed to take longer than the nights before.

Maybe because he really needed in that store. Mia's cough was worse, and he was now sure she had a fever.

One final light remained on over the store for hours after the other lights went out. But Mateo was patient. He knew how to wait. After all, he'd been waiting in the abandoned trailer behind the rickety old barn for more than a week now.

Waiting wasn't the issue. The real issue was his conscience. He knew that stealing was wrong, but he also knew that Mia needed some medicine for the fever. She hadn't even eaten the cupcakes he'd found in the Dumpster. Still wrapped in plastic, Mateo couldn't imagine why someone would toss them. Why did people throw away good food?

He'd wondered that question a hundred times in his life. It made no sense to him.

The light winked out.

He checked on Mia one last time, and then he slipped from the building, little more than a shadow creeping through a cold February night.

CHAPTER 14

*P*aul turned out the light, but he didn't go to sleep. His mind was abuzz with details. They'd called the real estate agent from the shop's phone as soon as they'd arrived back home. Paul had made an offer, twenty percent less than the asking price.

The agent had whistled. "I'm not sure I can convince the family to agree to that."

"I thought the owner was a widowed man living alone."

"He was, but the property was willed to some distant relatives in Pennsylvania. You know what land is like there. I'm not sure they understand the difference between their land value and ours."

"Make them understand. This is a *gut* offer and you know it."

The agent's answer was a sigh.

"The longer they wait, the worse the place will look. I hear that your spring weather can be unpredictable. One good storm, and the house will fall over."

"I'll call you back on Monday."

Paul thought the family would take the offer. Obviously, they weren't interested in moving to Oklahoma or they would already be here. The price he'd offered was fair. Also, it was what he had. If his staying in Oklahoma was *Gotte's wille*…

He should have been able to go to sleep on that thought, but instead he tossed and turned. Thinking of the barn, making a mental list of what repairs to tackle first, remembering Sarah Yoder struggling under a large sack of flour.

But just because he lived next to the family didn't mean he had to adopt them. He would help when needed, of course. The Amish helped one another. However, his days would be full trying to carve a living out of the ramshackle place. He would need to focus on the task at hand and not allow himself to become distracted by a pretty girl raising four brothers. Or was she only raising three? Seemed he remembered that Andy was nearly as old as Sarah.

And the mother had recently left. His thoughts slid back to the bus station, the agent handing Mrs. Yoder a ticket for Sarasota, the furtive look she'd given him before turning away.

Paul must have drifted into a restless sleep. He was traveling on a bus, though when he looked down at the ticket in his hands, he couldn't see his destination. What if he was on the wrong bus? Then the driver swerved. Paul grabbed the seat back in front of him, glanced up, and saw a large suitcase about to fall out of one of the overhead bins. As he reached for it, something clattered across the bus aisle.

The remnants of his dream faded as he sat up abruptly. The noise he'd heard had been real.

Was someone downstairs in the store?

Were they being robbed?

He crept out of his bed and nearly collided with Rebecca in the hall.

"You heard it too?" she whispered.

He nodded.

"Joseph's still asleep. Should I—"

He shook his head and put a finger to his lips, which he hoped she could see in the darkness, and started down the stairs. She pulled him back and handed him a flashlight. The apartment stairs led to the back of the store—what they laughingly referred to as the employee work area. Actually, it was a large room where they kept extra supplies, a dolly for unloading things, and a worktable with two chairs. There was also a bathroom off to the side.

He distinctly heard running water in the bathroom.

Their burglar was using the facilities?

He thought of turning on the flashlight but decided to wait. Better to surprise the culprit. Paul crept across the room toward the bathroom's door and slammed his toe into the leg of a chair that had been pulled out into the middle of the room.

A groan escaped his lips as he clutched his foot and hopped up and down. He fumbled with the flashlight, nearly dropped it, and finally managed to turn it on.

But all he saw was the workroom as they had left it, the chair he'd knocked over, and the bathroom door ajar. And then, through the stillness of the night, he heard the back door latch and the sound of feet running across the parking lot. Behind him someone was hurrying down the stairs.

"Are you okay? What happened?" Rebecca turned on the battery lantern they kept on the worktable. "Did he knock you over?"

"I tripped on the chair." Paul put his hands on her shoulders. "Stay here, Rebecca. I'll check around outside."

"Are you sure you should?"

He didn't bother to answer. Instead, he hurried upstairs to his room, pulled on his work boots, practically ran down the stairs, and slipped out into the night.

Though he stomped around out there for a good twenty minutes, he found nothing for his effort. By the time he returned to the upstairs apartment, Joseph was up and Rebecca was heating water for tea.

"Find anything?" Joseph asked.

"Not much." Paul blew into his hands, trying to warm them. The day had been pleasant, but the temperatures had again dropped as soon as the sun had set.

Rebecca placed a hot mug of herbal tea in front of him, and Paul told them what he'd heard.

"You're sure it was water running?"

"*Ya*. No doubt about it. And I would have caught the person if I hadn't tripped over the chair."

"Why was it in the middle of the room?"

"To slow me down, I imagine. Maybe our thief has some experience."

Rebecca pushed back from the table and picked up the flashlight. "I'll be right back."

"Should I go with her?" Paul asked.

"*Nein*. Whoever was down there is gone, and Rebecca can tell just by looking what is missing. She has an uncanny ability to remember details like where things were left or how much of an item we still have."

She returned five minutes later, set the flashlight on the shelf by the door, and made herself a cup of tea. When she sat down, she admitted she hadn't learned much.

"Nothing was disturbed or missing, except maybe a bottle of chewable Tylenol."

"For a child?" Paul asked.

"*Ya*. I walked up and down the aisles. At the end of the day, we pull all of the stock forward to the edge of the shelf. The cold and flu shelf was the only one where I noticed an empty space."

"You're saying someone broke in, and all they took was Children's Tylenol?" Joseph shook his head in disbelief. "They could have asked, and we'd have given it to them."

"That might actually make sense." Paul glanced out the window, though it was still too dark to see anything. "I told you when I was outside I didn't see anything, but maybe I did."

"Meaning what?" Joseph yawned. He obviously wasn't concerned about them being killed in their sleep. As he'd explained while Rebecca was downstairs, it was a small town. Everyone knew everyone else, and they'd never been burglarized before.

"I saw some footprints in the mud left from the snowmelt, but they were small." He held up both forefingers, positioned about six inches apart. "I thought they must have been from earlier in the day, from some child playing out back."

"Unless..." Rebecca fiddled with her mug.

"Unless our thief was a child."

CHAPTER 15

*M*ateo huddled outside—cold, waiting, and afraid to move. He'd watched the tall man run outside and look carefully around, shining his flashlight down into the dirt. Apparently, he hadn't found anything because he'd gone back upstairs. Mateo thought about leaving then, but something told him to stay where he was. Good thing he had. The woman had come downstairs next, stared out into the night for a few moments, and then closed and bolted the door. Would she notice the missing bottle of Tylenol? Would she call the police?

Mateo knew it was wrong to steal, but he couldn't think of what else to do. His sister's forehead was hot to his touch. She slept a lot and didn't answer when he spoke to her. That was why Mateo was scared. He'd been alone before, though maybe not for this long. But he'd never seen his sister so sick.

Once the lights again went off upstairs, he hurried from the bushes where he was hiding and ran across the street and into the old barn. A tomcat sat inside the entrance, blinking at him in the night. His sister was exactly where he'd left her, curled up next to an old hay bale. He set the small flashlight in a corner, propping it up so that it would cast a little light. The flashlight was the only thing his mother had left with them. That and a few dollars. He'd spent those in the first two days.

Somehow, he managed to pick his little sister up, stuff the flashlight in his pocket, and carry her over to the trailer. Once inside, he placed her in their fort of boxes. Then he sat down beside Mia and pulled out the wet washrag he'd taken from the bathroom. Placing it across her head, he spoke to her softly. "*Es la hora de despertar, Mia. Despertarse. Tengo la medicina.*"

But she wouldn't wake up. He laid her back down and concentrated on opening the Tylenol bottle. He had decided to take chewables because they were grape flavored. Mia liked grape juice. Plus chewables were safer. He didn't trust himself to give her the right amount of the liquid, but he knew to give her two tablets. His mother had done that for him once.

He took off his jacket, rolled it in a ball, and placed it under her head. Mia finally blinked her eyes, which looked sunken and didn't seem to focus on him at all. He had to push the pills into her mouth. When he did, she slowly began to chew. Mateo had also filled up their water bottle when he was in the store. He pulled it from his pocket and tried to persuade her to drink a little. But Mia shook her head, curled on her side, and soon was once again asleep.

CHAPTER 16

Sarah was surprised at how difficult it was to get four boys ready for church. Andy was late coming in from the barn. Their chicken coop had withstood the night, and they hadn't lost any more of the chickens. "But they're skittish and not laying," he said. He'd also fed Dusty and harnessed him to the buggy. That had all taken longer than he'd expected. Probably the falling snow had slowed him down. It was light at the moment, but she suspected from the heaviness of the clouds outside the window that they were in for a good foot or more of accumulation.

"You should have taken Henry up on his offer to help."

Henry was looking rather chipper after sleeping in thirty minutes longer than usual, but dressing had been a problem. Sarah had failed to remove all the pins from the pants she'd sewn for him. He hadn't found that out until he'd tried to put them on, and then he had insisted she search them thoroughly before he stuck himself again.

Luke had refused to get up at all, claiming he was too tired from his extra chores the day before. He finally tumbled out when she told him that Andy had brought the buggy around. Isaac was out of bed but not ready. Sarah saw him fiddling with a shoe box, which he quickly slid under his bed when she ran upstairs to check on him. There wasn't a doubt in her mind that critters were inside the box, but there wasn't enough time to pursue that topic. So she let it go and told him to hurry.

They made it into the buggy with no time to spare, she and Andy up front and the three younger boys in the back. Fortunately, the services were held at Brian and Katie Walker's, which was just two miles from their house.

"Might have been quicker to walk," Andy mumbled.

"With those three?" Sarah tossed what she hoped was a serious look toward the backseat. "Not a one of them would have been dry by the time we got there. They attempt snowball fights out of the tiniest bit of snow, which ends up being mudball fights."

"We can hear everything you say." Henry leaned forward over the front seat. "And I'll have you know I'm much more careful with my appearance than my brothers, especially now that I know you're hiding pins in my clothes."

Sarah didn't mind the teasing. It proved that her family was healing, that even though they were orphans—the word seemed strange to her—they were managing.

By the time they reached the two-lane road that ran in front of their property, a small line of buggies was heading to the Walkers' place. They fell into line with the others and soon reached their destination. Andy said he would park the buggy, and Sarah hurried into the barn with her brothers.

The place was bright and cheery from many lanterns. The benches they sat on had been placed in rows facing a heater that was positioned to the side of the large room. Some were afraid of heaters in barns, but Brian had been careful to brick the floor under and around the heater. It was cozy and warm, and the barn was filling quickly with the people from her community.

What Sarah hadn't expected was for so many people to ask about her mother. She tried to answer noncommittally. She certainly didn't want to lie, but she also didn't want to admit that her mother had gone to Florida. Instead, she thanked them for their concern and left it at that.

She thought she noticed Paul Byler glancing her way a few times during the singing. Possibly she was imagining that. Several times he rubbed his right hand up and around his neck. As usual, his expression was quite serious. She wondered if she'd ever seen him smile, but then she hadn't exactly been staring at him the two months he'd been in town. He'd arrived the weekend before Thanksgiving, immediately after Joseph's heart attack. She did remember that well enough.

Turning her attention to the preacher, she focused on his words. "Religion that God our Father accepts as pure and faultless is this: to look after orphans and widows in their distress and to keep oneself from being polluted by the world."

She'd just been thinking about orphans. Plainly, she was to look after her brothers, but her mother was now a widow. How could she look after her? Deborah was gone, and even when she had been here, she wouldn't allow anyone close to her.

Their services were still in German, though Sarah had heard that some Amish communities were now conducting services in *Englisch*. She liked hearing the old language. The words brought back good memories of her mother and father when she was a child, when things were simpler. Her mind must have wandered at that point, because suddenly they were standing and singing again.

Luke was fidgeting.

Isaac reached into his pocket for something, smiled, and carefully pressed the pocket closed. Surely he hadn't brought some animal to church. Had he?

The final hymn was sung, and then Sarah was busy helping with the meal while the men moved chairs and created tables by putting planks across sawhorses. The meal was also held in Brian's barn, which she had thought might be cold. It wasn't, though. Between the number of people and the stove in the corner that had been going long before they arrived, it was actually pleasant.

She didn't notice Paul walk up behind her until he said, "Brian's house is a bit small, but the barn is nice."

How did a person answer that?

And why was he even talking to her?

"*Ya*, that's true," she mumbled and nearly dropped a dish of potato salad.

"I'll carry that for you."

"No need."

"I'm happy to. Should I put it over there? With the vegetables?"

Well, you wouldn't put it with the desserts! Sarah thought. But instead of saying that, she thanked him and hurried away.

Mealtime after Sunday service was always hectic for a few moments. Once everyone began eating, everything slowed down. Sarah sat next to Becca and Joshua, though she made sure she could see the boys a few tables over. It was her responsibility to keep an eye on them now.

"I saw Paul speaking with you," Becca said in a low voice.

"Have you ever met a more sour man?" Sarah realized how that must sound, and she quickly amended it. "What I mean is, he doesn't seem terribly happy."

"He's happier than he was last week, is what I hear." Joshua's plate was heaped with food. She didn't remember him eating that much on the mission trip, but then he'd been worried about his brother at that time. Now Alton lived in Texas and worked full-time for Mennonite Disaster Services.

"He doesn't look happier," she said, grateful that no one else was sharing their table.

She didn't want to seem to be gossiping about Paul Byler. She didn't want to gossip about anyone. She hadn't even started this conversation.

"He looked happier when he took that bowl of potato salad from you," Becca said. She was five months pregnant and had the glow that expectant mothers had after they made it past their time of morning sickness. "He was grinning."

It was plain her friends were teasing her, but Sarah didn't know about what.

Joshua leaned across the table and said, "I heard he made an offer on Leon's old place."

Sarah had just swallowed a forkful of ham and macaroni casserole, and she promptly started coughing. Becca patted her back and Joshua waited, apparently amused by her reaction.

When she'd stopped coughing and caught her breath, she said, "Paul? Buying the place next to ours? But, it's…it's…it's falling apart!"

"*Ya*, a *gut* place for a bachelor to start." Joshua winked at Becca and resumed devouring the mountain of food in front of him.

"Don't look so flustered." Becca took a sip from her glass of water. "You'll have neighbors again. That will be a *gut* thing."

Indeed, but it wasn't what she'd prayed for. She'd prayed for a friend—a *female* friend. The conversation turned to Becca's pregnancy and the progress on the home they were building. Sarah didn't notice Andy walk up behind her until he leaned down and said, "The bishop would like to speak with us."

"Is everything all right?" Becca asked.

"*Ya.*" Sarah had meant to tell her friend about their situation at home, but she'd been waiting for the right moment. "I'll come find you later."

And then she was hurrying beside her brother across the yard and through the snow. The February sky looked ominous, even as the snow continued to fall thick and wet around them.

They walked up on the porch and into the front sitting room, where the bishop was waiting.

CHAPTER 17

*S*he just left? She…" Bishop Levi's voice trailed off.
Sarah had never seen him at a loss for words, and he'd certainly never exhibited any degree of anger.

His face turned slightly red. He pushed himself up from the couch by leaning heavily on his cane and limped to the window. He stood there awhile, studying the low-lying winter clouds. Sarah looked at her brother, but he only shrugged and waited.

Finally Levi said, "I know several of the bishops in Sarasota. I'll make some inquiries."

"The thing is…" Sarah cleared her throat and tried again. "Maybe she needs this time away. Perhaps it will help her to cope."

He didn't answer that immediately. He glanced outside again, as if the clouds worried him. Sighing, he walked back over to the couch and sat down heavily.

"It's *gut* that you're worried about your *mamm*, and that you're thinking about what's best for her. But she has responsibilities as a parent. She can't just abandon her children."

"We're hardly abandoned," Andy said. "Sarah and I have been taking care of the younger ones for years. *Dat* wasn't able, and *Mamm* was busy taking care of *Dat*."

"It's not as if this is new to us," Sarah agreed.

Levi stared across the room, his complexion again reddening. Once he had his emotions under control, he confided, "Sometimes I am guilty of the sin of anger. I understand that the men and women in my flock occasionally struggle. But when they put their own needs before others, as your mother has done, it upsets me."

Sarah and Andy began talking at once, defending their mother, but Levi stopped them. After a moment of silence, a moment where they all could hear the wind in the trees and the muffled sound of snow falling, he spoke again.

"Your reaction is commendable. I know that you love her, as Scripture commands. And maybe you are right…maybe Deborah needs a little time away in order to heal. I will speak to my friends in Sarasota and ask, confidentially, how she's doing. In the meantime, will you be okay handling the farm, Andy?"

"*Mamm* wasn't much help with that side of things anyway. I'll be fine."

"And Sarah, will you be all right with the younger boys?"

"*Ya*. Sure I will." She could have added that her mother hadn't been much help in child-rearing matters either, but she had a feeling Levi had guessed as much.

"Then it's settled." The bishop thumped his cane against the floor and smiled at them both. "Let's pray—that you have the strength and wisdom to navigate the road ahead, and that you will remember our heavenly Father has a purpose in all things."

By the time the three of them made it back to the barn, it was snowing heavily and the lane was nearly obscured.

"Are you still okay driving the buggy home?" Andy asked.

"Of course. Why wouldn't I be?"

He jerked a thumb toward the weather.

"Andy Yoder. I've been driving a buggy since I was—"

"Fifteen. I know. Same as me. I just thought I'd check."

He went off to stand with three of the other young men who were talking crops and probably girls from the way they were eyeing the group across the room. Instead of joining those young ladies, Sarah found Becca, pulled her over into a corner, and explained their situation at home. After they'd cried, laughed, and prayed together, she felt immeasurably better. She might not have a friend living next door, but she did have a friend—a very good one—in Becca Kline.

An hour later, she rounded up Isaac and Luke.

"Why can't we stay with Henry and Andy?" Luke asked.

"Because you're not old enough."

"I'm out of school in three months."

"And in three months you can stay for the singings if you like."

"I'm not that fond of singing, and girls are just plain weird." Isaac took another peek at his pocket.

Sarah was sure she saw something green in there.

But she had little time to worry about it. They ran toward the buggy, making tracks in the snow and talking about dinner as they pulled out onto the two-lane.

They'd driven to Brian Walker's house via a dirt road that cut between several properties. Given the heavy snowfall, Sarah turned left instead of right out of Brian's drive.

"Going through town?" Luke asked. He was sitting beside her in the front seat. He had occasionally driven the buggy in the last year, but only when someone else was with him. He was interested in all things driving related.

"*Ya*." Sarah wondered if she'd be able to convince him to wait until he was fifteen to drive alone. Luke could be stubborn at times.

"It's longer this way."

"True, but the roads are better." Cody's Creek was a relatively small place. It wasn't as if you could get lost there. And though it meant a longer drive, Sarah actually enjoyed riding in the buggy, which kept them dry and relatively warm.

Their small downtown area was basically closed up on a Sunday afternoon. The sky had turned dark, and the snow was blanketing everything so that it looked rather like a whiteout. The roads were still good, though. Apparently the Cody's Creek street department had plowed through just before them.

Sarah drove slowly and carefully maneuvered the buggy to a stop in front of the blinking red light. Sure that no car or buggy was going to come barreling through the intersection, she pulled forward cautiously.

She'd just passed Byler's Dry Goods and was allowing Dusty to settle into a nice trot when a small shape darted into the road in front of them.

Sarah pulled on the reins with all her strength. Dusty neighed and tossed his head, but he came to a stop, causing the buggy to jerk forward suddenly. Isaac fell off the backseat with a thud.

"What's going on up there?" he asked.

Luke was leaning forward, peering out through the front windshield of the buggy. "Was that…was that a child?"

"*Ya.* I think it was." Sarah's hands were shaking. Instead of giving Dusty the signal to continue, she guided him over to the side of the road and under the limbs of a giant oak tree, which at least provided some shelter for the horse. She set the buggy's brake.

"What are you two talking about?" Isaac was now leaning over the seat, trying to see what they had.

"He went into the abandoned barn." Luke wiped at the condensation on the front window.

"But why?" Sarah couldn't see anything at all now that they were standing still. She felt as if she were inside a snow globe as the last of the daylight waned.

"I don't know, but it can't be warm in there."

"Or dry."

"Maybe we should check."

"I think we should." Sarah grabbed her purse and turned to Isaac. "Stay here and wait for us."

"I'm not staying here alone."

"Let him come," Luke said. "No telling what we'll find. Could be that we'll need him."

Which was how Sarah found herself walking into the abandoned barn with Isaac on one side and Luke on the other. They had barely made it inside the door when she heard the cry of a child.

CHAPTER 18

*M*ateo didn't know what to do. They had seen him, he was sure of that, and now Mia was crying.

He swiped at the water running down his face, water from where he had slipped in the snow. He knew it wasn't tears because he was the big brother. It was his job to help, to take care of Mia. Crying was for babies.

Clutching her hand, he pulled her farther into the back of the barn. And though she resisted, he insisted they go out into the snow and up into the old trailer. They had left footprints, which provided a clear path to where they had gone. But maybe the people who had stopped wouldn't look so hard. Maybe the snow would cover their tracks quickly. Maybe it would be okay.

His sister continued to cry. Would they be able to hear her?

"Please, Mia. *Por favor, silencio.*"

She only cried harder. She didn't feel as hot, but now she was clutching her stomach, which was why he'd gone back to the store. He'd been surprised to find the door still locked from the night before. He knew the store was closed on Sundays, but it had never been locked during the day. Apparently, the owners were being more careful. Mateo didn't know how to break through a locked door, so he'd hurried back, and that was when the horse had nearly run him over.

He couldn't make out anything Mia said because of her tears and the snow and the wind. Suddenly, over the sounds of the storm and his sister, Mateo thought he heard voices.

Were they hidden well enough? They were inside the cardboard box. Anyone coming in might not notice them. Except why would a perfectly good box be sitting in the middle of the floor of an abandoned trailer?

Mateo closed his eyes, put his arms around his sister, and tried to think of a way to make them invisible.

CHAPTER 19

*I*t was a kid crying. No doubt about it." Luke pushed in front of Sarah and pulled a small flashlight out of his pocket. "Wow. This place is a mess."

"You're not kidding." Isaac actually laughed. "But it would make a great place for hide-and-seek."

"We're not playing games here." Sarah looked left and right, but there wasn't much to see. Some trash that a homeless person must have left. A lot of dust on shelves. Droppings from rats. Snow falling through the roof.

She didn't remember the barn being used. The person who had bought the property years ago had put the old trailer out back with the intention of repairing the barn later. No doubt they'd envisioned large harvests and a fat bank account. They had eventually moved and abandoned the place when she was a small girl. There had been talk of developers purchasing the lot, removing the barn and trailer, and adding tourist shops, but nothing had ever come of those plans.

"Why are we here?" Isaac asked.

"Because…because I saw something."

"Over there." Luke pointed the beam of his flashlight toward wet tracks leading to the back of the barn.

Sarah didn't even hesitate. She followed the tracks until they were standing at the back door and looking over at the abandoned trailer.

"That's where he went."

"They," she whispered. "Look. Two sets of footprints."

They walked across to the trailer, stopped in front of the door, and discussed whether they should go inside. Finally, Sarah pushed past her brothers and opened the door. Inside was not much better than outside. Several of the windows had been broken and were covered on the inside with cardboard. The floor was wet from snow dripping through a small hole in the roof. It was a single room, and in the corner was a stack of boxes.

When she looked closer, Sarah saw that it wasn't exactly a pile of boxes. It was more like a hideaway built of boxes, and they were newer—not rotten and torn like the other items in the room.

She held up her hand to quiet her brothers, who had begun to argue about whether it was illegal to be in the trailer. Stepping closer to the boxes, she listened, holding her breath to still even the sound of her heartbeat. But she heard nothing.

Turning to her brothers, she said, "I guess I imagined it. We should go before you two catch a cold."

They had nearly made it back to the door when the cry of a child pierced the afternoon's gloom. Sarah, Luke, and Isaac all stared at one another, and then they hurried back toward the fortress of boxes.

Luke insisted on crawling inside first. He backed out, shrugged his shoulders, and said, "No one there now, but I think there has been."

Thunder crashed—snow thunder—and lightning split across the sky. Extreme Oklahoma weather. Sarah had learned not to be afraid of it years ago, though she did listen carefully to weather warnings. She had checked the forecast before they had left the church gathering. The storm had already done its worst and was predicted to move through within the hour.

Sarah pushed him out of the way. Kids? Living in a box? Maybe Luke was playing a joke on her.

But she'd heard the cry of a child, and she had seen someone dart across the road.

Sarah dropped down on her hands and knees and forced her way through the opening. She had to blink several times to understand what she was seeing.

The light from Luke's flashlight revealed a bottle of water, an empty Tylenol box, and trash from what they had been eating. She saw cupcake wrappers and a few unopened cans of vegetables. Where had those come from? The Bylers' store across the street?

She backed out. Luke and Isaac were glancing around the trailer. It was so small they could see the entire room from where they stood.

"No one's here, Sarah." Isaac resettled his hat on his head.

"I could have imagined seeing someone run out in front of the buggy—"

"You didn't," Luke said. "I saw it too."

"Well, I certainly didn't imagine the cry I heard. It was a child."

She focused the beam of the flashlight on the floor. There were tracks from where they had walked in, tracks leading to the box, and then—

"Back door," Isaac said.

The three of them glanced at one another and then rushed over to open it. At first Sarah saw only a farm in the distance, the silo and outbuildings rising up out of the snow. Then she realized that two children were walking toward the farm—a girl in a pink coat and an older boy.

"Maybe they were playing here."

"Maybe."

But why the box that had once held chewable Tylenol? Food wrappers could possibly be explained by children playing, but not medicine.

Luke was once again saying they should leave, and Isaac was complaining that his feet were cold. Sarah continued to watch the two children walking away from the trailer when over the wind and snow she heard the girl call out and then collapse to the ground.

They reached the children quickly. Both were Hispanic. The boy looked to be Isaac's age, and the girl appeared to be his younger sister. He didn't look up as they approached, only remained kneeling in the snow, trying to convince the girl to stand up, to keep moving. The girl continued to cry.

It was obvious to Sarah that they had been living in the trailer, and now they were running away.

She knew it was foolish to try to talk to them outside in the storm with the snow swirling around them and the wind cutting through their thin clothes. With gestures, she convinced them to turn around and go back into the trailer.

Once there, the boy huddled in a corner of the room. His arms were wrapped around the girl, who was wearing jeans and a pink coat. The boy's clothes were so soiled it was difficult to tell much about what he was wearing other than he had on pants, a filthy shirt, and a coat which was ragged and too large. The girl was crying and clutching her stomach, and the boy was murmuring something to her that Sarah didn't understand. Both were thin and dirty, and they smelled bad. From what she had seen in the box and how he was acting, Sarah could tell that the boy had tried to take care of his sister.

"My name is Sarah. Is there something wrong with your sister?"

The little boy shook his head. His black hair was long and dirty and wet. He'd been the one they had nearly run over, there was no doubt about that.

"No. We're okay. *Pero no hablo Inglés.*"

Plainly they were not okay. Sarah understood enough Spanish to know what the boy had said, but she couldn't think of how to answer him. Instead, she turned her attention to the little girl. She clutched a dirty blanket. Her long black hair was matted to her head. When Sarah touched her forehead, she wasn't surprised to find it slick with sweat.

How long had they been here? What had they been eating? And what was she supposed to do?

The morning's sermon came back to her as clearly as if the preacher were standing right beside her, whispering the Scripture in her ears.

Religion that God our Father accepts as pure and faultless is this: to look after orphans and widows in their distress...

"Where are your parents?" She asked. *"Mamá?"*

"Nuestra madre tenía que ir. Se supone que debemos esperar aquí."

Sarah shook her head. She had no idea what he was trying to tell her. The boy was becoming visibly agitated, and the little girl continued to cry. Luke had squatted down beside them. Did the girl have something contagious? Should Sarah insist that her brothers leave?

Isaac waved at the small boy and girl and asked in a stage whisper, "Who are they?"

"I don't know," Sarah said. "But they can't stay here."

Convincing them to leave was no easy task. The boy kept speaking in Spanish, arguing, and saying something about his mother.

Was he worried his mother would come back? How long had they been in the old trailer? Perhaps if he could leave her a note…

Sarah pulled a pen from her purse. She pantomimed writing on one of the boxes. At first the boy would only shake his head no, but then his sister began coughing in addition to her crying. The boy looked from Sarah to his sister and back again. Finally, he took the pen and began to write.

CHAPTER 20

Sarah somehow managed to get the children to her house. Once there, she heated leftover soup for the boy and gave the girl some weak tea and bread. She wanted to give the tiny thing milk and soup and cheese, but she didn't think the child's stomach would keep it down. She did give her more of the Children's Tylenol Mateo had offered to her when they sat down at the table.

After they had eaten, she insisted the boy try to clean up. "Isaac will show you where the bathroom and towels are."

Isaac shrugged. "Okay. C'mon."

But he'd come back five minutes later. "Do you want Mateo to put on the same clothes?"

"Mateo? That's his name?"

"I guess."

"You guess? What…was his name sewn into his clothes?"

Isaac started laughing. Somehow her little brother helped her to see the humor in even such a tragic situation as this.

"I pointed to myself and said, 'Isaac.' He pointed at himself and said, 'Mateo.' It's not that hard to figure out. By the way, his sister's name is Mia."

Sarah had stared at him, stunned at how she could make something so complicated and he could make it so simple.

"Sarah? Hello?" Isaac waved his fingers in the air to get her attention. "Clothes? Mateo? Should he put the old ones back on?"

"*Nein.* Give him something of yours."

The boys were approximately the same size. For all she knew they were the same age, though Mateo was pitifully thin.

Mia was lying on the couch, staring at Sarah with large brown eyes. She crouched down in front of the little girl and pointed at herself. "I'm Sarah," she said softly. "And you're Mia."

Mia reached out and touched Sarah's face before promptly sticking her thumb back into her mouth. She'd stopped crying after she'd had some tea and bread, but her eyes darted around constantly. The poor thing was as frightened as a doe separated from its mother. She wouldn't allow Sarah to bathe her, though she did hold still long enough for Sarah to get a good swipe at her hands and face. Because she had no little girl's clothes, Sarah found an old shirt of Isaac's and put it on her. It reached to her ankles, but at least it was clean.

Mia became noticeably calmer when Mateo walked back into the room in a pair of Isaac's pajamas looking like a different kid.

He sat beside Mia on the couch until Luke coaxed him into a game of checkers. Isaac laughed when Mateo won the third game. "I guess it's the same in Spanish or *Englisch*."

Isaac and Mateo began another round of checkers, Luke worked on some homework at the kitchen table, and Sarah tried to resume her crochet work. But her eyes constantly returned to the children. Her attention was captivated by their plight and a thousand questions that she might never know the answers to.

A little while later, Sarah gave the boys milk and cookies and then scooted them off to bed. She'd made Mateo a pallet on the floor in Isaac and Luke's room. It had been several hours since she'd brought the children to her house, and she thought that perhaps Mia could stomach a little more food. The child's expression brightened at the sight of a large oatmeal cookie, but she only managed to eat half before her eyes were drooping. Sarah felt her forehead—if she'd had a fever before, it was gone now. Perhaps she only needed food and a good night's sleep. When Sarah went to help her out of the kitchen chair, Mia wrapped her arms around her neck. Small and sticky and warm, her hands found the back of Sarah's hair braid and played with it.

And in that moment Sarah stopped thinking of the problems with language barriers and an overcrowded house and financial issues. In the instant when Mia's little hands were clasped around her neck and her head was resting on Sarah's shoulder, all Sarah could do was thank the Lord that she had found these two and that they wouldn't be spending the night in the abandoned trailer.

An hour later, Henry and Andy found them sitting in the rocker, Mia snoring softly and Sarah making a valiant attempt to stay awake.

Isaac and Mateo were asleep, but Luke came downstairs and began to describe the evening's events to his older brothers, beginning with their search in the old abandoned trailer.

Sarah said softly, "Perhaps you should let me tell Andy what happened."

"It was radical," Luke said.

She cringed at Luke's slang, but Andy didn't seem to notice. He told Henry and Luke to get upstairs.

"You have school tomorrow," he said to Luke.

"Don't remind me."

Andy shrugged and turned to Henry.

"I know. I know." Henry's hands went up in a surrender gesture. "Our day starts before the rooster crows."

"As if we had a rooster," Luke mumbled.

But the two boys went upstairs, leaving Sarah, Mia, and Andy alone.

"You left a note?" Andy paced back and forth in front of Sarah. "For who? Where? How?"

"Sit down and I'll tell you. But lower your voice. It took me forever to convince Mateo to go upstairs with Isaac."

"Mateo? Who is Mateo?"

"Mia's brother. Weren't you listening to Luke? Mateo is the one who darted in front of our buggy. At least, we think that Mateo and Mia are their names. It's all a bit iffy since they don't speak much *Englisch*, and we don't speak much Spanish."

Andy had stopped pacing and was staring at her as if she'd sprouted rooster feathers and was about to start crowing. "There are two of them?"

Sarah suppressed a sigh with great difficulty. "For the third time.

Yes. There are two children. Mateo is in Isaac and Luke's room. I made him a pallet on the floor, which is a big improvement over the box he was living in. I'd rather have a bed for him, but—"

"Sarah, what are you talking about? Surely you're not thinking about them staying here. We can't possibly take in two homeless kids."

She glanced down at the child in her arms. After another dose of medicine, little Mia was finally sleeping and her fever had definitely broken. Perhaps it was merely a cold. Maybe she'd simply needed some hot food and dry clothes. Sarah thought about arguing with her brother. She almost reminded him of the sermon from that very morning. She very nearly told him that they, more than anyone else, understood how it felt to be abandoned.

Instead, she said, "Hold her for a minute. I need to make some tea."

Andy sank onto the couch. She gently placed Mia in his arms. Though she wanted to look back to be sure they were both okay, she didn't. Instead, she set the kettle on the stove and dropped two bags of herbal tea into two mugs. As she waited for the water to boil, she pulled out the peanut butter bars she'd made the afternoon before. Just one wouldn't keep them awake. The sugar would give them a temporary burst of energy, perhaps enough to talk this through, and then they would all sleep.

She set everything on a tray. By the time she carried it into the sitting room, Andy had laid Mia on the far end of the couch and covered her with a lap quilt.

"She's a small thing."

"That she is."

"And they were living in the old trailer? In a cardboard box?"

Sarah nodded and handed him one of the mugs of tea.

Andy accepted it and a peanut butter bar. "You'd better start at the beginning."

So she told him about the storm, taking the longer route, and seeing the boy dart in front of their buggy.

"That must have scared you."

"*Ya.* I was sure and certain that Dusty would run right over him."

"But he didn't."

"*Nein*. Dusty still has plenty of stopping power."

She described walking into the barn, observing the state of disrepair they found there, following the footprints to the trailer, and seeing the fort of boxes.

"Supposing we could keep them, and I'm not saying that we could or even that we should. But supposing we could, how do we know that their parents aren't looking for them?"

"You think they're runaways?"

"If it were just the boy, maybe, but most runaways don't take their baby sister with them." He finished the peanut butter bar. "You say he's Isaac's age?"

"Looks to be."

"Makes no sense. At nine years old boys are thinking about playing ball and catching frogs." He ran a hand up and down his jawline.

Sarah realized as she watched him in the dimness of the lantern light that her brother was no longer a boy. Somewhere along the difficult road of the past few years, he'd become a man.

"We're going to have to tell the police and the bishop, and get a translator."

Sarah nodded as if she agreed with him. "But he left a note on one of the boxes. Maybe their mother will come back. Maybe she's just been away for a few hours."

"You think she was living in the trailer too?"

There had been no sign of a mother, but it was possible. Sarah shrugged. "I'm only saying that maybe we should give it a day or two."

"I don't know if that's legal." Andy stood and stretched. "I could sleep on the couch, but I suppose it's best to drag myself upstairs."

"Carry her for me?"

"Sure."

As Sarah followed her brother up the stairs, she prayed that Mia's health would improve, that Mateo would be less frightened in the morning, and that somehow they could learn what had happened to the children's mother. One thing she knew for certain. Though a language and probably a faith separated them, her family had more in common with these two children than they did with any other Amish family in their district. They were all abandoned. Perhaps they could look after one another.

CHAPTER 21

*M*ateo's first thought on waking was that he was still dreaming. His head was on a pillow, he was under a blanket, and he could smell biscuits cooking. His second thought was of Mia.

He bounded out of his cover, causing Isaac to laugh.

"No need to run. We still have a couple of minutes."

"Mia?"

"She's okay." Isaac exaggerated the last word exactly as Mateo had the night before.

Mateo sank back onto his makeshift bed. He'd lied to Sarah the night before. He'd told her that he didn't understand English, but he did. He'd been to school before, and he'd lived in the U.S. all of his life. It was only that he didn't speak it very well. He understood most of the words he heard, but his thoughts were in Spanish. By the time he came up with the English word for something, the conversation had usually moved on. He'd found it was best to keep quiet.

He had somehow lost track of what day of the week it was, but as he saw Isaac getting ready, he figured it must be Monday. There wasn't any doubt that his new friend was getting ready for school. What would that be like? To live in the same place year after year and go to the same school the entire time?

Mateo was trying to imagine that when Isaac squatted down beside his bed and pulled out a shoe box.

"Come look."

At first Mateo thought it might be a trick, but these people had been nice to him. They had cared for Mia and given both of them food. Hesitantly he moved closer to Isaac, and then he was right next to him, their heads touching as they peered into the box.

"I'm thinking of starting a colony of them."

Mateo laughed when Isaac picked up one of the frogs and it peed on him. He'd filled the box with grass and rocks and even a small dish, which held water.

"I found them out by the water pump next to the barn."

Luke stuck his head in the door. "Better hurry before she burns the oatmeal again. And don't even think of bringing that box to school with you."

"Remember, it's a secret." Isaac closed the box, and then he held up his hand for Mateo to high-five.

Some things were the same, whether English or Spanish—like frogs and secrets and high fives.

CHAPTER 22

Sarah hadn't burned the oatmeal, but she had cooked it a little too long. It resembled paste more than breakfast. Fortunately, no one complained, at least not to her face. For many months, there had been one empty place at the kitchen table—their father's. Then their mother had left. Two empty places to remind Sarah that her family was crumbling into pieces.

With Mia and Mateo, all of the chairs were once again full.

Sarah scrubbed a hand over her face, trying to throw off the weariness she felt. Three times during the night, Mia had woken up. Once, she'd been crying. Twice, she had snuck out of the bed and hidden—the first time under the bed and the second time behind the opened door. What would possess the child to do such a thing? Probably she'd simply had a nightmare, but who knew? Perhaps she missed her mother.

Andy and Henry stomped their boots clean in the mudroom. When they walked in, they stopped to stare at Mateo and Mia.

Henry raised a hand in greeting.

Andy walked over to the boy, squatted down by him, and said, "We're glad you and your sister are here, Mateo."

He didn't make him any promises, and he didn't try to pump the kid for information. That was Andy's way, honest and straightforward. He washed his hands at the sink, they all bowed their head to pray, and then they were eating.

Sarah had peeked at Mateo while they silently gave thanks. The boy was showing Mia how to put her hands together to pray. That image remained on Sarah's heart as she prepared the boys' lunches, talked to Andy of spring crops, and cleaned up the spills which seemed to occur with every meal.

Soon Luke and Isaac were out the door on their way to school. Sarah thought she saw something akin to longing in Mateo's eyes, but when he noticed her watching, he stared down at his hands.

"Henry and I hope to get the tractor working today. The part is supposed to be in, so we'll go to town first thing this morning to get it. Do you need anything while we're there?"

"Nein." There were a hundred things she needed, especially if she was serious about the two children staying in their home. Mia couldn't exactly walk around in a boy's shirt all the time, and Mateo kept tugging at Isaac's clothes. No doubt the child was accustomed to T-shirts. Could they even adjust to Amish life? Would they want to?

"We'll talk after lunch. All of us." He smiled at Mateo and went outside.

Belatedly, Sarah remembered what she wanted Andy to do. "I'll be right back," she assured Mateo and Mia, and then she hurried out the door after her brother.

"You'll go by the old trailer? I promised Mateo that we would check to see if his mother had returned."

"I can check, but I'd be surprised to find her there."

"So would I."

"Sarah, we have to go to the police with this."

"I know we do, but maybe check the trailer first. Give me a few hours to think of how to handle their situation."

"They're not our children to keep—"

"You're right. I know you are." Why did she feel so strongly about this? How had they claimed her heart so quickly? "All I'm asking for is one day to figure out what to do next."

"What we do is contact the police." Andy shook his head, and then he reached out to tug on her *kapp* string. "You can have one day. The children would have been hiding in that cold trailer if it weren't for your quick thinking and kind heart."

"*Danki.*" When she came back inside, her cheeks stinging from the cold air of the early morning, she sat beside Mateo and waited for him to look at her. When he did, she began talking, slowly and with an effort to mitigate her German accent. She felt a little silly. After all, she didn't know if he understood a word she was saying.

"My *bruder* Andy will stop by the trailer. He'll check inside, in your fort, to see if your mother has been there."

The boy only shrugged, but it seemed that a little of the worry left his eyes.

She found some paper and crayons and set them on the table for Mateo and Mia. Sarah could clearly remember Isaac at three years old. She'd been seventeen at the time, and her parents had claimed she couldn't get a job because she was needed at home. They depended on her to tend to her little brother. At first she'd been upset about that, but she'd found it impossible to stay angry around Isaac. He'd been a sponge, soaking up everything from how to color to his ABCs to the names of different animals and what sort of habitat they preferred. Which might explain the critters in his pocket at church.

Sarah cleaned the breakfast dishes and prepared a chicken casserole for dinner. She needed to wash clothes, but that would require spending most of the morning in the mudroom and much of the afternoon hanging wet clothes on the back porch. She didn't want Mateo or Mia to feel alone or scared or worried, but then again she needed to take care of the dirty laundry.

She compromised by asking Mateo to help. You would have thought she'd handed him the moon.

"What should we do with Mia while we work?"

"*Un momento.*" He dashed back into the living room and returned with an old Amish doll that Mia had picked up from Sarah's room. Taking his sister by the hand, he led her into the mudroom, made her a pallet in the corner with an old blanket he found on a bottom shelf, and handed her the doll. He stooped and kissed the top of her head.

Sarah blinked back the tears that pricked her eyes. "You take good care of Mia. You're a good *bruder.*"

Whether he understood her words or just her tone, Mateo smiled hugely. Within minutes, they were knee-deep in dirty laundry. Mateo ran up to each room and retrieved bundles from the clothes baskets, something that always wore Sarah out. She showed him how to separate the dark colors from the light. Her brothers made for a lot of dirty laundry. It wasn't that they had many sets of extra clothes, but with five in the house, plus Mia and Mateo, the piles were high. Sarah also washed sheets every other week in the winter, so she pantomimed pulling sheets off a bed, and Mateo dashed off to retrieve them.

The mudroom was actually fairly large, accommodating the hot water heater, the washing machine, a wringer machine, and a large sink. Across the outer wall were cubbies for each person's shoes and various items such as umbrellas and baseball bats. Above each cubby was a peg for hats or *kapps*.

Fortunately, their washing machine was a newer model that tapped directly into the hot water heater. Sarah measured half a cup of laundry powder, added it to the water that was already filling the tub, and pushed in the first load of laundry, which included Mia's and Mateo's clothes. No doubt they would feel more comfortable when they were again wearing their own things. She yanked the starting cord and almost laughed at the expression on Mateo's face.

"It's the Amish way." She motioned for him to come over and take a look at the machine. "We don't have electricity, so the washer operates off of a small gasoline engine. Like when you pull the cord to start a lawn mower."

She continued explaining the process to him as the machine began to agitate. On the wall shared with the kitchen was a large sink. She filled two buckets with water for rinsing, adding fabric softener to one and leaving plain water in the other. Mateo laughed out loud when he saw her run the first pair of pants through the wringer that sat next to the washer. After that she dipped them into the water with fabric softener, put them back through the wringer, and rinsed them a last time in the water-only bucket.

It was a long process, but one she was used to. Mateo quickly got the hang of using the wringer. Together they made quite a productive team. Soon, the lines strung across the back porch were filled with clothing, Mateo was a pro, and Mia was sound asleep.

Sarah sank onto an old wooden chair they kept in the room, and Mateo plopped on the floor, his back against the now silent washer and his eyes taking in the mudroom, his sleeping sister, and Sarah. She knew she was a mess, but what woman wasn't after a morning of laundry? The humidity had caused her hair to pop out of her *kapp* in haphazard, lazy waves. The sleeves of her dress were damp, and though it was cold outside, she was still sweating from the work they had done. Glancing down, she saw that she'd also managed to get a good bit of the casserole she'd made onto the front of her apron. No harm. It wasn't as if they were expecting visitors.

Mateo stood and walked across the room, gingerly touching a baseball bat in Luke's cubby.

"It's okay. You can take it outside if you want."

Grinning as if she'd just handed him the world's best gift, he turned and tried to hurry from the room. But he was still wearing Isaac's pants, which were a tad too long. He tripped, bumped against the table, grabbed for something to steady himself and pulled the bucket of rinse water down on his head.

He sat there, stunned and dripping, and apparently worried he was in trouble.

"It's not a problem, Mateo. It's just water."

As she hurried across the room to help him, he pointed toward where Mia had been sleeping. Only she wasn't there anymore. She'd once again disappeared.

And then, when Sarah thought things couldn't get any crazier, she heard a knock at the back door.

CHAPTER 23

*P*aul had no idea what to say to Sarah when she opened the door. He couldn't make sense of what he was seeing.

A small Hispanic boy waited near the counter, dripping wet and struggling not to burst into tears.

Sarah stood in front of him, a look of complete bewilderment on her face. Her apron was soiled. The sleeves of her dress were pushed up and wet, and her hair was poking out of her *kapp* in a dozen directions. She was a complete mess.

Paul felt sweat break out under the rim of his hat, between his shoulder blades, and even on his palms. He wanted to back away. Why had he thought it would be a good idea to knock on the back door? He should have known when he'd dodged through the rows of hanging laundry that now would be a bad time—apparently a very bad time.

"Oh. I'm sorry. Come in." Sarah abruptly turned away from him and hurried to the corner of the room, where she picked up a blanket and shook it out, as if she was looking for something. "Mateo, I have to find Mia."

She left the room and then darted back in. "Your clothes are still wet. Why don't you run up to your room and change into some of Isaac's things?"

The boy looked past Paul at the laundry lines spread across the back porch. He glanced back at Sarah. Though the room was warmer than outside, the lad had begun to shiver.

"Don't worry. Paul will help you." She turned to him, still clutching the blanket that had been on the floor. "Could you...could you go with him upstairs and help him find something to wear? I have to..."

She turned and hurried from the room.

The boy looked at Paul and shrugged. It was simple enough to find him some clothes. But why was a Hispanic boy staying with Sarah? They went upstairs together, Mateo showing him which room was Isaac's. Together they pulled out a pair of dark pants and shirt from the chest of drawers.

The boy accepted the clothes with a timid, *"Gracias."*

"De nada," Paul replied.

The boy looked surprised, but he didn't question him. Instead, he bundled up his clothes and a dry towel and disappeared into the bathroom.

Paul returned to the laundry room, wondering what had just happened. Spying a mop in the corner, he grabbed it and cleaned up the water that had apparently spilled from a bucket. He squeezed the water out into the sink and put the mop back in the corner.

Still no Sarah.

Glancing around the room, he could see the bottom shelf where the bucket belonged. When he squatted down to put it there, he found himself eye to eye with a small Hispanic girl.

"Cómo estás?"

The girl's eyes were large and brown, and she looked frightened. Though she didn't answer him, when he held out his hand, she took it and crawled out from the shelf where she'd been hiding.

"We'd best go and find Sarah."

He walked into the kitchen and nearly laughed at the sight of her, opening each cabinet and looking frantically inside.

"Is this what you're searching for?"

Sarah twirled toward him, her eyes widening in disbelief. Hurrying across the room, she pulled the girl into her arms. "Where did you find her?"

"Bottom shelf. Mudroom. Say, what's going on here?"

The child laid her head on Sarah's chest as if it were the most natural thing in the world, and stuck her thumb into her mouth.

"It's okay, Mia. It's okay." She settled the child into a chair at the table. "Maybe she's hungry. I just don't know if I'm doing this right, and sometimes she disappears."

"Disappears?"

"Hides. Why would she hide?"

He could see that her hands were shaking as she pulled out bread, homemade peanut butter, and a pitcher of milk. What was it about this woman that made him want to fix things? Normally, he made a point of staying out of other people's problems.

Paul crossed the room in three long strides. "Go sit down by her. I'll bring over whatever you need."

Sarah's hands fluttered to her *kapp*, her hair, and finally dropped at her side. "*Ya. Gut* idea. There are strawberry preserves in the refrigerator."

He gathered up the sandwich fixings and set them on the table. Then he retrieved the pitcher of milk and poured three mugs full. The girl had climbed into Sarah's lap, and the boy was standing in the doorway to the kitchen.

His eyes brightened when they landed on the food.

"*Lava tus manos,*" Paul said.

The boy walked straight to the kitchen sink, but Sarah choked on the sip of milk she'd taken.

"You know Spanish?"

"A little."

"How—"

"I worked more than ten years in the RV factories in Indiana. We had a fair number of Hispanic workers. Almost as many as Amish."

The little girl reached up and touched Sarah's face, saying the same phrase over and over.

"I don't…I don't know what she wants."

"Her mother. *Quiero que mi mamá.* She wants her mother." Paul sat down at the table as Sarah began to make sandwiches. She offered to make him one, but he shook his head. He needed to get out of this house as quickly as possible. He didn't want to leave her in a predicament, though.

"Explain to me who these two are and why they're staying here."

He forgot about the fact that he was now officially purchasing a farm. He pushed away thoughts of the needs next door, the house that looked ready to fall in on itself, the barn that he was moving into within the week, and even the tractor that he'd hoped to get Andy to fix. His attention was captured by Sarah's story.

She picked at her sandwich while the children devoured theirs. Soon Sarah was done explaining how they had found the children and brought them home, and she was wiping the little girl's mouth with a washrag. "Could you...that is to say, would you mind..."

He took the little girl from Sarah's arms. She was small and thin and stared up at him as if he knew the answers to any question.

"No llores," he said, rubbing her back as he'd seen Rebecca do with the grandchildren. *"Está bien."*

The words seemed to soothe her, or perhaps she was exhausted by the morning's ordeal.

"I'll be right back." Sarah hurried from the room and up the stairs, calling over her shoulder, "If you could stay just another minute, please."

So he found himself alone with the boy and the girl.

"Dónde está tu madre?"

The boy shrugged, but then he began to speak—hesitantly at first and then gaining momentum with each word, his story spilling out of him like water gushing over river stones.

By the time Sarah returned, wearing a clean dress and apron, and with her hair tamed into some semblance of control, Paul had a pretty good idea what was going on.

CHAPTER 24

Sarah sat staring at her brothers and the children and Paul.

She'd returned from changing clothes to find Paul talking with Mateo. Before she could question him, Andy and Henry had walked in and set about making their own lunch. Though he had politely refused to eat with Sarah and the kids, he'd had no problem putting down two sandwiches with Andy there. Was she too scary to eat around? Every time he glanced at her, she was certain he frowned.

As they ate, the conversation had turned to the Fisher place next door. Paul had stopped by, looking for Andy, hoping he could fix the tractor he'd found behind the barn.

"So it's true?" Sarah continued to hold Mia in her lap. "You're buying the Fisher place?"

"*Ya*. Received the call this morning that they accepted my offer. The real estate agent has power of attorney, so the deal should close quickly."

"And they're allowing you to work there before the sale is finalized?"

"What's the harm? The worst I could do is improve something. If the sale didn't go through—and it will—then the family has received a few days of free labor."

Paul seemed to be enjoying dropping such momentous news on her, or maybe he was just happy about the farm he'd purchased.

Mateo and Mia finished their meal, so Sarah told them they could go into the living room, sit on the couch, and read or draw.

"I hope to move in by this weekend," he added, studying his now empty plate.

"We'll be glad to have you as a neighbor." Andy poured another glass of milk and reached for the peanut butter bars.

They had neighbors on the other side of their property and to the back—though one family was *Englisch* and the other an elderly Amish couple who would probably sell soon. Still, it wasn't as if they were alone.

But none of that was her most pressing concern. She leaned forward and waited until Paul met her gaze. "You said you know Spanish? Can you talk to Mateo?"

"I already have." Paul drummed his fingers against the table. "Guess I got caught up in farm details, which is why I came over to begin with. Can't tell you how relieved I am, Andy, that you're willing to look at the tractor."

"I'm not promising we can fix it."

"But we'll give it a try." Henry looked pleased at the thought.

"Henry can fix most things," Andy explained. "My *bruder* is good with mechanical problems."

Paul accepted a peanut butter bar when Henry passed the plate his way. "I also wanted to see if it would be possible for me to hire Henry for the spring planting."

"Henry will be busy here," Sarah said.

"There's plenty of Henry to go around," Andy assured her. "It's an effort some days to find enough work for him, which is why he's working at the restaurant in town."

"I'd rather be working on a tractor—or even farming. Anything beats asking folks if they want their whoopie pie to go."

"I can keep you busy two days a week," Paul said. "Let me close on the place, and then I'll see what I can afford to pay."

"Sounds *gut* to me. I won't turn in my apron at the Dutch Pantry until I hear from you." Henry grinned and moseyed off to the living room.

Sarah heard him collapse on the couch where Mateo and Mia were sitting. Leaning back in her chair, she could just see the three of them. Henry had his eyes closed. Mia was talking to the doll she'd found in Sarah's room, and Mateo was drawing on a sheet of paper.

"Our farm simply isn't that big," Andy added, returning to the subject of hiring Henry out. "I'd rather have Henry at home than in town, and it will be *gut* for him to earn a little extra money. I predict a *wunderbaar* partnership between the two of us."

Paul appeared satisfied with the arrangement.

Great. Her brother and the man who set her teeth on edge were best buddies now.

Sarah shook her head to clear it. "I can't believe we're talking about farming and tractors while I have two abandoned children in my living room. Paul, what did you learn when you spoke to them?"

"Apparently they arrived in town a little over a week ago. They'd hitched a ride from someone because they had no money for a bus ticket."

"Where were they going?" Andy asked.

"He didn't know. He only knew that they were dropped off here. The mother's name is Elisa Lopez."

Sarah dropped her hands to her lap. She could feel a tremor start in one of her hands and creep all the way up her arm. Why was she upset? It would be a good thing if they found the children's mother. But what kind of mother abandoned her children?

A mother like her own.

She bit back the thought and continued to question Paul.

"Why did she leave them? When is she coming back? Did she know that Mia was sick, that Mia could have died of pneumonia in that barn?"

Paul held up both hands in a surrender gesture. "I'm not a translator, Sarah."

Had he ever used her name before? She closed her eyes and ignored the shiver dancing down her spine. She was tired. The last few days had been stressful.

"But you're sure…about their mother?"

"*Ya*. The boy was told to wait with his sister."

Sarah was stunned. She was feeling a hundred things at once and tears pricked her eyes, which was embarrassing. Why would she be crying? This was good news! The children's mother was alive and well, or had been a week ago.

"How old are they?" Andy asked.

"The boy is eight. The girl just turned three." Paul drained his mug of milk and added, "He couldn't tell me anything about his father."

"That's all we need to know." Andy pushed back from the table. "Henry will go into town and fetch the sheriff. This is officially not our problem."

"How can you say that?"

Andy had stood and was walking toward the back door. Now he turned to face her, and Sarah could see the puzzlement on his face. Things were that simple for him.

"These children were in an abandoned building, Andy. At least when our mother left, we were in a home."

"The authorities will take care of them."

"Will they? So they'll shuffle Mateo and Mia to another home? Or to several other homes because no one wants to keep them for very long? Or even to separate homes because no one wants two children?" She fought to lower her voice, afraid they would hear, afraid she would hurt them more than they already had been. "This is what we're supposed to do, as Christians, as *gut* neighbors. Didn't you listen at all to the sermon yesterday?"

"That does not mean that we're to jump in the middle of every problem we see!" Andy shook his head and glanced at Paul, who was obviously trying to stay out of this family argument. "We don't know anything about keeping orphans. You find someone who can advise us, and I will listen. But they need to be here by this afternoon. I can stall a few hours, but that's all. Before the afternoon is over I have to send Henry to town to alert the authorities."

Sarah tried to still her emotions, to make her expression a blank slate. She failed miserably. Turning away, she wiped the tears from her cheeks and hurried into the sitting room.

"Time to go back to work, Henry. But…where is Mia?"

Henry had apparently fallen asleep.

Mateo was sitting beside him on the couch, thumbing through a primer reading book.

And Mia?

Mia was nowhere to be seen.

CHAPTER 25

*Y*our *schweschder* becomes attached quickly."

"*Ya*. She has a big heart. Maybe too big."

"Cute kids."

"They are, but in case you haven't noticed, I already have a houseful of those."

Paul laughed, at ease with Andy in the same way he had been with his own brothers. Women? They were a different matter entirely. Why would Sarah cry because two children she'd known less than twenty-four hours still had a mother?

"I wish I could help you today," Andy said. "But I need to get my own tractor running."

"Not a problem. Technically, I don't own the tractor or the place yet."

They had reached the door to the barn, and Andy had stopped to study him. "It's a big thing you're taking on. Fisher's place was never in what you'd call good shape."

"And it's been empty since he died. *Ya*, I know."

"Will you be staying in the house?"

"I doubt it. The place is likely to fall down around me as I sleep."

They stepped into the barn. Paul had ducked his head in earlier, but now he took a moment to study the work area, storage bins, clean tables, and supplies for their horse.

"You only have the one gelding?"

"*Ya*, and he's getting on up there in age. Don't mention that to Sarah…you'd think the horse is another child."

"Easy to grow attached to a buggy horse."

"It is. We also have a donkey to keep the gelding company. We once tried goats on the place, but…" Andy hesitated, and then he apparently decided to be honest. "My *dat* had a gambling problem, among other things. The goats were doing well, but he lost them in a wager."

Paul let out a long, low whistle. Compared to Andy and Sarah's family, his family of seven brothers was calm and predictable. "You've had a lot to deal with."

"Yes, we have, but maybe things will turn around now." Instead of elaborating, he walked over to his tractor, which had recently been disassembled.

"How did you ever get used to driving tractors?"

Andy's laugh was full and unrestrained. "I was raised with tractors. It's the Amish who move into Cody's Creek from somewhere else who have to get used to the mechanical beasts."

They spent the next half hour talking tractors, crops, and Oklahoma weather. At some point Henry appeared and slipped under the tractor, asking Andy for various tools and generally making a lot of noise.

"Does he know what he's doing?"

"He does, and it's my *bruder* you'll want working on your antique. I'm the farmer in the family. He's the mechanic."

Paul was surprised to find himself whistling as he walked back toward his place, or at least it would be his place soon. He only whistled when he felt no pressure, had no worries. He definitely would feel the stress as soon as he had a barn to renovate, a tractor to fix, and a crop to plant. But he wasn't worried. Maybe that was because he was outside again, doing what he'd been born to do.

The sun crept behind a cloud and a cold wind swept across the fields, causing him to fasten his jacket. It was good to be outside, even when he would prefer a warmer spring day. Those days would come soon enough.

He puttered around in the barn for two more hours. Then he

hitched his brother's mare to the buggy and turned toward the dry goods store. He'd opted to take the buggy, in case Rebecca or Joseph needed the tractor. As he drove back toward town, he admitted to himself that he was more comfortable with a horse and buggy. The clip-clop of the mare's hooves, the gentle rocking of the buggy, the feel of the leather seat and even the small battery heater—it all made for a pleasant and soothing experience. He waved a hand to a tractor that passed him, a teenage Amish boy driving. The kid looked happy as a clam. Paul tried to imagine himself contentedly wrestling the rusty machine in his barn down the two-lane, but failed.

The store was empty of customers, which was pretty common at that time of day. Things picked up again around three and stayed that way until close. Paul had suggested that Rebecca close the shop during the middle of the day. She'd laughed and asked, "What would I do? Take a nap?"

Which didn't sound like such a bad idea to Paul. He'd soon be working from before daylight until past sunset. With that thought in mind, he headed toward the upstairs apartment, but Rebecca caught him before he made it through the storeroom.

"I'm putting labels on our new shipment. Come and help me and tell me all about your morning."

"Where's Joseph?"

"Placing an order for more books. Anything you want?"

"Not unless there's something on how to restore a homestead in three easy steps."

"Haven't heard of that title, but I'll keep my eyes open."

It was while he was applying stickers to gardening tools that he told her about Andy and Henry. "They both agreed to help with the tractor and repairs around the place."

"Did you see Sarah?"

"*Ya*, she was there too." Paul stopped and scratched at the nape of his neck, remembering the scene he'd walked in on. "Her and two orphans."

"Orphans?"

"Mateo and Mia."

Rebecca put down her labeler and placed both of her hands on her hips. "Are you telling me that Sarah Yoder has two orphaned children at her house? And you didn't think to tell me this first?"

"I suppose I could have led with that."

"Indeed you could have." Rebecca was taking off her apron and pulling on a shawl she kept near the register.

"There's no use going out there."

"Of course there is. She might need help."

"*Nein.* Andy told her that he was sending Henry to town to alert the police. They're probably gone by now."

Rebecca dropped her purse on the counter and sank back onto the work stool. "Tell me everything, Paul. From the beginning."

Ten minutes later she was gone, mumbling that if she hurried she just might get there in time. Paul was looking out the front window as she pulled the tractor out onto the street, and the funny thing was…she turned in the opposite direction of the Yoder place.

CHAPTER 26

Mateo didn't know what to think about the group of people staring at him. There was a sheriff, whose name was Bynum. Mateo could remember that because the man wore a name tag. There was also a social worker. In his experience, that was never a good thing. When he was younger, a social worker had taken him away from his mother. He didn't want to be taken away from Sarah or Mia.

Sarah sat on the couch, between him and Mia. They were squeezed together tightly because Andy was also in the room, as was someone Sarah had called Bishop Levi. He wasn't sure what a bishop was, but the old guy seemed nice enough. Plus, he chewed bubble gum. Mateo was pretty sure that bad guys didn't chew gum.

Mateo would have felt better if Isaac was in the room with him, but the three youngest boys had been sent to the barn to finish their chores. Probably Sarah didn't want everyone in the room. Things were confusing enough.

"The Department of Human Services has a specific protocol for this," the social worker said.

Mateo suddenly remembered that his name was Tommy. Though his skin was white like Sarah's, he dressed differently. He dressed normal, but in the last twenty-four hours Mateo had sort of become used to long dresses, dark pants, and suspenders.

"We have a very good foster care system here in Oklahoma. We will relocate Mateo and Mia with a Bridge family."

"But why can't they stay here?" Sarah asked. "They're already settled."

"After less than twenty-four hours?" Tommy's eyebrow arched up over his thick black glasses. "I appreciate that you've bonded with the children quickly, Miss Yoder, but this is the very situation we have Bridge families for—to provide a safe passage from less than optimal conditions to reunification with their birth parents."

Mateo only understood about half those words. He wanted to answer, but his English wasn't very good. What if he made things worse?

"We wouldn't want the children to be placed in two different homes," Andy said.

"Neither would I. We'll do our best—"

"Where will you take them? To Tulsa? How could living in the city be better than living here?"

"As I said before, we have a specific process, and it works. I can promise you that both Mateo and Mia will be well cared for."

Mia crawled into Sarah's lap at this point, putting her head on Sarah's shoulder and staring at Mateo. He didn't know what to do. He thought they should stay here, close to where their mother had left them. Besides, he liked it here. He liked being with another boy his age and having food to eat.

Sarah was brushing at her eyes. Was she crying? Did she care about them so much?

Mateo realized he had to say something. He might not have another chance because the man named Tommy was already standing up and speaking with the police officer.

"We want to stay with Sarah."

His voice came out smaller than he expected, but that didn't stop him. "Please," he added.

Everyone was staring at him now.

Sarah was the first to react. "You speak English?"

"*Un poquito.*"

"He said that he understands a little." Tommy squatted down in front of him. "Can you tell us where your mom is, Mateo?"

"No. She said...she said she would be back...*en poco tiempo*." He tried to think the last three words in English, but they wouldn't come.

"Is this the first time your mom has left you alone?"

Mateo shook his head. He didn't want to say anything bad about his mom, but he didn't think he should lie either.

And though he'd fought hard against giving in to the feelings of hopelessness and uncertainty, his eyes filled with tears. He allowed himself to be pulled into Sarah's arms.

"It's okay, Mateo. We're going to work this out. It's going to be fine."

He heard Tommy sigh and sit back down. "It's plain the children have bonded with you, and I'd like to leave them here. I can't, though. I don't have the authority to make a decision like that. Maybe if we had a Bridge parent close by…"

"I'm a Bridge parent."

Mateo raised up his head.

It was the bishop who had spoken. Now he was blowing a bubble with his gum. He popped it and tapped his cane against the floor.

"Mary Beth and I went through the training years ago."

"I never knew that." Andy had been looking pretty miserable. But now, when Mateo peeked at him, he saw that Sarah's big brother was smiling. Surely that was a good sign.

"It's not something we put in the *Budget*." The bishop laughed. "Check your system. Levi and Mary Beth Troyer."

"And you'd be willing to take these two children on a temporary basis?"

"Of course. They will be close to Sarah, and she can visit until we work this out or the mother is found."

It wasn't the answer that Mateo wanted, but Sarah seemed to trust this man, and Andy was definitely smiling.

He squatted in front of the little boy. "Levi is our bishop, Mateo. He's a *gut* man, and his wife cooks even better than Sarah."

"But we want to stay here."

"I know you do, and I would let you if it was possible. Sometimes we have to accept *Gotte's wille, ya?*"

Mateo didn't know what he meant by that, but he nodded because Andy seemed to be waiting for him to do so.

It wasn't as easy for Mia. She cried and clung to Sarah's neck as they tried to place her in the buggy. Eventually, the bishop peeled her arms away and placed her in the backseat next to Mateo.

Sarah stuck her head in the buggy and said, "I'll come see you tomorrow. I promise."

And then they were following the police car into the dark evening. A soft rain had begun to fall, and Mateo realized they were fortunate not to be in the cold, dilapidated barn or the abandoned trailer. But as they turned the corner, with Tommy's car behind them, he looked back at the house he'd been in since the night before, and he wished with all of his might that they would be able to return.

CHAPTER 27

*S*arah was up well before her normal time.

She had the boys' lunches packed and breakfast on the table. She tried to clean the mess she'd made in the kitchen, but her emotions were tumbling up and down—excitement over seeing Mateo and Mia again, followed by deep sorrow over all that had happened to the two children. Her stomach rebelled when she tried to eat a piece of toast, and her hands shook as she swiped at the counter with a dishcloth.

"How are you doing?" Andy asked.

"*Gut*. I...I miss them."

"I know you do. This will work out, Sarah. Somehow it will."

"I'd like to drive over to the bishop's. See how they're doing."

"I thought you might. I'll harness Dusty to the buggy after breakfast."

Everyone was somber that morning. Andy tried to tease Isaac about his hair sticking up, but her youngest brother only stared at the two of them and asked, "When can I see Mateo again?"

"I don't know. We're working on that."

"That's a terrible answer, Sarah. It's bad enough about *Dat* and *Mamm*, but now I finally have one *gut* friend, and you gave him away."

Sarah started to answer, but Isaac wasn't listening. He bounded up from the table and shot out the back door.

"Leave him be," Andy said.

Luke reached for the bowl of oatmeal. When he tried to dump some onto his plate, it stuck stubbornly to the large serving spoon. He took his own spoon and pried it loose, before smiling at Sarah. "At least you're attempting to feed the troops."

"We're not troops," Henry pointed out. "We're family."

"Well, I'm pretty sure that Isaac thought Mateo and Mia were family too."

"After only one night?" Andy shook his head. "I liked them, honestly I did, but they're not pets, you know. They're children, and they need a *gut* home."

"We have a *gut* home," Luke said. He shoved a spoonful of lumpy oatmeal into his mouth so he wouldn't have to explain himself.

"We do, but that doesn't mean *Gotte* intends us to share it with every homeless person we meet."

"Not that many homeless folks in Cody's Creek." Henry reached for a handful of raisins. Instead of putting them on top of his oatmeal, he tossed them into his mouth.

"Everyone will feel better this afternoon," Andy promised. "We'll get back to normal faster than you can say Peter Piper."

But no one was interested in alliteration games. Luke continued to pry his oatmeal out of his bowl, and Henry focused on the raisins and nuts. Sarah didn't see Isaac again until Luke had started down the lane, headed toward the schoolhouse. As she watched from the window, Isaac ran from the barn and joined him.

She wished she knew how to comfort her brother, but she was in no place to encourage someone else. She'd spent most of the night falling asleep, only to wake and wonder where Mia was hiding. Suddenly she would remember all that had happened, and an ache would pierce her heart. After a time, she'd slowly fall back into a restless sleep only to repeat the cycle an hour later.

All that was behind her, though.

This morning she was going to see the bishop.

She wanted to learn what she had to do in order to bring Mateo and Mia home.

The drive to the bishop's house calmed her nerves. She'd barely knocked on the door when Mary Beth answered. The woman could be a storybook illustration of an Amish grandmother—matronly, neat, calm. "Levi's gone to town, but I suspect you're here to see the children."

"Is that all right?"

"Of course." She led Sarah into the living room, where Mateo was sitting on the couch reading a book to Mia.

When they looked up and saw her, a smile burst through their formerly serious expressions.

Mia ran to her, arms lifted high, and said, "Up, please."

Mary Beth seemed surprised. "First words I've heard from her."

Mateo was a little more reserved, but not much. When she walked to the couch, he threw his arms around her waist, and then he quickly stepped back as if embarrassed by his show of emotion. "Hi, Sarah."

"Hi, Mateo."

They grinned at each other a moment. Then Sarah sat and patted the seat beside her. "Say, why didn't you tell me you can speak English?"

Mateo shrugged. It was a habit of the child's. Before she'd thought he was merely disinterested. Now it occurred to her that perhaps he was buying time to search for the right word.

He settled for, "I don't speak well." As if that was explanation enough, he picked up the book and showed her what he'd been reading.

When they sat together on the couch, the anxiety Sarah had been feeling melted away.

Mary Beth kindly murmured, "I'll give you all a few moments alone." She busied herself in the kitchen, and twenty minutes later called them all to the table for a snack. She'd brewed hot tea for her and Sarah and poured milk for the children. In the center of the table sat a plate of oatmeal cookies.

Mia ate half a cookie and proceeded to break the rest into tiny crumbs on her plate. Mateo ate two, and though they tried to steer the conversation to safe topics, he asked, "When can we come to your house, Sarah? *Yo quiero*...that is, I want to see Isaac."

Mary Beth sipped her hot tea and allowed Sarah to answer.

"I don't know at this point, Mateo. I don't want to lie and say I do know. But I can promise you that I'm trying. Okay?"

"*Ya*, okay."

Sarah and Mary Beth exchanged a smile at the Amish emphasis on his first word.

"Will you take Mia to wash her hands, Mateo?" Mary Beth stood and collected their dishes. "After that maybe you can finish reading the story to her."

Mia was already rubbing at her eyes, but she allowed herself to be led into the other room.

They had barely left the kitchen when Sarah turned to her bishop's wife and said, "Tell me how to be a Bridge parent. I want to bring Mateo and Mia home."

CHAPTER 28

*I*t's not a decision to be made easily," Mary Beth cautioned.

"I'm sure it's not, but…but if it meant that Mateo and Mia could come home, I will commit myself to doing whatever is required." When Mary Beth didn't respond, Sarah pushed forward. "I'm sure they'll be fine here, but I would like to bring them back to our house, at least until their mother is found."

Mary Beth pulled out some crochet work. "Tell me about finding them."

So she did. She described Mateo running out in front of her buggy, how it had terrified her, how she'd known in that moment that the boy she'd seen was not a figment of her imagination.

"You went into the old trailer?"

"*Ya*, with Isaac and Luke. Perhaps that's why they feel so close to Mateo and Mia. We found them there, living in a tower of boxes in the middle of that abandoned trailer. Actually, they ran away when they first saw us. They were frightened, I suppose. Then Mia tripped and began to cry. It was all we could do to convince them to go back inside, and then to leave with us. Mary Beth, they were so cold and wet and hungry and desperate. It's not a thing you easily forget."

"I'm sure it's not. I'm also sure…" she leaned forward and tapped the table with her crochet needle. "I'm sure *Gotte* meant for you to find the children. If you hadn't stopped, if you hadn't gone in…well, there's no telling what would have happened."

Sarah thought about that for a moment. She felt restless and needed something to do with her hands while she talked, while she worked out what she was feeling and what steps she planned to take next. She spied a bowl full of potatoes in the sink.

"Do you need those peeled?"

Mary Beth nodded, not the least surprised. *"Ya, danki."*

Once she'd washed the potatoes, located a paring knife, and sat back down at the table, Sarah was ready to tell the rest of her story. As she peeled the potatoes, she described the first night, how Mia had fallen asleep in her arms, and the next day's laundry fiasco, with Paul walking in on a dripping Mateo and a missing Mia.

"He found her squatting on a bottom shelf in the mudroom. I'm not sure why she hides."

"It's happened twice here already. Once she was behind the couch, and another time she'd hopped into the tub and laid down with her blanket. I found her sound asleep there."

"I can't fathom what's going through that child's mind."

"We've had a lot of different children over the years."

"I always assumed they were distant family."

Mary Beth smiled. "They felt like family."

"Why did you never tell anyone about your being Bridge parents?"

"It was a small thing we were doing, and not something we wanted to brag about. There seemed no need to share the children's story. It was only necessary to love them for a time until they could find their forever home—whether that was back with their natural parents or with an adoptive family."

"You never wanted to keep them? For your own?"

"Oh, they claimed my heart, some more than others, if that's what you're asking. But Levi and I knew from the beginning that our role was to provide a smooth and safe transition, not a permanent home."

"Would it even be possible?" Sarah paused mid potato. "Could I be a Bridge parent? And if I manage to do that, would they allow me to keep the children, either temporarily or...or permanently?"

"I don't see why not. It's true that you have an unconventional home." Mary Beth picked up her mug of tea, long gone cold, and sipped it. "You've been through a lot in the last few years, Sarah. The DHS, Department of Human Services, won't hold that against you. If anything, it proves your resilience."

"But…we've had to accept help from the church just to get by."

Mary Beth waved away that concern. "Andy will turn your place into a productive farm. He's a *gut* worker, and the land will produce if it's cared for."

"Then there's the fact that they're not Amish, and we're not Hispanic."

"Other Amish have adopted before. There are other concerns, much more important than if you share the same ethnic background or how much money you make."

"Such as?"

"Can you provide a safe, healthy home?"

"*Ya*, of course we can."

"You'll have to pass a background check, and everyone in the house will need a physical exam."

"Why?"

"The state wouldn't want someone who is physically unable to care for children to take on such a task."

"Can't they tell that by looking at us?"

"Not always."

Sarah didn't know what to say to that. She focused on finishing with the potatoes, quartering them when Mary Beth indicated she should. She rinsed them again, placed them in a pan, covered them with water, and set the pan on the stovetop. It stilled something inside her to know that she'd helped to prepare the children's meal.

She peeked back into the living room. Both Mateo and Mia were asleep on the couch.

In response to her unanswered question, Mary Beth said, "It will take a while for them to recover both physically and emotionally. Being abandoned, at that age, is not an easy thing."

When she sat back down at the table, Sarah said, "I know something about being abandoned."

"For sure and certain you do. I'm sorry about your mother."

"The worst part? It's easier without her."

"And that is not how things should be, but we make the best of what we're given." Mary Beth put aside her crocheting, walked around the table, and sat down beside Sarah. Reaching for her hands, she held them, squeezed them, and spoke in a calm voice. "The question at this point isn't whether you can be a Bridge parent. If *Gotte* has chosen that path for you, He will make it possible. I want you to search your heart. Are you doing this to heal something inside of you? Or are you doing it for the children?"

"Maybe both?" Sarah's voice sounded incredibly small, even to her own ears.

"That's certainly possible, but you won't always be a twenty-three-year-old woman raising her *bruders*. Andy and Henry and Isaac and Luke will all be on their own within a few years. What you're taking on, especially if you're considering permanent placement, is for the rest of your life. Be sure that's what you want, and that it is what *Gotte* has called you to."

"And if it is?"

Mary Beth's smile eased an ache deep in Sarah's heart. "We will pray that *Gotte* makes smooth the path before you."

CHAPTER 29

*P*aul's purchase of the Fisher place closed on Friday morning. The real estate agent claimed it was the fastest sale he'd ever brokered. As for Paul, he was simply relieved that the legalities were done with and he could get to work in earnest.

He didn't need any help moving in, as he only had a duffel of clothes to take with him and a few items Rebecca had found in their storage room. So he was surprised when he and Rebecca and Joseph drove out to the place in Joseph's buggy and found a line of tractors and buggies in the yard.

No one had gone inside. Men, women, and even children were milling around, waiting on their arrival. Indeed, they weren't sure if Paul would be living in the house or the barn.

"The barn," he admitted. "At least there the rain won't come through the roof."

There was much backslapping and congratulations, offers of help and suggestions for contractors. Paul couldn't explain that he wanted to do the work himself, to do it slowly, and watch life come back into the neglected place. So he thanked them for their suggestions and accepted slips of papers with names and phone numbers, but he doubted he would be contacting anyone.

Once he opened the door to the barn, the women fairly swarmed the place, stocking the shelves in the office with food, placing new sheets on the cot, leaving extra bedding and towels in the bathroom.

Half the women cleaned while the other half unloaded items and put things away.

"I didn't expect this," Paul confessed to his brother.

"*Ya?* The women enjoy helping an old bachelor settle down." With a wink, Joseph followed Paul around the barn to look at the old tractor. They were soon joined by Andy and Luke.

"Henry couldn't come," Andy explained. "He's working a shift at the restaurant in town, but he's already looked at it. Says it will take a bit of work to get it going, but that it is fixable."

"I suppose tractors are like horses." Joseph tapped a rusty spot on the tractor Paul had acquired along with the purchase of the property. Sitting next to it was the bed of an old white Ford pickup that could be attached to the tractor. "Once you make up for the years of neglect, they will last you a long time."

"Are you going to buy a horse and buggy?" Luke asked.

"One day, but money's tight at the moment."

"No doubt you'll want to get your crop in first," Joseph said. "*Gotte* will provide, Paul. Never fear."

They walked back outside, and Paul found himself looking for Sarah.

He'd heard from Rebecca what had happened to the Lopez children. His sister-in-law was one of the few who knew the bishop and his wife were licensed foster parents—Bridge parents they were called. She had hurried over to the bishop's house after Paul had told her about walking in on the laundry fiasco and discovering the two small children. It had been her idea that the bishop intervene and offer support if necessary. Paul doubted it took much convincing. Levi seemed the type to offer a hand whenever one was needed.

A passel of children had accompanied the women, and they were now playing tag in what had once been a horse pasture. He noticed Mateo in the middle of the children, but no sign of Mia. He turned and nearly bumped into Sarah. Mia was plastered to her side.

"I wanted to thank you," she said, glancing down at Mia and adjusting her coat. She looked everywhere but directly at him. "For helping the day you stopped by."

"You're welcome, of course." He didn't know what else to say. Though they were to be neighbors, he hadn't quite been able to figure out Andy and Sarah and their odd family. He'd never known a family to be abandoned by their sole surviving parent before.

Because he couldn't think of a thing to say to Sarah, Paul squatted down so that he was level with Mia. "How are you?"

He expected her to hide her face in Sarah's coat. Instead, she stepped closer to him, put one hand on each side of his face, and said, "Up, please."

It broke the tension between Sarah and Paul as they both laughed. He raised the little girl up in the air. She squealed and clung to his neck.

"She seems taken with you."

"*Ya*? I always thought children were afraid of me—too ugly."

Sarah's eyes widened, but she didn't counter his uncharitable description of himself. Now that he thought of it, he sounded like a teenage fool fishing for a compliment. He cast around for something else to say.

"They're staying with the bishop and his wife?"

"For now." Sarah's chin raised a fraction of an inch. "I began my training earlier this week."

"Training?"

"To be a Bridge parent."

Mateo called to Mia, and she squirmed to be released.

"No hiding," Sarah called after her.

Paul took off his hat and resettled it on his head. The day was sunny and unseasonably warm for the second week of February. Some of the children had even taken off their coats.

"A Bridge parent. So you want to be a foster home?"

"What I want is Mateo and Mia to stay with me, at least until their mother returns."

"What if she doesn't return?"

"We'll deal with that later."

"But you need to have a plan." Paul glanced around, as if he might see someone he could pull over, someone who could talk sense into this woman.

"My plan is to do what *Gotte* has called me to do."

"Such as raising your *bruders*?"

A clear look of defiance flashed over Sarah's features. "You think I can't do both?"

"I don't understand why you'd want to do both."

Sarah opened her mouth to argue. He didn't give her the chance.

"They're *gut* kids, Sarah, but surely *Gotte* doesn't expect you to take on so much."

"Is that so? Because I'm pretty sure the Bible tells us to look after the orphans."

"Well, yes, but—"

"Nowhere does it say to do so only when the road is easy."

"It certainly won't be," he muttered, but she wasn't listening. Nope. He'd hit a nerve in Sarah Yoder's heart, and she was now as prickly as a porcupine.

"I may not have the most money or the cleanest house, but at least they won't be living in a barn."

Instead of being offended, Paul had to resist the urge to laugh. As if he would bring children to live in his barn. His home might not be ready to live in for some time, but he was a bachelor and fully expected to remain so.

As for Sarah, he had to admit that his neighbor made a pretty picture, especially when she was angry.

But he didn't say any of that, because she had stomped away, gathering up her brothers, and saying goodbye to Mateo and Mia. She never once turned to look at him.

CHAPTER 30

*T*he next ten days passed in a flurry of activity. Sarah made a good dent in the twenty-seven hours of preservice training required by DHS. Twice she hired a driver to take her to Tulsa for all-day classes. When she tried to pay the woman, she'd been informed that Bishop Levi had already taken care of the charge. She completed about half of the classes on the computer at their small library. At first she'd been filled with trepidation as she sat in front of the monitor. Rebecca had accompanied her and patiently explained how to use the device. The librarian even stopped by to offer help.

"It's only that it feels wrong." Sarah worried the strings of her prayer *kapp*.

"To use the computer? Phooey. There are reasons for our rules, Sarah, for our *Ordnung*. It's not necessarily because something is bad. Sometimes it's only that we don't want a thing in our homes, distracting us from our family. But computers can be useful at times."

"I suppose," she mumbled, still unconvinced.

"Many of our men use them to read the latest in weather prediction or crop rotations. And I've known more than one woman who stops by when she is hankering for a new recipe."

"There are recipes? On here?"

"*Ya*. You can even find Amish recipes."

That made her laugh, and suddenly she wasn't intimidated anymore. Rebecca helped her to navigate to the DHS website and log on to the Resource page with the password Tommy Cronin had given her. She'd seen the social worker twice now, and though he seemed impossibly young and…well, *Englisch*…she did believe he had the children's welfare at heart.

The second time she'd gone to the library, she'd done so alone. The librarian smiled, assured her one of the computers was open, and offered to help if she had any trouble.

"*Danki*. I think I'll be okay." And miraculously she was.

The certification process was going smoothly, and Sarah found herself believing that everything might all work out.

Until the day that they had to go to the police department to be fingerprinted.

Luke was the only one happy about that. Apparently, it gave him new insight into the video games he wasn't supposed to be playing with the neighbor boy.

"This is totally radical," he claimed, staring at the Wanted posters lining the walls.

"There's no time for that." Sarah nudged him away from the harsh-looking photographs of unkempt men and women. "The officer is waiting."

Andy was restless, claiming he needed to be in the fields working.

Henry was covered in grease, which she hadn't noticed until they were already on their way.

And Isaac had thought they were going to see Mateo.

"Don't you see him at school every day?" Sarah had been quite pleased to learn that Mateo had started school at their small, one-room schoolhouse. She agreed that the boy needed to spend time with other children his age, and he also needed to be in school. She only hoped that it wasn't too hard for him.

"*Ya*, of course I do, but we have to work at school. I thought we were going to the bishop's house."

"I plainly said that we were going to help Mateo and Mia by getting fingerprinted."

"I guess I stopped listening at the word Mateo," he admitted.

They were a grumbly lot standing before the police station counter as they waited to be escorted to the back. The woman standing in front of them wore a uniform and sported a gun on her hip. The entire thing made Sarah nervous. Officer Holland was pleasant enough, though, and a few minutes after they arrived they were led to a back room where the fingerprinting was done.

"Each person has a unique print," Luke told her. "It's so they can catch us if we do anything wrong."

"I don't think that's why we're here today," Andy said.

Sarah wasn't exactly clear on how Andy felt about her desire to become a Bridge parent. He was so busy outside around the farm, and out occasionally with friends (which she thought meant a girl), that they rarely had time to talk.

Officer Holland, who was older with white hair, explained the process to them.

It turned out he only needed Sarah and Andy's prints. "To check against our database."

"What will that tell you?" Luke had been gravely disappointed that his fingerprints weren't needed until the officer showed him a Junior Officer pamphlet and printed his right index finger.

Isaac and Henry both passed on being printed, but seemed interested enough in what the officer was saying.

"Every time you touch something, you leave a fingerprint."

"Believe me, I see those all over the house," Sarah muttered.

The officer laughed, putting them all at ease. "Indeed, we do transfer dirt and residue to surfaces, but you also leave a unique fingerprint."

"And you keep a record of them all in that computer?" Henry asked.

"Actually, we upload them to a federal database—the IAFIS. That stands for Integrated Automated Fingerprint Identification System."

"Sounds awesome." Luke was practically bouncing on the balls of his feet.

"There are seventy million subjects in the criminal master file, plus another thirty-one million civil prints."

"What's the purpose of the civil prints?" Andy frowned at his right hand, each finger now smudged with ink.

"Employment background checks as well as firearm purchases.

Some employers, such as school districts or the government, require employees to be fingerprinted to ensure they are hiring people of good character. Law enforcement agencies can request a search, and, of course, civil searches can be performed as well for a small fee, which DHS covers." As he described the process, he'd printed Andy's other five fingers and now began on Sarah's.

She felt oddly invigorated as he pressed each of her fingers into ink and rolled them on the card where he'd printed her name. To look at those swirls and think that there wasn't another like it in the whole world…well, that was a humbling thing. She had heard often enough in church that they were "fearfully and wonderfully made," but those little swirls put a specific image in her mind.

The officer handed her and Andy each a disinfectant wipe to clean off their fingers.

She rubbed vigorously, but some of the ink remained.

"No worries. It'll wear off over the next few days."

Andy thanked him, eager to get back to the farm. Her brothers followed him out of the building, but Sarah hung back.

"How long does the process usually take?"

"In the old days it would take several weeks, but things are faster now. Three to seven days at the most."

She nodded her thanks and was almost out the door when the officer called her name.

She turned toward him, expecting that she would need to sign another form.

But instead he simply said, "What you're doing, Miss Yoder, is a good thing. Best of luck to you."

"Thank you."

Her words seemed inadequate. The man's unexpected kindness had eased her anxiety. But her gratitude was all she had, so she again said, "Thank you," and hurried out the door.

CHAPTER 31

*M*ateo had been going to the small Amish school for a week now. He still hated to leave Mia each morning, but he loved the school. He loved the subjects they studied, even though he had to work in the younger books. Brian had tried to reassure him. "It's okay, Mateo. You'll catch up in no time."

He loved that everyone called the teacher Brian, and Brian sometimes called them scholars. Mateo had never been called a scholar before. He'd often been put in remedial classes, and though the teachers thought he couldn't understand the conversations they had about him, he could. He understood English quite well when he was listening. It was only when he was talking that he sometimes forgot the word he needed.

Brian called that his expressive vocabulary. "You'll learn to express yourself in time. Your receptive vocabulary is good, and one inevitably builds on the other."

Mateo wasn't sure about that, but he trusted Brian, even though he'd only been in his class a short while.

Amish school was different in a lot of ways. He'd learned that's what the people were who had rescued him—Amish. They dressed differently, didn't own cars, and their school was a completely new experience for him. For one thing, all of the grades were together in the same room. Mateo was a little intimidated by the older kids, though they seemed nice enough. But the math they did? He wasn't sure he would ever be able to do that.

The amazing thing was that sometimes he could help the younger kids.

Brian had asked him just that morning, "Would you sit next to Simon and look over his addition? Check his answers and explain to him what he did wrong if something isn't right."

The first graders' math included very simple problems. Two-digit numbers. He'd learned to do those long ago. So he nodded that he would do as Brian asked. Simon had all the answers right except two, and he listened closely when Mateo explained what he had done wrong on those.

It was a very odd experience. Mateo had never helped someone learn before.

Mary Beth fixed him a lunch every morning, which he took to school. He no longer had to show a card to get his free lunch. As he carried that little pail with a sandwich and piece of fruit, Mateo felt more normal than he'd ever felt in his entire life.

The very best part about school was that he was once again able to see Isaac. He was surprised the first day when Brian had told him to sit with other students his age, and he couldn't believe his luck when he was assigned the desk next to Isaac.

They were in the same class, though Isaac was ahead of him in every subject. It didn't seem to matter. No one was worried that Mateo sometimes took a paper home to finish. There weren't any embarrassing tests to take where he had to bubble the answers on narrow sheets. He'd done that the year before in a school in Texas. He must not have done very well, because the teacher had frowned when he turned his sheet in.

"Ball game is starting," Isaac said. A slow grin started spreading across Isaac's face, and Mateo thought he knew what that meant.

"Want to play? You hit the ball pretty good yesterday."

"We could." Isaac glanced left and then right. "Or we could look for bugs. My frogs need to eat, and it's still too cold to let them outside."

"How long have you had them?"

"Since last fall."

"And they've been in that box all that time?"

"*Nein.* When Sarah isn't looking, I put them in the tub and let them hop around."

That sounded smart to Mateo, though he wasn't sure Sarah would agree.

"Okay. Let's look for bugs."

It was cold outside, but the sun was shining. Mateo still couldn't believe that they were given a full hour for lunch, and they always went outside. Well, probably they didn't when it was raining or snowing, but otherwise they were outside playing ball, or taking turns on the playground equipment, or looking for bugs.

They must not have heard the bell calling them back to class.

Luke came looking for them.

"Don't know what you two are doing, but class is back in session."

Mateo had been in trouble in school before, when he'd gotten lost in the building and been late for class. He didn't want to be in trouble again.

They followed Luke back to the classroom and slipped into their seats.

Brian was reading to everyone from a book called *Treasure Island.* Mateo liked the book even though he'd missed the first part while he was still living in the old trailer. Today Brian was reading about a cook named Long John Silver.

Maybe Brian didn't know they were late.

If he did know, maybe he would forget.

He didn't forget.

After the reading and when they'd started their writing work, Brian stopped by and said in a low voice, "You two stay after class and see me."

Mateo's eyes must have betrayed his fear, because Brian touched his shoulder and said, "Don't worry, Mateo. I just want to talk to you."

He did worry, though.

All through his writing exercise. As they were doing map work. And finally through cleanup time.

When everyone filed out, he and Isaac stayed in their seats.

As Luke left, he had said, "You know your way home, so I'm not going to wait for you." Then he'd added, "Good luck," and grinned as if he found the entire thing very funny.

Before Mateo could process how much trouble he might be in, Brian pulled around a desk to face them and sat in it. He was a big man with red hair and a bushy red beard. He looked funny sitting in that desk. Somehow it helped Mateo relax a little.

"So what happened, guys? Why did I have to send someone to find you after lunch?"

"We were looking for frog food," Mateo explained.

"And we thought we saw something hop under the woodpile—"

"So we were trying to get it."

"But then we knocked a lot of the wood down."

"So we restacked it."

"And were waiting to see the bugs again."

The boys fell silent and waited for Brian's reaction.

To Mateo's surprise, he grinned at them.

"You're keeping a frog?"

"Three of them. In a box under my bed." Isaac squirreled his nose. "Might be better if Sarah doesn't know about it."

"You think she doesn't know?"

"She's a little afraid of frogs. I'd have heard about it if she did."

"It's a nice box," Mateo added. "He has rocks and water and grass and stuff in there."

"So you've built a terrarium."

Both boys shrugged.

"What kind of frogs?"

They shrugged again.

Finally, Isaac said, "Just frogs."

Brian tapped on the desk a few times before standing and walking to the bookshelf. He pulled out a book and said, "I can't send this home with both of you, so I want you to read it a few minutes during lunch each day."

On the cover of the book was a picture of a frog peeking out from tall, green grass.

Mateo could read the title *Frogs!* easily enough.

When Brian handed it to them, he traced the top words with his finger, slowly sounding them out, "Na-tion-al…"

"Geographic!" Isaac high-fived his teacher. "These books are cool."

"They are. When you finish, we'll talk about what you've read."

"We have to read it during lunch?" Isaac asked.

"You have to do it during part of lunch. Come inside when I do, about ten minutes before everyone else, which will also ensure you're not late again."

Isaac acted as if this was a terrible punishment, but Mateo thought it was pretty fair. And it would keep them out of future trouble.

They were almost at the door when Brian called out to them.

"And Isaac? Tell Sarah about the frogs."

"Okay."

Mateo almost laughed. Isaac sounded as if his frog home was doomed.

"She'll *comprende*...I mean, understand," Mateo said. "Sarah's cool."

"You don't know how much she hates frogs."

CHAPTER 32

Sarah suspected that Bishop Levi had pulled some strings.

Her application to be a Bridge parent was proceeding at lightning speed. She had been able to finish her twenty-seven hours of training in record time. The background checks on her and Andy had been sent and were due back any day, and everyone had passed their physical. The bishop had stopped by earlier that afternoon to tell Sarah that her in-home study would happen within the next forty-eight hours.

"They don't give you the exact time so that it's a surprise, but they give you a window." He'd popped his gum and assured her she had nothing to worry about.

Nothing to worry about?

She'd separated the dirty laundry into piles, but she hadn't had time to wash it. She'd gone to Tulsa the day before to finish up her training, and so she had missed her regular wash day. It wasn't a big problem as everyone had extra clothes, but it made for some large piles.

The dinner she made had been a disaster—not only had she burned the casserole, but dishes were piled everywhere. She'd sent Isaac upstairs to take his bath, and asked Henry and Luke to clean up the kitchen. From the sounds coming from the next room, she suspected they were playing more than washing. Andy came inside grumbling about the tractor and had forgotten to stomp the dirt off his boots. The result was a smudged track of large boot prints from the back door up to his room.

At least she'd have tomorrow to clean before Tommy Cronin, their social worker, arrived.

The thought had barely crossed her mind when there was a knock on the front door. At six thirty in the evening? Who…

Her hand flew to her mouth, and she thought about not answering the door.

But it could be that something had happened to Mateo and Mia, or maybe their mother had been found.

When she opened the door, though, it was only Tommy standing there, holding a clipboard. "I'm here for your home visit."

She nodded, momentarily speechless, and motioned for him to come inside.

If he was surprised to see the chaos that was their living room, he didn't say anything.

Instead, he waited while she cleared a place for him to sit by moving a pile of dirty laundry off the couch.

"Would you like some hot tea?" she asked.

"That would be great. Thank you." He pushed up on the large glasses he wore. Tommy was probably her age, maybe a little older. He had black hair that looked as if it could use a trim. He was also terribly thin.

Sarah rushed into the kitchen, thinking she would bring him some of the cookies Rebecca had sent over. And that was when she caught Henry and Luke throwing dish suds at one another. Water was puddled on the floor, and no one had yet cleared the dirty dishes from the table.

"Start cleaning," she hissed. "The social worker is here. What if he sees this mess?"

Henry shrugged and Luke patted her shoulder, leaving a wet handprint. "It'll be okay, Sarah."

"Just clean this up!"

She set the kettle on the stove, found the tea bags, and turned to look for the cookies.

"Where are they?"

"What?" Henry asked. He at least had his hands in the soapy water now, though she didn't see any dishes there.

"The cookies Rebecca brought us."

"Umm. I think we ate those."

Sarah closed her eyes in disbelief. There had been two dozen.

"Dinner was pretty bad," Henry pointed out.

"Not that is was your fault," Luke said. "We know you're busy, and we don't mind eating cookies for dinner."

"Stop talking!" What if Tommy was listening? Would he think she always fed them dessert for supper?

She hurried out of the room.

Tommy was sitting on the couch, making notations on a notepad.

"I didn't realize you'd be here so soon," she admitted, sitting across from him. "Should I call Andy?"

"I'd love to speak to your brother before I leave, but we can start without him."

There was the obvious noise of a shower running, and then Andy hollered something at Isaac. It sounded like, "I mean it! Get those out of here." But she couldn't be certain.

"Tell me about your family, Sarah. How did you come to be in charge of raising your brothers?"

She wasn't sure if what had happened in the last year would count against them or for them, but neither could she lie. So she explained about her father's death, skirting around the subject of his bipolar disorder.

"And your mother?"

"She's gone…for now."

"Do you have any idea when she'll be back?"

"*Nein.* I mean no. I don't think…that is to say, it doesn't seem as if she will be back anytime soon." In truth, they didn't actually know where their mother was. She'd told Sarah she was going to Florida. An aunt had sent a letter that she'd stopped by and quickly moved on. Where would she have moved on to? Another state? Or a different community in Florida? What, exactly, was she looking for? Sarah pushed those questions from her mind and attempted to focus on the man sitting across from her.

"All right. How do you feel about all of this?"

"What do you mean?"

"Well, some young women might be bitter or resentful." When she didn't answer he added, "Maybe you had other plans for your life, something other than taking care of your siblings."

Sarah almost laughed. "Amish girls are raised waiting for the moment when they can care for a family."

Glancing around, she had a sudden urge to apologize, but why? This was their life, and if it wasn't perfect…well, what life was?

"I'm not the best housekeeper," she confessed, waving a hand at the pile of laundry. "But I'm usually better than this."

"All I see is laundry that you're about to wash, Sarah. We're not concerned about that. We just want to know that you can provide a safe and loving home for Mateo and Mia."

At that moment, Luke walked in carrying a tray with two mugs of hot tea, a stack of crackers, and some freshly cut cheese. She could have hopped up and kissed him.

"You're Isaac, right?"

"Nope, I'm Luke. Isaac's the baby of the family…though I guess he won't be anymore when Mateo and Mia come back." Luke grinned at the thought and sauntered off toward the kitchen.

Tommy sampled some of the cheese and crackers. "This is great cheese."

"*Ya*, it's fresh from one of the members of our church. Henry sometimes helps the neighbor with his cows. In exchange, we receive cheese."

"Do you have animals on your farm?"

"Only the buggy horse, Dusty, a donkey who keeps him company, and a few laying hens. When I was younger we had goats and also a rooster…"

"Who crowed hours before sunrise," Henry hollered from the kitchen.

Tommy seemed to find that funny. He added another note on his pad of paper.

Was a crowing rooster good or bad?

They spoke for a few more minutes about Sarah's goals and hobbies, things she hadn't spent much time thinking about. Finally, Tommy said he'd like to speak with Andy.

Sarah had just stood and started toward the stairs when Isaac came barreling down. He was holding a box in his hands, and Andy was yelling after him, "The barn, Isaac. Take them to the barn."

Isaac stopped, apparently unsure whether to continue down or turn and go back up.

And that was when Sarah saw the box bounce in his hands.

CHAPTER 33

Sarah didn't have very many fears. She could kill or relocate a snake as fast as her brothers. Storms didn't bother her, in spite of the fact that her father had died during one. Spiders weren't a problem. But when Isaac dropped the box and three frogs hopped out, she nearly fainted.

"Oh. Oh!" She jumped to the left and to the right, and then she turned and went to the front door.

Isaac was saying, "I've got them, Sarah."

Andy was calling out, "What did you do now?"

And Henry and Luke were standing in the kitchen doorway laughing.

Without even thinking, Sarah ran out the door and hollered, "Get those out of my house this minute, Isaac Yoder!"

Standing on the front porch, shivering and wondering what her brother was doing with frogs in the house, she suddenly remembered Tommy.

She'd left the social worker in the living room in the midst of a plague of frogs.

Gathering all of her courage, she pulled up the skirt of her dress—maybe she could see the green monsters before they jumped on her—and marched back into the living room.

Henry was holding on to his sides, howling with laugher.

Luke had his head under the couch. "I see him."

And Tommy was holding one of the frogs in his hands.

Andy appeared in the room, assessed the situation in seconds, and managed to get all of the frogs back into the box. "You can explain all this to Sarah later. Now take them to the barn."

Isaac walked off, shoulders slumped.

Tommy stood and shook hands with Andy.

"You have an active household."

"*Ya*, we do. But that's to be expected with three younger brothers. I'm not sure they could do anything to surprise me, but Sarah? They are no doubt hard on her."

Sarah could feel her face radiating heat, but she sat down and tried to look like a grown-up. "I wasn't expecting that," she admitted.

Tommy looked amused, but he quickly returned to business. He asked Andy about his future plans, his goals, and his hobbies. Andy answered much more succinctly than she had, but that was her brother's way. Life was not complicated for him.

"Are you bothered by the thought of being responsible for two more children?" he asked Sarah.

"*Nein*. Children are a blessing from the Lord—always."

Tommy seemed to consider that for a minute and wrote something else on his form. Finally, he closed his folder, put everything back in the messenger bag he carried, and leaned forward, his arms on his knees and fingers steepled together.

"This is a bit of a unique situation for us. Of course we have Amish Bridge parents. Levi and Mary Beth are a fine example. We've also had single women and single men approved to provide a temporary home for children in need. What we haven't had, at least as far as I can tell, is a single Amish woman apply to participate in our program."

Andy sat back and crossed his right leg over his left knee. "Not surprising. We don't have that many single Amish women in a Plain community."

"It's true," Sarah said. "Though I might seem young by *Englisch* standards, most Amish women my age are married and beginning their own family."

"So you see why this is an unusual state of affairs." Tommy pushed up on his glasses. "I want to be clear that it is Sarah who is applying for certification. Andy, we're interviewing you because you will have daily contact with the children, and also because you provide the means of support."

"*Ya*, and I'm happy to do so."

"Would you have applied for certification if Sarah hadn't?"

Andy wasn't offended by the question. "Hard to say. I'm not the one who found Mateo and Mia. I don't have the connection to them that my sister does, but I can see they are in need, and I'm happy to help where I can."

"So you're supportive of what Sarah is doing?"

"Sure I am."

Tommy seemed to be struggling with a question, or how to ask it, or whether he should ask it.

Sarah's impatience won out over her initial nervousness. After all, he'd seen their home at its absolute worst. If the man was still here, and he had a question on his mind, she was more than willing to answer it.

"Might as well share what you're puzzling over."

"There is an aspect of this I can't quite get my mind around. You've obviously been forced into a situation where you have to put others first. You've taken on the responsibility for your brothers—both you and Andy have. You've put any dreams or plans of your own on hold."

"Why." Now Andy uncrossed his legs and sat up straighter. "You're wondering why she would want to."

"Yeah. I suppose I am."

"They're special children," Sarah added. "I feel a deep sympathy for them."

Andy threw a smile at Sarah, and leaned forward to meet Tommy's gaze. "*Gotte's wille*. That's what you're struggling with."

"Excuse me?"

"Sarah feels…correct me if I'm wrong, *schweschder*…Sarah feels that it was *Gotte's wille* for Mateo to run out in front of her buggy, for her to go inside, for Isaac and Luke to notice the stack of boxes. She feels the call of *Gotte* on her life in this matter."

Sarah nodded, stunned that Andy was able to put into words the certainty that had pierced her heart these last few weeks.

"And why would I support her? Because I wouldn't dare to thwart *Gotte's wille*. If He wants the children in this house, we'll gladly welcome them here. We'll find a way to provide for two more. We'll love both Mateo and Mia for as long as they need us."

CHAPTER 34

*P*aul had owned his own place for exactly two weeks. There was more work to do than he had imagined, and it was more satisfying than anything he'd ever done before. As he repaired the roof on the barn, he pictured the cattle and horses he would own in a few years.

As he mended fences around his fields, he thought of the crops that would grow there by fall.

And as he lay down to sleep in his cramped office, he sometimes allowed himself to imagine a family that would one day live in the house. He would wake later with images of children and animals and crops in his mind. And the woman? Well, he tried to deny to himself that the woman looked anything like Sarah Yoder, but that was foolishness.

Somehow as he'd been going about his own business, she had invaded his dreams, his thoughts, and his heart. How had it happened? Because he'd seen her in the laundry room with her hair popping out of her *kapp*, her apron askew, and the hem of her dress wet? Or maybe because of her close proximity and the fact that he sometimes caught a glimpse of her as he was walking the fence line? It could be explained by the fact that Andy and Henry sometimes mentioned her and how the foster parent application was proceeding. Perhaps he was lonely and simply needed to invite one of the ladies from church to dinner. Possibly it was time that he settle down.

But he couldn't imagine doing that. Who would live in this wreck of a place? Maybe in a year or two. Maybe after he'd been in the community longer. Maybe not. He was a confirmed bachelor, and the thought of a woman walking into his life and *setting things right* didn't sound too inviting.

Regardless the reason and how he tried to explain it away, his thoughts turned to Sarah time and again. He'd even taken to thinking up crazy ways to help her family—ways where they could be contributing and wouldn't see it as charity.

He could buy a cow, and ask them to care for it, splitting the milk between them. This seemed like a big expense and something that he wasn't quite able to do until he'd harvested his first crop.

He thought about the herd of goats their father had lost in a wager. Wasn't it Andy who had told him that? But a herd of goats was as far outside his financial means as a cow.

His mind brushed back over something Andy had mentioned, about losing most of their chickens. "Only two left now, so we'll be hoping they lay an abundance of eggs." He'd laughed and changed the subject, but Paul had thought at the time that he could afford a few chickens, even though he had no time to take care of them. The idea had merit. It was something that would benefit them both.

On a slightly wet and cold Friday morning, Paul decided to make his way over the rickety fence that separated their places. This time he walked up to the front door, not wanting to catch Sarah unaware doing laundry. Not that he'd ever known a woman to do laundry on a Friday.

He wasn't surprised that the tractor was gone. Andy had mentioned that he and Henry were heading to a neighbor's to work on a tractor and muck out stalls. They had an arrangement to help the *Englischers*, a Mr. and Mrs. Tripp, with whatever the older couple needed in exchange for seed they could plant for the spring crops. Perhaps in the back of Paul's mind, he'd known that he would find Sarah alone. What he hadn't known was that she'd be in a state of complete panic.

Sarah jerked open the door, saw it was him, and fled back into the living room.

He followed her inside but stayed near the entry. Obviously he'd picked a bad time—again.

The house was a complete wreck. Dirty laundry, board games, and old copies of the *Budget* littered the coffee table, floor, and both chairs. Sarah plopped onto the couch and immediately jumped back up, pacing the area between the couch and the large potbellied stove.

"This is a disaster. A real disaster. I should walk to the phone booth, but then I'll be soaked and the judge will decide I'm unfit to be a mother."

"Sarah, what's wrong?"

She was crossing and uncrossing her arms and muttering to herself. When she looked up, he saw the depth of misery in her eyes.

"I'm going to miss it."

She rushed over to the window and peered out, turned, and paced back toward the stove. "After all we've done, and it comes down to a broken radiator…"

He crossed the room in three long strides. "Sit down. Tell me what's happened. What's wrong?"

Though the house was a disaster zone, Sarah was impeccably dressed, not a strand of hair out of place, and wearing a fresh apron and *kapp*.

"What's wrong? Everything's wrong. I'm going to miss the hearing, and then they're going to send Mateo and Mia to some foster home in Tulsa. That's what's wrong. If Andy doesn't get here soon—"

"Andy and Henry are over at the Tripp place. Remember?"

Her hands flew to her mouth. "It's their Friday at the Tripps."

"So they told me."

"Oh. Oh, no." She sank back onto the couch. "I'd forgotten. How could I have forgotten? He mentioned it just this morning, but I wasn't paying attention. Isaac had lost one of his shoes, and Luke was angry about having to go to school at all. I knew Andy and Henry had left, sure. It didn't matter. I had a ride. But now—"

"This is about Mateo and Mia?"

The words came out in a rush, mimicking the rain now tapping against the roof. "We got the call last night…well, someone delivered a message to the bishop, and he sent one of his sons by here to tell us. The judge is going to hear our case at…at eleven. And I wasn't supposed to ride with the bishop. Something about not unduly influencing the children."

"All right. It's only nine. There's still plenty of time."

"*Nein.* There's not. Amelia Stark was supposed to give me a ride. She drives—"

"The white van. I know."

Paul sat beside her on the couch. It seemed as natural as the sun rising in the morning for him to reach for her hands, for him to find a way to calm her nerves. Her fingers were freezing. Had she been pacing on the front porch? He covered them with his own and rubbed some warmth into them.

"I learned Amelia couldn't take me after Andy and Henry had gone. They offered to go with me to Tulsa, but I know how much Andy is counting on the seed he will receive from the Tripp family."

"Tell me about Amelia."

"She sent someone by with a note. Her radiator is broken, and she can't come. I was waiting for Andy to return home." She glanced up at him, seemed to finally realize that he was there, in her house, holding both of her hands in his. She hopped off the couch and stood in front of the stove. "I thought Andy could take me to town or go to the phone booth."

Glancing around the room, she spied her shawl, grabbed it, and headed for the door.

"Where are you going?"

"There's a list of drivers inside the phone booth."

"I've seen it."

"So I need to go and call someone. I need to find a ride to Tulsa."

"You don't want to go out in the rain. I'll go. I'll call them for you."

She seemed to hesitate but then nodded in agreement. "*Danki.*"

"It's not a problem. Promise me you'll stay here and wait. Don't try walking to town or harnessing Dusty."

She gave him her word, and he hurried from the house. Twenty minutes later he was back, soaked through and through, and Bob Johnson was on his way. "Said he'd be here in ten minutes. Said it would be no problem to get you there in time, not at this hour. Barely any traffic at all."

"Go with me."

"What?" Paul had found a towel in a pile of laundry. It looked clean enough to him, so he was using it to dry himself off.

"Please?" Sarah stepped closer, near enough that he could smell the soap she'd used that morning and something else—probably a type of lotion, something with a hint of springtime flowers. "It's only that I'm so nervous and there will be no one...no one to sit on my side. They have Mateo and Mia on one side, with the bishop and his wife, and I'll be on the other side—"

"I'm soaked."

She seemed to notice his wet clothes for the first time. "Andy's clothes will fit you. Please, Paul. If you could, I would be...that is to say, I am forever grateful."

He nodded once and headed up the stairs to Andy's room. It wasn't too hard to find. They were approximately the same size, though Andy's trousers were a good inch too short for him. Not that he expected anyone would be looking at his pants.

He changed quickly, hurried down the stairs, and arrived in the living room at the same time that a knock was heard at the door. Five minutes later, they were speeding down the road, headed west toward Tulsa.

CHAPTER 35

Sarah felt relieved, terrified, and embarrassed all at the same time. What had come over her? She'd practically begged Paul to come along. For all of her independence and determination, she'd melted at the thought of standing alone before the judge.

Which was ridiculous. Levi and Mary Beth were on her side. Tommy was on the children's side. The Lord was on her side. She would not be alone in the courtroom.

She glanced at Paul, who was sitting beside the driver. They'd had a conversation about the Oklahoma City Thunder basketball team for the last twenty miles. How could there be that much to say about basketball?

Finally, they pulled up to the courthouse. The rain had stopped once they had reached the outskirts of the city, but the sky was still gray, and the forecast promised heavy storms with a drop in temperatures before morning. She'd heard that much on the driver's radio.

Paul helped her out of the van. "Everything's going to be fine," he assured her.

She nodded once and reached for the money in her purse.

"I already paid him." Paul steered her toward the courthouse steps. "Fortunately, he has some errands to run here in town. He said he'd be back here in two hours."

Paul held open the door of the courthouse and motioned for her to go before him. Once inside, she stopped, frozen.

"I don't know why I'm in such a dither. This is what I've wanted, what I've prayed for and now...well, now I'm a basket of nerves."

"Anyone would be."

"Why?"

"Because this is a big deal."

He glanced up at the clock, which she saw read ten thirty. They had made it. By some miracle they had made it and with time to spare. He pulled her over into an alcove.

"Sarah, don't be so hard on yourself. This is a very big thing you're doing, a *wunderbaar* thing. But it's just like having a baby—"

"What would you know of that?"

"Lots of nieces and nephews, and every time—absolutely every time—the family is full of nervous energy. It's the adrenaline in your system, and it's completely normal."

She took a deep breath, forced her heart rate to calm, and pushed the thousand and one things that could go wrong from her mind.

"*Ya.* I suppose you're right."

"First time you've said that."

Sarah closed her eyes. When she opened them, she looked at Paul directly. "I haven't been a very *gut* neighbor. I'm sorry."

"Nothing to apologize for." Paul rubbed his chin thoughtfully. "Though you did insult my house."

"Which is a disaster."

"Indeed."

They smiled at one another, and all of the tension inside of Sarah melted.

"Let's go up to the courtroom. I doubt they'll let me in, but I'll wait in the hall for you. I'll pray the entire time you're there."

She wanted to thank him, but she found herself at a loss for words. She had completely misjudged Paul Byler—taking his serious nature for a sour one, not bothering to get to know the man. Perhaps she'd even been afraid to know him better. Maybe her father had left a scar on her heart that prohibited her from even being friends with another man.

Which was ridiculous. She had been friends with Charlie Everman when they had worked on the mission team in Texas. Joshua and Alton Kline were both good friends. The bishop was a man, and he was like a grandfather to her. As they climbed the steps to the second floor courtroom, she almost laughed at her emotions, which seemed to be all over the place.

Completely normal she reminded herself, and then she glanced at Paul and smiled.

When they gained the second landing, Sarah saw a group of familiar faces and felt her world settle back onto steady ground. Mateo and Mia noticed her first and rushed to meet her. Mia threw her arms around Sarah's waist and demanded, "Up!" Mateo stood there grinning, shifting from one foot to the other.

"Today's the day, Sarah. Maybe we can come back and live with you."

"I hope so, Mateo."

They walked down the corridor and joined Levi and Mary Beth. As Paul explained about her transportation problems, a young woman with curly black hair cut shoulder length and an irrepressible smile hopped up from the bench and walked over to say hello. "I don't know if you remember me…"

"*Ya.* Of course. You're the newspaper reporter."

"Chloe Vasquez. I married three months ago. I was Chloe Roberts when I covered Anna's story."

"The girl who was healed?" Paul asked.

"*Ya*, that was before you moved to Cody's Creek, Paul." Levi's smile broadened as he sat back down on the bench. "A special time in the life of our community, for sure and for certain. Chloe was a *wunderbaar* help in getting the word out about our auctions and benefits. Still is, in fact."

"Why are you here today?" Sarah asked Chloe as she set Mia back down.

Even as she was speaking to the reporter, Sarah noticed that Mary Beth had found another set of clothes to fit the children. They weren't quite Plain, but they were close. Dark pants and a long-sleeved white shirt for Mateo, a knee-length, long-sleeved dress for Mia. The young girl twirled in a circle, causing the floral print to fan out like an umbrella.

"I heard through the grapevine that you are trying to adopt these two."

"Actually, this is a temporary placement hearing."

"Our foster care system needs more families to step up and provide a home for those in need. By reporting on your case, I can bring some attention to the Rainbow program and the children who want for a home."

Sarah glanced toward Levi, who nodded in agreement.

"I suppose, if it helps the children, then *ya*—I'd be willing to speak with you."

"Awesome. I'll wait here in the hall, and then after the judge's ruling we can set up a time to speak."

Sarah nodded, though her mind was flashing back on the mess she'd left in the house. There simply hadn't been enough time with the certification hours in addition to trying to cook meals and care for her own brothers. She suddenly remembered that Paul had seen her house that morning. As if he were reading her thoughts, he squeezed her arm in reassurance and sat down on the bench next to the bishop.

She thought they might have to wait awhile. She'd heard that court cases could even get postponed to another day.

But suddenly the door to the courtroom opened, and a bald man with thick white eyebrows and a large belly stepped out.

"Mateo and Mia Lopez?"

Levi and Mary Beth stood. They didn't seem the least bit hesitant to enter the courtroom and proceeded to usher the children forward.

"And Sarah Yoder."

Sarah also stood, though her knees were practically knocking against each other.

"I'll be here, Sarah." Paul walked with her toward the courtroom door. "I'll wait here with Chloe, and I'll pray."

CHAPTER 36

Mateo didn't think he'd ever been in a courtroom before. This one was a little scary. For one thing it was huge, the ceiling reaching up so high that he had to crane his head back to look up and see the top. There was a lot of dark wooden furniture, and their steps echoed as they walked to the front and sat on a bench.

There weren't many people in the room. There was the man who had brought them in and a woman at the front, typing on a little machine. Tommy, their social worker, sat in front of them. He'd been by the bishop's house a couple of times, and he'd also stopped by the school one afternoon. Fortunately, it was during lunch and the other kids didn't seem to notice. He'd asked Brian later if he was in trouble, and Brian had said, "Not even a little bit."

Tommy said hello to Levi and Mary Beth, and then he asked Mateo and Mia how they were doing.

"Good, I guess." Mateo cleared his throat and tried to sound surer of himself. "Good."

Mia slid closer to Mateo. She had been clingy all morning. He knew that meant she was scared. He was scared too.

Sarah sat on the other side of the aisle. He hated that she was sitting alone, but he guessed her brothers couldn't come with her.

Someone walked in through the side door and said, "All rise for the Honorable Judge Murphy."

The judge wore a long black robe. She wasn't old or young, and she had light brown hair. She wore purple glasses, and she smiled at everyone as she sat down at the front of the room, up on a raised platform and behind an important-looking desk.

"You may be seated. How is everyone this morning?"

"*Gut.*"

"Great."

"Fine, your honor."

Mateo didn't know what to say, so he settled for bobbing his head up and down. He'd been scared the night before when Levi told them they were coming to the courthouse. Levi had explained that the judge was going to decide where they would live.

"What if she decides wrong?" Mateo had asked.

"We will pray that *Gotte* gives her wisdom." The bishop talked a lot about praying. Mateo wasn't too sure. He'd prayed for stuff before, like food or a place to stay or even for his mom to return. Didn't seem like his prayers made it all the way up to God. Maybe he was doing it wrong.

"This is a temporary placement hearing for Mateo and Mia Lopez. Mr. Cronin, let's speak first about the children's mother. Have you been able to locate her?"

"No, your honor. We're still working on it."

"All right. Any other family that has been notified?"

"No. We found birth records for both Mateo and Mia in Texas, but neither lists a father. Both do list the mother as Elisa Lopez, current age twenty-three, born in El Paso, Texas."

"Thank you, Mr. Cronin." The judge studied some sheets of paper before she pushed them to the side and directed her comments to the bishop. "Mr. and Mrs. Troyer, it's good to have you in my courtroom again."

"Likewise," Levi said, and Mary Beth smiled.

"I want to thank you on behalf of the State of Oklahoma for opening your home to these children. You've done so in the past, and your continued participation as a Bridge parent is appreciated."

"It's our privilege to do so, and these two have been a real blessing to have with us." Levi patted Mateo's hand.

For some reason, that made Mateo want to cry. When had anyone ever said they were a blessing? When had anyone ever wanted them? He remembered some arguments between his mom and her boyfriend, him saying that he didn't need two brats hanging around. Stuff like that. Mostly, he'd tried to distract Mia and keep her from hearing, but some of it had leaked through.

While he'd been remembering that, the judge had asked Tommy a few more questions. He only caught the words *background check* and *home study*.

The judge had then asked Sarah a question, and Sarah had smiled at them and answered, "Yes. Yes, I do."

It seemed to Mateo as if all the conversations around him were happening at the end of a long tunnel. Or maybe his ears were clogged up. He heard just fine when Judge Murphy called his name, though. "Mateo, I'd like to speak with you and Mia in my chambers. Miss Yoder, I would appreciate it if you would join us."

Mateo didn't realize the judge meant Sarah until she stood, walked over to where they were, and reached out her hand. Mateo and Mia practically jumped off the bench. Together, the three of them followed the judge into a little back room.

It looked less scary than the large courtroom. There was another big desk, though it was smaller than the other. One wall was covered with framed stuff—pictures and fancy-looking sheets with gold seals on them. The other wall looked like a library.

"You have a lot of books," he said.

"Yes, I do." The judge sat behind her desk and took off her glasses, indicating that they should sit in the chairs opposite her.

Mia climbed up onto Sarah's lap, and Mateo perched on the edge of the chair next to them.

"Do you like books?" the judge asked him.

"Not usually, but Brian has some books on snakes and frogs and stuff." Mateo wanted to tell her how he and Isaac had been in trouble and had to read the book. It had been the coolest punishment ever. But he couldn't slow down his thoughts enough to think of the words, so instead he said, "We're reading *Treasure Island.*"

The judge smiled at that. "One of my favorite books."

She turned toward Sarah. "The Amish educational system has proven itself to be exemplary in teaching children reading and writing and math. I suspect Mateo is doing very well there."

"*Ya*, Brian, our teacher, keeps both myself and Levi and Mary Beth up to date on Mateo's progress. He's doing very well."

They talked for a few minutes about Amish life and how Sarah felt about providing for so many even though she was only a young woman. Twenty-three seemed awful old to Mateo, but he didn't think he should correct the judge.

"And do you like the school, Mateo? Or would you rather be in an English school?"

He swung his foot and thought about that for a few moments. He knew his answer, but he wanted to find the right words. Finally, he said what was on his heart. "I like our school. I don't get lost going to the bathroom. No one makes fun of me or calls me *estúpido*. I even help the younger kids sometimes."

"Sounds like a good place to be."

Mateo nodded his head. It was a good place to be, and he didn't want to leave it. He didn't want to move again unless he was moving to Sarah's house.

"Tell me about Sarah's brothers."

Mateo nearly started laughing. "Isaac is most like me. We're in the same grade, and he's kind of like *mi hermano*. When there's snow, we sled down the hill on all sorts of things—feed sacks, trash can lids. You name it, and Isaac can sled on it."

"Sounds like a lot of fun."

"Luke is older and laughs at us, but not in a mean way."

The judge looked down at a sheet of paper. "And there are two older brothers?"

"Andy and Henry. They're like *mi tíos*."

The judge nodded and Sarah smiled. Maybe he'd said the right thing. He hoped so.

The judge asked Mia a few questions, but she still wasn't saying a lot of words—in English or Spanish. She pulled Sarah's arms around her waist. Maybe it wouldn't take words for the judge to see how much she trusted Sarah.

"I have one more question, Mateo. If we could find you a home with a Spanish family, would you like that better?"

Mateo had thought about that. He'd never had a family of aunts and uncles and grandparents, but his mom had hung out with other people like them. Everyone spoke a mix of Spanish and English, and the food was good. But none of those people had wanted them. They had been nice enough, for a little while, but then they had been ready for them to leave.

"Maybe it doesn't matter that Sarah is white and we're brown," he said. "Maybe it only matters that she cares about us."

CHAPTER 37

Sarah sank onto the couch, shoving aside the laundry that she had to find time to fold the next day. Shirts, pants, underclothes, and quite a few mismatched socks tumbled to the floor, but she had no energy to pick them up. After what she'd been through emotionally in the last twenty-four hours, laundry could wait another twelve hours without causing anyone permanent harm.

"I'm sorry we weren't there, Sarah. I didn't know it would be important for us to go." Andy scrubbed a hand across his face.

She could tell how tired he was, and also that he regretted not traveling with them to Tulsa that morning.

"You couldn't have known that my ride would break down before it even got here. Amelia has never had trouble before."

"Regardless, I should have been there. This is important to you and to the future of Mateo and Mia. Somehow in my mind it was only a matter of signing a few forms. I never imagined you having to go into the judge's chambers. It would have been nice to have someone with you then."

She thought of Paul, waiting in the hall, and the way his eyes had lit up the moment he saw her. He'd known before she uttered a word that Mateo and Mia would be going home with them.

"The reporter—Chloe—is going to come and interview me. She wants to draw attention to the fact that more children need homes."

"And Levi approved of that?" Andy asked.

"He did. Chloe is familiar with our ways." Sarah smiled and added, "She didn't even try to take our picture."

"If it's okay with Levi, it's okay with me."

"We have to appear before the judge again in six months. It would be *wunderbaar* if our entire family could go together then."

"Sure. Of course." Andy yawned.

"*Gut* thing you had us move things around in Isaac's room." Henry had been pretending to read the *Budget*, but she'd seen him rub at his eyes several times.

"*Ya*, those two are as thick as pigs in a pen, and Luke is there to keep them out of trouble." Andy hesitated and then added, "We need to prepare Isaac for when Mateo leaves."

"I've been wanting to talk to you about that."

"Uh-oh." Henry stood and stretched. "Sounds like an adult talk. Think I'll pretend I'm still a kid and head to bed."

"*Nein*. This affects you too, Henry. It affects everyone, but I wanted to speak with both of you first since you're the oldest."

Andy stretched his legs out in front of him and crossed them at the ankles. "I knew something was on your mind during dinner—you kept worrying your thumbnail."

"I did?"

"It's a nervous habit of yours." Andy grinned. "When you're angry, you turn red in the face. When you're nervous, you fidget with your nails."

"If she does both, watch out." Henry folded up the newspaper he hadn't read and sat down once more. "Out with it. What's on your mind now?"

"It's Mateo and Mia. While I was meeting with the judge, I spoke to her about permanent placement for them, here, in our house." She held up both hands when Andy and Henry started questioning her at once. "It won't happen right away. As I said, we have another review in six months. But there are steps we can take if we want to give them a permanent home."

"Let's start with seeing how they do here on a temporary basis." Andy sighed. "I like the kids as much as you do, but they have a parent."

"Only one, apparently, and no one can locate her."

"All right. She's missing. So is ours. Doesn't mean we'll never see her again."

Henry scoffed at that. They hadn't talked much about their mother since she'd left, but Sarah knew that each of them still thought of her. You didn't just forget your mother.

"We're old enough to take care of ourselves—the three of us are. And of course we will take care of Luke and Isaac, but Mateo and Mia have no one else."

"You don't know that," Henry pointed out.

"They were living in an abandoned building, not with relatives. And Tommy has done a search. He's tried to find family. He'll continue to do so, but he told the bishop that family is usually located within the first week if they're located at all."

"Let me see if I have this straight." Andy began ticking points off on his fingers. "You think their mother is not coming back, they have no other relatives, and we should be their permanent family."

"*Ya*, that's what I think."

He settled back into the rocker. "I have to admit I hadn't thought much past today's hearing and providing a place until—"

"But what if there isn't an *until*? Some kids stay in foster homes for years and years, never feeling like a real part of a family. I don't want that for Mateo and Mia. I want them to know that they will always have a home with us, and that we care about them permanently—not only until another solution is found."

Andy stood, picked up their empty mugs, and carried them to the kitchen. When he returned, he was once again smiling. "It's *gut* you brought this up, Sarah. We all need to pray on the matter. If you feel *Gotte* leading you in the direction of being a permanent parent, perhaps that is what we should do."

"But I realize it doesn't only affect me. That's two more mouths to feed, two more bodies to clothe, and probably additional doctor bills somewhere along the way. You and Henry are working long hours as it is just to make a living for the five of us."

"If *Gotte* will provide for five, then He'll provide for seven." Henry shrugged. "I heard someone at church say as much when they announced that their *fraa* was expecting twins."

"Our *bruder* is wise beyond his years," Andy said, leaning over to ruffle Henry's hair. "Let's see how the children settle in and talk about this again in a few weeks."

Henry and Andy sauntered off to bed, where they would no doubt drop off to sleep in less than a minute.

Sarah walked up to her room and tucked the covers more tightly around Mia. She'd made the girl a pallet adjacent to her own bed. They would have more space if they moved down to her mother's room, but Sarah wasn't ready to do that yet.

She changed into her nightgown, made sure a flashlight was next to her bed, and lay down. She didn't fall to sleep for some time. Instead, she tried to imagine where her mother was and what she was doing. Was the life she was now living so very different than their life in Cody's Creek?

And what of Elisa Lopez? She was the same age as Sarah, and yet she'd had two children, become homeless, and for some reason abandoned them.

Her mother and Elisa had felt unable to be a parent any longer. What caused a person to come to such a desperate conclusion? One *Englisch* woman and one Amish—both running from something. When you were frightened enough to run away from those you loved, perhaps it didn't matter if you were *Englisch* or Plain. Either way, you were lost.

With prayers for those two women on her lips, Sarah fell into a deep and restful sleep.

She awoke just before dawn when she heard Andy and Henry tromping down the stairs. And Mia? The little girl had crawled into her bed sometime during the night. She lay on her side, clutching an Amish doll.

CHAPTER 38

*P*aul officially joined the Plain community of Cody's Creek on Sunday morning. Because he'd already been a member of his church back in Indiana, there wasn't a need for baptism or new member classes.

Instead, Bishop Levi introduced him to the congregation. "You all know Paul already, Joseph's *bruder*. He's been here with us since Joseph's surgery, and now he is joining our congregation."

There were murmurs of *amen* throughout Joshua Kline's home. Paul noticed Becca and Sarah smiling at one another, though he had no idea what that was about.

"Paul's presence here today is one more example of how *Gotte* took something we would consider bad and turned it to our *gut*. No one would have wished for Joseph's heart attack, but through it we now have another member—someone to minister to us. Someone we can minister to. *Gotte* is faithful to build the body of Christ, and we trust that He will continue to do so."

More words of agreement from those gathered, and then Levi said, "Also, remember he has purchased the old Fisher place, so let's keep Paul in our prayers as he goes about the work of that restoration."

They sang the last hymn, and the bishop officially dismissed the service. Folks immediately came forward to congratulate Paul and welcome him into the community. He'd seen it happen dozens of times back home, only then he'd been the one sitting out on the benches watching.

The men filed past him, welcoming him, as the women began setting out the food. The day was rainy, windy, and cold. "Winter's last assertion," Joseph had said as they prepared for church. Now his brother stood beside him, grinning as if he'd been personally responsible for Paul's presence...and as the bishop had said, perhaps he was.

The meal was laid out on tables in the barn. Although it was slightly colder in the large building than in the house, where they'd had the morning's service, Paul felt more at ease there than in the crowded home. Why was it that he felt more comfortable in a barn? Could be because he lived in one, but Paul suspected it was more than that. He could breathe here, where in the house, in most houses, he often felt as if he needed to move carefully, worried he might knock something over. It wasn't that he was overly large or clumsy, only that he felt less hemmed in when outside or in the barn. Breathing space was what he'd longed for, and in Cody's Creek he had found plenty of it.

After he filled his plate, he ended up sitting at the end of a long table next to Andy and Henry.

Andy said, "Been meaning to thank you for helping Sarah out on Friday."

"Happy to do it."

"Yeah, I'm sure you were quite happy to sit in a car for an hour each way and spend the bulk of your day in downtown Tulsa." Henry made a sandwich out of a slice of ham and a large biscuit, took a giant bite, and grinned at him.

"Wasn't that bad." Paul had wanted to stop over and check on the kids the day before, but he hadn't felt it was his place to do so. "Saw Mateo standing with Isaac."

"And Mia is never far from Sarah."

"Both kids seem to be doing well."

They all turned to look at Mateo, who was sitting with a group of kids from school, though he always seemed to be right at Isaac's side.

Mia was shyly plastered nearly inside of Sarah's apron, who was walking toward a table of women.

"There's a singing tonight," Andy said. "You could ask her."

Paul nearly choked on his potato salad. "Are you talking to me?"

"You're the one watching my *schweschder*." Andy laughed as he picked up a piece of fried chicken from his plate. "Don't look so shocked. It's plain as the nose on your face that you've taken a fancy to Sarah."

"I think you've been under the hood of your tractor too long."

"Do you now?"

"Plainly it's affecting your thinking."

Henry and Andy shared a look. "Me thinks he protests too much," Henry said, and then they both laughed.

Paul didn't mind being the source of their amusement. But he did think he'd done a better job of hiding his feelings about Sarah. He didn't even understand what he was feeling. How could he explain it to someone else, let alone her brothers? Safer to change the subject.

"I'm a bit old for singings," he reminded them. "I gather you're both going?"

"Oh, *ya*. We go every time," Andy said.

"It's my *bruder*'s only chance to be alone with his girl."

"You have a girl?"

"I don't," Henry said. "It's still fun to go, though."

"And you, Andy?"

"You could say that I do." He leaned forward and confided, "She let me give her a ride home last time."

"Which meant I had to find another ride." Henry seemed to enjoy teasing his brother and not all that perturbed about finding another way home. "I suspect the same will happen tonight."

"Three's a crowd," Andy said, grinning.

"Does this girl have a name?"

"Sure does." Andy pointed a chicken leg toward Sarah's table. "Emma King. She's the pretty girl sitting on the other side of Sarah."

"Is it serious?"

"Could be." Andy focused on cleaning his plate and refused to say another word on the subject.

Which Paul thought was more telling than any outright confession. He wondered if Sarah realized that her brother was courting someone. She'd never mentioned it, but then all they had ever actually talked about was Mateo and Mia.

What did he even know about Sarah? That she was pretty, had four brothers, and no parents. That she had a big heart. But he didn't know what kind of pie she liked or whether she preferred sunny days to rain. She was special. He understood that, but if he were to try to describe her on the next phone call to his parents, he'd be hard pressed to do so.

There was no time like the present to change that.

CHAPTER 39

Sarah nearly dropped the dish of apple pie when Paul asked her if she'd like to go for a walk.

"It's freezing outside."

"Big barn. We could take a look at Joshua's horses."

How had he known that she'd been wishing for a few moments away from so many people? She pushed the plate holding the apple pie to the center of the table.

Mia sat on a stool beside the table, playing with an Amish doll. Paul squatted down in front of her. "Hello, Mia. How are you today?"

"Paul, up!" She practically threw herself into his arms.

Laughing, Paul raised her high into the air.

"I didn't realize she even knew your name."

"Well, of course she does. I carried her into the house when she was all sleepy on Friday."

For her answer, Mia patted his face and turned her attention to undressing her doll.

"Perhaps a walk would be *gut*." Sarah grabbed the shawl she'd placed over her bag. "Would you like to go for a walk, Mia?"

"Why?"

"Because it will be fun."

"Why?"

"Because barns always are."

"Why?"

Sarah shrugged and turned to Paul. "*Up* and *why*—they are her two favorite words."

"Why?" Mia asked, causing both Paul and Sarah to laugh.

Sarah was worried they would have nothing to say, but Paul brought her up to date on the work he was doing at his place. "The barn has been thoroughly cleaned out, with the help of your *bruders*, and I've begun mending fences around my fields."

"No progress on the house?"

"*Nein*. It will have to wait, which is okay. I'm comfortable enough in the barn."

"I suppose you're not the first bachelor to live in a barn."

"And probably not the last."

"You do want to move into the house, though. Right? Eventually?"

"I suppose. But it doesn't strike me as a priority at the moment."

He was just like her brothers. None of them seemed to notice piles of clothes, muddy tracks on the floor, or dirty dishes in the sink. Left to their own devices, each of them would probably choose to live in a barn.

They had reached the back wall, and Paul stopped in front of the last stall. Inside was one of Joshua's buggy mares, and across from them was the other. The mare nudged Paul's hand, looking for a treat, and he produced a cube of sugar.

"Do you always carry sweets in your pockets?"

"Comes in handy more often than you'd think."

He handed another cube to Mia, and they walked to the other mare so she could feed it to the horse. Mia started to put it into her mouth.

"No, honey. Give it to the horse."

"Why?" Mia puckered her lips and tried to feed the sugar cube to Paul.

In spite of herself, Sarah burst out laughing. It was such a funny sight—the small Hispanic girl, large Amish man, and a horse poking her head in the middle of the two. Eventually, Mia relented and fed the mare. Then she insisted on being let down and made a game of running from one side of the aisle to the other, touching the wall each time and saying "horse" when she did.

Paul spied a wooden crate and turned it over so Sarah could sit on it.

"Take a load off. You barely sat at all this morning. You ate in record time, and then you popped up to help with the dishes."

Had Paul Byler been watching her? The thought embarrassed Sarah, so she changed the subject, but she did sit on the crate. Her feet were actually tired from the long morning of church and serving.

"All right, but we need to keep an eye on little Mia. She's turned disappearing into an art form."

Paul sat beside her on the ground. "Still hiding?"

"Every chance she gets."

Paul started laughing. Mia turned to look at him, and the smile that spread across her face once again melted Sarah's heart.

"You're beautiful, you know." Paul's voice had turned husky. "When you smile like that, when you stop worrying about things...you're beautiful inside and out, Sarah Yoder."

She didn't know what to say. She stammered, she blushed, and she forced herself to look away from Paul's warm brown eyes and playful smile. And that was when she noticed that Mia was once again gone.

They found her ten minutes later. Somehow she'd managed to squeeze between an old slop bucket and a shelf in an empty stall.

"What if she'd gotten in with the horses?"

"That's impossible. She couldn't have opened the latch."

"I suppose."

For her part, Mia apparently thought it was great fun and clapped when they found her, throwing herself at Sarah and commanding that she lift her "up!"

"Mia, no more hiding."

"Why?" She stuck her bottom lip out in a pout and hid her face in Sarah's dress.

"We need to work on her vocabulary."

"It will come with time," Paul assured her.

"How do you know so much about kids?"

"Lots of nieces and nephews. I am the youngest of seven."

"You mentioned that in the courthouse." Part of Sarah's mind was still sitting on the overturned crate, listening to Paul tell her how beautiful she was. Had he actually said that?

"*Ya*, big family back home. Little children running everywhere. Couldn't sit down without squishing one."

"They're not bugs."

"Nope. I suppose not. My *bruders* think it's their job to ensure the growth of the Amish community."

"Meaning?"

"Kids. Every year there are more."

They walked slowly back to the front of the barn where lunch had been served. Maybe returning to a larger group caused Sarah to feel bolder because she asked, "Don't you like kids?"

"Sure I do. I like Mateo and Mia well enough. And I like your *bruders*."

"Just not any of your own."

Paul scratched at the side of his face as if he was deep in thought and frowned. It reminded her of when she'd seen him in the store, a few days before she'd found the children, before her life had changed. It had irritated her then, that frown. But now it made her laugh.

Paul looked at her in surprise. "What's so funny?"

"You are."

"Me?"

"That serious look on your face."

"You asked a serious question."

"I wasn't asking you to marry me."

"No?" Now there was a pronounced frown on his face, and Sarah knew he was teasing.

So instead of explaining herself, she gathered Mia up in her arms, found her purse sitting behind the tables, and went in search of Mateo and her younger brothers.

No doubt Andy and Henry would be staying for the singing, but Sarah wanted to be home. She wanted to change out of her church clothes, sit in the rocker as the rain splashed on the roof, and make some sense of the twists and turns her life had taken.

CHAPTER 40

*M*arch blew in with gusty winds and warmer temperatures, bringing afternoons balmy enough for the boys to shed their coats.

If Sarah had thought things would get easier once she'd been declared an official Bridge parent, she was sadly mistaken. It was possible she'd been so busy completing her certification that she hadn't had time to see what a mess their home had become.

The next few days, she dedicated herself to setting things to rights—unfortunately, their home was in a state of constant chaos.

She attempted to once more sweep and mop the floors. With the rain and the mud and five boys plus one little girl, it seemed to be an unending task. After Mia tracked in mud twice, she gave up and turned to the piles of laundry. Which was when the hose from the washing machine to the hot water heater broke and flooded the mudroom. Her cooking continued to worsen, which she was surprised was even possible. She'd never been a good cook to start with, and now she was distracted constantly.

Mia was a blessing for sure and certain, but she was also a three-year-old child with a lot of energy and no playmates. She pulled all of the pans out of the cabinet when Sarah was washing clothes, dumped out her sewing basket when she was sweeping the front porch, and managed to land in the mud when they were walking to the mailbox.

Sarah pulled out the mail and was surprised to see a copy of the *Mayes County Chronicle* with a picture of the courthouse shown on the bottom of the front page. Chloe had visited on Monday and interviewed her, but she didn't realize the article would appear that same week.

Amish Family Joins Bridge Program

The Amish in our area are well known for their good cooking, roadside stands, masterful quilting, and benefit auctions. But now the Plain people of Cody's Creek are also becoming involved in the Bridge Program, which seeks to match a child in need of a home with a family that has met the Department of Human Services requirements (spelled out on the agency's website).

Beverly Rivers, head of the Oklahoma DHS office, encourages anyone interested to contact her. "Bridge parents are what make this program work. It's because families are willing to provide a home, shelter, and, of course, love to a child in need that we are able to help the most vulnerable among us."

Ms. Rivers admitted this is not her first Amish Bridge family. "The Amish we have worked with are quiet, private people. You probably won't see their faces in the paper or read about their adopting needy kids in a local magazine. What's important is that we find a safe, stable home for children. We welcome people from all faiths and backgrounds."

Sarah would have liked to stand there and read the rest, but Mia began pulling on her hand and whining.

"All right. Let's clean you up—again." They turned toward the house, Mia now happy that they were on the move. Sarah thought of the news article and wondered if it would encourage others to become foster parents.

They slowly made their way back down the lane, Mia covered in mud and Sarah trying to coax her to walk. If she picked up the child, she'd be covered in mud herself. The mere thought of doing more laundry was enough to make her want to curl up and take a nap. The day was cloudy, wet, and a bit dreary.

They'd nearly made it to the porch when a red Chevy pulled into their lane. The driver came right up to where Sarah was waiting with Mia. She couldn't see who was in the passenger seat. The windows were tinted, and the woman ducked her head. She seemed to be rooting around in her purse. Then she reached forward and paid the driver. Who would pay a driver for a ride to come and see Sarah?

She waited, hesitating and curious. She thought she made out a prayer *kapp* and a woman's profile. Sarah's mind went completely blank. She couldn't think of anyone who would come to visit her. Her mother's image briefly crossed her mind, but she pushed it away. This woman was larger, and besides, her mother had given them no indication that she planned on returning to Cody's Creek. In fact, she hadn't written them at all.

The *Englischer* turned off the vehicle, got out, and waved. "Afternoon," he said as he walked toward the trunk and pulled out a large suitcase.

The woman in the backseat seemed to be gathering up packages. Sarah pulled herself together and hurried to open the door, peering closely through the glass.

A small gasp escaped her lips, and she wondered if she was imagining things. But no, it really was her grandmother from Montana— her father's mother. Fannie Yoder was solidly built and as energetic as a four-year-old, though she had just turned seventy. Sarah had spent very little time around her over the years. She remembered a woman who was kind but brokered no nonsense. The question was—what was she doing in Cody's Creek?

"*Mammi?*"

She had visited briefly for *Dat*'s funeral. There had been an argument between her mother and grandmother, something Deborah would never talk about. The next morning Sarah had woken to find her grandmother gone.

"Sarah. How are you, child?" *Mammi* enfolded her in a full embrace, and then she held her at arm's length. "You look *gut*. Something of a mess, but healthy."

"I didn't know you were coming."

"Didn't know myself until I woke up yesterday morning. The Lord pricked my spirit, surely He did, and I knew...I was certain that He meant me to be here, helping you."

At that moment, Mia stood up from where she'd been kneeling in the mud, making pies. She held up one in her little hands and offered it to Sarah, who backed away. If the child had been dirty before, she looked as if she'd positively rolled in the mud now. She was completely covered from the top of her dark brown hair to the toes of her small pink tennis shoes.

"Oh, Mia." What had she been thinking letting go of the child's hand? If she'd watched her closer, this wouldn't have happened.

"Up! Please, Sarah."

"No, you don't." Sarah held her at arm's length, and then she remembered her grandmother was watching.

Unperturbed by the sight of an extra child, *Mammi* said, "Best put that pie on the porch railing to cool, child. All pies go on the porch railing."

Mia ran up the steps to do as she was told.

When she ran back to them, *Mammi* patted the pocket of her coat, pulled out two pieces of foil-wrapped chocolate, and placed one in each of their hands. Then she adjusted her two bags on her shoulders, grabbed her suitcase by the handle, and thanked the driver. Without asking a single question, she marched up the porch steps and into the house.

Sarah took Mia's hand, holding the forgotten mail in the other, and followed her grandmother into her house.

Mammi had stopped inside the front door, her eyes taking in the wreck that was once their living room and tilting her head to see into the kitchen. Sarah expected a reprimand, but instead *Mammi* smiled, nodded her head, and proclaimed, "Looks like I was right to come. If you'll put my things in a bedroom, I'll see to cleaning up this little gal."

Sarah started to say that Mia was shy, that she rarely went to strangers, and that she would do it herself. But the little imp looked up at *Mammi*, smiled broadly, and said, "I'm hungry."

"Indeed? We'll find something for you to eat as soon as we wipe away the mud."

The two disappeared through the kitchen doorway and out into the mudroom. Sarah expected to hear cries. The one thing Mia fought was a good scrubbing, but instead she heard her *Mammi*'s voice and Mia's giggles. Shaking her head, Sarah carried the suitcase into her mother's room. It was the only place in the house that looked clean and orderly, probably because no one went in there. She had dusted it a couple of times, just in case her mother returned, but generally she kept the door shut—some part of her mind attempting to close off the memories and the questions, no doubt.

Hurrying back to the sitting room, she scooped up her grandmother's two bags, which were surprisingly heavy. Had she brought books with her? How long was she staying? Why was she here? Sarah deposited the bags next to the bed. By the time she reached the mudroom, Mia was nearly clean.

"Do you have another set of clothes for her?"

"*Ya*. Sure." Actually, she only had two, and she'd been washing one set out each night for the next day. Fortunately, the day before hadn't included a mud bath, so those clothes were reasonably clean—the blue jeans and pink top that she'd been wearing when they'd first seen her in the old trailer.

She scooped up a towel with the clothes and delivered them to *Mammi*.

"I'll dress her if you'll make us some hot tea, and I believe Mia would like a sandwich."

There wasn't any bread left. She'd intended to make some, but then Mia had dumped the sewing basket, and she'd become distracted cleaning that up. Sarah found some crackers and a jar of homemade peanut butter Mary Beth had sent over. She set the kettle on the stove and carted the breakfast dishes to the sink. Why were they still on the table? She had meant to clean it off when the boys left, but then she'd realized

Mia was missing and gone in search of her. Ten minutes later she had found her sitting in the bathtub, blessedly empty of water, playing with her doll. But she'd forgotten the dishes.

Mammi dressed Mia and set her on one of the chairs. "She's a mite small."

"Mia's three."

"She needs a booster seat."

"Oh. Well, usually she just sits on one of our laps."

"We'll get Andy started on something this afternoon. Where are the boys?" *Mammi* finished stacking dishes beside the sink, wet a dish towel, and wiped the table clean.

"Andy and Henry go over to help at the neighbor's a couple times a week."

"Deserted place next door?"

When had *Mammi* seen the Fisher place? Perhaps on the way to the funeral. It was visible from the road, but just barely.

"*Ya*. Paul Byler, the man who bought it, is slowly fixing up the place."

"Must be a hardworking young man."

"I'm not sure how young he is."

"Regardless, he'll make a good neighbor. Industrious people who aren't afraid of a challenge usually do."

The kettle on the stove whistled, and Sarah jumped up to fill their mugs.

When she placed them on the table, *Mammi* added a scoop of sugar to hers and said, "Now, catch me up on everything, including little Mia."

CHAPTER 41

*P*aul's tractor was finally working well enough to drive it to town. After Henry and Andy left, he fired it up and headed toward his brother's dry goods store. He still wasn't convinced that tractors were the way to go, but every man in their congregation had assured him he would change his mind in a few weeks when he began planting his first crop.

"Paul! What a nice surprise." Rebecca rushed out from behind the counter to greet him.

"Needed to pick up more coffee." He was both pleased and embarrassed by the smile on his sister-in-law's face. In truth he'd been missing them too, but he hadn't realized it until he walked into the store.

"I have a chicken roasting upstairs in the oven. There's more than enough for all three of us."

He didn't even bother to resist the invitation. He might be good at rebuilding barns and fences, but he was a terrible cook. A man could only eat so many cans of soup.

An hour later, he helped her clean the dishes as his brother pulled out his pipe and studied it.

"Still pretending to smoke that thing?"

"If he ever tries putting tobacco in it, he'll have to fight both me and the doctor." Rebecca set a coffee cake on the table, causing both Joseph and Paul to perk up. They were plenty full from the meal, but both had grown accustomed to a little dessert after dinner. When Paul had been staying in their apartment, Rebecca had been trying to break her husband of that habit, but he'd fought her all the way.

"It's reduced sugar, and I even tried some of those healthy egg substitutes." She set about slicing the cake. "It was futile trying to convince Joseph to give up his evening dessert. This is made with applesauce to sweeten it, so surely it can't hurt him. Let me get the coffee."

Paul had eaten one piece and was contemplating a second when he got around to the real reason for his visit.

"I'm thinking that Sarah is short on supplies for the young ones—clothes, shoes, stuff like that. For Mateo she's been able to scrounge up a few things that were Isaac's, but I don't believe he had that much extra. For Mia, it seems she has nothing."

"I should have thought of that." Rebecca hopped up from the table, found a pad of paper and a pen, and began making a list. "What else?"

"Jackets for the children. They probably don't need coats now that the weather is turning."

"They had coats. Didn't they?" Rebecca's pen hovered over the sheet of paper.

"*Ya*, but somewhat threadbare."

"What else?"

"Two more mattresses and bedding to go with them. Apparently, there wasn't much extra in the house to begin with, and now…"

"Sarah told you this?" Joseph clamped the pipe between his teeth.

"*Nein*. I spoke with her on Sunday, but she didn't mention needing anything."

"Sarah is a fairly private girl." Rebecca added two more items to the list, and then she set down the pen and studied Paul. "How well have you gotten to know them?"

"Not that well. Both Andy and Henry are hard workers. Andy has his hands full keeping their place running, but he still comes over to help me as much as he can. Henry is working for me two days a week, and I'm going to pay him by giving him a portion of the seed I'll buy for my fields."

"That's *gut* of you, Paul." Joseph smiled and tapped his pipe against the table. "Those children need someone in their life. It's a real shame what they have been through."

"The reason I'm telling you all this is because Henry let a few things slip. Sarah has to do laundry every night because the children only have two sets of clothes—the ones they were found in, and the set Mary Beth gave them."

Rebecca refilled their coffee cups. "Mary Beth has been distracted with the birth of another *grandkinner*, or she would have been out to check on them by now."

"It's only been a week," Joseph pointed out.

"True, but a week can seem like a long time when you are dealing with small children. We were all so excited that Mateo and Mia were placed with Sarah. We didn't stop to think that she might not be prepared for them."

Paul cleared his throat and stared down into Rebecca's strong coffee. He used to worry it would keep him awake, but somehow, when he had lived here, he always passed out soon after dinner.

"Out with it, Paul Byler." Rebecca leaned forward. "I can tell something else is bothering you."

"It would seem that Sarah is a bit overwhelmed—between the cleaning and cooking and sewing."

"It hasn't been that long since her mother left, leaving her in charge of the house and the boys. And after that, Sarah took on the care of two more." Now Rebecca sat back, studying the ceiling as if she might find answers there. "Sarah has a big heart, but no experience with little girls or foster children."

"Couldn't you ladies do a pounding?" Joseph returned the unused pipe to his shirt pocket.

"That's a *wunderbaar* idea. I'll go downstairs and call the phone shacks and leave a message at each one."

"Word will get around quickly." Joseph stood and stretched. "It's a *gut* thing you brought this to our attention, Paul."

"Wasn't sure I should, but I hate to see her struggling."

Rebecca and Joseph shared a smile.

"What?"

"Nothing." Joseph walked over to the sitting area and picked up a well-worn copy of the *Budget*.

"Now he's ignoring me."

"*Nein.* Joseph doesn't like to stick his nose into other people's business."

"Sarah's?"

"Yours."

"What does this have to do with me?"

It sounded like Joseph laughed at that, but Paul couldn't be sure.

"Walk downstairs with me," Rebecca said.

It was when they were standing at the back door, looking out at the moonlit yard, that Rebecca broached the subject of Sarah.

"It's only that she's a very sweet girl, and we both were thinking that perhaps you cared for her."

"For Sarah?"

"*Ya.* Why not?"

"Well, of course I care for her, but…"

Rebecca waited, expectantly, patiently.

"She's very young."

"Only seven years younger than you are, which is nothing."

Paul squirmed under her scrutiny. He thought of when he'd taken Sarah for a walk in Joshua's barn, of telling her she was beautiful. Had he misled her in some way? He'd only meant to cheer her a little. He certainly wasn't interested in courting the woman. The last thing he needed was an instant family.

"I'm a bachelor, Rebecca. Haven't even had a serious girlfriend in the last five years."

"And whose fault is that?"

"Maybe it's mine, or maybe I prefer things that way."

"Do you?"

"I don't know. Sometimes I do. Other times…" He let the thought fade away, and suddenly his mind flashed back on something else entirely—Tylenol missing from the shelf, stubbing his toes on a chair in the middle of the workroom, small footprints in the snow.

"It was Mateo who broke into the store that night."

"Probably."

"They were living across the street, and we never even noticed."

"It's easy not to see something."

"But Sarah saw."

"She did, and not only did she see, but she did something about it. She's a special woman, Paul, and don't be worrying about her lack of things for the children. Our community pulls together in times like these. By Saturday, she'll have everything she needs."

Paul nodded, thanked his sister-in-law, and walked across to his tractor. As he drove home, past Sarah's place, he thought about what Rebecca had said. Was it his fault that he was still a bachelor? Had he chosen this solitary life? And did he still enjoy it, or was he ready for things to change?

CHAPTER 42

*O*nce they had dinner, cleaned the kitchen until it sparkled, and everyone was in their pajamas, *Mammi* called a family meeting.

Sarah hadn't had a chance to speak with Andy alone. Each of her brothers had been surprised when they walked into the house and found their grandmother cooking and cleaning, but they were more surprised to hear that chicken spaghetti casserole was for dinner with fresh bread and green beans.

"Wow, you can cook, *Mammi*."

"*Danki*, Luke. Sarah has her hands full with little Mia. It's no wonder she's had to resort to tuna and macaroni."

Ack. She'd seen the cans in the trash. It was the one thing Sarah knew how to fix when in a hurry, and she'd been in a hurry a lot lately.

Mateo had stood back as Luke and Isaac hugged their grandmother. She smiled at him and said, "You must be Mia's *bruder*. She chatters about you all day long."

That was all it had taken to break down Mateo's wall of resistance. Like her brothers, he was also easily swayed by a warm meal.

Now all eight of them were gathered in the sitting room. *Mammi* began the family meeting by walking around the room and handing out chocolate, which she apparently kept in her large apron pockets. Had she done that before? Certainly not when she'd visited for the funeral, and Sarah had only fuzzy memories of her visiting before that.

"A little bit of sweet is a *gut* thing. *Ya*?"

No one argued. They all accepted a piece of chocolate, unwrapped it, and popped the candy into their mouth. Isaac hopped up and collected all of the silver wrappers.

Sarah had thought that *Mammi* would wait until the younger ones were asleep to explain what she was doing here and how long she planned to stay. Wrong. *Mammi* thought everyone in the family, right down to the youngest, should be involved in family discussions.

"We eat together, pray together, and discuss life together. It's natural and *gut* for us to do so."

Mateo and Isaac were sitting on the floor a safe distance in front of the big stove. Luke had pulled in a chair from the kitchen. Henry, Andy, and Sarah were perched on the couch. *Mammi* was in the rocker, and Mia was sitting beside her, playing with several old thread spools from her mother's sewing kit—something *Mammi* had found, hastily penned faces and hair on, and given to her.

"Children need toys or they'll find mischief. We'll scour the house for more tomorrow." That had been several hours ago. Now they were sitting and waiting.

Mammi sipped her tea. She seemed to love tea more than anyone Sarah had ever known. She nodded her head in contentment, smiled at each of them, and then set her mug on the end table.

"I told Sarah when I first arrived that the Lord brought me here, and I think it's true. For sure and certain it was His guidance that spoke to me. My son, your *Onkel* Tobias, wanted me to stay in Montana, but I told him that I had to come, that I had to check on his *bruder*'s family."

"Why now?" Sarah asked. She didn't mean the question to be rude, but those were the two words that had been circling round and round in her head since her grandmother had stepped out of the red car.

"*Gut* question. I can't say as I know the answer. Many times over the last twenty years, I have tried to come and help. Each time, your father told me not to. He insisted you all were fine. He insisted that I stay where I was."

She shook her head and again sipped her tea. "I knew he was sick. Melvin struggled even when he was a young man, and I warned your mother about his condition. But they were *in lieb* and no one, no argument, could convince them not to marry, move away, and start their own family."

Mammi rocked, her eyes drifting out the window to the moon-lit night. "Maybe I should have insisted that they wait. It would have given your mother a few years to understand what she was going to need to deal with."

"*Dat* was *gut* at hiding things from people," Andy said.

"Indeed he was." *Mammi* let go of her memories and focused again on those in front of her. "When he passed, I asked Deborah to let me come and stay, but she also insisted that I wasn't needed. I'm afraid we had a bit of an argument about it, and I ended up leaving without say-ing goodbye. I apologize for that. It was wrong of me."

The fire crackled, and Mia tapped the thread spools against the floor. Everyone else was mesmerized by *Mammi's* story.

"I didn't know until last week that she had left you all alone. I won-dered why she hadn't answered my letters, but then Deborah never was that *gut* about writing."

"I didn't know if I should open them or not." Sarah understood now that she should have opened them, and she should have thought to write her grandmother herself. Why had she tried to deal with every-thing on her own? "They weren't addressed to me."

"It's *gut* that you value your *mamm's* privacy. *Ya*, in spite of the chal-lenges this family has endured, it's plain to see you were raised correctly."

"Wait until she catches Isaac with frogs in his pockets," Luke said.

Mammi nodded but didn't address that particular topic. "You have all done a *gut* job without either parent, and taking in Mateo and Mia—well, from what Sarah has told me, *Gotte* placed these children on her heart. We're glad you are here, Mateo."

Mateo ducked his head and stared at his hands.

"And little Mia."

"Why?" Mia asked, and everyone laughed.

She barely looked up, squirming onto her tummy to better see her tiny people, as she called them.

"I am glad I came to help. Your grandfather died before your parents married, but he was a wise man, and I loved him very much. He used to say that it takes many people to raise a family. It takes the community." She held her hands out, far apart from one another, and moved them steadily closer to one another.

"The church, our neighbors, and finally…" now her hands were clasped together. "Family. Kinfolk. Those who share your blood and know your deepest hurts as well as your grandest joys."

"We're not family," Mateo pointed out.

"You are a special addition," *Mammi* said. "And although we don't share blood, we share something just as important—a path that *Gotte* has put us on at the same time."

"How long will you stay, *Mammi?*" This from Andy, who probably remembered their father's mother better than anyone else. She had visited a few times over the years, but Sarah only remembered that the visits were somewhat tense and short. Now she saw that her father had probably been to blame for that. His illness, both the highs and the lows, caused him to want to experience those things alone, with only his immediate family near. Some part of him must have been ashamed of his condition.

"The short answer is as long as you need me. The long answer? As long as you want me, as long as I'm helpful, as long as I feel that the Lord desires for me to be here. But know this…I'm prepared to stay permanently if that's what we as a family decide is best."

Sarah felt tears pricking her eyes and glanced away, but *Mammi* was still talking, still binding their wounds with her words of love.

"I won't be running out on you. You can trust me, *kinner*. Maybe there haven't been a lot of adults in your life you could count on, but you can trust me. And while I haven't been there much in your past, I'm here now. I'm here, and I'm ready to make up for lost time."

CHAPTER 43

*M*ateo had never had a grandmother before, not that he could remember. At first, he'd felt shy around *Mammi*. It was plain how much she loved her grandchildren, but he wasn't family. It was obvious that *Mammi* and Sarah were related. Though *Mammi* was larger, they both had eyes the same color and shape—blue and oval. He'd learned that word in math class last week. Oval—like a squished circle.

He had heard Luke say they didn't need another adult telling them what to do, but he'd laughed when he said it, so maybe he didn't mind *Mammi* being there. Andy and Henry seemed happy to have clean clothes and better meals. She'd arrived on Thursday, and Mateo woke up Saturday morning to the smell of cinnamon rolls. They had to be the best thing Mateo had ever eaten—that and the fresh milk a neighbor had brought over.

As for Sarah, she was finally smiling again, and the dark circles under her eyes were disappearing. Plus, she was remembering to wear the same color socks. He hadn't realized how hard it was for her, caring for them all. He decided it was a good thing that *Mammi* had come, because Sarah was starting to look more rested and less worried.

It didn't take long to see that *Mammi* did care for him and Mia. She was kind and patient with his little sister, and though Mia still seemed attached to Sarah's side, she also ran readily to help *Mammi* whenever she was called.

For the first time in his life, Mateo felt as if he was surrounded by an entire group of people who cared about him and Mia, who would support them no matter what. He thought of *Mammi*'s hands—fingers intertwined, palms pressed against each other. He remembered the way she had talked about family. That's what they were, the eight of them. They were two hands clasped together.

"Mateo, would you take this saucer of milk to the porch?" *Mammi* poured the extra little bit that Mia hadn't finished into a small plate. "I saw a small barn cat yesterday who looked as if he could use fattening up."

"You like cats?"

"I like how they keep the snakes and mice away. Wouldn't want one in the house, but we can still care for the little guy."

That made sense to him. He walked out the front door, carefully holding the saucer of milk so as not to spill it. The cat appeared out of nowhere and began meowing and winding between his legs. He'd barely set the saucer down when the little thing greedily began lapping. He reached out a hand and stroked the cat from the crown of its yellow head, down its back, and to its white and yellow tail. The cat purred like the engine of a car. He'd never had a pet before.

"I'm going to call you Motor," he said.

The clatter of buggy wheels broke the morning's quiet. He looked up to see not one or two, but three buggies headed down their lane. Was something wrong? Had they found his mother? But if that had happened, he would see probably Tommy's car or maybe the bishop's buggy. But it wouldn't take three buggies.

He turned to fetch Sarah or *Mammi* and nearly bumped into them.

"Looks like we have visitors." *Mammi*'s tone told Mateo that she liked having company.

"I'm not expecting anyone." Sarah hurried down the steps. When she turned to smile at them, Mateo knew that everything was okay. "Looks like a ladies' visit."

"I love those. And we have a few leftover cinnamon rolls. I'll run inside and put on the teakettle."

Mateo sat on the step beside Motor.

"What's up?" Isaac asked, coming out and sitting down beside him.

"Beats me," he said. "I named the cat Motor."

"Great name! Can we keep her?"

"Him according to *Mammi*, and she says we can as long as he stays outside."

"Awesome!"

They high-fived, and then Sarah called out to them.

"We're going to need Luke and Henry, and even Andy if you can find him."

She'd hugged the three women. He knew Rebecca, who owned the dry goods store. He heard Sarah refer to the other two as Becca and Suzie. They looked alike, though Becca was bigger than her mom—at least her stomach was. The women began pulling sacks of items out of the buggies.

"Better do as she says." Isaac tugged on his arm. "If we don't go now, we'll end up dragging all that stuff inside by ourselves."

As they hurried past the buggies to the barn, Mateo saw that two mattresses had been secured to the storage areas at the back of the buggies. Already, it seemed normal to him to place groceries or food in the little boxes rather than in the trunk of a car. Already, he preferred the horses to an automobile.

Thirty minutes later they had taken the larger mattress to Mateo's room, the smaller one to Mia's room, and were separating the clothes into what fit him and Mia now and what they would save for later.

"How about these pants, Mateo?" Becca's stomach was like a small volleyball. She was Sarah's close friend. She often put her hands on her stomach, and once she'd even grabbed Sarah's hand and placed it there. He had no idea what that was about. "There's black and dark blue and brown."

"Do you like them?" Sarah asked.

"*Ya*. They look just like Isaac's."

"Say, Mateo. There are *Englisch* and Amish clothes here." Sarah carefully folded another shirt. "We're going to put several sets of both in your room, and you wear whatever you feel most comfortable in."

Mateo nodded, and suddenly he couldn't swallow at all. Fortunately, he was saved from crying in front of everyone by Mia. She had found a bag with clothes for her and pulled out a prayer *kapp*. He had asked Sarah about those last week, and she had explained that Amish girls kept their head covered when they were in public. Mia apparently liked the idea because when she found the *kapp*, she plopped down on the floor and tried to put it on her head.

Everyone laughed, including Mia, and then the older woman, Becca's mom, helped her to put it on correctly.

Mateo didn't think either he or his sister were going to want the *Englisch* clothes. Who wanted to look different from everyone else? No, he'd be leaving those in the drawer. Unless his mother came back, which was something that he didn't want to think about. So instead, he accepted a piece of chocolate from *Mammi* and followed the boys out to the barn.

But later, when he saw the women preparing to leave, he gathered his courage and approached Rebecca.

"You run the store, the one across from the barn and trailer?"

"I do, with my husband, and sometimes Paul helps."

"Paul's our neighbor now."

"He is."

"I...I need to apologize." Mateo wanted to stare at the ground, but he forced himself to look up and into Rebecca's eyes. He saw only kindness there, and perhaps that gave him the courage to confess.

"I took food and stuff from your Dumpster in the back. And once...once I came inside and took some Tylenol. It was for Mia, because she was sick, but I knew...even then, I knew it was wrong."

Rebecca squatted down so that she was at eye level with him.

"I accept your apology, Mateo, on one condition."

He nodded, hoping he could do whatever she wanted. Perhaps she would ask him to work to pay for what he'd taken, or even go to the police station and tell Sheriff Bynum.

"The condition is if you will forgive me."

"For what?"

"That we didn't notice you were in need. That we were too busy to find you and care for you."

Mateo didn't know what to say. Had anyone ever apologized to him before? On an impulse, he threw his arms around Rebecca's neck and hugged her tightly.

As the women drove away, Mateo felt better than he could ever remember feeling. He hadn't realized that the memory of what he'd stolen had bothered him so much. He hadn't understood that he needed to make things right.

But now he knew, and he'd learned his lesson.

The next time he needed help, he would ask.

CHAPTER 44

Tuesday was the first day that Sarah hadn't had a major mess to deal with. After Becca, Suzie, and Mary Beth had left on Saturday, they had spent the morning rearranging the boys' room to make space for one more bed. "There was a time I had four boys in one room." *Mammi* helped to move the dresser so that they could put Mateo's new mattress along the wall and between Isaac's and Luke's beds. It looked like a U-shaped sleeping arrangement.

They placed the dressers at the end of the two beds. There was enough room, but just barely. Fortunately, Isaac hadn't minded cleaning out half of his drawers for Mateo.

"They even brought sheets." Sarah felt a deep satisfaction as she made up the twin-sized bed. Apparently, someone had sent out a call, and they had received donations from nearly every family in their church.

"Remember what we said about community? We help one another, and no doubt they would have done so sooner if they had known that you needed these things."

"I didn't think to tell them."

"Someone must have," *Mammi* said. "I wonder who?"

Not her brothers. That was for certain. They wouldn't have noticed if Mateo was sleeping on the couch. It seemed to her that the males in her family were oblivious to most things as long as they had clean clothes and a hot meal.

"I have no idea."

"Well, it was someone who cares about you. That much is certain."

They put up the donated items Saturday morning, scrubbed the house Saturday afternoon, and rested on Sunday since there was no church service. It had taken all day Monday to do laundry, but with *Mammi* there the entire process had gone more smoothly, and they only lost Mia twice.

Now it was Tuesday, and Sarah was looking forward to a day of sewing and maybe even beginning to plant their vegetable garden if the day warmed up enough.

All thoughts of gardening flew away when an *Englisch* car pulled up in front of the house. She glanced out the window and saw Chloe Vasquez walking up to their porch. "I forgot about the newspaper reporter coming today."

She had shown *Mammi* the initial article in the *Mayes County Chronicle*, worried she might disapprove. *Mammi* had simply nodded and said, "*Gut.* People will know that children need homes."

Now *Mammi* smiled at her and said, "Why don't you two do your interview in the kitchen. I'll watch over this little one."

So she'd hurried to the door and then spent thirty minutes answering Chloe's questions.

What was the hardest part so far? Finishing the twenty-seven hours of classes.

What was the best? Seeing the children smile whenever she did the simplest thing for them.

Did she regret getting involved? No. Not at all.

What worried her the most?

Sarah hesitated, and Chloe set down her pen. "Something you want to talk about?"

"It's a small thing. Maybe it's small. It seems big to me…"

"Just tell me."

"Sometimes Mateo speaks in both Spanish and English, interchanging the words."

To Sarah's surprise, Chloe laughed. "Some people call it Spanglish. I think that's pretty natural. Teens do it all the time. Even my husband does, and he just turned thirty-five."

"Your husband?"

"Hispanic, remember? My last name is now Vasquez."

"I forgot!"

"It's okay. I'd love for him to come out and meet the kids sometime. When you feel like they're settled."

"Could he…or could you…maybe teach me some Spanish words?"

"I'd be happy to, and you know what? I imagine Mateo would like to teach you some too."

The next hour passed quickly. When Chloe drove away, Sarah's head was filled to the brim with English and Spanish. She was thinking of that when Mia and *Mammi* appeared in the kitchen, and Henry tromped in through the back door.

"You might want to come and see this." He grinned impishly and ducked back outside before she or *Mammi* could ask any questions.

Grabbing a shawl, both holding on to one of Mia's hands, they hurried in the direction of the barn. Sarah was surprised to see Paul's tractor parked outside the front door of the barn, and even more surprised to see him unloading a crate.

Squawks came from the crate, and *Mammi* clapped her hands. "Chickens!"

Chickens? Paul had brought them chickens? He looked up, met her gaze, and smiled, as if he had brought them a Christmas present, as if she wanted chickens.

Sarah did not want one more thing to feed or clean up after.

Mammi and Mia were enchanted.

"This is *wunderbaar*, Paul."

Had they met already? Apparently, sometime in the last five days, they had. Already their family was back and forth so much that it seemed as if Paul's place was merely an extension of their own. Sarah wasn't sure if that was a good thing or not. Her brothers were getting awfully attached to Paul. What if he packed up and left? Could they deal with being abandoned again? Which was a ridiculous thing to worry about. She couldn't protect her brothers against all of life's changes, and Paul gave no indication he was doing anything other than settling in.

She returned her attention to the chickens.

"I appreciate the thought, but we already have two…"

"Hardly enough for such a large family, and I heard they weren't producing many eggs."

"Where did you hear that?"

Ignoring her question, he added, "You had six a while back, didn't you? Before the coyote problem?"

"Yes, but—"

"Someone offered me a *gut* deal on them." Paul smiled.

To Sarah it seemed as if he were delivering a well-rehearsed line.

"I can't look after them at this point," he continued. "But I thought if I gave them to you that maybe the boys could take care of them, and you know…share the bounty."

"It's a perfect chore for Isaac and Mateo." *Mammi* clapped her hands together. "Isaac, in particular, has shown a real interest in animals."

"Yup. Caught a squirrel last week." Henry noticed Sarah's look of dismay and added, "We convinced him to let it go."

Sarah finally found her voice. "Where are we going to keep them?"

"Need to make a bigger and better chicken coop," *Mammi* said. "I'm sure Andy has some extra lumber."

"And I brought chicken wire. It…uh…occurred to me that you might need some."

Sarah wasn't buying it. She didn't believe that Paul had simply come across a "good deal" that included six laying hens, one rooster, and chicken wire. She waited until everyone else, including Mia, had followed the chickens into the barn, and then she stepped in front of him.

"I should probably help," he mumbled.

"Tell me again where the chickens came from, Paul."

"Where they came from?"

"Uh-huh. Who offered you a good deal?"

"Who?"

"You sound like an owl. Answer the question."

"Oh. Well, Rebecca got some in at the store."

"Your sister-in-law does not carry live poultry in her store."

"True, but—"

She glanced into the pickup bed attached to his tractor. "And your deal included both chicken wire and several bags of feed?"

Now he was looking anywhere but directly at her.

"You ordered them."

Paul squirmed uncomfortably, but he didn't deny what she'd said.

Sarah remembered something her grandmother had said earlier, when they'd been discussing how the donation drive had started. *Mammi* had said their needs must have been shared by *someone who cares about you.*

"Did you have anything to do with the two mattresses and sacks of clothes and a box of toys for Mia?"

"I might have mentioned to Rebecca—"

"And now you've bought us chickens."

"It's a small thing, Sarah. Every family can use fresh eggs, and I know that you all will take *gut* care of them."

He was frowning again, no doubt worried that she was going to argue with him, possibly concerned that she was going to send the squawking birds back.

She didn't do either.

Suddenly she realized that Paul was a *gut* neighbor. Maybe even more than that. It was possible that the frown he often wore covered his concern, that he wasn't comfortable sharing his feelings. She understood that well enough. And was it so necessary to say a thing when one's actions plainly displayed it?

So instead of thanking him for the seven birds she did not want, birds that would feed her family and be a good experience for Isaac and Mateo...instead of trying to find words for any of that, she stood on her tiptoes, kissed him on the cheek, and before he could reply, hurried into the barn.

CHAPTER 45

$\mathcal{P}$aul didn't want to stop planting, but he realized he needed to eat, and the tractor might overheat if he didn't turn it off for a few minutes, and Sarah was waiting.

He arrived at the barn at the same time Andy did. "How's it going with the corn?"

"*Gut*. How's it going with the alfalfa?"

"Same."

The two tractors sitting side by side appeared rather old and pitiful, but they worked. Without them, it would be difficult to till the fields and plant the crops. As folks had warned him, the Oklahoma dirt was more difficult to farm than it looked. It dried out as soon as you broke a row open. He couldn't imagine doing what they'd done this morning with horses, though when it came time to mow and rake the hay in the fall, he was determined to have two workhorses to do it. For some reason, even as he drove and was grateful for the old tractor, it became more and more important to him to retain as much of the old ways as possible.

Sarah stood under an elm tree, placing lunch on the battered picnic table. Andy and Henry fell on it like vultures. Paul washed his hands and waited for her to head back into the barn for more supplies. When she did, he followed her inside.

"I wanted to thank you for feeding us yesterday and again today."

"Thank me? They are my *bruders*, you know." She smiled prettily at him, and Paul felt something in his heart lighten.

"*Ya*, sure, but you could have brought food for them and made me eat more eggs."

She laughed at that. "Who would have ever thought your six hens plus our two could produce so many? *Mammi* was making a twelve-egg pound cake when I left, Mia at her side stirring the batter. They are a sight."

"It's been *gut* since your *mammi* came. Hasn't it?"

"She's more help than I can even begin to explain. And having her here—well, it seems to settle us as a family once more. The boys suddenly remember to take off their muddy boots before coming in, and everyone helps to keep the place tidy." Sarah tucked a strand of blond hair back into her *kapp*. "We'll see how long their helpful attitude lasts, but for now I'm grateful."

She picked up a pitcher of lemonade, and Paul carried the glasses. They sat at the picnic table with Andy and Henry, and soon the conversation turned to crops.

"We'll be done this afternoon if we push until dark." Andy finished off his first sandwich and began to make himself another—thick, fresh bread, turkey from the deli, and locally made cheddar cheese.

"Maybe. Twenty acres of corn and another twenty of alfalfa doesn't sound like much, but in this dirt…" Paul shook his head as he plopped a large spoonful of potato salad on his plate. "We could finish tonight if we stay at it."

"*Mammi* is making a large stew," Sarah said. "We could bring some over…"

"*Nein*. There's no need to do that. End of the day? It would be easier for me to drive to your place."

Henry laughed. "I see you're not turning down her cooking. The woman is a saint. Not that I'm saying anything bad about your kitchen skills, Sarah."

She laughed with them. "Actually, I'm learning from *Mammi*."

"Recipes?" Paul asked.

"Some, but the main thing I'm learning is not to be distracted by anything while I'm cooking."

"And to set Mia to helping," Andy added.

"*Ya*, that keeps her from finding mischief."

Paul listened to the banter and glanced out over his farm. Things were going well, better than he had expected. He had much to be grateful for.

"Tomorrow we'll start on your place," he said.

Andy refilled his glass of lemonade and nodded in agreement. "Between the two of us, and the *gut* Lord willing, we'll both have a fine harvest by fall. I realize that no one likes to talk about this, but when *Dat* was here the farm was never very productive."

No one disputed his observation, so he pushed on. "He had *gut* intentions, of course, but if we planted at all, it went in late, and we rarely finished what we started. This is the first year that I've been hopeful about the crops in a long time."

"Still depends on the weather." Paul stared out across their fields, as if he could look hard enough to see the future.

"But that is the one thing we can't control." Henry reached for several cookies. "Do what we can and don't fuss over the rest, that's what *Mammi* would say."

Four hours later, they were still at it. Every muscle in his arms and back and legs hurt, but Paul wasn't about to stop when they were so close to finishing. Who would think that driving a tractor could be so exhausting? Between the constant jostling, stopping to work on the mechanical beast, and the warm temperatures, by five o'clock he felt completely depleted. He looked up and spied four small figures walking toward Sarah, who was crocheting under the elm tree. He had tried once to send her home, but she demurred, saying she was actually enjoying a day away from their place.

When he saw Luke, Isaac, Mateo, and even Mia, Paul pulled the tractor up to the barn. He didn't shut it off, but he hopped off to grab a glass of water.

"We came to work, Paul."

"Did you now?"

Luke nodded, helped himself to one of the cookies, and took off to the south pasture, where his older brothers were still planting.

"And did you two come to plant as well?"

Mateo and Isaac both shook their heads, but it was Isaac who answered. "Actually, we came to see if you'd picked up the piglets."

"Nope, but I heard from the guy. He's supposed to deliver ten tomorrow."

"Ten? We thought you were only getting four." Mateo reached for a cookie, handed it to his sister, and took another for himself.

"The price was better than I thought." Paul glanced at Sarah, who only smiled. They had a running joke about farm animals since he'd gifted her the chickens.

"We've been reading one of Brian's books at school—all about pig-pens and that sort of thing." Isaac shuffled from foot to foot. "Learned some interesting stuff."

"You're welcome to take a look behind the barn to see how I did."

That was all the permission they needed. Each boy snagged another cookie before trotting off in the direction of the pens.

"And what about you, little Mia?"

Sarah answered as Mia climbed up into her lap. "Apparently, *Mammi* thought some time out in the sunshine would do this little girl good."

"Is that so?"

"Why?" Mia asked.

"Because sunshine is good for you."

"Why?"

"Vitamin D."

"Why?"

Glancing at Paul, Sarah said, "I read recently that the average four-year-old asks four hundred and thirty-seven questions a day."

"And Mia's only three, which means she's either ahead of her age group—"

"Or the questioning is just getting started."

"Why?"

"Maybe you should eat your cookie." Sarah kissed Mia on top of her head.

Paul picked up two cookies, slugged down an entire glass of water, which he would sweat out before he reached the end of the field, and headed back to the tractor. The last thing he saw, the thing he would remember four hours later when their lives were once again turned inside out, was Mia sitting in Sarah's lap, reaching up to touch Sarah's face, as the child tried to feed her a cookie.

CHAPTER 46

$\mathcal{M}$any things had improved since *Mammi* showed up on their doorstep over two weeks earlier. She seemed such a natural part of their life, and Sarah didn't want to take her for granted. That was one reason she was working on the shawl today, and at Paul's instead of at home, though *Mammi* had eyed the cloth bag slung over Sarah's shoulder as she was leaving that morning.

"Taking some handwork with you?"

"I am. The barn is already spick-and-span. You would think Paul expects an inspection any moment. There's nothing for me to do there, and his house—well, I wouldn't know where to begin."

"It's *gut* to have work with you." *Mammi* had slipped a silver-wrapped chocolate into her hand. "Enjoy your day, dear."

And she had. She'd loved watching her brothers and Paul out in the field. The breeze had tickled her hair and swept away the worries of winter. Spring seemed like a miracle to her, and it was bursting everywhere she looked.

Now, with Mia in her lap, Sarah put aside her crochet work and focused on the little girl. They sang their ABCs. They counted birds on the fence post. They spied wildflowers that were colored green and blue and yellow. When Mia began to grow restless, Sarah attempted to occupy her with singing one of the hymns from church, but Mia was having none of it.

"Home, Sarah. Home to *Mammi*." Her vocabulary was expanding as quickly as her appetite.

"Not yet. See all these dishes?" She'd piled them neatly at the end of the table, all except the plate of cookies and glasses for lemonade. "I have to take them back. We need to wait for Andy."

"Sarah…" Mia began to pull on her arm and her voice took on an all too familiar whine. Soon she'd escalate into a hearty cry.

"Let's count again."

"No. Home, please."

"Can you find the color purple?"

"No, Sarah. No." As the pitch of her voice climbed higher and higher, lines formed between her eyes, and she pulled on Sarah's hand with all of her might.

"What's wrong, Mia?" Mateo plopped down on the bench next to Sarah.

"She wants to go home already. Maybe you could play with her?"

"I could take her home."

"Weren't you—"

"Looking at the pigpens with Isaac. Yeah, I was, but now he's drawing a sketch of how Paul can make it better. I got bored."

"Oh."

"I'll take her home. It's no problem."

"You won't get lost?"

"Sarah." Now he sounded comically like Mia, who was hopping from foot to foot and had taken to pulling on Mateo's arm. "It's next door. How can I get lost?"

"You'll have to go around by the road. Mia can't climb over the fence."

"Okay."

"Hold her hand the whole way."

"I will."

"You know how she likes to h-i-d-e."

"I promise to watch her the whole time." He'd begun walking backward, smiling at her, his right hand holding Mia's, and his left holding a stick which he banged against the ground.

"I'll be right behind you." Already the sun was lower and the afternoon cooling. "Tell *Mammi* I'll be there before dark."

He gave her a thumbs-up and turned toward the direction they were walking.

She watched the two of them strolling down the lane.

It was a good sign, it seemed to her, that Mateo sometimes went off without Isaac. She thought of what Andy had said, about needing to prepare Isaac for when Mateo wasn't there. But Sarah couldn't imagine such a time, and she didn't think Isaac needed preparing. Regardless what happened with the judge and whether or not they attempted permanent placement, Mateo and Mia would always have a place in their hearts. Mateo and Isaac would always be friends.

She gathered up the glasses, took them into the barn, and rinsed them off. Once the boys were done, she'd be ready to go. She was looking forward to a nice quiet dinner at home, not to mention a full bowl of *Mammi's* stew.

CHAPTER 47

*M*ateo didn't pay much attention to the white car at first. It was parked across the road from their house. When he did look more closely at it, he thought it must be broken down. Anyone visiting would turn down the lane, and there was no other reason to stop on the side of the road here. Nothing to see but fields, soon to be planted with corn and alfalfa and sorghum and soybeans.

He was looking forward to seeing the plants push up through the soil. He'd never watched anything grow before. He understood where food came from, but he'd never participated in planting or harvest. Sarah had said that on Saturday they could plant their own garden. He and Isaac had made up several diagrams—Isaac loved to draw things out on paper. *Mammi* had teased that they needed to save room for her to plant a chocolate candy tree.

He was thinking about that, about sweets growing on trees, when the door of the old car opened and his *mamá* stepped out.

Mateo froze where he was. He couldn't have moved if he'd wanted to. His feet felt as if they'd been planted into the earth. He was stuck on the side of the road with Mia pulling on his arm. A dozen different emotions swept through his heart in the span of a heartbeat—relief, joy, puzzlement, and even fear.

Mia finally noticed what he was staring at, but she didn't immediately recognize their *mamá*. Mateo did though. He knew her instantly. She looked to Mateo as she'd always looked—slim, rather short, long

195

brown hair pulled back in a simple ponytail, dirty-looking jeans, and a T-shirt that had seen better days. His *mamá* was beautiful. He'd heard enough men say so, but looking at her now he thought she looked tired and too thin.

"Mateo. Mia. *Rápidamente*."

She held out her arms, and it was like an invisible string pulled Mateo toward her. He was powerless to resist it, though he did remember to check both right and left before crossing the road.

"*Cómo estás?*" She crushed them against her, kissing the tops of their heads and breathing in the scent of them.

For just a moment Mateo pushed away the questions and savored the smell and touch and comfort of her.

The joy of at last being reunited didn't last.

His *mamá* ducked her head into the open door of the car and said, "Aren't my children handsome? I told you."

The man said something that sounded short and impatient.

"Let's get in the car." A pickup drove past them, the driver tapping his horn lightly to warn Mateo out of the road. "Hurry, hurry."

"Where are we going?" Mateo asked, even as he climbed onto the backseat of the car. By the time he had fastened the seat belt around Mia first and then himself, his mother's friend had put the car into drive and sped away, spewing gravel. Sarah's farm faded into the Oklahoma countryside.

"How long are we going to be gone?" He tried to keep the tremble out of his voice. He didn't want Mia to pick up on how frightened he was.

"When did you start questioning me?"

"Sarah will worry."

"She's not your *familia*."

"Yes, but—"

His mother turned around in the front seat and studied him. "You did good to find a place for you and Mia to stay, Mateo, but don't sass me. I'm still your *madre*."

"How did you find us?"

"That snoopy social worker was looking for me. Didn't take too long for me to figure out why, and then it was only a matter of finding the article in the newspaper."

The man snickered and raised his eyes to the rearview mirror to study Mateo.

Though he wanted to, Mateo didn't look away.

This man was older than his mother. He had lines around his eyes and gray hair in his mustache.

"Are you sure he's eight? Looks small."

"He takes after his father, but he will grow. Once he becomes a teenager, he will shoot up and put on the pounds like my father. Won't you, honey?"

Mateo nodded dumbly. He felt as if he were stuck in a bad dream. He didn't know why he'd crossed the street and climbed into the car. His *mamá* was acting as if she hadn't abandoned them.

Mia had started to cry and was attempting to unfasten her seat belt. She held her arms out to their *mamá*, and that more than anything scraped against Mateo's heart.

"Stay where you are, Mia. I can't be holding you right now." She turned around in the seat, reached into her purse, and pulled out a bottle in a paper bag.

And suddenly all the times they had been left, all the things they'd had to do without, and all the ways they had suffered built up in Mateo's heart and spilled over.

"You just left us! Mia was sick, and you never even came back. You didn't care—"

He never saw the slap coming, but he felt the sting. Tears filled his eyes. He brushed them away, anger overriding every other emotion.

"Do not speak to me with that tone, Mateo."

He had forgotten so much—the fear, the constant knot in his stomach, the feeling of hopelessness.

"I did my best, and you will not speak to me in such a way." She turned toward the front again, now speaking more to the dashboard than him. "I came back, didn't I?"

It had been a mistake.

He'd been temporarily blinded by the thought of *familia*—a blood relation who had come back for them, who cared enough to find them. But that wasn't what this was about.

Mia had stopped fidgeting and begun sucking her thumb. He hadn't seen her do that in weeks.

Mateo sank lower in his seat, tried to make himself invisible, and listened. He heard the words *benefit check* and *new start*, and then a word he'd long ago learned to dread—*casino*.

The last thing he heard before the man—Orlynn, that's what she'd called him—before Orlynn turned up the radio so that it blared and shut out every other sound was his *mamá* saying, "I found my kids. I think this is our lucky day."

CHAPTER 48

*I*t was nearly seven when Sarah ran up their front steps. She should have been home long ago. The time had slipped away from her, and then there was some problem with the tractors that Henry insisted would only take a minute, and then another, and then still another.

It wasn't unusual for dinner to be late on planting or harvest days, but Isaac and Mateo and Luke had school the next morning. She wanted them in bed on time or they would be a bear to wake up. After asking Henry to slow the tractor so she could jump off at the front of the house, she hurried through the door of their home, threw off her shawl, and made a mad dash for the kitchen.

The house was unusually quiet.

She abruptly stopped on seeing the kitchen. Dinner was on the stove with a lid on the pot. Bread sat on the counter, cooling. *Mammi* was in the rocker she'd recently moved into the kitchen, knitting a pastel blue-and-green baby blanket.

She looked up, smiled at Sarah, and then she seemed to realize that something was wrong.

Sarah said, "Mateo and Mia...where are they?"

"They're with you."

"*Nein*. I mean they were, but I sent them home..." Sarah stared out the window, trying to process how much time had passed. Already it was dark. "I sent them home more than an hour ago."

Mammi dropped the knitting on top of the basket next to her chair. "They never got here."

"But…I saw them. I saw them walk down Paul's lane and then—"

"Did someone say my name?"

"Sure smells *gut* in here."

"I'm starved."

"Out of my way. I'm the hungriest."

The bantering fell over and surrounded her, but it didn't pierce the block of ice that had formed around her heart.

"What's wrong?" Paul pushed through the boys, took her by the arm, and forced her to turn and look at him. "Tell me what's wrong, Sarah."

"Mateo and Mia, they never…they left your place. Mia wanted to come back to *Mammi*, and I wanted to stay and enjoy the afternoon. Mateo said that he could find his way, that it was just next door."

Andy had crowded into the middle of the room. "He didn't get lost, Sarah. He knew his way home well enough. Maybe he became distracted by something and then as darkness fell…"

"We'll look." Paul squeezed her arm and turned to her *bruders*. "We'll all look."

"I'll take the barn," Isaac said.

"And I'll look down the lane, both sides." Henry turned to Luke. "We both will."

"*Ya.* Of course."

"You'll all need flashlights." *Mammi* hurried into the mudroom and returned with half a dozen flashlights. Just yesterday she'd insisted that Sarah test each one and be sure they were working.

"Paul and I will take the road and travel back along the lane of his place." Andy was already walking out the front door, Paul close on his heels.

"Sarah will stay on the porch."

It was as if *Mammi* read her mind. She couldn't sit at the table. She couldn't just wait inside as if nothing was wrong.

"We'll put a lantern out there. If the children look up and see the light, if they see Sarah, they'll find their way back." *Mammi* clapped her hands out in front of her. Andy and Paul had stopped at the door. Luke,

Isaac, and Henry were nearly out the back. *Mammi* stood in the doorway between the kitchen and sitting room and held her hands out wide, and then she brought them together until her fingers were interlaced.

"We're a family, *ya*? As we search we will pray, and *Gotte* will lead us to them."

Each person nodded. Sarah found herself hoping, believing, and praying that it was so.

But two hours later there was still no sign of Mateo or Mia.

Mammi agreed it was time to call the authorities. Paul and Andy left to take a tractor to the phone shack. Within an hour, a Cody's Creek police cruiser made its way down their lane.

Sheriff Bynum took down the information as well as a description of the children.

"Two hours isn't much time," he pointed out.

"Yes, but it's only been two hours since we started looking." Sarah rubbed her forefinger against her thumbnail—back and forth, back and forth. "They could have been missing three hours or a little longer."

They were all in the living room. The boys had eaten, but Sarah couldn't imagine swallowing a bite. Now they were together, all sitting in a circle around the sheriff.

"We usually don't put out an alert unless it's been at least six to twelve hours, preferably twenty-four."

"But—" Sarah's heart rejected the idea of waiting any longer.

"I know. I know the situation is different with the Amish. However, do you remember a few years ago?" He looked at Sarah and then Andy. "The Stutzman girl went missing. We even brought your teacher in for questioning."

"Stella had run off with some *freinden* to Tulsa." Sarah closed her eyes and forced the tears back. "*Ya*, I remember."

"Surely this situation is different." *Mammi* sat up straighter and crossed her arms. "Mateo is a young child. He'd have no reason to run away, no one to take him in a car."

Bynum scratched the side of his face. "I agree with you. I'm going to go ahead and issue a limited alert to our officers in case they see or hear of anyone matching Mateo's and Mia's descriptions. Since the children are involved in the social services program, we'll have pictures of them to distribute as well."

Sarah remembered the day they'd had those pictures taken. She remembered the way Mateo had insisted she cut his hair first, and Mia had wanted to wear her dress *like Sarah's*. She remembered, and another piece of her heart broke.

"We also have the ability to issue a local area alert. It's not an Amber Alert. In my opinion, we're not there yet."

"Why not?" Paul asked.

He had refused to leave even when Sarah told him he could go. She was glad to have him there. In fact, she was grateful that the room was full of those she was closest to, almost as if together their love for Mateo and Mia could bring them home.

"Because there's no evidence of an abduction having occurred...yet. If anyone saw something, we can proceed with the Amber Alert. You'd be surprised what people notice. The folks of Cody's Creek keep an eye on one another. It can be helpful in situations like this."

Everyone agreed, and the sheriff left to make some phone calls. He promised them he would alert Tommy, their caseworker, as well as get word to the bishop.

Mammi reminded them that they had done all they could do. Now was the time to pray and to believe that God had a plan for Mateo's life. That He cared for Mia. "He hasn't forgotten or forsaken these two small ones. He brought them to us for a reason, and He watches over them still."

He watches over them still.

Sarah wanted to believe that—she did believe that—but all the same she trembled at the thought of them alone and frightened. She stepped into the backyard, needing a moment to clear her head. A battery-powered lantern blazed from each window and cast her shadow across the lawn. *Mammi* had placed all of their bedside lanterns in the windows in case the children were somehow lost in the fields.

Sarah didn't realize Paul had followed her out until he cleared his throat, stepped up behind her, and set a hand lightly on each of her arms.

His touch settled her, and his voice calmed her jumpy nerves.

"We will find them. This time tomorrow, they'll be home again. You can trust and believe that, Sarah." When she didn't respond, he added, "Like *Mammi* said. *Gotte* cares for His children."

She pivoted toward him and found herself in the circle of his arms, looking up into eyes colored with concern. "Was *Gotte* looking after them when they were living in the old trailer? Where was *Gotte* then?"

Paul wasn't offended by her doubt. He cupped her face in his hands, leaned closer until his forehead was resting against hers, until his voice was only a breath away. "That's when He sent you."

CHAPTER 49

Mateo tried to eat the food the waitress brought—waffles and syrup and a glass of water. He'd never liked waffles. They were too sticky, and the sweetness made his stomach hurt. Mia had no such reservations. She had covered hers with syrup and was now pulling it apart with her fingers.

They had driven around for a long time—Orlynn was mad about somebody who was supposed to meet them. Only the man wasn't where he said he'd be. Orlynn tried to call him a few times and finally said, "We've got an hour. Let's feed them while we can."

The roadside café they stopped at looked dirty and tired, if a café could look tired. Mateo thought maybe it could. How many people had eaten here? How many families had sat on the cracked vinyl seats?

Only the woman sitting across from him wasn't his family—not in any meaningful sense of the word. He'd come to terms with that as they had sped away from Cody's Creek. He was supposed to love his *mamá*, and a part of him did. A part of him always would. Perhaps it wasn't her fault that she would rather take sips from the bottle than eat. Maybe she had a sickness.

He tried to remember the times the bishop had talked to him about praying for his *mamá*. Sarah, too, had said that they should ask the Lord to watch over her.

But what could God do for someone like her?

How do you help someone who won't even listen?

"But we liked it there. I got to go to school, and Mia is learning stuff, like how to cook."

His *mamá* blew out cigarette smoke with an exasperated sigh. Orlynn had stepped outside to make more phone calls. From where they sat, Mateo could look across the street and just make out the word *CASINO* in bright neon letters.

"You want to know the problem with you, *hijo*? You think about yourself too much." She stubbed out her cigarette in the tray and immediately lit another. "While you were enjoying the good life, I was trying to find a way for us to get back together."

"Down, *Mamá*." Mia sat in a high chair, but she wasn't happy about it. She was too big to be in a high chair and only fit because she was small for her age. She didn't like the confinement. "Down, please."

When her *mamá* ignored her, she began to finger paint the tray with her sticky fingers.

At Sarah's, Andy had made a block for Mia to sit on, and *Mammi* had sewn a little cushion for it. They laughed and called it "Mia's throne." That memory made Mateo's heart ache.

His sister had made fast work with her waffle, though she wore as much as she had eaten. Mateo glanced at the clock over the cook's window. It read fifteen minutes after nine, long past the time for Mia to be taking a bath and putting on her pajamas.

"Orlynn has a plan. He's good with cards, and I'm good at distracting people. We could get ahead here." She pointed the glowing end of her cigarette at him. "Then you and I and Mia could find a nice place to live. Isn't that what you want?"

"You could come back with us—back to Sarah's. She would let you stay, and we could start over there."

"Don't be ridiculous, Mateo. It's time for you to grow up. People like your Sarah? They're not interested in the likes of me."

She'd been drinking steadily from the bottle, and now he realized that her eyes had taken on an all too familiar glassy look.

He would have argued with her, even at the risk of another slap across his face. There was no time though. Orlynn arrived, excited about their plan. "This is going to work, baby. She's your size and every-thing. But…uhhhh…they said no about your kids staying there."

"That's okay." His *mamá* laughed, handed Orlynn the empty bottle, and accepted the new one he'd apparently had in the trunk or the glove compartment. Mateo hadn't seen it. If he had, he might have tried to grab it and throw it out the window. "Mateo and Mia are good kids. They'll wait in the car."

He didn't hear the details of their plan because Mia needed to go to the bathroom.

"You take her. Orlynn and I have some things to work out."

So he'd helped Mia out of the high chair and led her to the bath-room. Peeking into the men's room, he decided it was too dirty. There was no one in the ladies' room, so he took her in there and locked the door behind them.

"I want Sarah, Mateo." Mia rubbed at her eyes, smearing more syrup on her face. "I want *Mammi*."

"I know you do." He pulled off three paper towels and held them under the tap water. When he was washing her hands and face, she started to cry.

"I want to go home."

"We will. You don't have to cry, Mia." He finished cleaning her up and then helped her use the bathroom. Once she was finished, he did his best to straighten her clothes, though his *mamá* had yanked off the prayer *kapp* when they'd first pulled up to the restaurant.

"Looks like a lost prairie girl," she'd muttered.

Mia's hair was still in a long braid wound around her head—like *Mammi* combed it every morning. That sight, that memory, somehow calmed Mateo's heart.

"We'll get back to Sarah. Don't worry."

"When?"

"Soon, Mia. Very soon."

He unlocked the door and reached for her hand. As they walked toward his *mamá* and Orlynn, Mateo vowed to himself that he would find a way to get Mia home. And then he did something he'd never done before. He began to pray that God would show him what to do next.

CHAPTER 50

*W*ithin the hour they had their first lead. It wasn't much, but it was something, and something equaled hope. Paul wanted to fall on his knees and thank *Gotte* for that.

"Someone driving by saw two small Hispanic kids being helped into a late-model white Buick." Sheriff Bynum was reading from notes he had scribbled on a pad of paper.

Paul was sitting next to Sarah. *Mammi* had put on a fresh pot of coffee and set out snacks on the table. No one was hungry, though. No one wanted to act as if life was normal, even if their stomach was growling.

"*Helped?*" Sarah dropped her face into her hands and rubbed at her temples. Sitting up straighter, she waited until Bynum met her gaze. "What do you mean *helped*?"

"Our witness, a man who was driving through to his brother's place ten miles from here, he said it looked as if the children went willingly."

"Did he see anyone else?" Paul asked.

"Couldn't make out who the driver was, too much glare on the windshield, but there was a small Hispanic woman standing beside the car."

"Their mother. She came back." Sarah's voice sounded so lost, so forlorn, that Paul had to fight the urge to take her in his arms.

"This is *gut* news, Sarah." Andy stood and began pacing back and forth. "At least we know who to look for, right?"

"Right. We have a partial plate on the vehicle, and a description of the mother. We know she wasn't driving—so we're looking for two adults and two children."

"Can she do that?" *Mammi* had returned to her knitting, though she was doing so with furious speed. "Can she just come back in and steal the children?"

"Yes and no. Yes in that Elisa Lopez has not surrendered her rights to Mateo and Mia. No because social services is now involved, and she has to prove to the courts that she can provide them with a safe place to live."

"So you will look for her?" Sarah's voice had gained some strength and the color was coming back into her face.

"We've already released a full Amber Alert." Bynum was interrupted by a knock at the door.

Paul immediately recognized Chloe Vasquez, the young news reporter from the temporary placement hearing.

"Sarah." Chloe rushed across the room and enfolded Sarah in her arms. When they finally parted, Chloe unashamedly wiping at the tears on her cheeks, Sarah introduced her friend to Sheriff Bynum.

"I was there at the children's initial hearing," Chloe explained.

"I saw the news article you wrote. The general consensus down at the department was that it might help to find more homes for those little ones still waiting on a family."

"There was a good response, yes." Chloe nodded hello to Sarah's brothers and Paul and *Mammi*, and then she turned her attention back to Sarah. "We'll lead with this story on our front page tomorrow. If anyone knows anything, they'll call."

"Tomorrow—"

"I know." Chloe's hair was a wild chaos of black curls. They bounced when she nodded her head in agreement. "I know. We want this resolved well before then. Don't worry. We've updated our online website as well. Between that and the Amber Alert that was issued, we're going to find them."

Andy offered Chloe and Sheriff Bynum a mug of coffee. The three walked off into the kitchen, discussing tip hotlines and police procedures.

Mammi remained focused on her knitting. Henry, Luke, and Isaac were draped over various pieces of furniture—refusing to go to bed but barely staying awake.

Paul stepped closer to Sarah. "Would you like to walk out on the porch?"

"*Ya*. That would be *gut*."

They stepped out into the cool March evening. Rain was coming. He could smell it in the night air. According to Andy, it was predicted to rain steadily for the next three days. They would get Andy's crops planted, but they wouldn't do it until the next week. Neither of them was worried. Together, they could and would get the work done in time.

Sarah sank into a rocker and dropped her head into her hands. Paul didn't realize she was crying until her shoulders began to shake.

"Hey. Don't do that. Look at me. Sarah, look at me." He squatted in front of her and gently raised her face, thumbing away the tracks of tears. "Mateo is a smart boy. He'll find a way to contact us."

She nodded, gulping and pulling in a deep breath. "It's only that my emotions feel so raw. It's so hard…so hard to keep them reined in."

He pulled a chair in front of hers, sat in it, and reached for her hands.

"I know it is. You care about those two, and they know you care about them."

"Why would he get in the car with her? Why would he do that?"

Paul propped his elbows on the arms of his rocker, but he didn't relinquish her hands. Instead, he rubbed them gently, hoping his touch would calm her somehow.

"I can't answer that," he admitted. "But let me ask you a question. If your mother were to show up on the side of the road, would you walk past her? Or would you stop and speak to her?"

"Of course I would stop, but—"

"And if she said to you, *Sarah, let's go somewhere and talk*. Or maybe, *Sarah, come with me, just for a moment*. Would you go?"

"*Ya*, probably I would."

"Because you love her. Because she's your mother. Not because you don't love the people here. Right?"

"I guess."

"Mateo is only an eight-year-old boy, and he's had a lot of upheaval and confusion in his life. I can't imagine what he was feeling when he saw his mother step out of that car, but one thing I do know." He stood and pulled her into his arms, never wondering what *Mammi* would think, though she was sitting facing the window. *Mammi* would understand. Somehow he was sure of that.

"Mateo and Mia love you. That's plain to anyone who sees them when you're around."

"I care so much for them, Paul. I can't stand the thought of seeing them hurt or scared."

"It's hard to let go of those we love, especially the young ones."

She was sniffling into his shirt, making a mess of it, and he didn't care one bit.

"I never expected to have a family, not like this."

"Oh, you didn't? No hidden beaus I should know about?"

She laughed and hiccupped at the same time. Then her voice grew somber so that he had to lean his head down close to hers to make out her words.

"When I first saw them, I felt sorry for them. Then after they were in my home, I was sure that it was my duty to help them. But now?" She raised her eyes to his, and Paul knew in that moment that he would never be able to resist loving her. He understood that he already did.

"Now, it feels as if my heart is walking around outside my body. As if I would do anything to be in their place, and have them here—safely at home."

He smiled, kissed her softly, and said, "You know what you sound like?"

She shook her head, but she didn't pull away from his embrace.

"You sound like a *mamm*."

CHAPTER 51

*W*hen they left the café, they drove away from the casino. That should have made Mateo feel better, but it didn't. His mother was drinking steadily from the new bottle. Even Orlynn noticed. "Take it easy, honey. You won't do me any good passed out in the car."

His *mamá* laughed as if Orlynn had just told the best joke ever. Orlynn glanced in the rearview mirror and winked at Mateo. There was much of his childhood Mateo didn't remember, and there were a few special moments that stood out as happy times. But the bulk of his memories were of nights just like this. When his *mamá* had a plan to make a better life for them. Always a man was involved, and always it ended with *Mamá*, Mia, and Mateo standing on the side of the road watching someone's taillights as they drove away.

Orlynn turned left and then right into a large downtown area—the signs said *Tulsa*. Then they wound their way through a maze of lights, streets, and junky-looking stores. Mateo was sure he would never be able to find his way out. Finally, Orlynn pulled up in front of a small house with no yard at all and several cars parked haphazardly.

His *mamá* nearly fell out of the car when she opened the door. That produced another round of laughter. She shut the door, walked toward the house, and then stopped as if she'd suddenly remembered something. She stumbled back to the car, tapped on the window beside Mia, and pointed her finger at Mateo.

"Stay here and watch your sister. This won't take long."

He thought about running then, but the neighborhood they were in was not a good one. Two kids walking down the road would be noticed in a minute, but he wasn't sure he could count on anyone to help them. A lot of the houses they had passed actually had bars on the windows. Why would someone want bars on their windows?

Mia began to whimper. "I'm cold, Mateo."

Oh, how he wished he had worn his jacket to school that day. *Mammi* had told him to, but he'd laughed and said he didn't need it. If he had it now, he could put it around his sister. But he didn't have it. He closed his eyes, thought of *Mammi* lacing her fingers together and saying, *Maybe there haven't been a lot of adults in your life that you could count on, but you can trust me.*

He brushed the tears away, grateful for the darkness and glad Mia couldn't see. She'd crawled into the circle of his arm.

He couldn't trust his mother, but he could trust *Mammi*. He could trust all of Sarah's family, and the bishop and Paul too. They were all people who cared about them. What he had to do was find a way back home.

"Tell me a story, Mateo."

"A story, huh?" He stared out the car window. The words found their way out of his heart slowly—about planting seeds in the ground, watching the corn grow tall, spying rabbits on an early summer morning.

By the time his *mamá* came out of the house, looking cleaner and more sober and wearing different clothes, Mia was asleep.

And Mateo? He had figured out exactly what they were going to do.

They drove back the way they had come, past the houses with bars on the windows, through the downtown streets, and onto the freeway. After twenty minutes—Mateo was now watching the clock on the radio—Orlynn exited the freeway. Mateo looked out his window and saw the diner they'd eaten at earlier. They passed it and drove slowly around the tall building next door.

Orlynn circled the casino three times before he settled on a parking space as far away from the bright lights as he could get.

"Won't be any cameras out here. The last thing we need is to get in trouble for leaving your kids in the car."

"They're my kids, and what's wrong with leaving them in a car? They're dry and they're safe. Aren't you, baby?"

Mateo nodded. Mia snored softly.

His mother opened the car door and stood up. She was definitely more sober now. She managed to stand on bright red high heel shoes. Adjusting the silky black top over her sparkly blue jeans, she paused to check her lipstick in the reflection of the glass. Then she leaned into the car and said, "Back in a flash, kids."

She slammed the door and walked away, Orlynn's arm around her shoulders.

CHAPTER 52

Mateo forced himself to count to a hundred once, then again, and finally a third time. He knew his mother. More often than not, she forgot something and came back. He couldn't risk that she might catch them as they tried to run away.

Mia was curled up against his side. The late hour and the motion of the car had lured her to sleep. He was thankful that she hadn't seen their mother walk away. Perhaps this would all seem like a dream to her once they were back at Sarah's—and he didn't doubt for a minute that they would find a way back.

The bishop had told him that everyone, in every situation, had something to be grateful for. The bishop said that God was always on their side and always looking out for them. Mateo didn't understand why their mother couldn't be normal, but he did believe the bishop. After all, Sarah had found them, and she had taken them into her home and loved them.

He was grateful for that even as he huddled in the back of Orlynn's car with the rain tapping against the windows. He started over at one, counting to a hundred one last time and thinking about all the other things they had to be thankful for.

Sarah was probably looking for them right this minute.

Next week, he and Isaac would design the rows of vegetables and flowers for the spring garden.

Brian had recently asked him to look after a new kid in their school who was one year younger.

Paul was going to have pigs that he and Isaac would help with.

It was his responsibility to help look after the new chickens.

Mia was learning how to cook—to stir things and pat out biscuits and decorate cookies.

Mateo thought of all the wonderful things in their life, and he vowed that they would not give them up now. When he'd finished with his counting, he nudged Mia awake. She squirmed and moaned and finally sat up and rubbed at her eyes.

"I need the bathroom." She didn't seem to realize they were in a car.

"Okay. But you have to wake up. We have to walk a little ways."

The light rain had turned into a steady downpour. Mateo found the prayer *kapp* that Mia had been wearing, the one that his mother had thrown onto the floorboard. He brushed it off and placed it back on her head. She smiled, and said, "All ready."

"Yup. We're all ready."

Her good mood didn't last long.

"Bathroom, Mateo."

"I know. We're almost there."

"Bathroom *now*."

"In a minute, Mia."

In truth, he wasn't sure exactly where they were going. He didn't want to head back to the diner. He couldn't go into the casino. But there were other businesses out toward the road. He led her down the edge of the parking lot, walking as fast as she could. The first place they stopped at, a Starbucks, was closed. He peered in the window at the small tables and chairs and displays full of wrapped baked goods. But no one was there. The place was closed up tight.

Mia began hopping from foot to foot. "I need to go."

"Okay."

"Now!"

"Don't worry. We'll find something."

Next door was a nail salon and after that an auto parts store. Both were closed.

Mateo could see the lights of a large gas station, but it was farther down the road. The rain continued, and they were both soaked to the skin. Mia seemed to have forgotten about going to the bathroom. She had also started to cry.

They made it out to the main road. No one was following them, but cars were whizzing by, splashing water in their wake. At one point, Mia sat down on the curb and refused to go any farther.

He squatted in front of her.

"We have to keep going, Mia."

"I'm tired."

"I know you are. See those lights over there?"

She squinted past him and nodded her head.

"We need to get over there, and then we're going to call Sarah."

"Promise?"

"I promise."

"Okay."

When she stood up, he noticed a puddle under where she'd sat. "It's okay, Mia. *Mammi* will clean you up."

Her mood seemed to improve, and they made quick time to the gas station. They were nearly to the door when Mateo saw a white car drive up. He pulled her into the shadow of a vending machine, but it was only an old man stopping to fill up his car.

A small bell rang when they pushed into the store.

Behind the counter was a Hispanic man with long hair and an earring in one ear. He peered down at them. "*Cómo estás, amigos?*"

"We're okay, but we need to make a phone call."

"Did you drive here?" The man—his name tag said *Javier*—was smiling at them. "Bet your driver's license is pretty new because you're kind of *poquito*."

Mateo shook his head.

The man's teasing smile turned to a frown as he glanced past him. "Are you two alone?"

"Yes."

"I'm tired," Mia declared.

"No parents or anything?"

"We need to call someone."

A woman waiting at the cash register cleared her throat impatiently. Javier glanced her way, and then he said to Mateo, "Hang on just a second. Don't go anywhere."

He rang up the woman's purchases and gave her some change. Glancing again at the children, he pulled out his phone and checked something on the small screen.

"What's going on?" This from a young black woman who was working the other register.

Javier showed her his phone.

"You think that's them?"

"It is. It has to be."

"We'd better call someone, then."

They both glanced at Mateo. He didn't know what was on the phone, what they could be looking at, but he knew who they should call.

"Sarah Yoder is our foster mom. She lives in Cody's Creek, and she'll come to get us."

CHAPTER 53

*B*ishop Levi had come by and prayed with them. He'd wanted to stay, but Paul insisted they would be fine. "Perhaps tomorrow, if—"

He didn't dare to voice the rest of that thought.

Levi had run his fingers through his beard, nodded, and made them promise to send someone if they needed anything at all.

Sheriff Bynum occasionally left the room to make a call or check something on his phone. He had apparently gone off shift, but he refused to leave them. "The first twenty-four hours are the most important."

The minutes ticked slowly by, the hands on the clock relentlessly ushering in another day. Rain splattered against the roof. No one spoke. There was nothing left to say. It was only a matter of waiting together, of being there to support one another whatever happened.

Sarah was sitting across from Sheriff Bynum when his phone vibrated. She could tell by the look on his face that it was about the children.

He jumped to his feet, listened for a moment, and then began firing questions. "Where? You're sure it's Mateo and Mia? No signs of injury?"

Sarah's throat closed on that last question. She hadn't allowed herself to think about what might have happened to them while they were gone. But as fast as the dreadful thought appeared, it fled. Bynum was smiling and nodding his head.

"Get an officer to the site and don't let the clerk go off duty. We'll want to ask him some questions."

Paul, Sarah, *Mammi*, Andy, and Chloe all stood up at once.

Bynum said a few more things into the phone, but Sarah couldn't make them out. Everyone was talking.

"They found them."

"Praise be to *Gotte*."

"I knew it would be okay."

But Sarah held back, not yet ready to believe this horrible event was about to end.

Bynum pushed a button on his cell phone and stuck it in his shirt pocket. "They're at a gas station on the east side of Tulsa, near the casinos."

"And they're all right?" Sarah could barely breathe.

"They're fine. A little tired and a little wet, but they're fine."

Chloe threw her arms around Sarah, who finally accepted that the nightmare was over. Paul and Andy were slapping each other on the back, and *Mammi* was raising her hands to the heavens.

Bynum stepped outside to make more phone calls. By the time he returned, *Mammi* had roused Henry and Luke and Isaac, and sent them upstairs after telling them the good news.

"They'll be home when I get up? You promise?" Isaac lingered on the bottom step.

"I promise. Now up to bed. You still have school tomorrow." *Mammi* turned back toward their little group. "We have much to be thankful for this night."

Bynum was preparing to go and pick up Mateo and Mia.

"Can I go with you?" Sarah asked. "To get them? I want to be there."

"Of course."

"I'll go too." Andy stepped close to her side. "We'll both go."

She nodded and ran to get a shawl. *Mammi* put together a sack of clothes for Mateo and Mia, and then stuck in a container of cookies. "They might be hungry," she said, pushing the items into Sarah's arms.

Paul stood there, looking at her, and although Bynum and Andy had already walked outside, Sarah didn't. Instead, she walked over to this man she'd only known for a short time. Somehow he felt like family. The things they'd been through, the unusual twists and turns of her family, had bound them together.

"*Danki*, for everything."

"You are more than welcome, Sarah."

His voice sent a river of warmth through her veins. She wanted to throw her arms around him, to tell him that he'd been a rock in her storm. Instead, she smiled, clutched *Mammi*'s sack of goodies to her chest, and hurried out the door.

It took forty-five minutes to reach the casino area.

When they pulled to a stop in front of the gas station, Sarah noticed that a police cruiser was parked near the door.

She didn't wait for Bynum to tell her she could go in. She didn't look to see if her brother was following. She bolted out of the car, through the front door, and to the counter.

No Mateo. No Mia.

Just a middle-aged black woman, a young Hispanic man, and a police officer.

"You must be Sarah," the young man said. His name plate read *Javier*. "Same..." he touched the top of his head. "Like the little girl."

Sarah gulped, aware that Andy and Sheriff Bynum had caught up with her.

"Are they here? Are Mateo and Mia here?"

"Yeah," Javier said. "And, boy, are they going to be glad to see you. They kept saying, *Sarah will come and get us*. I'll show you where they are."

Sarah followed him to the back of the store, down a short hall, and into an office.

For a moment, she couldn't see anything except Javier. He filled the doorframe, but then he stepped aside, and she saw them. It was an image that would remain etched on her heart if she lived to be one hundred.

The two were sitting side by side, wearing large Hoosier sweatshirts. An uneaten package of donuts and two cartons of milk sat on the table beside them.

A female officer stood across the room.

Mia was rubbing her eyes, leaning against Mateo.

And Mateo? He was watching the door.

The instant he saw her, his face lit up like a child at a picnic. For a moment, he became what he was—an eight-year-old boy who was relieved that his parent had arrived. For a moment, Sarah saw a child—happy, joyful, and without the unnatural burdens of an orphan.

He started to hop up, but then he remembered Mia was leaning against him.

Sarah was beside them, kneeling in front of them, before Mateo could fully wake his sister. She was putting her arms around them, running her hands over their heads, listening to their exclamations. She was allowing all of the broken places in her heart to heal.

Gratitude washed over her, through her, and filled her heart.

CHAPTER 54

 ou're okay. Thank *Gotte* you're okay." She didn't try to hide the tears running down her cheeks. She clutched the children to her. Mia's arms wound around her neck, and Mateo relaxed in the circle of her arms.

"I want to go home, Sarah."

"Home, Sarah."

"*Ya. Gut* idea."

Mateo finally noticed Andy. He darted across the room and threw his arms around Andy's waist.

Andy crouched down and said something to the boy, something that Sarah couldn't hear. She was busy running her hands up and down Mia's arms, assuring herself that no harm had come to the child.

Javier and Sheriff Bynum had crowded into the room.

Sarah realized it was an office of sorts. There was a computer on a desk, and a chair behind it. With the four of them, plus the two officers and Javier, it was quite crowded.

Bynum motioned to the chairs, and Sarah reluctantly sat down. She didn't want to stay here one minute longer than she absolutely had to. She wanted to take the children home—to Cody's Creek, to their cozy, warm beds in her snug little house. Mia crawled onto her lap, and Mateo positioned himself next to her, as close as he could get.

"Could we get another chair?" Bynum asked.

"I'm fine." Andy crossed his arms and leaned against the wall. "All that time in an *Englisch* automobile. Feels *gut* to stretch my legs."

He winked at Mateo, who laughed.

It was a beautiful sound to Sarah.

How traumatized had they been by the night's events? Was it her fault for letting them walk home alone? And under those questions an even more disturbing one—how would they keep this from happening again?

"Want to catch us up?" Bynum nodded to the officer to sit behind the desk.

"Should I stay?" Javier asked.

"We have your statement." The woman's name tag said *Wilson*. She looked to be around forty, with hair pulled back by a simple rubber band and black bangs hanging across her forehead. It looked strange to Sarah, to see a woman in an officer's uniform. Wilson's said *Tulsa Police Department* and was a slightly darker shade of blue than Bynum's.

Regardless how she was dressed, Sarah was overwhelmingly grateful to the woman—that she'd been there to watch over Mateo and Mia. She supposed mothers came in varying shapes and sizes and occupations.

"If there are any other questions we'll come and get you," Wilson assured Javier. "How long will your shift last?"

"Until five a.m." Javier turned toward the door and then reversed directions and stopped in front of Sarah. "I'm glad your kids are okay."

"We appreciate everything you've done, for calling us and taking care of them. For realizing they were in danger."

"It was the Amber Alert that did it. I had just looked at their pictures on my phone when they walked into the store." Javier waved goodbye to Mia and Mateo and hurried back out to the store.

Officer Wilson was now sitting behind the desk. She began to recite what she'd learned. "The children walked into the store at approximately forty-five minutes after eleven. The clerk, Javier Rodriguez, recognized their photos from the Amber Alert that had gone out. He immediately called 9-1-1, and then he brought them back here to the office."

"Why did he do that?" Andy rubbed at his eyes, the long hours catching up with him as his adrenaline ebbed.

Sarah knew exactly what he was feeling. She suddenly thought that she could sleep for a dozen hours, now that the children were safe, now that they could go home.

"Why not leave them out front until the police arrived?" Andy asked.

"I didn't want them to find us." Mateo spoke up for the first time. He swung his leg back and forth, staring at the floor. "I didn't want my mom and that man she's with to find us, so I asked Javier if we could wait somewhere else until he called Sarah."

"Good thinking, son." Officer Bynum had sunk into one of the chairs. How long had he been on duty? Surely he was as tired as Sarah felt, and yet he had insisted on coming with them.

"We were wet from walking in the rain, and he gave us these sweatshirts." Mateo pushed up on the arms of the shirt that kept falling over his hands. "He gave us the donuts and milk too."

Bynum nodded at Officer Wilson to continue.

"I arrived within seven minutes of the initial call. After questioning Mateo, I requested backup. Two squad cars arrived and patrolled around the casino in the area the boy described."

"They'd parked at the back," Mateo whispered. "Away from the cameras, that's what Orlynn said."

"Who is Orlynn?" Sarah asked.

"The man driving." Wilson again consulted her pad. "We don't have a last name yet, but Mateo gave us a good description. We suspect they returned to the car and discovered the children missing, and then they left the area. No sign of the vehicle Mateo described. Of course, there were any number of late-model white sedans, but there were none parked out at the edge of the parking area."

Sarah had suddenly heard enough. She wanted the children home, warm and dry in their own beds. She stood and looked directly at Sheriff Bynum. "We'd like to go home now."

When he nodded, she thanked the female officer. Andy picked up Mia, and Sarah clasped Mateo's hand as if someone might try to snatch him away.

They walked out through the store and were nearly to the door when Sarah retraced her steps to the counter.

"I will wash the sweatshirts and return them to you." She just then remembered the sack of dry clothes and cookies that *Mammi* had sent. In her hurry to see the children, she'd left them on the backseat.

"My boss said to keep them."

"Okay. *Danki*, for being kind to my children."

"I only did what anyone would do."

"*Nein.*" Javier didn't look to be twenty, which wasn't that much younger than Sarah. But she knew, perhaps better than he did, how many people would have simply looked away, wished not to become involved, or done so but without kindness. "You gave them dry clothes and food. You stayed with them until the police arrived. You calmed them when they were frightened. That was more than many people would have done."

She made her way outside. Rain continued to splatter against the pavement. Though it was now close to two in the morning, cars continued to swish past on the freeway. She climbed into the backseat of the police car. Someone had provided Bynum with a child safety seat for Mia. Sarah buckled her into it, settled herself in the middle, and made sure Mateo was safely buckled to her right. Andy sat in the front next to Bynum, who started the patrol car and drove away from the convenience store, away from the casino, and back toward home.

CHAPTER 55

Sarah didn't know whether she should send Mateo to school the next day. "You can stay home. Brian won't mind."

"But I want to go, Sarah. I'm okay."

Mammi nodded in agreement. "Perhaps it would be *gut* for everyone to get back to their normal schedule."

She didn't have to tell Isaac and Luke to stay near Mateo, to be sure he got there safely. Everyone was on alert, afraid that Elisa Lopez would show up and try to snatch them away again.

Mateo calmed her fears before heading out the door.

"It's my fault, Sarah."

"No, it isn't."

"I shouldn't have got in the car."

She thought of what Paul had said. Of the natural emotional pull from one's parents. "I might have done the same."

"I want you to know it won't happen again. I know now…I know that it's not safe for us to be with her."

"We'll talk about this more later. For today, try to enjoy school."

Mia acted as if nothing had happened, though she was a bit more clingy than before and three times that morning she hid—the first time in the mudroom, the second time under a kitchen cabinet, and the third time under her own bed.

"It seems to be her way of feeling safe," *Mammi* said. "What else can a child do but hide?"

"But she is safe with us. Doesn't she realize that?" Sarah had finally convinced Mia to lay on a pallet on the living room floor, and now she was fast asleep.

"*Ya*, she is safe here, and I think in her heart she knows that, even at her young age. But her mind has to find a way to deal with what happened to her."

"I can't imagine what it must have felt like—to see her mother and then just be left, again."

"Maybe you can."

Sarah and *Mammi* were sitting at the kitchen table, preparing lunch for Andy and Henry. Paul had stayed at his place to work on pens for the new piglets. They would try to plant the next day if the fields dried out enough. At least it had stopped raining. From where she sat, Sarah could watch Mia—could keep an eye on her. But she knew that she couldn't watch her all the time. At some point, she was going to have to trust that God would take care of her, as He had the night before. Suddenly Sarah's hands began to shake, so she stuffed them in her lap.

"Paul said something similar."

"What your mother has done, what Mia's mother has done—it's not a natural thing." *Mammi* paused, as if she were choosing her words carefully. "I won't be judging either of them. In my heart, I believe they are doing the absolute best they can. It's only that, to us, it seems as if their best isn't very good."

"I don't know why she left. Why would my mother be better off somewhere else? At least if she were here, we could take care of her. We were taking care of her."

"But here she was reminded daily of her failures, and maybe…" *Mammi*'s eyes met hers. "Maybe she knew that being here was holding you all back from healing."

"Healing?"

"Over the loss of your father. Over the childhood you endured."

"Those things weren't her fault."

"I agree, but I imagine Deborah is still struggling with that truth."

Sarah allowed those words to sink in. She didn't know if she agreed with her grandmother or not, but she could tell that *Mammi* believed what she was saying. She wasn't simply saying it to ease Sarah's worries.

"And Mia's mother? How could she be so selfish as to grab her own children? If she wanted to see them, all she had to do was ask." Sarah sat at the table and began aggressively slicing cheese from a large block, the knife thudding down onto the cutting board with each pass of the blade.

"I can't answer your questions as to what her motivation might have been."

"I love Mateo and Mia as much as my own *bruders*, but if she truly wanted to be their mother, if she could provide them a safe home, it wouldn't be my place to keep them here."

"All we can do is offer grace and forgiveness as we're commanded." *Mammi* stood, walked over to Sarah, and placed both of her hands on her shoulders. She bent over so that they were eye to eye. Sarah could clearly see the dear woman's map of wrinkles branching out from her eyes, across her forehead, down her cheeks.

"What you just said? That shows you've truly learned to love Mateo and Mia, and that you're willing to put their well-being above what you want. That, Sarah, is what a parent is supposed to do."

Mammi walked out onto the porch, leaving Sarah staring at Mia, who was clutching her Plain doll close to her heart as she slept.

Thirty minutes later they were seated at the kitchen table for lunch. Sarah enjoyed hearing her brothers discuss the crops, their chickens, even how Dusty seemed to have perked up over the last few days. The last thing they needed was to have to replace the buggy horse. Not to mention how much they would miss the gelding if anything happened to him. He was as much a family pet as the yellow cat *Mammi* insisted on feeding.

The men had trooped back outside, and Sarah was beginning to run dishwater in the sink when there was a knock on the door.

"That must be Tommy." *Mammi* nodded toward where his car was parked. "Go and speak to him in the living room."

Sarah invited him inside. As he walked in, she saw their sitting room as he must see it. No more clothes piled on the couch. No issues of the *Budget* scattered across the floor. It was a classic image of a Plain home—clean, uncluttered, welcoming. But what did that matter if she couldn't even keep the children safe? That question echoed through her mind every few minutes.

It had been her fault. She should have been more careful.

Tommy didn't waste any time getting down to business. He opened his messenger bag and pulled out a folder. From the folder he removed an eight by ten glossy photo. "This is Elisa Lopez, Mateo's and Mia's mother."

"Why am I just now seeing this?"

"Because you need to now. Normally there is no interaction between Bridge parents and birth parents, at least not at this stage of the process. I know how carefully you are looking after the kids, but it's hard to do so if you don't know what or who to look for."

She studied the photo. Elisa had brown hair and dark eyebrows. Her eyes looked exactly like Mateo's, and the smattering of freckles across her nose and cheeks reminded Sarah of Mia. She seemed young, incredibly so.

"Should you see her, you're to contact the police immediately. Send someone to the phone shack and keep the children inside until authorities arrive."

"She has no rights to her own children?"

Tommy studied her for a moment before answering with an observation of his own. "Many Bridge parents feel strongly that birth parents don't need to be near their children, that it's the parents' fault the children are in such a dire situation."

Sarah thought of what *Mammi* had said. "*Ya*. I understand that perspective, and certainly the most important thing is for Mateo and Mia to be safe. But what I'm wondering is…does that mean she will never see her children again? Because she's made a mistake—"

"Several," Tommy said softly.

"*Ya*, several mistakes, especially taking them last night. But does that mean she gets no other chances? What if Mateo and Mia…" She brushed at the tears slipping down her cheeks. "What if they want to see her? They're frightened now, but when they're older, then…well, then they might feel differently."

Tommy wrote something in his folder, and then he put the picture in the folder and the folder in his bag. Finally, he sat forward with his elbows on his knees and his hands clasped together. "Mateo and Mia will always have a right to see their mother if they wish and if it is safe. However, Elisa will have to prove that she's taken the necessary steps to change her lifestyle. She'll have to show that she can provide an adequate living arrangement. We will help her, but she has to be willing to make the changes."

Sarah nodded, relief flooding her heart. She wanted Mateo and Mia with her forever, but she didn't want to be responsible for severing a bond as natural as that of a mother and child. She didn't want to have that on her conscience, burdening her soul. She didn't want to be the person who had refused to give Elisa Lopez one more chance.

"For now she is not allowed contact with them until she is evaluated by DHS. What she did yesterday was wrong. It wasn't your fault or Mateo's fault...it was Elisa's fault. We'll do everything within our power to make sure it doesn't happen again."

CHAPTER 56

*P*aul stayed away from the Yoder household the first full day the kids were back. He told himself they needed time alone, but his eyes kept drifting toward their farm, his mind kept wandering to thoughts of the entire family, but especially to Sarah.

On Thursday afternoon the piglets were delivered, and he knew he wouldn't be able to resist any longer. He snatched up the newspaper Rebecca had given him and grabbed the keys to the tractor. He could walk, but he wanted to be able to bring Isaac and Mateo back to see the piglets. He didn't think Sarah would want them walking.

Sarah surprised him though.

"Careful walking on the road," she called after Luke, Isaac, and Mateo. All three had insisted on going as soon as they heard the news.

She shook her head and sat back down in the rocker chair where she'd been hand-sewing a new dress for Mia.

"Seems they've all grown since I saw them last."

"Two days ago?"

"*Ya*, I'm sure Mateo is an inch taller, and Luke looks more like a man than a boy." He laughed at himself and then nodded toward her sewing. "I thought the ladies brought you plenty of clothes."

"They did, but...well, I had some material left from my dress and thought Mia would like something new."

"I'm sure she'll love it." Paul cleared his throat. "It surprises me a little that you're letting them walk to my place. I was worried that after what happened—"

"That I would try to keep them under my wings?" She tucked her chin and glanced up at him, reminding him comically of his mother. Sarah Yoder was nothing like his mother. Or was she? Physically they were certainly very different. Paul's mother was tall and heavy from years of birthing children and cooking for a large family. But their attitude and demeanor? Both had a healthy dose of common sense, didn't mind showing their emotions, and were hard workers. Yes, they were more alike than he had realized.

Sarah had returned her attention to her project, though she was still answering Paul's unasked question. "I can't keep my eyes on them all the time. If anything, the last week has taught me that. But Mateo...he's a smart boy. He'll be more careful now, and I can trust him whether he's alone or with Mia. He's a *gut* boy. He'll watch out for his *schweschder*, just like he did Tuesday night."

"While we're on the subject of the other night, Rebecca sent this over for you." He held up the paper, folded to show the front page story.

He knew Sarah recognized Elisa immediately because she dropped her fabric into her lap and reached for the newspaper. "I didn't know they were going to print anything about it."

"The story was written by your friend Chloe."

He'd read it through several times himself, but he listened as Sarah read it aloud.

> On Tuesday evening an Amber Alert was issued for two children taken from a Cody's Creek home.

Sarah glanced up at Paul. "She doesn't mention their names?"

"*Nein*. It's not allowed to put the names of young children in the newspaper. Not unless their parents approve it."

Sarah nodded and continued reading.

> Taken by Elisa Lopez, the children were recovered unharmed several hours later and returned to the Yoder family. Sheriff Bynum from the Cody's Creek Police Department would like to extend his sincere thanks to those who called in tips and facilitated the return of the children.

She continued reading silently for a moment, information about Elisa's car, a description of her companion, and a brief history of Amber Alerts and how many were issued each year. Shaking her head, she returned the paper to Paul.

"You don't want to keep it?"

"*Nein*. I'd rather not dwell on what happened."

"I'm sorry. I thought you'd want to see it."

"I am glad you brought it. Don't misunderstand me. It's only that I think we have to move on."

"Well, at least local folks will have seen Elisa's photo."

"And they'll have a description of the car."

"If she's spotted anywhere in the area, I'm sure they'll call it in." Paul finally sat in the chair next to Sarah. He wasn't sure that she'd want him to stay, but she seemed to be enjoying their conversation almost as much as he was. It occurred to him that she had little chance to talk to many other adults except her brothers and *Mammi*.

"The article will put people on alert. That is a *gut* thing, but the publicity? We could do without that. I want the children to have a normal life, and they can't do that if they're in the newspaper."

"Spoken like a true Amish *mamm*," he teased.

Instead of rising to the bait, she gave him another look. This one caused Paul's hands to sweat. He thought about leaning forward, about kissing her, and then those thoughts were interrupted by the banging of the front door.

Mia ran across the porch, clutching something in her hand. She squatted down in front of him and smoothed out a sheet of paper that had become quite rumpled. "Paul! Look what I drawed."

"What you drew," Sarah corrected.

"What I drewed." Mia climbed up onto Paul's lap, clutching the paper. "That's you—"

"With the big head?"

"That's Sarah."

"Our arms are longer than our legs."

"That's Mia!"

Mia had drawn herself between the two larger stick figures, who were each clasping one of her stick hands.

"Very *gut* drawing," Paul said.

"And Mateo, Andy, Henry, Luke, Isaac." She pointed at a different blob with each name. They were drawn to the side, standing together in a large group with a giant sun beating down on them.

In truth the image struck a chord deep in Paul's gut. Did Mia think that they were a family? Did she think he and Sarah were more than friends? He supposed she had no way of knowing what a real family, a normal family, looked like. To her, it would seem natural for him to leave and reappear every few days.

"I forgot *Mammi*."

Sweat broke out on his brow as she scrambled off his lap.

"*Mammi*! I need cwayons!" She was gone with another bang of the door.

"She's talking more these days, but still working on the *r* sound," Sarah said. "I'm sure she'll get it eventually."

Paul wanted to invite Sarah to see the piglets. He wanted to sit beside her on the porch until the sun set in the western sky. He wanted to stay.

Instead, he mumbled an excuse about needing to check on the boys. But as he drove his tractor back down the lane, he was thinking about a little stick girl, holding hands with a stick mommy and stick daddy.

CHAPTER 57

Mateo and Isaac hadn't wasted any time getting into the enclosure with the pigs, though Luke warned them they had best not get dirty. In the end, he couldn't resist and joined them.

"I thought they would be bigger," Mateo confessed.

"Still plenty heavy." Isaac was trying to scoot one off his lap. The pig happily rolled over on to its back, apparently waiting for a tummy rub.

"How old are they, Luke?"

"About six weeks. Paul said they were weaned at twenty-eight days."

Mateo nodded wisely. He wouldn't have known what weaning was a month ago, but he and Isaac had been reading Brian's books. It was plain enough from the pictures that weaning meant the piglets no longer received their mother's milk.

"Will they grow up to have piglets of their own?" he asked.

"*Nein*. Paul bought these for slaughter."

"I like bacon, but I don't think we should talk about it here." Isaac's voice was so serious that they all started laughing.

The piglets squealed at the sound and took off like a flock of geese, trundling across the pigpen.

"It is important to remember that they're not pets."

They all turned around in surprise at Paul's voice. Mateo had been focusing so hard on the piglets he hadn't even heard the tractor.

"*Ya*, but…we should take good care of them. Right?" Mateo thought they were about the cutest things he'd ever seen—all pink and chubby with curly tails and little brown ears.

"Of course we will. They're our responsibility now."

"We'll give them the best life a pig can have." Isaac jumped up and stuck his hands in his pockets, and then he remembered that they were covered with mud and jerked them back out.

"We will do that. People have to eat, but we can still be kind and be *gut* stewards of what *Gotte* has given us." Paul waved at the enclosure. "So what do you think? Does it meet your approval?"

"Sure it does." Mateo reluctantly pushed his piglet away, and it took off after the others. "You have a covered area with lots of straw."

"So they won't get cold." Isaac nodded in approval.

"Do you know why we have the lower area filled with water and mud?"

"Because pigs don't sweat," Mateo and Isaac said in unison.

Luke rolled his eyes, but Mateo could tell that he was enjoying this as much as they were. They spent the next few minutes walking around the pen as Paul showed them what he'd done to accommodate the little creatures.

He'd attached a water trough to a sliding bracket on the side of the fence. "So we can move it up as they get taller."

"Why not just put it on the ground?" Luke stuck his hand in the water and then shook it dry.

"My *dat* raised pigs every year. No matter how we secured the water trough to the ground, the pigs would uproot it, spilling it. I might be in the field and not notice. If that happened, they could be without water all day."

"A pig's body weight is one half water." Isaac had practically memorized that book. He'd been quoting it to Mateo for over a week.

"Correct. If they don't have access to clean water, they can get very sick."

"What will you feed them?"

"*Mammi* said she would start a slop bucket. Can I count on you two to bring it over every day?"

In answer, Mateo and Isaac high-fived one another.

"The majority of their diet will come from grain. We'll need to measure and watch each day. We don't want to waste it, but we want them to have all they need."

All three boys sat down on top of the fence rail, and Paul stood beside it.

"There's going to be enough work here for all three of you. I'll admit to you right now, it's hard work. You have to scoop out the manure each day."

Luke glanced at Mateo and Isaac. When they both nodded, Luke asked, "And you're going to share the money with us?"

"I will. One pig will provide meat for the winter for your family, and one will be for mine—for me and Rebecca and Joseph."

"What about the other eight?" Isaac asked.

"We'll sell them to neighbors. I can put up a sign at the store. Half the money will go to you boys, and I'll keep the other half."

Again Isaac looked at him, and Mateo could feel his head nodding. He'd never actually earned money before. Maybe he could help Sarah with their fall school clothes. He and Isaac had even talked about using the money to purchase some goats. There were a lot of different things they could do with their half of the money. Even split in thirds, it would be more than he'd ever had. The possibilities sometimes kept him awake at night.

"We're in," all three boys said simultaneously.

"Will you ever let them out of the pen?" Mateo asked.

"Actually, I was hoping you boys could help me with that." Paul showed them a fenced cattle pen that as yet had no cattle. "The grass will come up good in here. I need to add some fencing around the bottom so they won't get out. Want to lend a hand?"

Of course they did. Luke claimed he needed to get back to the house and take care of Dusty's stall, but Mateo and Isaac stayed. They handed Paul nails, made sure there weren't any gaps in the fencing, and then promised to come back the next day to see how the piglets liked it.

"I'm counting on you two. I have fields to take care of, but with your help, we should be able to provide these piglets with a nice place to live."

Mateo and Isaac promised they would help, and then Paul told them they should get home before dark. "You don't want to keep Sarah or *Mammi* waiting."

It was Isaac's idea to cut across the field rather than go by the road. Mateo thought that maybe it was to avoid cars. Was there even a chance that his mother would try to come back again? Mateo didn't think so. He was pretty sure that he wouldn't be seeing her for a long time, and while one part of him felt sad about that, another part—a bigger part— was relieved.

Isaac insisted that he go over the fence first. "Just step in my hands and hold on to that post."

"How are you going to get across?"

"I'll climb up. I've done it plenty of times."

Maybe he had. Maybe what happened next was simply because they were in a hurry. Mateo had landed in the weeds on his back-side, laughing and standing up, trying to brush off the pieces of grass. Unfortunately, the grass was stuck to the mud he'd managed to splash on his clothes earlier.

He was thinking of that, and of how he would offer to clean them in the sink so Sarah wouldn't have to, when he heard the tear of fab-ric. He looked up to see that Isaac had ripped a hole in his pants across the entire seat.

And while they should have been worried, instead they laughed more and ran across the field, toward their home, as the sun set over their family's farm.

CHAPTER 58

The letters began arriving on Friday. At first the mailman left them in their box at the end of the lane. Then on Saturday he left a note, saying there were more to pick up at the post office. And finally, on Monday, he brought a large bag and set it on their porch.

Fortunately, the mail came early in the day, so Sarah had been able to hide it from the children.

"You're going to have to tell them." *Mammi* was baking a pie, and the smell was distracting Sarah from the problem at hand.

She hadn't realized how much she had missed good cooking until *Mammi* arrived. Actually, they had never enjoyed very good cooking. They had been the Amish family with few sweets on the counter and barely adequate meals on the table. She realized now that many of their prior difficulties had probably been owing to her mother's depression as much as their father's illness.

"*Ya*. I will tell them. Tonight, I guess."

Andy wasn't there for their family meeting. He'd cleaned up and taken off in the tractor, claiming he had friends to meet. Sarah was pretty sure it was one friend by the name of Emma, but she didn't call him on it. Maybe it wasn't serious, and that was why he hadn't brought up the subject himself.

Henry, Isaac, Luke, and Mateo sat on the couch—yawning and making an obvious effort to keep their eyes open. Mia was curled in

Mammi's lap, and the gentle motion of the rocking chair assured she would be sound asleep in no time. Sarah sat in the chair where her mother had always sat. There was a time when she'd felt a spike of anger every time she used something that was her mother's. Those times were fewer and farther between. Perhaps she was healing.

"Let's get on with this," Isaac said. "I'm tired."

"*Ya*, the pigs got out again today. Took forever to catch them." Mateo leaned his head back in mock exhaustion—or maybe it was real exhaustion.

"Next time we won't leave the gate open for even a second."

"Who would have thought a piglet could run so fast? They're like flies or bees or—"

"Torpedoes?" It was the first military word Luke had used in several weeks. He wasn't spending as much time at the neighbor's house, not since *Mammi* had arrived. Had she talked to him about it? Regardless, Sarah was glad. She was also happy to see the neighbor boy in their yard, playing on the trampoline or enjoying a game of baseball.

"Don't know, but they're fast." Mateo yawned, covering his mouth at the last second.

"I'll be quick about this," Sarah promised. "We've been getting a lot of mail since the piece about Mateo and Mia came out in the paper."

There had been no keeping Chloe's article from the boys. It seemed that every family in their community had seen it, though very few of them subscribed to the paper.

"How much is a lot?" Henry sat up straighter and focused his attention on the group. He was their dreamer, often reading or thinking of other things. But when one of his family was in any sort of trouble, he was all ears and quick with a plan to resolve the situation. Just out of school one year, and already he acted like a grown man.

"At first there were only a few, but today the mailman brought a large sack."

"All for us?" Isaac squirreled up his nose. "Who would want to write us?"

Sarah still wasn't sure exactly how to explain this, so she chose her words carefully. "People. Some people who want to encourage us, who think it's a *gut* thing we're doing by having Mateo and Mia live here."

Mateo's eyes widened, and he looked suddenly awake.

"Other people think both Mateo and Mia would be better off somewhere else."

"What do they know?" The question burst from Mateo. "They've never even met us!"

"That's true, but sometimes when people read about others they feel like they know them." *Mammi*'s voice was calm, quiet, and reasonable. "I suppose that because of the pieces in the newspaper, these people do think they know something about you."

"But I don't get it. Why would we be better off with someone else?"

"It's a question of your being Hispanic and us being Plain." Sarah hadn't known how to broach the subject of ethnicity, but after worrying over it she had prayed and determined it was best to meet it head-on. "Some people think you'd be better off with a Hispanic family."

"Why would the color of our skin matter?"

"I don't think it's your color so much as your heritage." Henry drummed his fingers against the arm of the sofa. "Am I right, Sarah?"

"*Ya*. I haven't read them all, mind you, and we won't even try to answer them, but many of the letters seem to say that what we're doing is wrong because you will never..." She dug in her apron pocket and pulled out a piece of paper to check the wording. "The children will never be able to fully embrace their own culture."

"We'll call Chloe!" Mateo jumped up, his eyes filled with excitement. "She can interview me, and we'll tell them how much we like it here and how...how you all are learning some Spanish."

"*Yo quiero dormir*," Isaac said with a yawn.

"See?" Mateo fell back on the couch. "Isaac totally knows what he just said."

"I want to go to bed."

"You want sleep. *Dormir* means to sleep." Sarah couldn't help smiling at their enthusiasm.

"That's not a bad idea. This all started with Chloe, and perhaps it can be resolved there." Mia was now snoring softly from her spot on *Mammi*'s lap, and *Mammi* bent down to kiss the top of her head. "Although I don't know that I would want you to be the headline of another news story."

"Plus, some people won't be convinced." Henry ran his fingers back and forth across his chin. "Some people will find something wrong with anything."

"True." *Mammi* resumed her rocking. "But what if Sarah spoke to Chloe and told her about the letters. We hadn't received a single letter until her last article—the one that spoke of your mother taking you to Tulsa."

"Chloe was only trying to help," Sarah said.

"And apparently she has. There was that sighting of Elisa in Oklahoma City, and they have a license plate number on the car now. Perhaps the police can find the driver."

"She probably isn't even with him anymore." Mateo flicked the couch with his thumb and forefinger. "She does that—moves around a lot."

"I'm only agreeing with Sarah that Chloe meant well. As a result of her articles, the Bridge program has received a lot of attention, not to mention we know a little more about Elisa's whereabouts."

They had thought of keeping the most recent information about Elisa from the children, but in the end Sarah agreed with her grandmother. It was best that they know, and that they be assured it wouldn't change anything in their daily life. Not for a long time, if ever, according to Tommy.

"Sarah, perhaps you should call Chloe tomorrow." *Mammi* repositioned Mia on her lap. "Maybe she will want to set the record straight. It seems to me that any adoption—whether it be temporary, permanent, within races, or between races—is a blessing."

There was nothing else to say on the subject, so *Mammi* told everyone to go on to bed and to remember to say their prayers. When she'd handed Mia to Sarah, she patted her apron pocket and gave everyone a piece of chocolate.

"Remember to brush your teeth," Sarah called after them.

The boys nodded that they would and stumbled up the stairs. Sarah carried Mia upstairs and tucked her into bed. But she didn't go to sleep herself, though she was tired enough that her eyes were beginning to droop shut.

Instead, she walked back to the kitchen, heated some of the leftover coffee on the stove, and poured it into a mug. Pulling the bag of letters closer, she began to read.

CHAPTER 59

Though the rains had slowed them down, Paul and Andy and Henry managed to finish planting the Yoders' fields by noon on Thursday. Andy was ecstatic.

"It's been years since we did this," he admitted. "*Dat* would start often enough. He had good intentions, but he rarely managed to finish. Maybe one field out of three would be planted. It was never enough to live on."

Paul might have guessed that such memories would make a person depressed or angry, but Andy was looking out over the recently planted corn and grinning as if he'd just opened a longed-for Christmas present.

"This is *gut*, Paul. And though I might have attempted to do it myself, it's been much better with you here to guide me. *Danki*."

"Don't thank me. If anyone deserves thanks, it would be my father. Without him, I wouldn't know a thing about crops or planting or running a farm, for that matter."

"Then I will thank him if I ever make my way up to Indiana, which I seriously doubt."

"You never know where life will take you, Andy. I certainly never expected to end up in Oklahoma." They had laughed about that, and then Andy had walked toward the barn and Paul had walked toward the house.

Sometimes he felt positively drawn there.

He only managed to stay away with a great deal of effort, and he still wasn't sure about why a part of him insisted on avoiding the girl next door.

There was no one or no thing he thought of more.

He wanted to see Sarah.

She was sitting next to their yet-to-be-planted vegetable garden, studying a sheet of paper. Beside her was a basket, filled with seeds and gardening tools.

"Need me to show you how to use those?"

Sarah glanced up, her bottom lip pushed out in a pout. "I know how to plant a garden."

"What's the problem, then?"

"In a moment of weakness, I told Mateo and Isaac I'd use their diagram."

"Huh." He dropped to the ground beside her, enjoying the feel of the sun and the fact that the woman who often visited his dreams was within arm's reach.

"I can't tell if this says *carrots* or *chrysanthemums*." She leaned closer to him, and he caught a whiff of lilac soap.

"Longer word—must be the flowers."

"According to the boys, the odor from the flowers will help keep away pests."

"*Ya*? Seems I remember my *mamm* saying the same thing." He hesitated before asking, "Can I help you with the planting?"

Sarah looked up from the piece of paper, a smile playing across her lips. "Are you telling me you're not tired enough from working our fields the last two days? Now you want to help with our garden?"

"You know how Amish farmers are—always happier with our hands in the dirt."

"The piglets don't need you at home?"

"The boys are doing most of what needs to be done there."

"What about work on the house?"

"I don't plan to start that right away. There's, uh, no hurry."

Sarah glanced down and away, and he thought she would politely refuse his help. But instead, she handed him a package of flower seeds and pointed to the far end of a row. "You can start there."

Planting the family vegetable garden was a simple thing he'd done for his mother each year. As he used the hand trowel to break the earth, Paul felt some restless thing inside of him relax. It should have frightened him, but it didn't. This was where he wanted to be, helping Sarah.

No doubt Andy or Henry would have been happy to have done the same thing, but Paul happened to know they both were busy. Andy was taking the horse to get reshod, and Henry had hurried to town to make his shift at the Dutch kitchen.

The afternoon was peaceful with only the two of them there working, and the next hour passed quickly. Suddenly he realized that perhaps it was too quiet.

"Where's Mia? Where's *Mammi*?"

Sarah was now kneeling in front of the adjacent row, facing him, her eyes focused on her work. "*Mammi* is sewing, and Mia is determined to help her."

"More clothes?"

"Table runners. She says we can sell them at our produce stand in the summer. Always planning ahead, *Mammi* is."

"I'd think helping to raise the Yoder family would keep her busy enough without taking on extra sewing projects."

"Yes, I would think so too. She has an amazing amount of energy for a woman her age, or a woman my age, for that matter."

At that moment the front screen door slammed shut. They both turned to see Mia tottering down the front steps carrying a glass of lemonade. "For you, Sarah."

Half of it was spilled down the front of her dress by the time she reached them. Sarah took a big sip and said, "Delicious. What about Paul, though?"

"I'll get it!" She was running toward the front porch before Paul could call her back.

"You did that on purpose," he said.

"Indeed. The more errands I think up, the longer her afternoon nap lasts."

Mia returned with another half-filled glass for Paul. She seemed to suddenly notice that her apron and dress were a wet, sticky mess. She pushed her fingers into the fabric and then pulled them away, tentatively licking them.

"Would you like some of my drink?" Sarah asked.

"No."

"Your dress is rather sticky."

"I know."

"Best get *Mammi* to change that before your nap."

"I'm not tired!" Mia turned around and backed up into Sarah's lap, landing with a plop and a smile.

"Not tired at all?"

"No!" Mia stuck her right thumb in her mouth and closed her eyes.

"Didn't know she was still doing that." Paul mimicked a thumb-in-the-mouth gesture.

"It comes and goes. *Mammi* says not to worry. She'll stop soon enough if we don't call attention to it."

Now Mia was rubbing her eyes with her left fist. "Sarah, I'm sleepy."

"Are you now?"

"Not tired, though."

She snuggled closer to Sarah, her thumb in her mouth and a blissful look on her face. Sarah kissed the top of her head and then continued planting, though it was an awkward reach with the child in her lap. Paul had never owned a camera, never even wanted one. But it occurred to him that if he did own one, he would take a picture of those two at that moment.

Sarah had dirt smeared across one cheek, and her blond hair had largely escaped from her prayer *kapp*. Mia was sticky, dirty, and obviously content. Together they were a beautiful sight.

Paul was so busy trying not to stare that he jumped when Sarah said his name.

"Paul, could you carry her inside?"

"Of course."

He gathered Mia up into his arms, trying to ignore the closeness and scent of Sarah. Mia woke enough to clasp her sticky arms around his neck. He carried her up the porch steps and *Mammi* met him at the door.

"She naps in my room." *Mammi* nodded toward the room at the front of the house.

"She's sticky and dirty."

"It's all right. I always lay an old sheet over my quilt before her nap."

When he stepped back outside, *Mammi* followed him.

"Are you going to tell her?" *Mammi* asked.

"Tell who?"

"Sarah."

"Tell her…"

"How you feel."

"Oh. I don't…that is to say, I'm not sure…"

Mammi smiled and patted him on his arm. "We all need something to do, someone to love, and something to hope for."

"My *mamm* used to quote that one."

"The proverbs are *gut* for guiding us."

"It's only that I don't know what I feel. I certainly don't know how she feels."

"Tell her, Paul. Never assume you'll have tomorrow."

CHAPTER 60

That evening Paul walked to the phone shack to call his parents. His mom filled him in on family news, they talked about the weather, and she asked after Joseph and Rebecca. His parents had a phone in their barn owing to the fact that his mother had been a midwife for the last twenty years. The bishop had decided if ever someone needed a phone, they did. It could be dangerous for the laboring mothers to wait while someone drove a buggy over to the Byler home.

He'd been calling them on Thursday evenings for years, but usually their conversations were fairly short. This time, Paul wasn't ready to hang up. He asked more questions about the farm, told his mother inconsequential things that had happened, and even returned to the subject of the weather a second time.

His mother finally asked, "What is it? What aren't you telling me, son?"

"I met a girl."

"Did you now? Well, I'm glad to hear it. We've been praying for many years that *Gotte* would place the right woman in your life."

"Oh, I don't know—"

"Perhaps this is a conversation you'd rather have with your *dat*."

He heard her whisper the news to his father, and then his *dat* was on the phone, and it was as though Paul were sitting beside him in the barn, asking how and when he realized he wanted to be a farmer.

"Want to tell me about her?"

No doubt he'd had this conversation many times—after all, Paul was the youngest of seven brothers, and all of his siblings were married, every one of them.

"I hardly know where to start."

"Well, what kind of person is she?"

"A kind one. Always puts others first, maybe too often." He found himself sharing about Sarah's parents, how one had died and the other left. He described how Sarah and her brother had stepped into the gap and had been attempting to run the house and the farm with no resources and little experience.

The church had helped. And *Mammi* had shown up.

He hesitated and then decided there was no point holding back if he wanted his father's advice. So he explained about Mateo and Mia and the process Sarah had been through to foster them.

His father didn't speak for a moment, and then he said, "Sarah sounds like a special woman."

"*Ya*, she is."

"And you live next door to her?"

"I do. Sometimes it feels as if we have one large farm instead of two separate ones. Her *bruders* and I help one another with crops and animals and such."

"As you should—a Plain community is committed to being one body, son. Regardless of what happens romantically between you and..."

"Sarah."

"Between you and Sarah, you need to commit yourself to helping the family."

"Of course."

"You've told me plenty about the family, about their situation, but there's something you're not telling me. Why this one? Why is Sarah different from any other girl you've met over the years?"

"She makes me smile."

He wanted to tell his dad everything. The first time he'd seen Sarah in the store, how she'd struggled down the steps with a twenty-five-pound sack of flour and a big canister of oats. How she had refused any help. The look of tenderness on her face when she spoke to Mia, her patience with the boys, her strength and determination. He wanted to describe her hands, her eyes, how unself-conscious she was. He wanted to share the way she'd looked earlier, sticking out her bottom lip as she studied the boys' map for her garden.

Instead of saying any of that, he repeated, "She makes me smile," and then he groaned at how he must sound.

His father laughed, and then he turned serious. "This life we choose is difficult. *Ya*, it may be Plain, but it certainly isn't simple. When you choose the one that you want to spend it with, choose carefully."

"Of course."

"She makes you smile? I'd say that's a pretty *gut* place to start because your *fraa* is more than someone who fixes your meals and births your children. She's someone who bears your burdens with you."

"She's so small, you wouldn't think she could bear many burdens."

His dad began laughing again. "The size of the girl isn't nearly as important as the size and strength of her heart."

The size and strength of her heart.

Never assume that you'll have tomorrow.

His father's and *Mammi's* advice echoed through Paul's mind, bounced off the walls of his heart, and stole his sleep for the next twenty-four hours.

By Friday afternoon, when the boys came over to check on the pigs, he had figured out what he wanted to do. He had already written out the note, folded it, and stuffed it in his pocket.

He had thought the afternoon's chores would pass quickly, uneventfully, but he was wrong. The boys set about moving the piglets to the cattle pen as they were prone to do for several hours each afternoon. They had read that allowing the pigs to range about would make them more content and also help to increase their weight.

Mateo thought Isaac had the gate, and Isaac thought Mateo had it. Fortunately, only two of the piglets escaped before Luke slammed the gate shut.

"They're headed toward the cornfield!" Luke called out.

Mateo and Isaac were over the fence in no time, sprinting after the escaped pigs. Though they had only had them a short time, the animals had put on a good amount of weight already, but Paul knew from experience that pigs were fast and incredibly intuitive.

Isaac had closed the gap on his escapee. At the last possible second, he made a flying leap toward the pig, who abruptly stopped, squealed, and turned right.

Isaac closed his arms around empty air and landed on the ground with a thud.

"It's getting away!" Luke shouted. He had taken a seat on top of the fence and was calling out directions like a rodeo announcer. "Better head yours off, Mateo!"

"Where did he go?" Mateo had circled the barn and lost sight of his prey. He came to a halt and looked left and right.

"He's headed for the trees."

Mateo didn't bother to answer. He pivoted to his left and took off after the blur of pale pink headed toward a small stand of trees.

In the meantime, Isaac had caught his piglet near the water pump. He slowly walked back, both of them completely covered in mud.

"This one's gaining weight for sure. I can barely carry him."

Luke opened the pen, and Isaac dumped his captive in with the others. The piglet squealed once and sped off toward his littermates.

Isaac attempted to brush mud from his clothes, shrugged, and climbed up on the fence next to his brother.

"Shouldn't you two be helping Mateo?" Paul asked.

"Nah. Mateo's the fastest kid in our grade."

"Yeah, that pig doesn't have a chance."

The piglet had circled back toward the pen.

"Maybe you can chase him in," Paul called.

But the pig had other ideas. He sprinted left, then right, and then left again, almost as if he was aware that Mateo was gaining ground.

Isaac and Luke had begun cheering Mateo on.

"You can do it!"

"You almost had him that time."

"Don't give up."

Paul remembered Sarah saying that Mia slept better if she'd had more errands to do. He wished she could see the boys now. They would probably fall asleep with their head on their dinner plate. Mateo made one final lunge at his pig as he started up a hill beside the house. The pig turned around and squealed, and then Mateo was on him, laughing and telling him to calm down.

Paul went back to work in the barn while the boys did the various chores related to the pigs. They were certainly earning their share of the profits—which it seemed they would have plenty of at the rate the pigs were growing.

He caught up with the boys an hour later, as they stood by the pump attempting to brush the mud off their clothes.

"I'm telling you, Sarah's going to make you take a bath," Luke said.

"Not if we can get it out of our hair." Isaac dumped a cupful of water over Mateo's head, who shook it off and then returned the favor.

Now they looked wet and muddy. Paul wasn't sure it was an improvement, but he shrugged and pulled Luke aside.

"I was wondering if you could take something to Sarah."

"Of course." Luke's eyebrows shot up when Paul handed him the folded note. He grinned and said, "I guess this is private."

"Now that you mention it, yes, it is."

For his answer, Luke grinned even wider and stuck the note in his pocket.

CHAPTER 61

I would think you have that memorized by now." *Mammi* chuckled and continued slicing ham for their luncheon the next day.

It was their off Sunday as far as church, but they had been invited to eat at Suzie Troyer's. Sarah was looking forward to seeing Becca and catching up with news of her pregnancy. Her friend was now only six weeks away from delivering if Sarah had the date right.

She suspected, by the way *Mammi* was grinning, that Paul had been invited as well.

Everyone was in bed except for *Mammi*, Sarah, and Andy, who was once again out with a friend.

"I can't think how to answer him."

"Probably a simple yes or no will do."

Sarah sat down at the table and smoothed the note out with the palm of her hand. "He wants to take me on a picnic tomorrow after we return home from the Troyers'."

"And…"

"He doesn't mention the children, so I assume it would be just the two of us."

"Most dates do involve only two people."

"Oh, I don't think it's a date."

"No?"

Sarah felt her cheeks coloring. "Honestly, I don't know. I haven't been asked on many dates, so I'm not an expert at it."

"Why is that?"

"Why aren't the boys interested?"

"I suppose I was wondering why you aren't interested in the boys." *Mammi* brought over two mugs of herbal tea and placed one in front of Sarah. Sitting down across from her, she pulled off her left shoe and rubbed her foot. "What about when you were younger?"

"While the other girls were beginning to go to singings and picnics, I was dealing with *Dat*. He…well, he didn't make such things easy."

"I'm sorry. I wish I had been here then to help you all."

Sarah sipped the tea and stared at Paul's note. "*Dat* accused me of being pregnant once."

Mammi didn't interrupt. She let the story unwind. Sarah loved that about her grandmother. She was a good listener.

"I was so offended and a little scared. I wasn't even interested in boys at the time, and I would have never done anything inappropriate."

"Of course you wouldn't." *Mammi* made a *tsk-tsk* sound.

"I was shy and somewhat insecure, I suppose. It was when *Dat* accused me that I first began having eating problems. In my mind, I couldn't control my family life, but I could control what I did or didn't eat. And maybe…I can see now that maybe I was trying to punish them a little."

"I remember Deborah writing me that you'd gone away for a while."

"To a center the bishop found. They helped me a lot. I learned that what I was struggling with had a name—anorexia. My emotions interfered with my being healthy. In my mind, if I could stay small enough, my father would never accuse me of such a thing again. But then, later, it became difficult to eat normally even if I wanted to. At the center, I learned to distance myself from issues here in my home, and the doctors helped me find more constructive ways to cope with my *dat*'s problems."

"You were quite young then."

"I was. It seems like forever ago and yet also like yesterday." Sarah turned her mug left and right. "My *dat* was only worried about me and my future, though it came out as an accusation. The odd thing is, now that I'm in the role of parent, I understand that urge to worry about every possible thing."

"Still, he should never have accused you."

"It could be why I didn't date. I always was quiet and shy in school. I spent most of my time with a couple of other girls. When they began drifting toward boys, I didn't."

"And then you went on a mission trip."

"I still think about that trip to Texas. Helping the people who were in the path of Hurricane Orion changed me. It made me realize my problems weren't the only problems."

"Something not everyone understands."

"After that I came home, and there were the same old troubles with *Mamm* and *Dat*, but I was stronger. You know? I was better able to handle them. But I guess…I guess I just got used to being alone."

"You're not alone now."

"No." Sarah smiled past the ache of her memories. "I'm not."

"So how will you answer Paul?"

"I'd like to say yes. If you wouldn't mind—"

"Of course I don't mind. I can handle things here for a few hours."

"It would be *gut* to have a little time away from anyone who needs their face washed or wants to talk pig nutrition."

"The boys are quite excited about the pigs. It's *gut* of Paul to think of them, to give them this chance to learn and even earn money."

"But don't you see? That's part of the problem. My brothers have been through so much. So have Mateo and Mia, for that matter. I don't want them getting too close to Paul if this doesn't…well, if it doesn't work out."

"Why wouldn't it?"

"I don't know." Sarah rubbed at the muscle at the back of her neck. She'd slept wrong and woken with a crick. Every move felt unnatural. She was hoping by morning it would be better. "I don't know anything about him."

"It seems you probably do and don't realize it." *Mammi* replaced her shoe and washed her hands. Sitting back down, she pulled her basket of yarn closer and began to knit and purl. "We know he's a hard worker. He cares about the children. He's a fine farmer."

"But those things don't necessarily make a *gut* husband." Sarah blushed just saying the word. He'd asked her on a picnic. It was hardly a marriage proposal.

"True, but I think it tells you something about a person. If they are hardworking and dependable, then they care about others. If they are willing to help, then they are compassionate. The feelings a man has for a woman don't exist independently of who he is and how he relates to others. Rather, I think romantic feelings are an extension of those things."

Sarah thought about that a few minutes as she nursed her mug of tea. Finally, she voiced the worry that had been circling in her mind for weeks. "You said once that you wished my mother had waited longer. That if she had, she might have realized what she was taking on with my father."

"They were young. Younger than you are now."

"But how do you know? How do you know that you won't regret beginning a thing?"

"I suppose the best way is to pray, and to listen to the advice of your elders."

Now Sarah smiled. "Which would be you."

"Yes, I guess it would."

"And you think I should go."

"I think you should follow your heart, but if your heart is lightened by being around Paul, if you find yourself looking forward to time with him, then yes—I think you should go tomorrow and enjoy a few hours out in the sunshine." And then she added mischievously, "With no dirty faces to wash."

CHAPTER 62

$\mathcal{P}$aul was surprised and relieved the next day when Sarah told him yes. Actually, she'd said, "You can pick me up at three."

Which gave him his first dilemma. How was he to pick her up? He'd spent so much time gathering his courage and then worrying over her answer that he hadn't given much thought to the details.

He had picked out a nice spot beneath an oak tree. It was far enough from the pigpen that they wouldn't be disturbed by the raucous critters. They could make quite a noise when they felt the need. The first few times he'd heard their high-pitched cries, he'd run over, certain a coyote had jumped into the pen. But no. They'd simply decided to chase each other at top speed, circling the pen, trundling through the mud, squealing and oinking and generally kicking up a fuss.

So he picked the site for their dinner as far from the pen as reasonably possible, but still close enough to the barn not to necessitate a long hike across muddy fields. Rebecca had given him an old quilt, which he spread out underneath the tree. Then he debated between walking over versus driving the tractor. Sarah worked hard all week. Maybe she would enjoy being off her feet a while. So he'd hooked up the battered Ford pickup bed to the back of the tractor and at fifteen minutes before three he'd driven over to her place.

He hadn't expected all of the children to be out on the front porch playing. All except Andy. "He's at Emma's," Henry had explained with a wink.

Sarah had looked doubtfully at the pickup bed, but she'd climbed in with a smile. Perhaps she'd forgotten he didn't own a horse and buggy yet.

They waved at the kids and *Mammi*. Only Mia had complained that she wanted to go, and Isaac had distracted her by offering to take her to the garden to see what had sprouted. Paul doubted anything had broken through the dirt yet, but he didn't point that out.

Instead, he popped the clutch and drove the tractor slowly back toward his place. The motor was too loud for them to talk, so he focused on the lane. When he stopped beside the old oak tree and helped her out, Sarah smiled and said, "*Danki*," and something in his heart fluttered.

She sat on the quilt and ran her fingers over the faded patchwork pattern. "I love old quilts."

"This one was Rebecca's. She said you probably wouldn't like sitting in the grass." He hadn't been particularly keen on sharing his dating plans with anyone, but his sister-in-law had guessed.

He and Sarah talked about the crops, the kids, and the Klines.

"You went on a mission trip with Becca and Joshua?"

"I did, and with his brother, Alton." She added as an afterthought, "We also had a chaperone—Becca's *aenti*."

"What was it like in Texas?"

"Different, being on the coast, but the people…well, after a while I learned that people are the same everywhere. Hardworking and honest, and sometimes in need of a helping hand."

He told her again about his plans for the other fields, what he hoped to plant and when he hoped to plant it.

Finally Sarah said, "Would you like me to help you bring out the food?"

"Food?"

"This is a picnic, *ya*?"

"Um…" The day was sunny with a slight breeze. One of those rare days that was absolutely perfect—neither cold nor hot, but a cold sweat broke out along Paul's neckline.

"You forgot?" Sarah guessed.

"I suppose I got distracted thinking about where to have it and how to pick you up and I…well, yeah. I forgot all about food."

"I could have brought something."

"No, I didn't want you to do that." At her look of surprise, he added, "What I mean is that you cook all week long."

Paul took off his hat and rubbed his fingers through his hair. "Let me run inside and see what I can rustle up."

"I'll go with you. We'll do it together. That is, if you don't mind my coming inside…"

"Of course I don't."

If his first mistake was forgetting the food, his second mistake was inviting Sarah into the barn. She'd been there before. She'd helped set up his living area and stock his pantry.

As they walked from the bright light of an April afternoon into the cooler semidarkness of the barn, he showed her the shelves he'd built, how he'd repaired some of the stalls that had fallen into disrepair. He shared his plans to purchase a buggy horse in the fall.

Sarah nodded politely about these things, but when they walked into his living quarters, the look on her face said it all. First her eyes widened, and then her mouth opened in a small *O*, and then she pasted on a smile and said, "Well. Let's see what you have."

"Um. Maybe just check the fridge or the…the pantry there to your right." He hastily collected the dirty socks, two sets of soiled work clothes, and muddy shoes. While her back was turned, he shoved it all under his cot.

He needn't have worried about being caught. Sarah was staring at the overflowing pile of dishes in the sink. When he walked up next to her, she'd snapped out of some reverie and said, "Right. I'll check the fridge."

"I think I have crackers and maybe a few cans of soda."

"I found some sausage and cheese."

She turned to him holding both in her hands, a triumphant smile again on her face.

"I'm afraid that cheese is a bit old."

"*Ya*, but we can cut off the molded portion. It will be fine."

He found a cutting board and sharp knife, grabbed a crate off the bottom of his pantry shelves, and dumped the items into it along with two cans of warm soda.

Sarah added the sausage and cheese.

"Oh. There is one more thing." He opened his refrigerator and reached in the tiny freezer section. Holding up a Snickers bar, he said, "Dessert."

Sarah was quiet as he carried the crate back toward their picnic quilt. He thought her silence said a lot—how disappointed she was, what a terrible idea this had been, and that she wished the afternoon was already over.

They had very little left to talk about, and soon Sarah admitted that she was worried about *Mammi* and the kids. He offered to give her a ride home, but she waved him away. "It will do me *gut* to walk. I ate more than half of the Snickers bar, and you know how packed with calories those are."

She smiled and thanked him for the picnic, but as she walked away Paul understood that he had blown it. He wished she had just laughed about it, but that look on her face when she'd seen the disaster of his small living space…it said a lot. He folded up the blanket and went back inside. Shaking his head, seeing his place as she had seen it, he set about cleaning out the sink, adding hot water and dish soap, and washing the last week's worth of dishes.

He could plow and plant a field by himself. He'd learned to work on forty-year-old tractors. He knew that his barn was in tip-top shape. He'd personally mended the holes in the siding and roof and shined the windows. He was a good farmer. Those were all things he'd learned from his father.

But he was a terrible housekeeper. He didn't know what to pack for a picnic lunch.

And he was clueless about how to court a girl.

Somewhere along the way, he'd missed those lessons.

CHAPTER 63

Sarah was still awake when Andy came home later that evening.

"Where is everyone?" he asked.

"Asleep already."

"Oh. I didn't realize it was so late."

"Out with Emma?"

"*Ya.* Is there anything to eat? I'm starving."

"*Mammi* made snickerdoodle cookies. There's a container of them on the counter near the stove."

"Want me to bring you any?"

"*Nein.*" Some days it was all Sarah could do not to revert back to her old ways. When something was bothering her, when she felt nervous at all, it was tempting to choose not to eat. She understood that for what it was—an unhealthy coping mechanism. Control what you eat and you at least control something. But she also understood that such behavior was self-destructive. A better idea would be to pray about the things bothering her.

"I'll take a half glass of milk." It was a small concession, but she felt proud of herself nonetheless.

"Tell me about your picnic." Andy collapsed onto the couch, pulling off his shoes and dropping his socks on the floor.

It reminded Sarah of Paul's place, and she nearly started laughing.

"Making fun of my feet again?"

"*Nein.* It's only that…well, you reminded me of Paul for a moment."

"How so?"

She told him about the tiny area he lived in and the complete chaos there. "Mateo and Isaac keep a room cleaner."

"Huh."

"Huh, what?"

"Well, it's only that picking up your socks isn't the first thing on your mind when a person is worried about crops or pigs or neighbors."

"I guess. But how does he even eat? If you'd seen the dishes in the kitchen. I didn't know he owned that many plates and bowls. The sink was full and even overflowing."

"It's not a sin to forget to wash dishes a few times."

Sarah didn't know how to respond to that. Had she been adding up Paul's sins and assigning him a score? That was a terrible thing to do. More confused than ever, she changed the subject. "And what of the house on his property? When is he going to work on it? Or is he going to live in a corner of the barn the rest of his life?"

Andy ate two more cookies and drained his glass of milk. Finally he said, "I admire Paul. Most single Amish men wouldn't take on such a big project as the Fisher place, and he doesn't have any family in the area to help."

"There's Joseph and Rebecca."

"True, but they aren't farmers." Andy picked up his dirty socks and shook them at her. "Don't judge a man by how he keeps his house."

"Do you judge Emma that way?"

"It's different with a woman."

"Andy Yoder, I can't believe you just said that to me."

Now he was grinning at her. "So…what? Have you ever heard of an Amish man who keeps the house and an Amish woman who works in the barn?"

"It's not so clear-cut. We both know many women who help with harvest and the animals, and I've seen the bishop himself help with the dishes."

"I suppose." He flopped back onto the couch and covered his eyes for a moment. When he looked at her again, he said, "Do you fancy him?"

"Paul?"

"Unless there's someone else you went on a picnic with recently."

"I hardly know how I feel."

"Well, don't let your idea of what a perfect man looks like stand in the way of your feelings or your common sense." He stood and stretched. "And next time you're over there, check out the fences around his fields and the pigpens and the crops. You might understand why he hasn't had time to wash dishes."

He was halfway up the stairs when she called out, "You didn't tell me about Emma."

But Andy only waved good night and kept going.

Her brother had never been one to talk about his feelings. How serious was his relationship with Emma? Was he thinking about marrying? And if he did, where would they live? No doubt Emma would move in with them. Andy hardly had the money to buy his own place, and why would he want to? The fields, the house, the barn—they all depended on him and his success or failure with the crops.

Certainly Emma would come and live with them if they were to marry.

How would it feel to have another woman around the house?

Sarah had thought she wanted their house to herself when her mother had left. She'd thought she was better off handling everything on her own. Now she couldn't imagine life without *Mammi*. Perhaps she wouldn't spend the energy worrying about her brother and Emma. When had worrying changed even one thing?

Instead she rinsed out their cups, placed them in the drainer, and made sure the kitchen was clean. Her mind flashed back on what the house had looked like before *Mammi* came. It had been nearly as bad as Paul's. How could she have so easily forgotten?

The quilt under the tree had been a nice touch, though. She turned off both gas lanterns and made her way through the darkened room, up the stairs, and to her bed. Her last thought as she drifted off to sleep was that if Paul Byler invited her on a picnic again, she'd be sure to pack a basket of food.

CHAPTER 64

*M*ateo and Isaac were often the last to leave the small one-room schoolhouse. The first Friday in April, they had been searching through Brian's books looking up the diet for an owl. The night before they had found an injured one in the barn loft. Isaac had quickly fashioned a cage of sorts, and they had added a dish of water along with some hay. *Mammi* had shown them how to bind the damaged wing to the bird's body. "Give it time to heal," she explained, but she hadn't known exactly what owls eat.

Mateo didn't know anything about keeping owls. He was a little afraid the bird would peck him, but it hadn't. Instead, it looked at him with large, sorrowful eyes before turning its head in the opposite direction.

"Strange how owls can do that," Mateo said, which caused Isaac to burst out laughing.

He slapped his leg and pretended to fall over holding his stomach. "Some days I forget you weren't raised in the country."

On Fridays they didn't have to check on the pigs because they generally spent several hours over there Saturday morning. Instead, they liked to stay late and hang around the schoolhouse. So they'd spent the last half hour looking through Brian's nature books as he graded papers.

Finally their teacher stood and said, "Let's call it a day, boys. It's a special night at the Walker house."

"Special how?" Mateo asked.

"It's his wife's birthday. Remember when we saw him in town buying her gift?"

Brian opened his desk drawer. "I asked two of the girls to wrap it up today." He pulled out a package the size of a small book, now wrapped in colorfully decorated notebook paper.

"Awfully small present," Mateo noted.

"Sure she'll like it?" Isaac asked.

"I think she will. It's a journal with her name inscribed on the outside."

"Sounds like homework."

"To you maybe, but Katie likes to write a little every day."

They walked out of the schoolhouse together. The morning rain had caused water to run in the small creek, so Isaac and Mateo stopped to crouch by it and look for food for their owl. The book had said insects, worms, spiders, and frogs. There was other, bigger stuff too, but they had decided things on the ground would be easier to catch.

Isaac was already calling the owl Icarus, something they'd learned about the week before. Brian had read them a story about Icarus and Daedalus and how they had tried to fly to the sun. Mateo was thinking about that as Isaac looked for owl food.

Brian waved goodbye and started walking down the road. He often walked to and from school, leaving the tractor for his wife in case she needed it. Their home was only a mile away, and Brian said that the walk home helped to clear his head—whatever that meant.

Mateo heard the squeal of brakes and looked up to see a black truck speeding away. His mind couldn't process what had happened. He stood up as the truck faded from view, and his eyes tracked back the way it had come.

"Must have hit something," he muttered.

The words were barely out of his mouth when he realized he could just make out a man's hat—Brian's hat, lying in the ditch beside the road.

Grabbing Isaac's arm, he pointed toward the ditch. "It's Brian. I think he's—"

And then he took off running. By the time he knelt next to his teacher, Isaac had caught up with him.

Brian's leg was bent at an awkward angle, and he seemed to be asleep.

Blood gushed from a wound on his head.

He didn't speak or moan or move in any way, even when they shook him gently.

"What do we do?" Isaac dropped to the ground beside him.

"I don't know."

"Is he...is he dead?"

"He can't be." The words were a prayer more than a fact. Mateo shrugged out of his backpack and slipped it under his teacher's head. It seemed the right thing to do, though he realized it probably didn't help very much.

"Is he breathing?"

"Can't tell." Mateo put his hands on his teacher's shoulders and shook him again.

"Nothing."

"He could be...maybe, sleeping." Mateo put his face close to Brian's. "Wake up. Brian, are you okay? Open your eyes."

"I don't think he can hear you."

"He has to hear us. He has to wake up."

"We need something to put around his head."

Mateo shrugged out of his shirt and they wrapped it gently around Brian's head. Blood seeped through instantly, staining the white cloth red.

"Should we move him? What if someone else hits us?"

"We're well off the road—the truck must have thrown him." Mateo glanced behind and in front of them. There were tire marks where the truck had sped away, but no other traffic. "Anyone would have to drive off the road to hit us."

"That's exactly what happened, though."

"Probably wouldn't happen twice in the same day." Mateo sat back on his heels, suddenly sick to his stomach. "I heard brakes squealing and looked up and saw a black truck. Did you see it?"

"Uh-uh. I was staring down in the creek." Isaac looked as if he might cry. He looked like Mateo felt.

"We can't just leave him here," Mateo said.

"I'll stay with him. Go to the phone shack."

"Maybe we should get *Mammi*."

"I don't think *Mammi* can fix this."

It felt like they'd been talking forever, but Mateo thought it had only been a few minutes. He leaned closer to Brian, put his ear over the man's heart, careful not to put any weight on him. "I think he's breathing."

"You need to run for help."

"Me?"

"You run faster than I do, Mateo. Run to the phone shack and call the emergency people. Then stop and tell Paul. He'll bring you back. Hurry, though. He's bleeding bad."

"Okay." Mateo glanced around one last time, and then he was off—running faster than he'd ever run. Running and praying as tears coursed down his cheeks.

But he couldn't outrun the questions.

Would the accident have happened if they hadn't kept him after school late? What if Brian had been driving the tractor instead of walking? Why had the person who hit him sped away? And above those, pressing down on his heart was the only question that mattered—was their teacher going to die?

CHAPTER 65

$\mathcal{P}$aul was checking the field closest to the road when he glanced up and saw a small dot appear. It took him a moment to realize the dot was a boy, and he was running. By the time he realized the boy had no shirt on, he jumped onto his tractor and began driving toward the road. He reached the end of the lane at the same instant that Mateo did.

It was only when he'd climbed off the tractor and walked toward Mateo that he noticed the blood on his hands.

"What happened?"

"Can't...stop! Phone shack!"

Paul shrugged out of his shirt and insisted Mateo put it on. Though the boy was sweating, he'd begun to shiver. "Look at me. What happened?"

Mateo was pulling in great gulps of air. He bent over, his hands on his knees. "It's Brian. A truck hit him. They hit him and sped away."

"Climb on the tractor."

"Phone shack first!" Mateo hollered over the roar of the engine.

Paul didn't shut the engine off when they reached the little shack by the side of the road. It wasn't much more than a lean-to with a phone in it. No stool, though there was a counter with an answering machine and a jar to put money in.

He dialed nine-one-one.

"State your emergency."

"A man has been hit by a...by a truck..." He glanced at Mateo,

269

who was waiting in the doorway. Covering the mouthpiece, he asked, "Where did it happen?"

"In front of the schoolhouse, just a little this side of it."

Paul relayed the information as well as the crossroads.

He dropped the phone back into the cradle as the woman was advising him to stay on the line.

They jogged back to the tractor, and once more Mateo climbed up behind him. It wasn't the safest way for the boy to travel, but they had less than a mile to go. He didn't feel good about leaving Mateo alone, though he could have dropped him off at the end of Sarah's lane.

Get to Brian first and see just how bad the situation was.

Later he wouldn't remember pulling over to the side of the road, kneeling, and feeling for a pulse. He knew next to nothing about first aid, but his mother had taught him a few things over the years—though she'd been more concerned with birth than death.

"His heart is beating. You two did well. You did the right thing."

He knelt on one side of Brian. Mateo and Isaac were on the other side. Twice Mateo reached forward to wipe blood off his teacher's face, staining the cuff of Paul's shirt. There was nothing else they could do as they sat in the waning light. It was two minutes, maybe three when they heard a siren, and then they were being pushed back as emergency personnel took over.

Paul stood with the boys, one arm around each of them, as the paramedics took Brian's blood pressure, set his leg, started an IV, and transferred him to a backboard. One of the workers relayed all of this into a radio, and Paul could understand about half of what he said. It didn't sound good.

A police car arrived, and Sheriff Bynum stepped out. He spoke with the paramedics before walking over to question the boys. Their story came out in bits and pieces, what little of it there was.

"We'll take him to Tulsa," the taller of the two paramedics told them. He named a hospital on the west side of town that the sheriff seemed to know of. "Can you contact the family?"

"I'll go myself to tell the bishop," Bynum said. "He'll want to go with us to contact Brian's wife."

It was a small community in a small town. Paul shouldn't have been surprised that the sheriff knew the teacher, but he was. What surprised him more was the look of grief on the man's face.

The paramedic nodded once, climbed up into the back of the vehicle, and slammed the door shut.

They sped away, lights blaring and siren screaming.

Sheriff Bynum took down their names, though he knew everyone well enough. He'd sat with them when Mateo was missing. It occurred to Paul that he was doing a good job of questioning the boys, keeping them calm and not scaring them with the facts of Brian's condition.

They were interrupted by a second squad car that arrived. Bynum walked over to the officer and said, "I want photos and dirt samples of the tire tracks. That's about all we're going to have to go on for this one."

The officer set to work, first putting out emergency cones to slow down any traffic.

"Can I give you a ride home?" Bynum asked.

"*Nein*. We all live close, and I have the tractor."

"All right. I'll be in touch as soon as we know something." Bynum climbed into his patrol car. He blipped the siren once and drove away toward the bishop's house. An unnatural silence had fallen over the scene. A few people hurried down the road, looking to see what had happened.

But there was nothing to see.

There was no sign of the tragedy that had happened there other than a couple of tire tracks in the mud. Everything was the same as before, and nothing was the same as before.

How quickly life changed.

Mammi's words came back to Paul. *Never assume you have tomorrow.*

He squatted down and pulled both boys to him. "You did *gut*. It was a very sad thing that happened today, but you stayed calm and did the right thing."

"Is he going to be all right?" Mateo used the back of his hand to brush away his tears.

"I hope so. Let's pray that he is."

He held them close as each offered up their own silent prayers, and then he squeezed them once more and stood up. As they were walking toward the tractor, Mateo pulled away, hurried over to the fence, and picked up a package.

When he brought it back, Paul could see it was some type of gift.

"For Brian's wife," Isaac said.

"*Ya*," Mateo unzipped his backpack, the one that still had blood from his teacher's wound, and stuffed the gift inside. "He can give it to her when he comes home."

CHAPTER 66

$\mathcal{S}$arah hurried down the porch steps. She'd been standing there, watching for the boys, and now Paul was driving down her lane. When he came closer, she saw that both boys were with him, scrunched onto the little tractor. He was driving slowly, carefully.

But why was he bringing them home? Why weren't they walking, and why were they late? And what were the sirens she'd heard?

Those questions died on her lips when she saw that Mateo was wearing Paul's shirt, and Paul was standing there in his pants and undershirt. She ran toward the tractor. As soon as it stopped, Mateo and Isaac jumped off. At first they flew to her, wrapping their arms around her, but then they stepped back and glanced toward Paul.

"It's their teacher, Brian. He was hit by an *Englisch* vehicle."

She covered her mouth with her hand. "How bad is it?"

"They've already taken him to a hospital in Tulsa. Sheriff Bynum said he would pick up Bishop Levi. Together they'll go and tell Katie."

"Someone should be with her. She'll want someone to stay with the children so she can go and be with him."

The rest of the Yoders had spilled out of the house. Paul again repeated what he knew, and this time Isaac and Mateo chimed in with bits of information.

"We saw it happen," Mateo said, his voice shaking.

"Sort of."

"I saw the truck swerve and then speed away."

"And he realized it hit Brian."

"So we ran."

"And we tried to help."

"But he was bleeding." Mateo touched the top of his head. "And his leg was…"

"Broken."

Their story spent, both boys swiped at their eyes.

Sarah pulled them to her again. What a terrible thing for two children to see. How frightened they must have been.

"Katie's parents live close. They'll stay with the children so she can go to the hospital to be with Brian." Andy stuck his hands in his pockets. "This is a tragedy for sure. It's hard to imagine…"

They stood there for a minute, their lives temporarily suspended by tragedy in their midst. Luke and Henry and Andy shuffled their feet. Paul stared back the way they had come. Mateo and Isaac studied their hands. Only Mia seemed unmoved by the news, though she did drop her doll into the dirt and proceeded to pat it saying, "You're okay. Don't worry."

Sarah's emotions tumbled over one another—from grief for Brian, to relief that the boys weren't hurt, to guilt that she could feel relief when one of their community was even now speeding toward the hospital.

It was *Mammi* who took charge and broke through their shock. "Best get inside, boys. You'll need to clean up before dinner. Mateo, put Paul's shirt in the dirty clothes, and I'll wash it tomorrow."

"There's no need for you to do that," Paul assured her.

"The shirt has blood all over it, and I doubt you know how to soak and remove the stain. One of Andy's should fit you. Don't be arguing with me, Paul Byler, and I can see you're about to. Dinner will be on the table in ten minutes, and I expect you to join us."

No one would think of questioning *Mammi*, not when she used that tone. So they all went into the house, shock giving way to sadness. When the screen door had slapped shut behind Sarah, she stopped and looked around their home, surprised that everything looked as it had fifteen minutes ago. Tragedy had once again touched their lives. Their world had changed, and yet their home remained the same.

Dinner was as tasty as ever.

The boys ate, even Isaac and Mateo, though occasionally they would close their eyes and pull in a ragged breath. After the meal, *Mammi* suggested they join hands and offer silent prayers of healing for Brian, wisdom for his doctors, and comfort for his family.

It was only by chance that Sarah had sat next to Paul. When he reached for her hand, she couldn't meet his gaze. She didn't want him to see her tears, to see how vulnerable and raw she felt at the moment. But his hand? It calmed her, somehow settled her world that seemed to have tilted when she saw the boys with blood on their clothes.

Andy reminded Luke and Isaac and Mateo to complete their evening chores. For once they didn't argue. Andy and Henry went to the barn to check on the chickens and Dusty. Sarah and Paul helped *Mammi* with the dishes. When the last plate was dried and put away, *Mammi* said, "Perhaps you'd like to walk Paul out to his tractor. I believe the night air might do you good."

Sarah didn't argue, but she didn't agree.

How would she ever feel good again? Life was so precarious, and there was nothing she could do to protect those she loved.

But the evening air did help. Though it wasn't yet fully dark, the first stars had begun to prick the night sky.

She looked up and remembered the Scripture from Job, about how God had placed the constellations in the sky. Surely He would show mercy to Brian, would heal him, unless…unless it was his time.

Paul's thoughts seemed to mirror her own. "When someone passes, we say their life is complete. Hard to imagine that's true in Brian's case."

"Did it seem so awfully bad? Do you think…is there a chance he won't make it?" She'd held back the questions, not wanting to know, not wanting the boys to hear the answer.

Paul shook his head. She could just make out his expression in the fading light. "I'd like to tell you he's going to be fine, but I can't say that with any certainty. His leg was certainly broken in several places, but that alone shouldn't have caused his unconsciousness. I'm not sure...not sure how bad the head injury was."

"It's a *gut* thing you were there."

"I wasn't though." He told her then about seeing Mateo running down the road, how they'd hurried to the phone shack, and then their mad dash back to Brian's side. "I think...I think the biggest danger would be internal bleeding. His blood pressure was low when one paramedic called it out to the other."

"How do you know about blood pressures?"

"My *mamm* is a midwife."

"*Ya?*" Sarah had never thought about Paul's family, aside from Rebecca and Joseph. "Tell me about her."

"She's tough, like *Mammi*. I guess she had to be to raise so many boys."

"Seven of you?"

"*Ya.*"

"A *gut*-sized Amish family." Sarah laughed and then regretted it. How could she laugh when Brian was fighting for his life?

"It's all right, you know." Paul stepped closer, hesitated, and then he reached for her hand. "It's okay to still have moments when you feel happy or when something makes you laugh."

"It doesn't feel okay."

"Because you care about him."

"I guess you know he wasn't raised Amish."

"Rebecca told me a little."

"We were all surprised that he stuck with it. I've never known an *Englischer* who became Amish, though you read about such things often enough in romance books."

"You read romance books?" They were walking toward his tractor, and he nudged her shoulder with his.

"*Nein.* Of course not," she said in an exaggerated I'm-innocent voice. "I've only heard about them."

Paul stopped a few feet from his tractor, glanced back at the house, and then reached forward and cupped her face in his hands.

"I could tell how frightened you were when you first saw the boys, when you saw the blood on them."

Sarah's right arm began to shake. She clasped it to her side with her other hand, but not before Paul noticed.

"Hey. It's all right. The boys are okay."

Any other time, she might have resisted, but when he pulled her into his arms, the reserve she'd carefully constructed began to crumble.

"What's this about? Isaac and Mateo?"

She nodded, feeling foolish for sobbing all over his shirt—correction, all over Andy's shirt. But for a moment, she stopped fighting the fact that she might actually need someone else. Briefly, she allowed herself to lean on his strength.

He patted her back, mumbled something about how strong the boys were, and attempted to make a joke about how much better *Mammi*'s cooking was than his.

"I managed to burn soup last night. Can you imagine?"

She could, and perhaps that was why she pulled away from him, wiped her sleeve across her eyes, and straightened her shoulders.

"Danki."

"For?"

"For not telling me that Brian would be okay when we don't know yet. For allowing me to fall apart."

"Sarah, we all need to fall apart occasionally."

Tears continued to roll down her face, but she pulled in a deep breath and put on her best smile.

"Even you?"

"*Ya*, of course."

"And when was the last time you cried?"

He tapped his finger against his chin, as if he were deep in thought. Finally, he leaned closer to her and said, "*Old Yeller*. We read *Old Yeller* in class. I pretended I needed to go to the boys' room, sat down on the step, and cried for a good two or three minutes."

"You did not."

"*Ya*. Ask my *mamm*. I told her, and she said most everyone cries when they read *Old Yeller*."

"I did."

"See?" He stepped closer and used his thumbs to wipe away the last remaining tears. "Get some sleep. We'll know more about Brian's condition tomorrow."

Sarah was pretty sure she wouldn't sleep, but she did. And before she drifted off, her last thought was of a young boy, sitting outside an outhouse, crying over a fictional story about a dog that didn't even exist.

CHAPTER 67

*P*aul went to town first thing the next morning. He had arrived before the store opened, and now he stood at the counter as Rebecca checked to make sure the cash register had enough change for the day's business.

"We heard he passed," Rebecca said.

"Passed?"

"That's what the Hershbergers told us. Said he died on the side of the road. Real tragedy. I plan to go and see Katie this afternoon."

"*Nein*. Brian was alive when they loaded him in the ambulance."

Joseph joined them at the register. "You're sure?"

"*Ya*. I was there." He explained how Mateo and Isaac had seen the accident.

"Those boys have been through enough." Rebecca crossed and then uncrossed her arms. "It's a shame that they saw such a thing, but I suppose *Gotte* has His reasons."

"Maybe we could call the hospital to see how Brian's doing."

"No need for that." Joseph flashed him a smile and hurried to unlock the door.

Bishop Levi was the first to walk inside. He was followed by two other men and one woman from their community. For the moment, Paul's mind went blank, and he couldn't remember a single name. Joseph said good morning to each of them, calling them by name.

Paul was going to have to make an effort to at least learn who people were. After all, this was his community now.

"Do you have news on Brian?"

"I do." The bishop waited until everyone had quieted. "I stayed at the hospital through the night. Katie is doing okay, but she needs our prayers. She's understandably quite upset."

"And Brian?" Joseph asked.

"He's in critical condition. He had some internal bleeding, which they did emergency surgery to stop. The doctors also had to give him a transfusion because he'd lost so much blood. If it hadn't been for Mateo and Isaac…They saved his life by wrapping the shirt around his head and at least slowing the amount of blood loss."

"So he will live?"

Levi shrugged and tapped his cane against the floor. Paul could tell that he'd rather not answer the question, but it was the bishop's job to guide them, not protect them from the harshness of the world.

"The doctors couldn't say. They put him in a medically induced coma to allow his body time to heal. The leg will mend, but the internal injuries, especially those to his head…only time will tell."

They stood in stunned silence, and then the bell over the front door rang again. Paul looked up to see an *Englisch* couple walk inside. Slowly their group dispersed. Rebecca patted him on the shoulder. "Be sure to tell Sarah and her family what we know."

He shook his head. "She was so upset yesterday."

"And she'll be upset today, but it's better that you not try to hide this from her. She'll imagine something even worse. Trust me. It's what women do."

"Hard to imagine worse than this."

"Have faith. Brian has a chance, and we all know what a tough person he is." Now Rebecca's eyes took on a mischievous glint. "He did become Amish. How many are able to do that? Brian Walker is a strong and godly man. We can trust him to *Gotte's* care."

⌒ℴ⌒

Though he didn't want to, Paul stopped by and told *Mammi* the news.

"Sarah is upstairs with Mateo. The boy's been unusually quiet since it happened."

"Would it help if I talked to him?"

Mammi cocked her head to the side, and then she patted her pocket and pulled out a silver-wrapped piece of chocolate. She put it into Paul's hand and closed his fingers around it. "You're a *gut* man, Paul Byler. I'll suggest the boys come to see you later. Caring for those pigs might be just the thing to perk them up."

So he'd gone home, though he wanted to stay and speak to Sarah. *Mammi* hadn't said how she was doing. Paul thought of her soaking his shirt with her tears, and he vowed he would find a way to make her smile again.

It was just before lunch when Mateo and Isaac showed up to check on the pigs.

"Where's Luke?"

"Helping Henry take apart the tractor engine, though it doesn't need it. Henry's fascinated with mechanical things." Isaac had picked up a stick, and he despondently struck it against the ground.

Mateo sat down on an upturned feed pail and stared at his shoes.

The two had obviously been dwelling on what had happened. Paul's heart ached for them, but he also understood the wisdom of what *Mammi* had said. An afternoon's work wouldn't take away their pain, but it would at least distract them for a few hours.

So he set them to cleaning the pigs' pen. He also suggested they raise the water buckets that were attached to the side of the pen. "These pigs are growing faster than I can keep up with."

After they had done that, he thought they would come and find him, but they didn't. He finally went to the pigpen to check on them. Mateo was sitting on the ground, giving the smallest pig a belly rub. Isaac was whittling on a stick with a pocketknife.

It was a beautiful April day.

There had to be something he could do to raise their spirits. Suddenly he remembered something he'd seen in a back stall of the barn.

"I could use your help with one more thing."

Isaac shrugged and Mateo stood up, but neither showed much enthusiasm. When he led them to the back stall and began pulling out fishing gear, he finally got their attention.

"Where did this come from?"

"It was left here."

"So it's yours?"

"I bought the place. Anything on the premises automatically became mine."

"You need our help cleaning up this stuff?" Isaac frowned at a tackle box that he'd opened. It was a real mess. It almost looked as if someone had turned it upside down.

"Sure. That would be *gut*, but I was sort of hoping you could help me catch some fish."

Isaac's head jerked up. "I thought you needed to check the crops."

"*Ya*, I do need to do that, but it will keep until next week. Today I have a hankering for fried fish. Think *Mammi* knows how to cook it?"

"*Mammi* can cook anything," Isaac said, walking over to the fishing poles and choosing a plain bamboo one.

Mateo looked less convinced. "I've never fished before," he admitted.

"No? Then today is a *gut* day to learn."

Paul sent the boys to dig up some worms while he fetched three cans of soda, a jar of peanut butter, and half a loaf of bread. It wasn't the best lunch, but he supposed that didn't matter as much as raising their spirits. He placed everything inside a medium-sized cooler and took two small ice packs out of his tiny freezer. The ice packs went on top of the drinks.

Two hours later, they had caught six nice-sized catfish from the creek that flowed across the northwestern corner of his property. He had placed them in the now empty cooler, ice packs once again on top, which the boys insisted on carrying. They stopped outside the barn while he returned the poles and tackle.

"Tractor or walk?" Paul asked.

"Walk," they said simultaneously.

"Works for me."

"*Mammi* is going to be shocked," Mateo said.

"*Ya*. We brought home the bacon, only it's fish!" Isaac laughed at his joke, and then he covered his mouth. "Sorry. I didn't mean to laugh."

"It's okay to be happy, you know." They were walking down Paul's lane. They could have cut across the fields, but he'd heard about Isaac's pants getting caught on the fence the last time. He didn't want to add any additional work to Sarah's afternoon.

"I don't know about that. Seems like we should be sad. I mean, we are sad." Isaac frowned and squashed his hat more firmly on his head.

"Being sad is normal. Someone we love is hurting."

Both of the boys nodded fiercely.

"But at the same time, Brian wouldn't want you to go around looking like the world had stopped turning. There's still work to be done and fish to be caught."

"Sometimes I forget," Mateo admitted. "You know, I forget for a minute that he's been hurt. Then I remember, and I feel terrible all over again."

"Yup. That's your mind and heart coming to terms with what has happened."

They had reached the end of the lane and were now walking down the side of the road.

"Why did it have to happen?" Isaac asked. "Brian's a *gut* person. He didn't do anything wrong or anything to deserve this."

Paul didn't answer immediately.

Mateo said, "I've wondered that before. Like, why do I have a terrible mom? I'm grateful for you all—for my new family—but why did I get stuck with such a bad one to begin with?"

"Let's not be judging your mother. We don't know the details of her situation."

"I know she's not here, and she's a drunk! What else do I need to know?"

Isaac nodded in agreement. "My mom isn't any better. She's not a drunk, and she still left."

Paul stopped walking, scratched at his right eyebrow, and said a quick prayer for wisdom. They had reached the lane leading to the

Yoder house. He motioned over to the vegetable stand that was currently closed.

He sat on the lone chair inside. Mateo and Isaac both sat on the cooler. Each tugged on their straw hat at the same moment. It was almost funny, the way the two mirrored one another, and that they weren't even aware of it.

This time, instead of staring at the ground, they watched him expectantly.

Paul sighed and leaned forward, elbows on his knees. "I don't know the answers to your questions."

"That's not much help," Isaac said.

"So you're as confused as we are?" Mateo pulled off his hat and scratched his head. "But you're grown up."

"*Ya*, I am. No one handed me all the answers when I turned sixteen or eighteen or even twenty. I'm still figuring stuff out. I guess we all are."

"Not any help at all." Isaac nudged Mateo, and they both grinned. "Maybe we should ask *Mammi*."

"That's a *gut* idea. *Mammi* is a wise woman, and we're lucky she's here."

"Sure are," the boys said simultaneously.

Paul leaned back in his chair. "Though, if your mom hadn't left home, Isaac, *Mammi* wouldn't have come to stay here."

"I traded one mother for another?"

"I don't know about that. I only know that I'm glad *Mammi* came."

"I am too," Isaac admitted.

"So something *gut* came out of your mother's leaving, just like *Gotte* promised He would bring *gut* out of the things men intend for evil."

"That's in the Bible?" Mateo asked.

"Sure is." Paul allowed his words to sink in, and then he reminded them, "And if Mateo's mom hadn't left, then you two would have never met each other. Sarah wouldn't have Mateo and Mia to take care of."

"Sarah loves us," Mateo said.

Isaac nodded in agreement. "She loves all of us."

"But what about Brian? How can something *gut* come of that?"

"I don't know, but *Gotte* will find a way. You can always trust that

Gotte will find a way to bless us in spite of the bad stuff in life. And you know what?" He stood and indicated they should pick up the cooler and continue walking. "If Mateo hadn't come, and you two hadn't pestered me about piglets—"

Isaac gave him a sideways look. "Hey. Wasn't that your idea?"

"Maybe it was, but I might not have actually purchased them without you two around. Now those piglets have the best home this side of the Mississippi."

Both boys started giggling, and this time they didn't cover their mouths.

CHAPTER 68

Mateo didn't know what to expect on Monday morning. He vaguely remembered having substitute teachers when he was in school in Texas. It had never gone well. The teachers seemed a bit lost, and the kids acted terrible.

He nearly fell out of his seat when he saw that Becca's mother was their substitute teacher. She was a nice enough woman. She'd brought them clothes and toys for his sister. And she was expecting her first grandbaby soon. That was pretty much all he knew about her.

"How's she going to do this when the baby comes?" he asked Isaac.

"She's only here this morning. They switch off."

When they returned from lunch, it was to find that Bishop Levi was their teacher for the afternoon.

And the next morning it was Sarah, and Paul's brother Joseph covered the afternoon class.

The best part was that the week kind of went on as normal. The people filling in didn't teach the way Brian did, but the students went about their work as usual. They still had math in the morning, a story after lunch, and history and reading in the afternoon. The older boys still tried to chase the girls around the playground, and the girls still squealed as if they didn't love it. But Mateo could tell they did. They always smiled and giggled as they ran.

"Why would anyone want to chase a girl?" he asked Isaac.

"Beats me. Let's check the creek for frogs." Isaac was still feeding his owl, though *Mammi* thought it might be ready to release in another week.

So life proceeded pretty much as it had before. They didn't forget about Brian. Each morning, after they had the singing, whoever was teaching would update them on his condition. Always it was the same. Never better and never worse. But at least they were being told something. No one was trying to keep them in the dark.

It was Luke's idea that they create a banner of handprints to send to the hospital. Each student traced his or her hand on construction paper, cut it out, and added a get-well note on the palm. They fastened them together with yarn and staples. By the time they were done, the hand banner reached from one end of the chalkboard to the other.

Mateo thought it looked better than any card he'd ever seen. Surely, when Brian woke up and saw it, he would feel better.

Mateo wasn't real good at praying yet, but the teacher always set aside a few minutes at the end of the day for them to pray for Brian. Mostly, Mateo bowed his head and said, "Please, God" over and over in his mind. After a few days, he remembered to pray for Brian's wife and their kids and the doctors and the bishop, who was still making trips back and forth to the hospital.

The week passed with no real news, and then at church on Sunday, Mateo noticed a lot of adults smiling and slapping each other on the back. They were saying things like, "I knew it" and "*Gotte* is *gut*" and "Praise the Lord." Mateo didn't have to wonder too long.

Bishop Levi stood up after the first two songs, thanked them for coming, and then delivered the news. "Katie called the store this morning. She spoke with Joseph, so I'll let him share with you what she said."

Paul's brother stood in front of the group, a smile stretching across his face. "Brian woke up last night."

There were more *amens* and shouts of joy.

"He remembers nothing of the accident, but he knows his name, his family, and that he's supposed to be teaching."

Laughter spread across the congregation. Mateo turned to high-five Isaac. The guilt he'd been carrying vanished. Why had he felt guilty? It was the *Englischer* who had run into him, a man who was now in jail from what Andy said. Yet in the back of his mind, he'd felt a little as if it were his fault. If he hadn't stopped with Isaac to look in the creek, if they hadn't stayed late, maybe Brian would have left earlier. Maybe he wouldn't have been hit.

He had shared that with *Mammi* one night. She said, "A person can spend their whole life worrying about what might happen, or they can live the life they're given. I'd suggest the latter."

Joseph was still updating the congregation. "He has a long recovery ahead of him, but the doctors say that he'll be home within the next month, and he'll be able to teach again by next year."

Mateo couldn't have told anyone a thing about the rest of the service. He was so relieved. He had spent many nights awake in his bed, worrying about his teacher, but now he could finally relax. When Andy woke him up, they were singing the final hymn. This one Mateo knew. They'd sung it lots of times since he had moved in with Sarah. And the words seemed to fit.

Amazing grace, how sweet the sound...

CHAPTER 69

The next few weeks crept by for Sarah. She felt a despondency that she hadn't known since her first few weeks struggling with her eating disorder. She felt lost, adrift on a sea of terrible possibilities.

What if the children were hit by a car as they were walking home?

What if Brian didn't get well?

What if one of the boys were hurt on the farm? There were always farming accidents, and she couldn't think how to watch over everyone all the time.

Then her mind would return to Mia, who was still occasionally hiding in bizarre places. Once, they had found her in the hayloft of the barn. Sarah shuddered to think of her climbing up the rickety ladder.

Another time, she hid in the bushes and came in smelling of skunk. What if it had bitten her? What if it had been rabid?

She didn't share her fears with *Mammi*. She knew well enough how *Mammi* would counsel her.

Pray. Trust *Gotte*. Read the Bible.

Whenever she tried to do any of those things, her mind would wander until eventually she'd give up and take up another chore to try to distract herself. She had trouble sleeping, and though she forced herself to eat, she knew from the way that her clothes fit that she was once again losing weight.

Becca attempted to get her to laugh about it. "Look at me. I'm as big as one of Joshua's cows."

In truth her friend looked beautiful and happy and well rested. Pregnancy agreed with her, and Sarah had no doubt that motherhood would as well.

One afternoon she was at Becca's house, helping her to sort the infant clothes she'd received and place them in the baby's dresser. They folded and exclaimed over each item.

"Some are used, but they're all in *gut* shape."

"You certainly have plenty whether you have a girl or boy."

"My *mamm* says girl, because I'm carrying her low like she carried me. The midwife says it's a boy because of the heart rate." Becca shrugged. "I'll be happy no matter what it is."

"Do you…" Sarah lowered her voice. Mia was playing on the floor in the living room. She'd taken to listening closely and asking lots of questions, but she couldn't hear them from the next room. "Do you worry about the birth or the baby being sick or…"

"*Nein.*"

"I'm sorry. I shouldn't have even said that."

"It's okay, Sarah. You know, you can say anything to me. Our friendship goes way back, all the way to Texas."

"Some days I feel like a completely different person from the girl who rode away on that bus. Hard to believe I left home and actually went on a mission trip."

"But you did. We both did."

"And you ended up marrying Joshua." Sarah smiled in spite of the constant ache in her heart. "*Gotte* has been *gut* to you."

"He has, and He's been *gut* to you as well." Becca reached forward and clasped her hands. "That little girl in the other room adores you. And if I'm not mistaken, a certain neighbor of yours is quite interested too."

Sarah shook her head. "I can't—"

"Can't what?"

Instead of answering, Sarah pulled her hands away and busied herself folding cloth diapers. They also had a stack of disposables for church and such. Becca didn't push. Instead, she waited—in Sarah's mind that was certainly one of the marks of a good friend.

"I can't see the future. You know?" She folded a yellow onesie and sighed. "I can't see past today. There's enough to worry over without thinking about a husband. More change—"

She shook her head, causing her *kapp* strings to fall forward. "There are so many things that could go wrong."

To her surprise, Becca stood and left the room.

Had she finally offended her friend? Perhaps Becca could no longer tolerate her morose mood. She wouldn't blame her.

But Becca had only gone to fetch something. She thrust it into Sarah's hands. "Alice sent me this."

"Alice?"

"Our friend Alice, in Texas. She still writes. Alice knows about suffering, *ya*? She lost her entire home in that terrible hurricane and feared she would lose her grandchildren, but she didn't. She says that sometimes we experience a crisis of faith."

"I don't know what that means."

"It's sort of like an earthquake. Did you feel the one we had last week?"

"Barely a tremor. They say it's from all the oil drilling in the area."

"Well, Alice said that most people have a crisis of faith at one time or another. She sent me these prayer cards when I was worrying over not getting pregnant."

"I didn't know you worried about that."

Becca shrugged. "When it didn't happen right away, I was afraid something was wrong with me. I mentioned it in one of my letters to her, and she sent me this box."

Sarah pulled the lid off the box. Inside was what looked like a small deck of cards, only when she pulled one out she saw it had a Scripture from the Psalms printed on each side.

"I want you to have it. Promise me you will pull out a new card each day, read it, and allow it to minister to your heart."

"Okay, only…" She'd gone this far, she might as well spill it all. "Only when I read my Bible now, it doesn't seem to mean anything. It's like they are just words printed in a book."

Instead of judging her, Becca enfolded her in a hug. "*Gotte* is doing great things with you, Sarah. It doesn't have to make sense, and it doesn't have to feel right. Sort of like when I felt nauseated with the baby those first few months. Or now, when I can barely roll over. None of that feels right, but *Mamm* says it's a part of the wonders of childbearing."

Sarah laughed through her tears. "I wouldn't know about that."

"Try not to rush what *Gotte* is doing. Read a card each day, and I will pray that He will use them to restore your faith."

CHAPTER 70

*P*aul knew that Sarah was struggling.

Mammi said to give her time.

Andy said he didn't understand girls at all. Apparently, he'd had a falling out with Emma. He was determined to make up, but so far she'd refused to speak with him.

"What did you do?"

"I don't know."

"No idea? Seriously?"

Paul squinted in the morning sunshine. The crops they had planted looked good. He might even be able to afford to purchase a horse and buggy before fall arrived.

At the moment they were repairing pens on the Yoder place. Paul had managed to trade two of his piglets, which were hardly piglets anymore, for four goats that he gave to Sarah. Unfortunately, she hadn't seemed nearly as happy as he'd hoped. She'd smiled and thanked him politely, but there'd been no real joy in her words or her expression.

"Could be I forgot about promising Emma I'd take her to town for dinner," Andy admitted.

"Huh."

"It's our three-month anniversary. Whoever heard of such a thing?"

"Three months—"

"Since we started formally courting. I'm not sure how formal it is, but neither of us is seeing anyone else. When she told me, I laughed

293

and said we should celebrate, but then our neighbor's cows knocked down the fence on the other side of our place. I was afraid they would get in the corn, so after Henry moved them back, we set to fixing the fence."

"You could have asked me to help."

"You were working at the store that day."

"Oh, yeah. The day Joseph had to go back to the doctor's, so I watched the store."

Andy sighed, hammered the last of the gate crossbars, and closed it. Giving it a good shake, he said, "Looks like it will hold."

"I don't know." Paul studied the work they had done. "You know what they say about goat fences."

"Can't say I do."

"If water can get through it, so can a goat."

Andy laughed.

Paul said, "Maybe we should go to town and get some fencing to put along the bottom, over there, on the west side."

"*Gut* idea. But only if you let me buy. You already gave us the goats."

"Deal."

An hour later they were in town at the feed store. It was cheaper to buy a large roll of the fencing. Andy relented and allowed Paul to pay for half. "My pigs are so big, I think they could lean against our fencing and knock it over. This will work to slow them down a little."

As they were leaving, Paul spied potted flowers outside the front door of the feed store.

"Maybe we should buy flowers."

"Flowers?"

"Could get you out of the doghouse with Emma, and they might cheer Sarah up."

Andy started to say something, bit it back, and stooped to pick up a tray of pink ones.

"What are they?"

"I have no idea. What's Sarah's favorite color?"

"I don't know."

"She's your sister."

"Well, you're the one who is sweet on her!" Andy waited, as if daring him to deny it.

But why bother? Paul imagined everyone was aware of his feelings for Sarah. Everyone except Sarah.

He selected a tray with half yellow, half purple blooms and changed the subject to goat feed.

He didn't have time to stop by the Yoder place, so he let Andy off at the end of the lane. "I'll be over tomorrow. Can't leave the pigs for too long or they get into trouble."

"How much trouble can a pig get into?"

"You'd be surprised. Good luck with the flowers."

"I could give these to Sarah, and you could take yours to Emma."

"Which wouldn't help your situation one bit." Paul whistled as he drove the tractor home. He set the flowers next to the barn and went to check on the pigs. By the time he returned, they were looking a bit wilted, so he took them out of the flat and placed them in an old iron pot. He didn't look in the pot first. Instead, he fetched a pail of water, soaked them, and went inside to prepare his dinner.

His cooking wasn't getting any better, but he had started cleaning his dishes each night. Not that Sarah had been back over, but she might.

The next day he waited until lunch, until he thought Mia would be down for a nap.

"They actually look kind of nice in that old pot," he muttered. Picking it up, he set it on the floor of the tractor and drove next door.

When he knocked on the door, Sarah answered, but she didn't invite him in. He thought she looked tired, and it crossed his mind that she might be sick. Surely if she was, *Mammi* would have noticed.

"I brought you something."

"More goats?"

"Um, no."

She stepped out onto the porch and crossed her arms. "Does it need to be fed or looked after?"

His surprise must have shown, because she hurried to explain. "That sounded ungrateful. It's only that, well, I feel I have my hands full at the moment."

"You don't have to feed this, unless watering counts."

He wanted to reach for her hand, but she remained standing there, her arms crossed. Finally, she shrugged her shoulders and followed him around to the tractor.

The surprise on her face was enough for Paul.

The smile was a bonus.

"They're beautiful." She leaned forward to touch the petals, and then she leaned down to smell them.

And that was when a snake stuck its head out of the pot.

Sarah screamed and fell backward. He caught her before she hit the ground, but he couldn't hold her. She was gone, racing up the porch steps faster than raindrops fall.

"Paul Byler! You take those back right now!"

He wanted to laugh, wanted to tell her that it was only a harmless rat snake that must have been in the bottom of the pot before he set the flowers there.

Before he had a chance to explain, though, she'd turned and fled into the house. So much for cheering her up. He set the flowers on the front porch, carried the pot to the nearest field and released the snake, and then placed the empty pot back on the floor of the tractor. Perhaps she'd accept his gift if she could see there were no reptiles included.

And although the flower situation hadn't worked out as he hoped, he was grateful because for a moment the melancholy look had left her face.

CHAPTER 71

Sarah thanked the Lord with every report of Brian's recovery. He was moved from ICU, then released to rehab, and finally allowed to go home.

But her fear remained—every time she passed the accident site, when one of the children was late coming home, every time someone had a cough or sniffle.

Becca's little stack of Bible cards didn't immediately restore her faith, but Sarah did what she promised. She pulled one out each morning and read it as dawn broke on the horizon.

The LORD is compassionate and gracious, slow to anger, abounding in love.

Blessed are all who take refuge in him.

In Your presence is fullness of joy.

The words weren't new to her. She'd heard the Psalms since she was a small child on her mother's lap. Somehow, though, the words had stopped reaching her heart.

But she had promised her friend, so she continued to read one card each day.

The first week passed much as the one before it. The second week, she found her appetite slowly returning. And by the third week, she heard an unusual sound and realized it was laughter, coming from her, as Mia stood before her, covered in mud, proclaiming, "I'm dirty."

"You need to wash up."

"Why?"

"Because of the mud."

"Why?"

Her laughter had bubbled over then. Mia honestly saw nothing wrong with playing in the mud. Apparently, she'd been pretending she was a frog.

"Let's just take you to the bathtub."

"Okay." Mia skipped toward the bathroom.

"Don't touch anything."

"Why?"

Caring for a small child had its good and bad moments, but always there was joy to be shared. That joy struggled against Sarah's mood. On one level, she realized she had let fear take root in her heart. On another level, that fear seemed justified.

But joy was waiting around every corner—in the bloom of a flower, in the love of her family, in news that Becca's daughter was born healthy and weighing almost eight pounds.

By the time they attended the school picnic the second Friday in May, she felt more like herself than she had since Brian's accident, or maybe before. Possibly this malaise had been building up since Mateo and Mia were taken, since her own mother had left, since the death of her father.

Mammi never pushed. She baked and fried and roasted. She was a rock in Sarah's storm with her patience, wisdom, and silver-wrapped chocolates.

The end-of-the-year picnic was held in the school yard, and Brian was able to attend, though he still wasn't able to teach. His broken leg had given him more trouble than the internal injuries. He had graduated from a wheelchair to a walker and finally to a cane.

"Just like you, Levi," he joked.

And that, Brian's ability to laugh at himself, did more to heal Sarah's spirit than any other single thing. How could she live her life paralyzed by a fear of what *might* happen when Brian was living victoriously in the face of what *had* happened?

She'd seen him at church, but she hadn't spoken to him yet. When she walked over to where he sat and welcomed him back, he pointed to the bench next to him.

"Actually, I wanted to thank you."

"Me?"

Brian didn't answer immediately. His expression took on a faraway look. She thought that perhaps he had forgotten what he was going to say, or maybe he was too tired to visit. She stood to leave, and he pulled his gaze back toward her. The look in his eyes practically caused her knees to buckle.

"It's hard to look away from them. Don't you agree? The children? Whether it's my daughter or my son or one of my students, they're such a miracle. I think I had forgotten that before my accident. I was happy enough, but sort of…taking things for granted."

She nodded as if she understood, but she didn't. She had no idea what he was trying to say or why he was saying it to her.

"I have you to thank along with Mateo and Isaac."

"But—"

"If you hadn't taken on the responsibility of your siblings, Isaac wouldn't have been at school that afternoon. Perhaps he would have moved off to a distant relative or ended up in the foster system." He held up his hand to stay her protests. "I know. It's rare, but it does happen, even in Amish families. Any family can be broken and scattered, Sarah—whether Amish or *Englisch*."

"I suppose."

"And Mateo? If Mateo hadn't been here, if you hadn't taken in those two children, then Isaac wouldn't have stayed late. It was because they were together and there that I'm alive today."

"They care about you very much."

"And I care about them. But don't you see, Sarah? I met my destiny that Friday. The boys thought I stayed late because of them. They felt a little guilty about that." He paused at the look of surprise on her face. "I guess they haven't told you that, but they both came to me—separately— at our last church meeting. They said it was their fault. I told them what I'm telling you. If it hadn't been for Mateo and Isaac I would have bled out on the side of the road in Cody's Creek, Oklahoma."

Sarah wanted to say how glad she was that he hadn't. She wanted to assure him that someone would have come along, but in truth how did she know that?

"They bandaged my wound, ran for help, and returned to stay with me until the paramedics arrived. I owe them my life, which means that I owe you the same." He laughed. "You look a little shocked."

"*Ya*, I am."

"Don't be. I know that *Gotte* put you all in the right place at the right time, but you chose to do the right thing—and for me, it has made all the difference."

Katie arrived then, bringing Brian a little of the picnic food and chattering about something their daughter had done. Sarah managed to slip away.

The children were playing baseball, volleyball, and a dozen other games that she remembered from her childhood. The end-of-the-year school picnic was always a big event, but this year everyone had turned out—even those without children in school. They'd come together as a community to minister to Brian, and now they were joining together to celebrate his recovery.

She walked to the back of the playground, leaned against a live oak tree, and simply watched the scene around her, allowing it to bless her soul.

"Beautiful site, *ya*?" Bishop Levi offered her a piece of gum.

"*Nein. Danki.*"

"It's *gut* to see Brian back today. The Lord has provided, Sarah."

She wanted to ask about those who had died on the side of the road. It seemed every week there was another news story about a buggy accident in some other Amish community. Had God forsaken those who didn't make it? What of the ones who were hungry or lonely or abandoned?

But she didn't ask any of those questions. Instead, she nodded slightly as if she were agreeing with him.

"I was an inquisitive youngster. I must have driven my parents to distraction, questioning everything. But never once did they become angry." Levi scratched at his jawline. "They were human though, and

I remember a few days when I caused my mother to reach the end of her patience." He laughed. "She once told me I could only ask three questions a day. Any more, and I'd be given additional chores. I wasn't any bigger than Mateo."

Sarah had no idea why he was telling her this. First Brian and now the bishop. Did everyone suddenly feel an overwhelming desire to bare their soul to her? Would it be Paul next? She'd been avoiding him all day because she couldn't stand to see the concern in his eyes.

"They may have become exasperated at times, but my parents understood that I was made perfectly as I was. Our heavenly Father understands too. And I'm pretty sure He allows us more than three questions a day."

With a wink, the bishop limped away, leaving Sarah befuddled and wondering if the entire world had lost its mind. But she wasn't dense. Later that night, she sat in the front porch rocker, Mia sleeping in her lap, and watched the stars appear.

She had been questioning God, and certainly more than three times a day. She'd been questioning every single thing she didn't understand. Somewhere along the way, she'd decided God was untrustworthy, but what was the psalm she had read that morning?

Whenever I'm afraid, I will trust in You.

Sarah didn't know if she could do that, but she knew that for the sake of her family, for her own sake, she needed to try.

CHAPTER 72

For Mateo the summer flew by.

In June he helped with the harvest of the early crops that had been planted when he'd first come to Cody's Creek.

July was spent helping with Sarah's garden, fishing in Paul's creek, and caring for the pigs.

Mateo felt as if he were living in a dream. He no longer worried about Mia—Sarah and *Mammi* took care of his little sister. She was growing faster than the beans in Sarah's garden, though she still asked a dozen questions a day. Her hiding had become less frequent, and her laughter was a common sound in their home.

Their home—he dared to hope that this was permanent, that Sarah and Andy and Henry and Luke and Isaac were his family, that *Mammi* would be there for him always, and that the nightmare of his past was over.

The first week of August, Tommy drove down their lane. Mateo and Isaac were beside the barn, working on a design for a larger, better chicken coop. Their flock had grown, and they also wanted to weatherproof it for winter, which Isaac assured him was quite cold. Mateo didn't bother telling him that he knew how cold Oklahoma's winter was; he'd spent part of it in an abandoned trailer. Those were memories he'd rather not dwell on. As Bishop Levi had said at Sunday service, "Best to leave the past behind you. No need dragging it along."

When they saw Tommy's car kicking up a cloud of dirt as it came

302

down their lane, both stood, dusted off their hands, and exchanged a questioning look.

"Maybe it's only a house check again."

"*Ya*. Could be he wants to see that I haven't been eaten by a goat."

"Or trampled by one of the pigs."

"Or lost in a cornfield."

"Life on a farm is full of dangers."

They high-fived and then jogged over to meet the social worker. Tommy stepped out of his car as Sarah came out the front door of the house.

"Morning," Tommy said. He was carrying a box of donuts.

"Come on in. *Mammi* just made a fresh pot of coffee."

"*Ach*. I'll take milk," Isaac said.

Mia came running to greet Tommy. "See my baby?"

She held up a Plain doll that Sarah had finished sewing the day before. "She's like me. Same dress. Same *kapp*."

They sat around the table and enjoyed the donuts and milk and for the grown-ups—coffee. Once he'd finished off two of the chocolate cake donuts, Tommy got down to the reason for his visit.

"We have a little more information on Elisa that I wanted to share with all of you."

Mateo liked that he was included in these meetings, and though the older brothers weren't always present, Isaac was with him every time. But then they did nearly everything together, so it would have seemed strange if he wasn't there.

"What kind of information?" Sarah asked.

"She checked into a homeless shelter in Oklahoma City. She only stayed a few days, but it was long enough for them to do a few assessments."

"Assessments?"

Tommy opened a folder and shuffled through the papers. He pulled out one that looked like a form of sorts. "According to the doctor and counselor at Rachel's House, Elisa was brought to them by a police officer who found her sleeping in a public park. The doctor who makes regular visits to the shelter did a workup on Elisa."

Folding his arms, Tommy looked from Mateo to Sarah and back to Mateo again. "It appears that Elisa suffers from Alcohol Use Disorder."

"I've never heard of that." Sarah helped Mia into her lap. Mia proceeded to try to feed a piece of donut to her doll, oblivious to their discussion.

"It means Elisa has no tolerance at all for alcohol. If she has one drink, she's gone. People with Alcohol Use Disorder will often only remember that one drink. They might come to a day or a week later, and they often have no recollection of the time that has passed or what occurred. They're completely unable to control themselves once they start drinking."

"Is there any…treatment?" *Mammi* asked.

"Those diagnosed with Alcohol Use Disorder are sometimes encouraged to take Naltrexone, a drug that makes a person sick if they drink even the smallest amount of alcohol. It's not a cure, but it helps them while they're learning coping strategies."

"So Elisa is receiving this treatment?" Sarah brushed at the crumbs on Mia's mouth. Mia took the napkin out of her hand and proceeded to wipe sugar frosting from her doll.

Mateo was wishing he hadn't eaten two of the donuts. The sugar, or the conversation, was making him feel a bit sick to his stomach.

"No. The treatment plan was explained to her. According to the counselor's notes, she seemed agreeable to taking the medication, but the next morning she left the shelter and didn't return. This was last week, and no one has heard from her since."

There was silence around the table. Finally, Isaac asked, "What does this have to do with us? You wouldn't…wouldn't send Mateo and Mia back to…to someone like that. Would you?"

Tommy smiled reassuringly at him. "No, Isaac. You don't have to worry about that at all. This only confirms that Elisa isn't able to provide a safe home at this time. If and when she were to receive treatment, we could talk about monitored visitation, but Mateo and Mia would have some say in that." He directed his next comment to Mateo. "No one is going to force you to do anything that you're not comfortable with."

He stared at his empty plate as he digested what Tommy had said. Then he raised his eyes and looked around the table.

Isaac looked almost angry. He liked things to go as they were planned to go, and he had big plans for the fall—their chicken coop, school, more pigs next year.

Sarah was studying him. She'd looked less worried the last few weeks, and Mateo sometimes caught her pulling a small card out of her pocket and studying it.

Mia was oblivious.

And *Mammi*? She was watching him with a look of compassion. They had spoken several times about his mother, and each time *Mammi* had encouraged him to pray for her.

"I think I always knew my mom was sick. I guess that means what happened...that it's not completely her fault. And I might want to see her again one day...if she couldn't make me leave."

"Trust me, Mateo. That's not going to happen again."

"Because I want to stay here as long as Sarah will let me. I might feel bad about...about my mom." Tears stung his eyes, and he blinked them away. "But this is my home."

Tommy nodded, and then he pulled out another stack of papers. "Then I assume you want to move forward with the item we discussed last time I was here?"

Mateo knew what that meant. They had all talked about it again at a family meeting earlier in the week.

"I do," he said.

Sarah glanced at *Mammi*, at him and Isaac, and finally down at Mia. When she looked up, a smile covered her face, and it seemed to Mateo that it even reached her eyes.

She squeezed his hand. "*Ya*, we surely do."

"Great. I have some papers for you to sign."

CHAPTER 73

*S*arah sat outside the courtroom, glancing up and down the bench, and marveling at how much her life had changed in six short months.

The last time she'd stepped into this corridor, she had been alone, afraid, and almost at her wit's end. Looking back, she could see that she had taken the children because she'd felt immense pity for them hiding there in that abandoned trailer. Her sense of duty, or moral obligation, had propelled her through those first few weeks. But now?

Now she had learned to love them as if they were her own kin. They were as much a part of her family as *Mammi*. She wasn't the only one who cared for Mateo and Mia, who were sitting next to her on the bench. Andy, Henry, Luke, and Isaac had all insisted on coming to the hearing.

When she'd suggested that it wasn't necessary, Henry had said, "We're family, *ya*? Family stays together." And he'd brought his hands together until one palm clasped another and his fingers were intertwined.

That had brought back the memory of *Mammi* in their home, that first evening. So it was settled. They would all travel to Tulsa for the six-month hearing, even *Mammi*, who was at that very moment walking down the line handing out pieces of chocolate. It was a wonder they didn't all have a mouth full of cavities.

She nearly laughed when the bishop accepted a piece, walked over to the trash can, and spit out his chewing gum. Even he was susceptible to *Mammi's* endearing ways. Mary Beth had come as well—both she and Levi had insisted that they wanted to be there as a character reference in case the judge needed one.

The only person missing from that first court appearance was Paul. He'd offered to come along, but Sarah knew that his hands were full with work on the farm. She'd politely told him it wouldn't be necessary. Although he'd seemed disappointed, he had nodded and told her he would be praying for good results. It seemed that he had wanted to say something else, but in the end, he'd squeezed her hand and walked away.

Sarah wasn't ready to examine her feelings for him. Life was complicated enough. Perhaps when things were settled with the children.

Chloe appeared at the top of the stairs and hurried toward her. "Am I late?"

"*Nein.* The judge had one case before ours, and it's taking a bit longer than they thought it would."

The boys squished together so that Chloe could sit beside Sarah.

"Thank you for allowing me to come."

"Of course. You've been with us since the beginning."

"Any more letters criticizing you for taking in Mateo and Mia?"

"Only a few. The columns you published on adoption needs seem to have helped."

"I'm still receiving a lot of correspondence on that. Some days I wonder how people could not know the need existed, that there are plenty of children to go around." She pushed back her dark curls. "But then I didn't realize either—not until I received Becca's call about your situation. I guess some needs in our community just become invisible."

"Perhaps we don't see what makes us uncomfortable."

Chloe studied her a moment and then smiled brightly. "I think you might be right. You're a wise woman, Sarah Yoder."

And that made Sarah laugh, because most days she was fortunate not to feel lost in a sea of questions.

When they were called into the courtroom, everyone filed in with only a minimal amount of jostling and wisecracks.

Judge Murphy was already at the bench, signing sheets of paper. She glanced up when they had all settled into the first row. Smiling, she removed her glasses, folded her hands on the desktop, and peered down at them. "Well, our group has grown since last time. Perhaps you all would be so good as to tell me your names and who you are."

"Andy, and I'm the big *bruder*."

"Henry, second biggest."

"Luke. I guess I'm the middle kid—sort of."

"Isaac. I was the youngest, but now I'm not." There was no mistaking the pride in his voice.

"Mateo, but you know that."

Mia bounced in Sarah's lap. "I'm Mia, and this is Sally." She held up her doll and everyone laughed.

"I'm Sarah, the oldest."

"And I'm Fannie Yoder, but everyone calls me *Mammi*. And that suits me fine."

Sarah felt such pride in her family at that moment that it seemed as if her heart actually swelled to fill up her chest.

"Mr. and Mrs. Troyer. Still shepherding the flock?"

"We do our best."

"And I believe you're Chloe Vasquez."

"Yes, Judge."

"I recognized you from the picture in your news column. I've appreciated your recent articles on the need for more foster parents, and I'm happy to inform you that my courtroom has become a bit busier since you so thoroughly examined the topic."

"I'm glad to hear it."

The judge put her glasses back on, indicating it was time to get down to business. Tommy reported on his home visits, Mateo's progress in school, Mia's development, and ended with his recommendation that the children remain in the Yoder home.

So far the hearing had gone as he'd assured her it would. But now came the part that he wasn't so sure about. They had spoken of it before he'd left their home on his last visit.

"It will depend on a lot of factors, Sarah. I'm not going to lie to you.

It's no small thing to permanently place children in a foster home, to sever that tie between kids and their natural parent. However, in this case, I personally can wholeheartedly endorse it. How the judge will rule…well, we'll find out when we submit the request."

Judge Murphy pulled out another sheet of paper and studied it a moment. Then she said, "I have another motion from Sarah Yoder regarding Mateo Lopez and Mia Lopez. This motion is to place the children permanently in your home, and I see that it is approved and recommended by Mr. Cronin."

She again pulled off her glasses. "Before I make my ruling, I'd like a few moments to speak privately with Sarah's brothers, followed by Sarah, and then separately with Mateo and Mia. I realize this may take a few more minutes than you had anticipated, but I believe it will be worth our time. Not to mention that doing this correctly is more important than doing it quickly."

Everyone nodded in agreement, and then Sarah's brothers trooped into the judge's chambers. Sarah's heart began to beat more rapidly. She turned to *Mammi*. "Do you think that's *gut* or bad?"

"It's neither," Tommy said, moving over to their side of the aisle. "Judge Murphy likes to give everyone involved a chance to express their thoughts in a less intimidating setting."

"The judge's room is less intimidating?" *Mammi* asked.

"Well, at least you're not trying to be heard across the courtroom." Tommy placed his hand on Sarah's shoulder. "Don't worry. She's a good judge."

Mia began to hide her doll under the bench, and then inside *Mammi*'s large shoulder bag, and finally in the bishop's lap. Sarah suspected she would attempt to hide herself next and was determined not to take her eyes off the girl. But then her brothers trooped out and the judge was calling her into chambers.

CHAPTER 74

*P*aul had made an honest effort to focus on his work, yet he'd managed to spill the feed he attempted to put into the pigs' buckets, let the goats out of the pen, and stall the tractor twice. Finally, he decided he was creating more work than he was completing, so he had a quick lunch and took his fishing pole to the stream.

After he'd lost his bait three times, never once noticing that the line had been pulled, he gave up on that as well. Best to sit and think good thoughts for Sarah. Who was he kidding? Better to pray.

Paul had never experienced the crisis of faith that Sarah had struggled with, but neither did he consider himself especially spiritual. He prayed at church, thanked God for his food, and occasionally petitioned the Almighty regarding the weather.

But that afternoon, as he waited for the Yoder family to return, he found himself turning to God on his friends' behalf. He prayed that Sarah would remain calm and sure of God's plan. He petitioned God for the very best decision for Mateo and Mia. He prayed for safety as everyone traveled to Tulsa and back. Finally, he prayed that his feelings for Sarah would not be in vain, and that God would use him to somehow bless her.

When he could wait no longer, he walked over to the farm, hoping the exercise would use up some of his excess energy. He passed the *Englischer's* van as it was leaving, and he thought of retracing his steps.

"Now probably isn't the best time," he muttered.

But he could no more turn around and go home than he could ask the sun to set an hour early. So he continued down the lane and climbed the porch steps.

No children in sight.

No indication of how things had gone.

Tentatively he knocked on the front screen door, resisting the urge to peer inside.

Mammi opened the door. "Paul. Come in."

"How did it go? What did the judge say?"

Mammi's smile should have been enough to calm his nerves, but it was Sarah—walking out of *Mammi's* room with a relieved, "She's finally asleep," that calmed any fears in his heart.

"Oh, Paul. I didn't know you were here."

"*Ya*, he just came to check on us." *Mammi* patted her pockets, and finding them empty looked temporarily befuddled.

Sarah actually laughed. "I'll go and fetch a few of the oatmeal cookies you made last night. We can eat them on the porch."

But *Mammi* was suddenly too busy to join them. She might have winked at him, but Paul wasn't sure. He followed Sarah into the kitchen to help.

"You don't have to feed me." His stomach betrayed him with a loud grumble.

"Is that so?" Sarah added some cheese and crackers to the plate.

Since she wouldn't let him help, he stood with his back resting against the counter, arms crossed, enjoying the sight of her. The ache he sometimes experienced when he watched her resembled an actual physical pain. He'd made a miserable mess of showing her how he felt. The picnic and the flowers and the attempts to woo her with chickens and goats had all failed. Perhaps it was time that he speak candidly with her.

"Outside or in?" she asked.

"Here's *gut*." He loved their kitchen. Loved the way it was filled with tantalizing odors. Enjoyed looking at the many chairs around the table and remembering the meals he had shared there. If he were honest with himself, it felt more like his home than the corner of the barn he was living in.

"Where are the boys?"

"Scattered. They couldn't get out of the van fast enough. Andy and Henry had work to do. I believe Luke is playing with the neighbor boy, though he promised me it wouldn't be video games."

"Mateo and Isaac?"

"Still working on enlarging the chicken coop. They're making it three levels high this time."

She sat beside him, close enough that Paul had to resist the urge to reach out and touch her face, run his fingers down her arm, kiss her lips.

Confused, he crammed two crackers and a piece of cheese in his mouth, and then he realized he couldn't say a word until he chewed and swallowed.

He didn't have to ask, though. Sarah told him about Tommy's recommendations, the judge's questions, and how she had called them separately into her chambers.

"What did she ask your *bruders*?"

"If they resented having two more in the family. I think she doesn't truly understand what it means to be Amish."

"Or maybe she comes from a small family herself."

"Maybe so."

"Mateo and Mia?"

"If they were happy, how Mateo liked school, whether they were ready to move forward."

"And what did she ask you?"

"If I was sure. How I felt about taking on so much responsibility. I…I found myself telling her about Brian and how it had, well, unsettled me. She said it's normal to have that kind of fear, especially for new moms."

"*Ya*. I remember one of my sisters-in-law refusing to allow her newborn into a buggy. She was determined to stay home with that child rather than risk an accident." Paul hadn't thought of that in a long time. "We hadn't had a buggy accident in years. In fact, our community in Indiana has both the triangles and the lights on the back. I suppose it's normal to feel protective of one so young."

"Judge Murphy said the same thing. She said it doesn't matter that

Mateo and Mia are older. Part of my mind still thinks of them as newborns."

"And you asked her about the permanent placement?"

"I did." Sarah finally met his gaze. "She's going to consider it, and we return in six months."

"Is that *gut* or bad?"

"Tommy assures us it's normal. She's very careful regarding her responsibility to do what's right for the children."

"Surely they would be better off knowing they're here permanently, that their life isn't going to change again."

"Mateo and Mia are doing well right now. She assured me that slower is better as far as change goes."

"I suppose."

Paul suddenly realized that Sarah was staring at his shirt. He looked down to see if maybe he'd spilled something on himself.

"What?"

"Your button."

"Oh. *Ya*, that fell off last time I washed it."

"But—"

"So I sewed it back on."

"You sewed it wrong."

She leaned closer to examine the offending button. "You sewed it from the inside out."

"I know that—now. But at the time, it seemed right, and then later, when I put the shirt on, I didn't have time to fix it."

Her laughter spilled out and across the kitchen.

He wanted to be offended, but it was impossible to be anything but happy when Sarah smiled.

"So you're mocking my sewing skills."

"*Ya*. They are worse than your dishwashing."

"Oh, they are, now?"

"You need a wife, Paul Byler."

She said it in jest. He knew that when she clamped her hand over her mouth, but he couldn't resist teasing her, couldn't resist testing the waters.

"Would you know anyone interested in the position?" He pulled her hand away from her mouth, held it between his, and then he kissed her softly on the palm.

"Ewww. That's disgusting." Isaac shoulder-bumped Mateo, who was standing beside him in the doorway to the mudroom.

"Tell me about it." Mateo rolled his eyes. "I saw Andy kissing Emma after church on Sunday."

"I do not get it."

"I don't want to get it."

The boys grabbed a couple of cookies from the plate and made their way back outside, discussing whether to use goat fencing or chicken wire on the chicken coop.

Sarah jerked her hand away from him and jumped up, declaring she needed to be preparing dinner.

But Paul thought he detected a slight flush on her face, which he took to be a good sign. Now all he had to do was figure out a way to court her.

CHAPTER 75

*F*or Sarah, the months of fall passed like a train barreling down the tracks.

In September Mateo and Isaac returned to school, this time without Luke, who had officially graduated at the end of May. Rather than take a job at one of the restaurants in town, he opted to work with Andy. Their brother needed the help because the work on their farm had increased as they'd gained animals and planted winter crops. Plus, there was the fact that Henry wouldn't be around as much. He had decided to apprentice with a member of their community who had a small engine repair shop. Moses Miller's place was on the east side of their district, and he was of the opinion that there was enough work for Henry to hang out his own shingle on the west side of town.

"I have a lot to learn before I can do that," he'd assured everyone when they had their weekly family meeting.

"How will you get to the Millers' each day?" *Mammi* asked.

"Walk to town and catch a ride with Frank Meeks. He delivers orders for Rebecca and Joseph. I asked when I was in town yesterday, and Rebecca says that he starts on the east side and works his way back toward town. He can drop me off in the morning. In the evenings, I'll either catch a ride with Moses or walk home."

"Even with a ride, that will be a walk of two miles each way," Andy pointed out.

315

"It's not a problem." Henry bounced a tennis ball to Mateo, who sent it back. "Except maybe when it snows."

"We'll deal with that problem when and if the time comes," *Mammi* said. "For now, it sounds like you have a *gut* plan."

In October Sarah received her first letter from her mother. She sat staring at the envelope, unsure if she wanted to open it, convinced it could only hold bad news.

"You won't know until you read what she has written," *Mammi* said, and then she'd convinced Mia to follow her out to the garden to check on their gourds. Her latest project was to hollow them out and turn them into bird feeders. So far they'd sold several dozen on weekends when they opened their produce stand.

Sarah walked to the utensil drawer, fetched a knife, and slit the envelope. Then she sat down and smoothed the single sheet out with a trembling hand. So many different emotions were running through her heart that she could barely focus on the words in front of her. She closed her eyes, whispered a prayer, and tried again.

Dear Children,

I suppose that you know I am with my aenti in Sarasota. Mammi has faithfully written me once a week and kept me up to date on how you are. Please thank her for me. When I didn't have enough courage to call, to reach out to you, she eased my worries and soothed the ache within my heart.

There are so many regrets, so many things I wish I could do again. That's not possible, though, is it? So instead I will ask your forgiveness. I should not have left you when I did. No matter how sick I was, I should not have put my own needs first.

I am so proud of each of you. Andy and Sarah—Mammi tells me you have turned into fine adults. Henry, Luke, and Isaac—I think of you more than you can ever imagine. Mateo and Mia—I can picture you so well from Mammi's descriptions. I hope to meet you one day.

It seems inadequate to say I pray for you every morning when I rise and every evening before I sleep, but I do. Memories of you fill my heart, and I hope that one day when I'm better, we can be reunited again. For now know that the sunshine and the doctors are helping me, and I am improving every day.

If you decide not to write to me, I understand. However, if you can find it in your heart to forgive me...you can't imagine what it would mean to receive a letter from you.

With much love,
Mamm

Sarah read the letter twice and then a third time. Finally, she became aware of *Mammi* and Mia sitting on the front porch, singing songs. She folded the letter, slipped it into the envelope, and walked out onto the porch.

Sinking into the rocker next to *Mammi*, she said, "I didn't know that you were writing her every week."

"I write all of my children once a week, and Deborah is still my child."

"What...what is wrong with her? She mentioned doctors."

"The doctors determined that your mother has a fairly severe thyroid problem. They've been treating it with medication, and it seems the sunnier winter helped her with some of the depression."

"Oh." Sarah felt numb. She'd wondered about her mother every day. She'd imagined the worst things. She'd been angry, and she'd been worried. She had feared that her mother was lost to her forever.

"She wants us to write. Do you...do you think we should?"

"That's a decision you will have to make, Sarah. I wish I could tell you what to do." *Mammi* rocked and stared out across their land. "Only...only know that I am glad I came here. This family has been such a blessing to me. I imagine you wish your mother had acted differently, but if she hadn't left, I might not have come. So I am grateful, *ya*, it's true. I'm grateful that her troubles brought us together, though I would rather she had an easier path."

That evening Sarah wrote her first letter to her mother. After she'd read Deborah's letter to her brothers, each wanted to add to the letter she'd written, even Mateo, who hadn't met her, and Mia, who drew a picture filled with each of them, all with long arms and big heads. She'd insisted that Sarah label each family member. It wasn't lost on Sarah that Paul was included in the picture.

CHAPTER 76

As fall turned to winter, Sarah allowed herself to spend more time with Paul. She enjoyed their walks around both farms. She replayed their conversations over everything from ways to increase the production on the land to the beauty of a sunset over a snow-covered field.

She watched as the boys became even closer to Paul. It was plain to her that they looked up to him as they did to Andy. Soon it was time to kill the pigs. They had grown quite large, and the ones they had sold had fetched an excellent price. But they kept three to provide meat for the winter. The boys insisted on being there when they were butchered, saying they weren't babies and they had understood from the beginning that the pigs had been raised for food.

She appreciated the way that Paul explained the process to the boys, assured them that the pigs wouldn't suffer, and answered their questions. She thought perhaps she saw tears in their eyes, but within a week they were planning improvements to the pen for next year's piglets.

Paul assured her the boys would be fine, and they were. It seemed that he understood her worries before she did herself.

Twice he kissed her.

The first time was on Christmas afternoon, when he'd asked her to go for a walk and given her his gift. She'd been so surprised when she'd pulled off the wrapping and stared down at the wooden box.

"It's beautiful." She'd ran her fingers over the scene on the top. "Did you carve this?"

"*Ya*. It's supposed to be the scene from your front porch. I was thinking you could use it for small things you save from the children."

"Like the tooth Mia lost last week?"

"Exactly. It was actually my mother's idea."

He had talked to his mother about her?

"She told me a mother needs a place to put away special memories. That children grow so quickly, you'll be glad you saved a few things."

"I...I don't know what to say."

"Don't say anything."

And then he'd leaned toward her and kissed her softly, leaving her breathless and happy and confused.

The second time he kissed her was on the first day of the new year. "May this year bring you many *gut* things, Sarah Yoder."

His attention left her confused. She thought she should be focused on the children, on taking care of their home, on improving the relationship she had with her mother.

When she confessed as much to *Mammi*, her grandmother waved away her concerns. "Never think you are too busy for love, Sarah. Love is what carries us through the bad days and sweetens the good."

But Sarah wasn't so sure. There were too many questions, things she didn't even want to voice. Why did anything have to change? Finally life was good. They were able to pay their own way. In February they would again return to family court, and while Judge Murphy could postpone her ruling, Sarah thought she wouldn't. She thought that the judge would decide—one way or the other—when they saw her again.

It was on Valentine's that Paul asked her to marry him. She'd finally agreed to go to dinner, something he'd tried to convince her to do for many weeks. She almost laughed when he picked her up in his horse and buggy, and it seemed as if they were both remembering the first picnic they'd shared, the ride on his old decrepit tractor, the way the day had turned sour.

But dinner at the small restaurant downtown was *gut*. They never ran out of things to talk about, and Sarah felt herself relaxing around him—something that happened more and more often.

When he'd pulled into her lane, she'd gathered up her bag and tightened the belt on her coat.

Paul reached out and said, "I was hoping we could talk for a minute."

"Here?" Night had fallen, but a crescent moon shone on the snow-covered fields.

"*Ya*, so we could have some...um...privacy."

He'd pulled the buggy to a stop, checked the battery heater to be sure it continued to pump out heat, and then he turned toward her and removed his hat.

"I think you know how I feel about you."

"You're a *gut* friend."

"I want to be more than that."

She didn't know what to say, so she stared at her hands.

"You are an amazing woman, Sarah Yoder. I knew it the first time you came into the store, buying flour and oats and insisting you could carry it all yourself. I've probably loved you since then."

"Paul—"

"Let me say this. It's...it's important that I say it. I watched all of my *bruders* marry, but I thought it would never happen to me. I was happy being a bachelor, though I knew...I knew I wanted to be a farmer." Now he glanced out across the fields.

When he turned toward her again, Sarah thought that surely he could hear her heart hammering in her chest.

"Buying this farm brought me closer to you. I want to marry you, Sarah. I love you, and I want to be your husband."

"I can't...I can't answer that question right now."

"Okay." He frowned, reminding her of that first time in the dry goods store when she'd thought he was such an unfriendly person.

"We're about to find out about Mateo and Mia. And Henry wants to start his own business in the spring. Andy, he's broken up with Emma twice, but now—"

"Sarah, I love your family. I understand that you're under a lot of pressure. I don't want to add to that."

"But you are! I can't make a decision like this. Not now."

He'd pulled her hands into his lap and rubbed her fingers until they were no longer numb. He looked at her and said, "Just promise me you'll think about it."

"*Ya*. I will."

"That's all I ask."

It was two days before she shared the conversation with *Mammi*. She'd expected her grandmother to tell her to follow her heart or remind her again of the importance of love, but instead she'd simply put a piece of chocolate in her hand and said, "We'll pray about this, Sarah. Both of us will."

A week later they received a letter from the court, saying the date for their hearing had been postponed until May.

CHAPTER 77

Henry, Luke, Isaac, Mateo, and Mia stood in a line in front of the couch—fidgeting, tugging on their clothes, and whispering to one another. It was rare for the children to miss a day of school, but Sarah had readily agreed that everyone should go to the court hearing. To her each and every person in front of the couch was a part of her family. They looked related to one another, and it wasn't just because of their Plain clothing. They watched out for one another, loved one another. Even now Mateo was helping Isaac with something in his pocket.

"That had better not be a frog," Luke said. "No amphibians in the judge's courtroom."

"*Nein*, it's not," Isaac assured him.

"It's something much better, Sarah." Mateo and Isaac exchanged a high five, and Sarah decided what was or wasn't in the boy's pocket wouldn't matter.

What mattered was what the judge thought when she looked at the five of them, plus Andy and herself and, of course, *Mammi*. Surely Judge Murphy would see the affection that Sarah saw. It told the story of what they'd been through together. The way they interacted with one another was what mattered, not who their birth mother was.

But would it be enough? After all, their skin color told a different story. Mateo's and Mia's dark to their light. In the end, it would depend on what the judge chose to see.

"Everyone ready? *Gut*." *Mammi* marched into the room, wearing her dark blue dress and white apron, its pockets bulging with chocolate candies.

"You'll ruin their teeth." Sarah crossed and recrossed her arms as *Mammi* walked down the row passing out the treats.

"*Nein.* They brush their teeth several times a day and see Doc Jerry regularly. No worries about that, Sarah."

Andy pushed through the back door. "The van is here."

Sarah was relieved to see that he had somehow found the time to change into clean clothes. He'd taken on all the chores himself that morning—caring for the horse and donkey, goats and chickens, so Sarah wouldn't worry over the younger ones being ready on time.

In her heart, Sarah knew she couldn't convince the judge with proper clothes and clean hands. Judge Murphy seemed to be a wise woman, someone who looked past a person's words to their deeds. But the *Englisch* world was different than theirs. Sarah didn't know if Judge Murphy would decide that a more traditional family would be best for Mateo and Mia. As she'd done a thousand times in the last month, her soul offered up a prayer. *Mammi* had reminded her just the night before that the outcome was already determined. She believed her grandmother and vowed in her heart that she would do her best not to try to wrestle it away from God's competent hands.

They all fit in the van with one seat belt to spare. Why was there an extra seat? She'd carefully planned...

"Mia's gone." Andy immediately unbuckled and ducked out of the van.

"But she was just here." Sarah thought she'd watched the girl closely. How did she manage to slip away? And why?

Luke patted her on the shoulder. "I'll check the bedrooms."

"I'll check the kitchen," Henry said.

"We'll check the kitchen and mudroom." Mateo and Isaac hurried toward the back of the house.

They scattered out, searching in all of Mia's favorite hiding places.

It was Sarah who found her, standing in the middle of their garden, clutching a fistful of spring weeds that had bloomed beside their rows of vegetables.

"For you, Sarah." Mia ran over to her and held up her gift.

A smudge of dirt now marred her newly laundered apron, and a bit of her dark hair had escaped from her *kapp*. Small things. Unimportant things. Sarah focused on the gift and chose to ignore the rest.

"See? Flowers."

"I see. I do." She gathered Mia in her arms, making a show of smelling the flowers. "*Danki.*"

Mia rested her head on Sarah's chest, but for once she didn't stick her thumb into her mouth. Instead she whispered, "I love you."

"I love you too, Mia."

She hurried to the van, her brothers tumbling out of the house to join her.

As they pulled out on the two-lane, she glanced toward Paul's place. Her hands began to sweat and her heart thumped more forcefully against her breastbone. Why had she allowed herself to fall in love with Paul Byler? Didn't she have enough to deal with emotionally? She should be completely focused on the children, not on an adolescent dream of two people living happily ever after. Too often she found her thoughts wandering toward him, acting like a teenager who was moonstruck over a boy.

But she wasn't a teenager. She was an adult with the responsibilities of an adult. She was the mother of the children around her.

As if sensing the direction of her thoughts, *Mammi* reached over and squeezed her hand, but she offered no words of wisdom. What could she say that she hadn't already? Sarah understood. She knew it was her choice to accept *Mammi's* wisdom or struggle through this season of life figuring things out on her own.

And what had *Mammi* said just last night?

Either Sarah decided to trust Paul, to trust the life he offered, or she didn't. That was a decision she would have to make…but not today.

Today was about the children.

CHAPTER 78

*P*aul climbed into the SUV with Joseph, Rebecca, and Bishop Levi. They'd had a short discussion the night before as to whether they should go. Bishop Levi was going because he wanted to provide spiritual support whichever way the case was decided. Paul's brother and sister-in-law were going because they had come to think of Sarah as one of their own. And Paul? In the end he decided he would go because he'd been there since the beginning, since the day he'd walked in on Sarah doing the laundry, Mateo dripping in rinse water, and Mia hiding on a bottom shelf.

He hadn't realized that he'd lost his heart to the family that afternoon, but he had. It was something he was willing to admit now—finally. Though there was much work still to do on his farm, the work would be there the next day. Today, he would support Sarah.

They waited until the van Sarah was riding in had pulled in beside them. The two drivers worked out their route to the courthouse in Tulsa, and the van's driver took the lead.

He only caught a glimpse of Sarah. She was sitting in the middle seat, and glanced at him long enough for Paul to give her a thumbs-up.

"Try not to worry," Rebecca said.

"She still hasn't given me her answer."

Rebecca shared a look with Joseph. Then she pulled her knitting from her bag and said, "Sarah has a lot to deal with right now."

"*Ya*, that she does."

"And no answer is nearly a yes," Joseph said.

"That makes no sense."

"It does! If a customer tells me *no*, they don't want something, I respect their decision. But if they tell me *maybe*, then the door is open for me to sell them that item."

"But this isn't something I'm selling her. This is our future."

"Still, a maybe is better than a no."

Paul wasn't so sure. With a no, he could go on with his life—lonely existence though it might be. A maybe meant that his heart kept hoping.

As if sensing the desperate turn of his thoughts, Rebecca began chatting about the beautiful weather and how grateful she was that the rains had stopped.

Paul allowed his mind to drift to thoughts of the courtroom. Would today make Sarah's life better or worse?

If the judge decided against permanent placement, her heart would be broken. Would she be able to accept the decision? They had talked about it often enough. Paul knew that she ached for Elisa Lopez. She told him once that she prayed every night for the children's mother, that she might find help and healing.

But neither of them believed the children would be better in that situation—moving from town to town, subject to Elisa's relapses.

There was another reason the judge might rule against permanent placement. She might decide that the children would be better off with a Hispanic family. Could such a family love them more? No. But they could offer both Mateo and Mia more insight into their cultural heritage.

Paul had no idea how the judge would rule. The bishop had explained that she might again postpone making a decision. Everything would be done with the children's best interest in mind. Paul didn't understand the *Englisch* well enough to even hazard a guess as to what the outcome would be, and he certainly wasn't familiar with their legal system.

As much as he loved those two children, all of Sarah's brothers, in fact, his main concern today was Sarah.

Would she be able to handle another major disappointment?

Did she want to marry him?

Would she need time before moving on with her life?

Of course, there was a good chance that the judge would decide in favor of permanent placement, in which case Sarah would find herself a single parent to five children. That wasn't completely true. She had *Mammi* to help her. And Henry was a man now, able to care for himself. His small engine business was doing remarkably well.

Paul also didn't doubt for a minute that Andy would always provide for her. Even after he married, which Paul suspected would be sooner than anyone thought, Andy would still be there for Sarah and all of the children—including Mateo and Mia.

The two Lopez youngsters had worked their way into the heart of everyone, not just Sarah.

"Did Sarah like the honey you took her?" Rebecca continued to knit as they sped down the highway toward Tulsa.

"*Ya*. She said it would be *gut* for the children's allergies."

"It's true. Local honey helps in many ways."

Paul found himself looking for small things to take them when he visited. On the nights he wasn't there to help put the younger children to bed, he felt a hole in his life that he'd never noticed before. He didn't regret that he'd never married. Before Sarah, there had been no one he'd even considered himself suitable for. Was he a good match for her?

He found no answers as they made their way west, into the city, and parked next to the courthouse. As they poured out of the two vehicles, several people turned to stare at their group, which he supposed was larger than most.

Mammi shepherded the boys inside like a mother goose. Sarah had a firm grasp of Mia's hand.

"Have we had an escape this morning?" Paul asked.

"*Ya*, we have. I'm determined not to lose her in the courthouse."

"Paul! Pick me up."

Once he'd raised her in the air, she patted his face with her left hand. In her other hand she held a wilted clump of something.

"I got Sarah flowers."

"I see that."

They traipsed up the stairs to the second-floor waiting room and took a seat on the long bench. Had it been more than a year ago that he'd traveled here with Sarah? It had been a mercy trip then. She'd been so terrified of losing the children. Was she terrified still?

He caught her eye and smiled. He wanted to pull her into his arms and assure her that everything would be fine, but there was no time.

Chloe hurried over to them as soon as she turned the corner from the stairwell.

"I was worried you might be caught in traffic. I went downstairs to look for you and must have missed you."

"We were a few minutes late taking off," Sarah explained.

They both turned to study Mia, who was being led to a bench by *Mammi*.

"Well, I'm glad everything turned out fine." Chloe pulled Sarah into a hug and began to laugh, wiping at her cheeks. "I don't know why I'm crying. I'm just so excited for you all."

An *Englischer* stepped out of Family Courtroom 3. He was a bald man with a protruding belly. The man looked like a police officer, but Paul had learned the last time that he was in fact the courtroom deputy. He was there to make sure everything proceeded smoothly. His name was Carson, and he liked to fish. That was all he'd learned about the man before.

Deputy Carson raised an eyebrow when he spotted them. Perhaps they made an odd group for the adoption of two small children.

"Yoder and Lopez families?" He glanced down at a clipboard. "Immediate family only."

"That's us." Sarah motioned for her brothers and Mia and Mateo and *Mammi* to stand.

He didn't seem at all surprised to have Amish people in his courtroom. "Follow me, please."

But if the man had hoped to keep a professional distance, he failed miserably. Mia ran up to him, pushing the wilted flowers toward him and proclaiming, "I got Sarah flowers!"

Deputy Carson looked left, looked right, and then he hitched up his pants and squatted down in front of her. "Those are awfully pretty. Now who might Sarah be?"

Mia pointed to Sarah, whose cheeks turned a pretty pink.

"I'd say Sarah is one lucky lady."

Everyone else in their party had stood when Deputy Carson walked out.

Now Rebecca hugged Sarah. "We'll be praying while we wait."

Sarah nodded and glanced at Paul, but apparently she didn't trust herself to speak.

Bishop Levi followed the family into the courtroom, explaining to the court officer that he was their bishop.

Chloe sighed and crossed her arms. She sat down and pulled out her phone. She stared at it a moment as if she wasn't seeing whatever was on the small screen, and finally she stuffed it back into her purse. Closing her eyes, she leaned forward, elbows on her knees and palms pressed together, and began to pray.

The large wooden door to the courtroom clicked shut, leaving Paul on a wooden bench, in the hall of an *Englisch* courtroom, wondering what was to become of his life.

CHAPTER 79

Sarah's right arm began to tremble as she walked to the front row in the courtroom. She clasped it to her side. What if the judge noticed? She should be confident, not nervous. She stopped at the front row, and each of her brothers filed past her, pausing to give her a quick hug or squeeze her hand. Andy, Henry, Luke, Isaac, and Mateo. Her grandmother passed next, holding Mia's hand. *Mammi* winked, and Mia reached over and patted her face. Bishop Levi took a seat behind them, smiling at her confidently.

And suddenly Sarah was no longer afraid. With each gesture of appreciation, her confidence returned a little more until suddenly she wasn't merely pretending to be confident. She was confident. God had given her this family—all of them. It wasn't conventional. On paper, it didn't make much sense. But these were the people she loved the most…these and those waiting in the hall, including one man whose gaze told her that he was longing to share his life with her.

When she sat, Mia crawled onto her lap, yawning and resting her head against Sarah's chest. It was time for the child's nap, and she should have a snack first. Her mind skipped over the typical tasks of a Monday, and then her thoughts settled back on the courtroom.

Sarah didn't know what the judge would decide. She didn't have a vision of the future. God didn't whisper in her ear. He didn't have to. He'd already spoken to her—through His words in their family Bible and through the actions and words of those who loved her. And what exactly had everyone said?

Don't be afraid, Sarah.

God's got this, Sarah.

You can trust Him.

Fear not.

Mateo and Mia would be a part of her heart forever. She'd been changed by them. She'd become a person she didn't even know she was capable of being. Oh, she still made a mess when she cooked dinner, and she wasn't the best housekeeper, but she knew how to love children. God had given her that ability in abundance.

The courtroom clerk stood and said, "All rise for the Honorable Judge Murphy."

The judge wore the same black robe as before, but now she sported blond highlights running through her chestnut-colored hair. Chloe had told her the judge was forty-four years old. To Sarah she looked both young and old. Young in her appearance, including the brightly colored earrings and purple framed glasses. Old in her eyes, in the way she looked at children, and in her mannerisms—pausing before she spoke, nodding sympathetically as she listened to someone, her thoughtful expressions. Sarah didn't doubt for a moment that this woman loved children and strove to find the best home possible for them.

"How is everyone this morning?"

Nine heads, including Sarah's, bobbed up and down.

They were good. They were together.

"This is both a review hearing and a permanency hearing for the placement of Mateo and Mia Lopez into the home of Sarah Yoder."

"Yes, your honor." Tommy Cronin sat across from them. He seemed as pale as the last time Sarah had seen him, and if anything his red hair was cut even shorter than before. The large black glasses were the same. He stood, pressed his tie down flat, and cleared his throat. "We submitted all of the standard paperwork to the court, including the home visit reports, initial family medical evaluations and background checks, and letters of reference."

"I see that." Judge Murphy shuffled papers for a few moments before closing the folder and removing her glasses. She directed her comments to Sarah. "I've thoroughly reviewed the information Mr. Cronin sent me. Thank you for complying completely and quickly with this court's requests. You've made my job easier."

The court reporter sat at her small typewriter, recording every word said. She was young—probably Sarah's age—and rarely looked up from her work.

Now the judge turned her gaze toward the children. "At our last visit I had the opportunity to meet with your brothers."

Andy, Henry, Luke, and Isaac each offered a small wave.

"And I also visited with both Mateo and Mia."

Mateo offered a similar wave. Mia turned and whispered to Sarah. At first Sarah nodded, hoping to appease the child, but then she began to shake her head. Mia placed both hands on Sarah's face. "Please, Sarah. Please."

Tommy Cronin must have noticed what was happening because he hurried across the aisle to see what the issue was. Sarah whispered Mia's request. Tommy straightened up, turned to the judge, and said, "My client, Mia Lopez, would like permission to approach the bench, your honor."

"Oh. Well, that's a bit unusual, but all right."

Mia jumped from Sarah's lap and ran to the front of the room, pausing a few feet from the judge to straighten her apron. Sarah had thought perhaps Mia shouldn't wear her *kapp* today. She had even considered purchasing *Englisch* clothes for Mia and Mateo. In the end Mateo had claimed that would be a foolish use of their money, and Mia had insisted she wanted to wear her Plain clothing. "Like you, Sarah."

And so earlier that morning, *Mammi* had wound her dark tresses into a braid, pinned it in a coil, and fastened the *kapp* onto her head. Now Mia stopped a few feet from the judge, disentangled her *kapp* strings from where they'd fallen into the bunch of flowers, and smiled up at the judge. She hurried to the side of the bench, where Judge Murphy was waiting.

"I got these for Sarah," Mia was attempting to whisper, but as usual her excitement raised her voice. They could all hear the girl's explanation. "I want to give them to you now. Look! The purple matches your glasses."

She pushed the flowers into the judge's hands and added, "Sarah says it's okay."

"Why, thank you, Mia."

"They smell *gut*, see?" The young girl moved the flowers closer to the judge's face. When Judge Murphy laughed, everyone else in the courtroom did as well.

"I love them."

Pleased, Mia turned and scampered back to Sarah, practically bouncing into her lap.

The judge reclaimed her seat, put on her glasses, and once again shuffled through the papers in the folder.

"There has been one new development in this case since we last met. I would like to address this with Sarah and Mia and Mateo in my chambers." She pulled off her glasses and looked solemnly from Mateo to Mia to Sarah. Then she cleared her throat and said, "We were successful in contacting the children's mother."

CHAPTER 80

$\mathcal{M}$ ateo wasn't afraid of the judge, but neither did he want to leave his brothers and walk to the judge's office. Isaac, who always knew what he was thinking, pulled their school paper from his pocket and pushed it into Mateo's hands.

"Take this with you. Maybe it will help."

The paper had been folded a number of times and easily fit into Mateo's pocket. He nodded his thanks, and then he followed Sarah, his sister, and their social worker out of the courtroom.

Instead of moving behind her desk, the judge sat in a large upholstered chair with a footstool. She motioned to the other chairs that were positioned around her. Sarah sat in one, and Mia crawled onto her lap. Tommy sat in the other, which left the footstool for Mateo. He didn't mind, but he would have felt more comfortable just sitting on the rug.

"I wanted to read this letter to you in private, though it will be a part of your permanent record. Your mother wrote the letter in Spanish, but I had it translated into English. Can you read Spanish, Mateo?"

"*Ya*. My teacher has been working with me. He says it's good for me to be bilingual."

"Indeed it is." She handed a copy to Mateo. "I'll read it aloud in English, and you can follow along in Spanish."

When Mateo touched the paper, he felt so many things at once that he thought he might fall off the stool.

He felt relief that his mother was alive. She must be alive if she'd written a letter.

He felt fear that this would change everything, that he would lose his place in the Yoder family.

And a very small part of him, a part that was as young as Mia and as naive, felt hope that perhaps the letter would contain good news.

Judge Murphy cleared her voice and began to read.

Dear Mateo and Mia,

I am very sorry that I did not come back to the old trailer. I meant to, but I didn't—and that was wrong. I regret that. I also know that is was wrong to snatch you off the road and drag you to Tulsa. I regret many things in my life. The one thing I'm proud of is the two of you.

The social worker here explained to me that Sarah wants to take care of you. God is good.

Gracias a Dios. Mateo read the Spanish words and wondered if that meant his mother believed in God. He realized the judge was still reading and scanned down the page to catch up with her.

I want you to have what I couldn't give you—food and clothes and a place to stay. Maybe you can even go to school now.

Judge Murphy turned the paper over to the back, but she didn't continue reading right away. Instead she looked over her glasses at Sarah and Mia and Mateo. Sarah had tears in her eyes, and both of her arms were around Mia, who was sucking her thumb. Mateo tried to swallow the huge lump in his throat. He felt as if he'd eaten too many of Sarah's cookies all at once. He was glad the judge was reading. He couldn't see the words on his sheet very well because his eyes were full of tears. So he nodded and hoped she would continue.

I want to be with you both. I do, but I am too sick to be a mommy right now. I am doing better, so don't worry about me. I am living at the shelter. We have two meals a day here and are even able to see doctors. Some days I think that I will get better, but other days I'm not so sure. That's not what is important, though. The important thing is that I love you both, and I always will.

No one said anything for a few moments. Judge Murphy placed the paper in her folder, and she motioned for Mateo to keep the copy he was holding. He didn't know what to do with it—this goodbye note from his mother—so he folded it and put it in his pocket, and that was when he found the school paper. He pulled it out and unfolded it, staring at his writing and Isaac's.

And then he did something he had dreamt of doing. He handed the sheet to the judge.

"Is this something you wrote?"

"Yes. It was an assignment in school. Brian, our teacher, told us to buddy up with someone and trace each other's hands."

"Brian is Amish?" The judge had pulled off her glasses, but now she put them back on.

Mateo shrugged because he didn't know if Brian was Amish or not. He turned and looked at Sarah.

"He became Amish," she said. "He was raised *Englisch*."

Tommy leaned forward, to get a better look at the paper.

Judge Murphy motioned for Mateo to go on.

"So you trace and cut out the other person's hand. Inside the hand, you write three things that are special about that person. But you don't show it to them. Not yet. So we...we couldn't see what each other was writing."

The judge's eyebrow went up, and now Sarah was interested. She shifted Mia, who had fallen asleep in her lap and leaned forward. Mateo and Isaac hadn't shown the paper to Sarah when they brought it home. They had wanted to surprise her after the court day was over. Sarah always smiled at their work. She was proud of what they did and collected the papers in a box. So their plan had been to show it to her at dinner, later that day. But then Mateo had told Isaac about his dream.

In the dream he'd walked into the courthouse alone. The place was dark and quiet, and he'd been a little frightened. When he'd found the right courtroom and walked in, Sarah had been sitting at the back— crying. Mateo hadn't known what to do. He'd never seen Sarah cry before. So he'd walked to the front of the room, where the judge was washing dishes.

"There's no sink or dishes in the courtroom." Isaac had laughed and held his stomach and laughed some more. Eventually, Mateo had begun to laugh with him, and he'd felt less upset about the dream.

"Then what happened?" Isaac asked.

"I gave her the paper from school."

"What happened after that?" Now Isaac's voice was quiet and serious.

"I don't know. The rooster crowed and I woke up."

Isaac had insisted they should take it with them to the courthouse.

"This is your hand?" Judge Murphy pointed to the hand that was shaded brown around the edges.

"Yes. And that is Isaac's. When we were done, Brian told us to paste them together on a sheet. He told us to remember that God gave us friends and family as a blessing."

Isaac's handwriting was better than Mateo's, but Mateo was proud of his nonetheless. He wasn't in a special class anymore. He learned with all of the other kids, and he was keeping up.

Across Mateo's hand, Isaac had written—*he's brave, he can fish good, he's my bruder.*

Across Isaac's hand, Mateo had written—*he's funny, I can trust him, he's my hermano.*"

Mateo pointed to the Spanish word. "Brian says it's okay for me to use Spanish when I want to. I think of Isaac as my real brother—my blood brother—so I wanted to write it in Spanish."

He thought of his mother's letter in his pocket, written in Spanish, in the language that they shared. He pictured the words *Gracias a Dios* and hoped that she understood God would look after each of them, no matter their language.

"Thank you for showing me this, Mateo. You boys both do very good work, and it's nice to see how much you care for each other."

Judge Murphy handed him back his sheet. He refolded it and stuck it in his pocket, next to his mother's letter.

Sarah was studying him.

Judge Murphy had stood up and was placing her folder on her desk. Tommy was fiddling with his glasses.

Suddenly Mateo's eyes filled with tears again. He'd been so worried about this day, and now it was nearly over.

Judge Murphy returned to the chair she had been sitting in. She leaned forward and studied Mateo. Finally, she said, "You told me before that you'd like to stay with Sarah. That you felt safe and happy there. How do you feel now?"

Mateo swallowed past the lump in his throat and glanced at Sarah. She nodded her head. She gave him the courage to go on.

"I love my *mamá*. I always will, but I remember living in the old trailer, behind the abandoned barn, and before that behind the store where she worked, and before that in a tiny, dirty apartment. My *mamá* did the best she could, but maybe she needs to focus on taking care of herself."

"We can give you all the time you want, Mateo. This isn't a decision we have to make today."

"It doesn't matter if you ask me today or *mañana*." Sometimes Mateo's thoughts still came out in Spanish. Sarah told him that was a good thing. That he could be proud of being Hispanic and of being Plain. "I love my old family and my new one, but I want to live with Sarah."

The judge nodded, carefully considering his words, and then she said something that did make Sarah cry. That part of his dream came true too. "Then I'm going to approve permanent placement for you and Mia in the home of Sarah Yoder."

CHAPTER 81

The fact that they'd been in the courtroom an hour gave Paul hope. A simple no wouldn't have taken so long.

When he heard a small, collective shout, he dared to look at Chloe and Rebecca and Joseph. Their smiles were reflections of his own. Surely that shout was a positive sign.

But when Sarah walked through the door of the courtroom, the second that he saw her, he knew. Mateo and Mia were officially a part of the Yoder family.

Everyone began talking at once.

Rebecca and *Mammi* were embracing.

Joseph was slapping Andy on the back. Bishop Levi was reaching for a stick of gum and offering some to the children. Henry, Luke, Isaac, and Mateo were high-fiving one another and grinning as if they had just won the annual buggy race. Little Mia was rubbing at her eyes as if she'd just woken up.

And Sarah?

Sarah was standing in the middle of the room, holding Mia, Chloe's arms around her, encircled by her family.

Paul stood on the edge, gratitude swelling in his heart until he had to reach up and rub at his chest. Joy, unmitigated and flowing over, filled his very being. He fought the urge to shout in celebration. He blinked away hot tears.

Chloe glanced up and locked eyes with him. She squeezed Sarah's arm and motioned toward Paul with a nod of her head.

Sarah didn't look at him. She handed Mia to her friend, and then she turned and walked up to Paul.

When she reached his side, she simply said, *"Danki."*

"For?"

"Everything."

"I should be thanking you." He shook his head, unable to put into words all that he was feeling. Instead, he asked, "It's official?"

"It is."

The whoop erupted from him. Paul jerked his hat off his head and slapped it against his leg. He wanted to pull Sarah into his arms, spin her around, and kiss her pretty lips. But suddenly Chloe was saying, "She was just here," everyone was laughing, and they began the search for Mia.

It didn't take too long to find her squatting beside the far side of the water cooler and giggling.

"You found me!" She ran to Paul and raised her arms. He picked her up, raised her up to the sky, and the smile on her face felt like his own.

It wasn't until they were once again riding home in the van that Rebecca asked him, "Will you ask her to marry you?"

"I already have. You know that."

"I meant will you ask her again."

"Energy and persistence conquer all things," Joseph said.

"Haven't heard that one. Amish proverb?"

"Benjamin Franklin." Rebecca was once again knitting. "He tends to read whatever comes through the store, and we have a book of sayings by him."

"A wise man, even if he was an *Englischer*."

Paul stared out the window the rest of the way home. He would never claim to be an expert on courting. He had all the energy in the world, but persistence?

How were you supposed to keep after something when nothing seemed to work?

Or maybe…maybe it wasn't about finding the right gimmick to

win a girl's heart. Sure, his *mamm* had told him that every girl liked flowers, and Rebecca had suggested that a meal where a woman doesn't have to cook was special. No doubt both ideas were good. But maybe what he needed to do was apply himself to being the man he wanted to be—for Sarah.

Yeah, that sounded like the right path.

That made complete sense.

He knew exactly what he'd do, what he'd been longing to do. He'd thought he should wait until she said yes, but maybe not. Maybe he should start now, and be persistent.

Paul closed his eyes, and the miles from Tulsa to Cody's Creek slipped away. He might have even fallen asleep. Wishing Rebecca and Joseph a good night, he whistled as he walked out to his place. He could have asked the driver to take him there, but he wanted the evening walk.

He had some planning to do.

CHAPTER 82

Sarah sat on the front porch, thinking that summer was her favorite time of year. June had given way to July, and soon the children would be going back to school. Andy had taken the tractor to see Emma. He'd winked and told Sarah that he had dinner, ice cream, and a very important question on his mind. Her brother had grown up. Sarah didn't doubt for one minute that very soon their family would be increasing by one.

Henry, Luke, Isaac, and Mateo were playing horseshoes. Metal against metal rang out as the sun dipped toward the horizon. It had been a long week. In truth, every week exhausted her, but it was a good tiredness that coursed through her bones and caused her to fall asleep as soon as she lay in bed beneath her summer quilt.

Mia crouched on the patch of grass next to the porch, playing with her Amish dolls. She would occasionally hide one and a few minutes later send the others to find it. Sarah still did not understand her daughter's fascination with hide-and-seek, but there was no doubt that the child was happy.

Mammi called from inside, "Tell Paul I have extra maple cream pie."

"But he isn't—" The words died on Sarah's lips as he stepped out of the twilight.

Paul had changed in the last two months. She couldn't put her finger on how exactly. He was as courteous as ever. He still frowned when he was deep in thought. He was attentive to the children. But to Sarah it seemed he'd taken a step back. Was he regretting that he had once asked her to marry him? He hadn't brought it up again, and she was embarrassed to broach the subject.

Maybe his feelings had changed. Possibly the permanent adoption of Mia and Mateo had frightened him.

"Pretty evening to enjoy outside."

"It is."

Mia darted past them, one doll in each hand.

"Still hiding the third?"

"At least twice a day. That doll ends up in the laundry each week because Mia insists on putting her in the oddest places."

Mia stopped suddenly, turned around, and noticed Paul.

Without saying a word, she flung herself at him. He lifted her high in the air, laughed when she patted his cheeks, and then set her back down. "Best go find your dolly."

She traipsed away.

Paul sat beside Sarah, and they watched the sun make its westerly descent. She closed her eyes and breathed deeply of summer smells—fresh cut hay, blooming azaleas, Paul. Yes, she believed she would know the man had walked into a room even if she wore a blindfold. He never failed to clean up before stopping by. Was that courting? When a man washed up before visiting his neighbor?

"There's something I want to show you."

She opened her eyes slowly, studied him, and said, "I can't leave the children."

"I'll watch them," *Mammi* called out through the kitchen window.

They both started laughing at the same time. "It seems that I've been given permission to go."

"Don't need my permission." *Mammi* was humming a hymn from Sunday. Like Mateo and Mia, she had become an important part of their household. Sarah couldn't imagine life without her father's mother.

"You're a grown woman," she added.

Sarah was mortified, but Paul only laughed again and reached for her hand.

"Hey, Paul." Henry paused midthrow. "You wanna play horseshoes?"

"*Nein*. I'm going for a walk with Sarah."

One of the boys made kissing sounds, but Sarah couldn't tell if it was Isaac or Mateo.

"All right. But you need the practice. You lost four games straight last weekend."

Instead of going to the road, Paul led her across the fields, toward the fence line that bordered their two properties. Was he going to show her how Andy's crop had grown? The corn was nearly as tall as she was. It had been weeks since she'd been out here. And though she'd been thinking of how tired she was just a few minutes ago, Sarah experienced a sudden surge of energy, almost giddiness.

Perhaps it was the clean air, or the bounty before her, or the man at her side.

Paul stopped next to the fence.

Though the light was fading, she could make out well enough the gate that he'd installed.

"When did you do this?"

"Last week."

"And no one told me? You did a *gut* job." Sarah stepped closer, raised the latch, and opened the gate. "It even works."

"Imagine that."

She could hear the laughter in his voice. After he'd followed her through to his property and secured the gate, he once again claimed her hand.

"*Danki*, Paul. That will save the boys a good amount of time not having to walk around between the two."

"The idea came to me the day Isaac tore his pants trying to climb over."

"That was quite the mending job, and it was quite a long time ago."

"Yes, it took me a while to get around to the important things. I didn't do it only for Isaac or Henry or Mateo, though. I did it for us as well." He paused, as if he was expecting an answer from her.

But Sarah didn't know what to say.

She didn't trust herself to speak at all. Installing the gate was a small thing, not like flowers or a fancy dinner in town, but it was so thoughtful. It would certainly save everyone time.

It occurred to her then that their two farms had become inexplicably linked. And it wasn't only that her brothers passed back and forth each day. The two households constantly turned to one another, whether Paul had burned his dinner or Sarah needed a hand with a broken water pipe. Whether the boys had a question they felt only a man could answer, or Paul needed a lesson in how to sew on a button.

Somehow, somewhere along the way, it was as if they had become one.

CHAPTER 83

As if they had become one...

Those words echoed through her mind as Paul led her across his fields and up to the house. Not the barn. The house.

She could just make out a new roof, cleaned windows, and a battery-operated lantern shining from the kitchen window. Sturdy steps led up to a porch that boasted a new floor and freshly painted railings. She was even more surprised to see two rocking chairs and a small table. This from a man who had been content to live in a barn for more than a year?

"When...when did you find the time to do this?"

"Over the last two months."

She counted back and said, "Since the court day."

"*Ya.*"

So that was where he'd been, why he hadn't been stopping by as often, why he always seemed as if he had some secret that was lightening his step.

"Is the inside finished as well?"

"For sure and certain."

"Can we...can I see it?"

"I did it for you, Sarah. Of course you can see it." He was standing directly behind her now, his hands gently touching her arms. All she had to do was take one step back and she would be in his embrace. All she had to do was trust him.

She moved forward, and he opened the door.

Everything wasn't new, but it was repaired, painted, and cleaned. He'd taken a building that was literally falling in on itself, and he had turned it into a home.

They walked through the entire house. It was beautiful. It would make someone a fine home. It would make Paul a fine home, but she couldn't...

"Let's sit out front," he suggested.

He poured them two glasses of lemonade and carried them to the front porch. Sarah was grateful for the cool drink. Her throat felt as though it were being clenched by a giant fist. She held her glass with both hands, relieved that she had something to hang on to. Thankful he couldn't see her shaking.

But Paul knew her.

He'd been at her side since the first day when Mateo pulled a bucket full of rinse water over his head. He'd helped her find Mia back when Mia's hiding was something strange and terrifying. He'd listened to her fears and her hopes and her dreams.

She owed him an honest, straightforward answer.

"You've done a *gut* job here, Paul. It's really quite amazing, the transformation."

"I hear a *but* coming..."

"But if you did it for me, I don't see how—" She glanced out at the lightning bugs signaling the end of the day, and then she forced herself to meet the gaze of this man she had grown to love.

"You don't love me," he whispered.

"I do."

A smile wreathed his face.

"I do, but—"

He stood and pulled his rocker directly in front of hers so that they were sitting knee to knee.

"Sarah, do you love me?"

"Yes, but—"

He reached out and gently placed his two fingers against her lips.

"Do you love me?"

She nodded and tried to remember what she needed to tell him. He was holding both of her hands in his, and she thought of how she'd prayed for this—that God would see fit to give her a husband in addition to her family. She'd prayed for it, but she hadn't dared to believe.

"I love you. We'll make this work."

"How? We'd live here and the children there? I can't."

"Of course you can't, and I wouldn't ask you to."

"I don't understand."

Paul rubbed the backs of her hands with his thumbs. She didn't realize she was shivering until that moment. On a warm night in July, she was shaking like a leaf in winter.

"You can choose, Sarah. We can live here and bring the children with us. Or we can live there."

"What of your house?"

"Andy will need a place."

She very nearly gasped. She didn't realize until that moment how much she'd worried about Andy, about his wife and his family. About how they'd make it work.

"You would do that? Allow him to live here?"

"We'd be a family, Sarah. Our two places—they would be one. You and I can stay in your house, with *Mammi* and Mia and the boys. Or we can—"

But she didn't allow him to finish what else they could do. She threw her arms around him, laughing and allowing the tears to flow. Putting both hands on his cheeks, as she'd seen Mia do a hundred times, she said, "I love you, Paul Byler."

"Do you now?"

"And my answer is *yes*."

"Is it?" He helped her to stand, slipped into her rocking chair, and pulled her onto his lap. "Well, that's the best answer I've ever heard."

She felt safe there in his arms. She knew now that she could navigate the ups and downs of life alone, but she also knew that she could dare to live her crazy life with Paul at her side.

She'd finally come home. She didn't not know if her mother would ever return, but that no longer angered her. It was a miracle that her anger had melted away over the last year, through the writing of dozens of letters, learning to put herself in her mother's shoes.

Finally, she understood that she wasn't an orphan anymore and neither were her brothers or Mateo or Mia. God wouldn't abandon them. He never had. He'd sent *Mammi* and Paul, their friends and neighbors, a compassionate judge, and a dedicated social worker.

God had given them one another.

That was the grandest miracle of all.

AUTHOR'S NOTE

There have been instances of Amish families adopting children outside of their ethnic and religious group.

According to the Congressional Coalition on Adoption Institute, nearly 400,000 children are living in the U.S. without permanent families. Of those, more than 100,000 are eligible for adoption. Around the world, nearly 18 million orphans have lost both parents and are living on the streets or in an orphanage.

Amber Alerts began in 1996 in the Dallas–Fort Worth area after the abduction and murder of Amber Hagerman. As of 2009, all 50 states, the District of Columbia, Puerto Rico, and the U.S. Virgin Islands have Amber Alert plans.

The town of Cody's Creek does not exist in Oklahoma. The place I visited and researched was Chouteau, which was originally called Cody's Creek when it became a stop on the Katy Railroad in 1871. The Amish community in Chouteau does allow the use of tractors, both in the fields and in town. They still use the horse and buggy when traveling to church, a wedding, or a funeral.

I would like to offer a special thanks to all the people who wrote me regarding their experience with adoption. While I thoroughly researched the adoption process, I changed some details to fit the story line.

DISCUSSION QUESTIONS

1. Several characters are grieving at the beginning of this story—Sarah, Sarah's brothers, and even their mother. Each one deals with grief in his or her own way. In Ecclesiastes 3:1-4, we're told there is a season/time for everything, even a season to mourn. What can we do to help someone who is grieving?

2. Paul is excited about rejuvenating a run-down farm, but when he realizes it might include befriending a family of "orphans," he hesitates. Why is that? What is it about helping others and drawing close to them that intimidates us?

3. Mateo and Mia are living in an abandoned trailer behind an abandoned barn. Do you think that's possible in our day and age? Could there be homeless children living in abandoned buildings? Why or why not?

4. At the end of chapter 20, Sarah realizes that her family has a lot in common with Mia and Mateo—that they are all abandoned. Have you ever felt abandoned? What does Scripture say about our heavenly Father and His faithfulness to us? (You can begin by looking at 1 Corinthians 8:6 and Galatians 4:6.)

5. We meet Elisa for the first time in chapter 47. She's not an admirable character. She seems selfish, desperate, and even callous toward her children. She seems a lot like Sarah's mother. But in chapter 55, *Mammi* tells Sarah, "I won't be judging either of them. In my heart, I believe they are doing the absolute best they can. It's only that, to us, it seems as if their best isn't very good." How did you react to this statement? What does the Bible tell us about offering grace and forgiveness to others? Some passages you might

read over in your Bible include Matthew 18:21-22; Mark 11:25; and Ephesians 4:32.

6. When Brian is hurt, Mateo and Isaac struggle with the question of *why bad things happen to good people*. It's a question many of us have. What would you tell someone who asks you this question? What Bible verses could you point them to for answers?

7. Becca tells Sarah that she could be experiencing a crisis of faith. What things can we do for a friend who is struggling in this way? What can we do when we experience this sort of crisis ourselves?

8. When Sarah finally receives a letter from her mother, she is both relieved and a little upset. She's still dealing with feelings of abandonment. How would you have counseled her at this point?

9. Sarah and Paul have strong feelings for one another nearly from the beginning of the story, but Sarah's fears hold her back. Whether it's a friendship, a family relationship, or a romantic relationship, what kinds of fears hold us back? Find three Bible verses that discuss the topic of fear.

10. This book is filled with imperfect people. In fact, nearly every character has a flaw of some sort—Sarah's mother, Mateo's mother, even Sarah and Paul. Philippians 1:6 says we can be confident in this, "that he who began a good work in you will carry it on to completion until the day of Christ Jesus." In what specific ways does this give you hope?

RECIPES

Ham and Macaroni Salad

2 cups uncooked elbow macaroni
2 cups chopped ham
3 hard-cooked eggs, chopped
1 small onion, chopped
2 stalks celery, chopped
1 small bell pepper (any color), seeded and chopped
2 T. dill pickle relish
2 cups creamy salad dressing (you may also use Miracle Whip)
3 T. prepared yellow mustard
¾ cup sugar
2¼ tsp. white vinegar
¼ tsp. salt
¾ tsp. celery seed

Bring a pot of lightly salted water to a boil. Add macaroni and cook for 8 to 10 minutes, until tender. Drain and set aside to cool.

In a large bowl, stir together the ham, eggs, onion, celery, bell pepper, and relish.

In a small bowl, stir together the salad dressing, mustard, sugar, vinegar, salt, and celery seed. Pour over the vegetables, and stir in macaroni until well blended. Cover and chill for at least 1 hour before serving.

Peanut Butter Bars

1 cup peanut butter
⅔ cup butter, softened
1½ cups brown sugar, packed
1½ cups sugar
4 eggs
4 tsp. vanilla extract
2 cups all-purpose flour
2 tsp. baking powder
½ tsp. salt
1 12-ounce package dark chocolate chips

Preheat the oven to 325°. Grease a 9 x 13-inch pan and set aside.

In a large bowl, cream together the peanut butter, butter, brown sugar, and sugar until well blended and smooth. Make sure any lumps of brown sugar are dissolved. Then add the eggs and vanilla. Mix until smooth and creamy and thoroughly blended. Add the flour, baking powder, and salt. Mix thoroughly until the batter is once again smooth and creamy.

Spoon the batter into the prepared pan. Sprinkle the chocolate chips over the batter and put into the oven for 5 minutes. Remove from the oven and, using a butter knife, swirl the chocolate chips through the dough. Bake for 40 more minutes. Remove from the oven. The bars are done when a butter knife inserted into the center comes out clean (some chocolate may stick to the knife). Let cool for an hour before cutting into bars.

Chicken Casserole

8 oz. broad egg noodles
½ cup butter
8 oz. sliced mushrooms (optional)
⅓ cup flour
2 cups chicken broth
1 cup milk
salt and pepper to taste
2 cups cooked chicken, cubed
pinch of sage
⅓ cup freshly grated Parmesan cheese

Cook noodles as directed on package. Melt butter and cook mushrooms in a large skillet until lightly browned. Stir in flour and blend in with a fork or slotted spoon. Stir in broth and milk seasonings. Whisk sauce constantly until thickened.

Combine sauce, noodles, and chicken. Adjust seasonings to taste. Place in a 2-quart casserole dish. Sprinkle top with Parmesan cheese and bake at 350° for 30 minutes.

Applesauce Coffee Cake

⅔ cup flour
½ cup whole wheat flour
1 tsp. baking soda
1 tsp. cinnamon
¼ tsp. salt
1½ cups peeled, cored, and finely chopped apples
¼ cup fat-free liquid egg product or 2 eggs
¾ cup sugar
½ cup chopped walnuts or ½ cup pecans
¼ cup applesauce
¼ cup brown sugar
1 T. flour
1 T. whole wheat flour
½ tsp. cinnamon
1 T. butter
¼ cup walnuts or ¼ cup pecans

Lightly coat a 9 x 9-inch baking pan with cooking spray. Set aside.

In a medium bowl combine the ⅔ cup flour, ½ cup whole wheat flour, soda, 1 tsp. cinnamon, and salt. Set aside.

In a large mixing bowl toss together the chopped apple and egg product. Stir in the sugar, ¼ cup of the nuts, and applesauce. Add flour mixture and stir until combined. Pour the batter into the prepared pan.

Topping:

Stir together the brown sugar, the remaining flour, whole wheat flour, and cinnamon. Cut in the butter until crumbly, stir in the remaining nuts, and sprinkle the topping over the batter in the pan. Bake at 350° for 40 to 45 minutes.

Maple Cream Pie

1 can condensed milk
⅔ cup maple syrup
pinch of salt

Cook on low heat, very slow, stirring constantly until mixture bubbles. Pour into a baked pie shell. Chill for one hour.

Topping:

2 cups whipping cream
½ cup powdered sugar
2 tsp. vanilla
pinch of salt
1 cup pecans, chopped

Whip ingredients except pecans until thick. Pour on top of pie filling and sprinkle with chopped pecans.

Amish Oatmeal Cookies

2 cups brown sugar
1 cup butter
2 eggs, beaten
1 tsp. vanilla
1 tsp. baking powder
1 tsp. baking soda
1½ cups flour
3 cups quick-cooking oats
½ tsp. salt
Powdered sugar for rolling dough

Cream brown sugar and butter together. Add the eggs and vanilla. Mix until well combined.

In a separate bowl, stir together the baking powder, baking soda, flour, oats, and salt. Fold into wet ingredients. Chill for at least one hour.

Form into balls and roll them in powdered sugar. Place on a cookie sheet and press the balls down a bit. Bake at 375° for 8 minutes or so. Don't overbake them.

Snickerdoodle Cookies

1½ cups sugar
1 cup shortening
2 eggs
1 tsp. vanilla
2¾ cups flour
1 tsp. baking soda
½ tsp. salt
1 T. sugar
1 T. cinnamon

Cream together the sugar and shortening. Add the eggs and beat well. Stir in the vanilla. In a separate bowl, mix together the flour, baking soda, and salt and then add to the shortening mixture.

Stir together the 1 T. sugar and cinnamon. Roll the dough into balls and then roll in cinnamon sugar mix. Bake 8 minutes at 400°.

Twelve-Egg Pound Cake

1 pound butter
3½ cups sugar
¼ tsp. salt
4 cups sifted flour
1 tsp. baking powder
12 eggs
1 tsp. pure vanilla extract

Cream the butter thoroughly and then gradually add the sugar, beating until light and fluffy (about 2 minutes).

Mix together the salt, flour, and baking powder. Add ¼ cup of the flour mixture to the butter and sugar mixture and beat well. Alternate adding the remaining flour and the eggs until all have been added and blended well. Add the vanilla and mix well again.

Bake in two 10-inch tube pans for 1 hour at 325°.

GLOSSARY

Aenti—aunt

Bruder—brother

Dat—father

Danki—thank you

Englischer—non-Amish person

Fraa—wife

Freinden—friends

Gotte's wille—God's will

Grandkinner—grandchildren

Gut—good

In lieb—in love

Kapp—prayer covering

Kinner—children

Mamm—mom

Mammi—grandmother

Nein—no

Onkel—uncle

Ordnung—the unwritten set of rules and regulations that guide everyday Amish life.

Schweschder—sister

Wunderbaar—wonderful

Ya—yes

ABOUT THE AUTHOR

 **Vannetta Chapman** writes inspirational fiction full of grace. She has published more than one hundred articles in Christian family magazines, receiving more than two dozen awards from Romance Writers of America chapter groups. She discovered her love for the Amish while researching her grandfather's birthplace of Albion, Pennsylvania. Her novel *Falling to Pieces* was a 2012 ACFW Carol Award winner. *A Promise for Miriam* earned a spot on the June 2012 Christian Retailing Top Ten Fiction list. Vannetta was a teacher for 15 years and currently writes full-time. She lives in the Texas hill country with her husband. For more information, visit her at www.VannettaChapman.com.

When Disaster Strikes...
Hope and Love Rise to Meet It

When a tornado hits the farms surrounding Cody's Creek, Oklahoma, Anna Schwartz's life is changed forever. She suffers a devastating injury and suddenly finds herself learning to negotiate her world from a wheelchair.

Three people—Chloe Roberts, Jacob Graber, and Ruth Schwartz—join forces to help Anna through her darkest days. Chloe, an *Englischer*, writes for the local paper. Jacob, recently arrived in town, stays on as a hired hand at her uncle's. And Ruth, her grandmother, offers her deep faith and compassionate spirit.

Then one morning Anna wakes and finds herself healed. How did it happen? *Why* did it happen? And what is she to do now? Her life is again turned upside down as the world's attention is drawn to this young Amish girl who has experienced the unexplainable.

When Loss Seems Overwhelming...
Grace Ushers in Peace

Joshua Kline travels from his farm in Oklahoma to offer aid to an *Englisch* town on the Gulf Coast of Texas after a hurricane has ravaged the area. He takes his younger brother Alton with him because the last thing Alton needs is another brush with the law. Joshua is pleasantly surprised when he hears that Becca Troyer, the bishop's granddaughter, also plans on joining their team.

What will he find when he arrives in Texas? Certainly, *Englischers* and other Plain people, who provide fresh perspective on life as the Amish volunteers help restore order from destruction. But a budding romance? A call from *Gotte*? A possible healing of his relationship with Alton?

Joshua's Mission is a story of love, forgiveness, and the grace of God that carries us through even the most desperate situations.

Fall in Love with the Amish of Pebble Creek!

A Promise for Miriam, A Home for Lydia, and *A Wedding for Julia* introduce the Amish community of Pebble Creek, Wisconsin, and the kind, caring people there. As they face challenges to their community from the English world, they come together to reach out to their non-Amish neighbors while still preserving their cherished Plain ways.

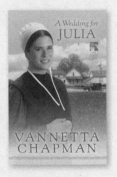

Enjoy These *Free* Short Story E-Romances
Download Them Today from Your Favorite Digital Retailer!

These two short story e-romances are an exclusive bonus from the Pebble Creek Amish by Vannetta Chapman. Fans of the series will enjoy this chance to briefly revisit Pebble Creek, and new readers will be introduced to an Amish community that is more deeply explored in the three full novels.

8-1 6

To learn more about Harvest House books and
to read sample chapters, visit our website:

www.harvesthousepublishers.com

HARVEST HOUSE PUBLISHERS
EUGENE, OREGON